BERYL BAINBRIDGE
OMNIBUS

BERYL BAINBRIDGE OMNIBUS

Beryl Bainbridge

Duckworth

This Omnibus edition
first published in 1989

Harriet Said first published 1972
The Dressmaker first published 1973
The Bottle Factory Outing first published 1974

Gerald Duckworth & Co. Ltd.,
The Old Piano Factory,
43 Gloucester Crescent, London NW1

© 1972, 1973, 1974 by Beryl Bainbridge

British Library Cataloguing in Publication Data

Bainbridge, Beryl *1934–*
    Beryl Bainbridge omnibus.
    I. Title
    823′.914   [F]

ISBN 0 7156 2328 1

Printed and bound by
BPCC Wheatons Ltd, Exeter.

Contents

HARRIET SAID...

1

———

Harriet said: 'No you don't, you keep walking.' I wanted
to turn round and look back at the dark house but she
tugged at my arm fiercely. We walked over the field hand in
hand as if we were little girls.

I didn't know what the time was, how late we might be. I
only knew that this once it didn't really matter. Before we
reached the road Harriet stopped. I could feel her breath on
my face, and over her shoulder I could see the street lamps
shining and the little houses all sleeping. She brought her
hand up and I thought she was going to hit me but she only
touched my cheek with her fingers. She said, 'Don't cry
now.'

'I don't want to cry now.'

'Wait till we get home.'

The word home made my heart feel painful, it was so lost
a place. I said, 'Dad will have got my train ticket back to
school when I get in. It will be on the hall table.'

'Or behind the clock,' said Harriet.

'He only buys a single. I suppose it's cheaper.'

'And you might lose the other half.'

'Yes,' I said.

We stood for a moment looking at each other and I won-
dered if she might kiss me. She never had, not in all the years
I had loved her. She said, 'Trust me, I do know what's best.
It was all his fault. We are not to blame.'

'I do trust you.'

'Right. No sense standing here. When I say run, you start

7

to run. When I say scream, you scream. Don't stop running, just you keep going.'

'Yes,' I said, 'I'll do that, if that's what's best.'

'Run,' said Harriet.

So we ran over the last stretch of field and Harriet didn't tell me to scream, at least I didn't hear her, because she was really screaming, terrible long drawn out sounds that pierced the darkness, running far ahead of me, tumbling on to the road and under the first street lamp, her two plaits flying outwards and catching the light. I hadn't any breath to scream with her. I was just wanting to catch up with her and tell her not to make that noise. Somebody came out of a house as I went past and called to me but I did not dare stop. If I couldn't scream for her then I could run for her. A dog was barking. Then we were round the bend of the lane and there were lights coming on in the houses and my mother on the porch of our house with her fist to her mouth. Then I could scream. Over her head the wire basket hung, full of blue flowers, not showing any colour in the night.

I did notice, even in the circumstances, how oddly people behaved. My mother kept us all in the kitchen, even Harriet's parents when they arrived, which was unlike her. Visitors only ever saw the front room. And Harriet's father hadn't got a collar to his striped shirt, only a little white stud. Harriet could not speak. Her mother held her in her arms and she was trembling. I had to tell them what had happened. Then Harriet suddenly found her voice and shouted very loudly, 'I'm frightened,' and she was. I looked at her face all streaked with tears and I thought, poor little Harriet, you're frightened. My father and her father went into the other room to phone the police. My mother kept asking me if I was sure, was I sure it was Mr Biggs.

Of course I was sure. After all I had known him for years.

*   *   *

8

2

WHEN I came home for the holidays, Harriet was away with her family in Wales. She had written to explain it was not her fault and that when she came back we would have a lovely time. She said that Mr Redman had died and that she had spoken to him only a few days previously. He had inquired what she was going to do when she left school. She said she might go on the buses. 'Likely you'll get more than your ticket punched,' he had replied. It was a nice farewell thing to say. Harriet said we should bow the head at the passing of landmarks.

His was one of the earliest faces Harriet and I remembered patrolling the lane down to the sea; in company with the Tsar, Canon Dawson from St Luke's and Dodie from Bumpy field.

Mr Redman, to be specific, never went into the lane. In winter he stayed in his bungalow and waved from the window, in summer he bent down to his garden. We talked to him a little, either over his hedge or his gate, about his nice flowers or his nasty weeds.

The Canon rode a bicycle, a big one with two back wheels and no crossbar. Typical, as Harriet said, seeing he was such a Child.

Dodie always walked down the lane, swollen ankles in apricot stockings, dressed forever in black. She would cry out to us as she passed our fence, 'Hallo Pets . . . How's my Pets?' She lived in a bungalow next to the lunatic asylum, handy for Papa, her husband, as Harriet said.

The Tsar had been walking down to the sea the first evening

that Harriet and I had gone to collect tadpoles from the ponds below the pine trees. Slightly unsober, slightly dishevelled, always elegant, he swayed moodily past us through all the days of our growing up. We acknowledged him briefly, as indeed we acknowledged the Canon whom we detested, and Mr Redman and darling Dodie. But it was only twice he spoke to us: once to admire our captured tadpoles that he said were like prehistoric embryos, and another more memorable time when looking away from us toward the sea, he had said,

'Years ago I visited Greece . . . beautiful beyond compare.'

Harriet, watching his face and perceptive to his mood, had cried, 'What were the statues like, all those lovely statues?'

It was then the Tsar looked at me, not a shadow of doubt, though it was her he answered.

'Scarred beauties, Harriet, chipped no end. Figures with noble noses and robust limbs, but beautiful.'

Harriet stood on one leg when he had gone, pointing her finger and hopping in a circle round me. 'He thinks your nose noble,' she sang, 'noble and robust, but beautiful, my dear, so beautiful.'

I said I did not care to be compared to Grecian ruins, then ran away among the trees, delighted with myself.

Later Harriet said his name was Peter Biggs and we should call him Peter the Great. But I thought the name Peter was daft so we called him the Tsar.

Without Harriet I was irritable and bored. I did not have any other friends, partly from inclination and partly because none of the families I knew sent their children to boarding school. I was a special case, as Harriet observed. I had gone when younger to a private school in the district, but I was a disgrace owing to the dirty stories found written in my notebook, and everyone agreed I was out of control and going wrong and in need of supervision. I did know, even without Harriet to tell me, that I had learned the shameful stories at school in the first place, that I did not have an original idea on the subject and that really they were scared of me and Harriet being so intimate. We were too difficult. Nothing else.

10

So I was sent to boarding school and heard new dirty jokes which I learnt by heart instead of committing them to paper. After a time I did not mind being away from home but it was a dreadful waste of money and my parents were not rich, not even wealthy. However I did speak nicely and I had a certain style.

The third morning I was home my father offered to drive me in his car to see the grave of Mr Redman. He was being kindly, but Harriet always said it was an insult the way he bought black-market petrol when other people suffered deprivations. However, she was not there to observe me.

When I entered the graveyard of the small Norman church there was the Tsar, head inclined a little to one side as I approached. A gentle breeze blowing from the pines lifted the thin hair on his head as he turned to greet me. My father sat in the car in the road and watched us shake hands in the sunlight.

'Ah, my dear child . . . Harriet said you were due home.'

'Why hasn't Mr Redman got a head stone?'

'It's expensive, you know.'

'More like no one's bothered.'

'Quite.'

Later, returning to the house, my father drove angrily, curving the car viciously round corners, asking, 'What did you say to him, eh? What did you find to say to the blighter?'

'Only that I had not seen him for years.'

'He's a scoundrel. Nothing but a damned scoundrel.'

He hunched his back in wrath over the wheel. He thought most people were scoundrels for one reason or another, mostly that I knew them. Burying my face in the warm leather seating I murmured to myself, 'A damned scoundrelly Tsar,' and thought complacently how fine it sounded.

That evening after my tea I went out in the rain to walk to the pines. There were two ways to the sea. One was straight down the lane past Harriet's bungalow on the left and the Tsar's house on the right, over the railway crossing and on to the cinder path leading directly to the pines with the ditch to cross. Once there had been a stream, but now it was just a cut in the ground, choked high with weeds and grasses.

Or you could go by the park bordered by privet, very neat with its clock-golf course and bowling green, two hard tennis courts, a wooden pavilion with thatched roof, and up the hill to the station. That was nice because there were railings and you could drag a stick across them all the way down the other side of the hill until you came to the Sunday school hut made out of tin with a bell on the roof; some ponies in the fields to the left, the Barracks away to the right and a single line of pines turning a corner of the road to the church fence.

It was a longer route but a good one.

I climbed over the stone wall, crossed the graveyard and went through the gate into the woods. I sang as I began to climb the slope among the trees, 'All through the night there's a little brown bird singing, singing in the hush of the darkness and the dew . . .' It was practically the only song I knew all through and it had the right note of melancholy suitable to a summer evening. The ground was nut brown with needles, but further along the sand had blown up from the dunes over the years and slid along the rise, a second sea, seeping in a white pool amongst the second row of trees. There were potholes in the earth left by the soldiers training there during the war. Once by mistake the Germans dropped a bomb, but the sand soon filled up the crater. On the other side of the road the woods covered the ground from the railway crossing to the beach. Here, at the end of the ridge, the ground dropped abruptly away to a flat hollow of grass and water. Behind that another rise of trees and then the dunes, half a mile of them, undulating up and down till they pushed the shore and the flat edge of sea.

I rolled all the way down the slope and reached the bottom covered with sand, breathless, not from exertion but because the Tsar was sitting by the tadpole ponds with his back to me. I was shy.

The ponds were no more than long puddles of rain-water set in the grass. In winter the rain fell endlessly, the pools

12

thickened, mud formed. When the frost came, the ground hardened, the edges of the pools shrank, the ice pinched closer; the low bushes snapped at a touch, the tall dune grasses froze in clumps. Once, in the centre of the largest pool, Harriet and I saw two frogs, dead, bloated with water, floating, white bellies upward, like pieces of bread. Now in summer the water was warm to the touch. I crouched down in the sand and trailed my fingers back and forth waiting for him to speak first.

'Aah,' he said, letting out a sigh, as he lay back with his head in the grass, his trilby hat, which he never wore, beside him, its brim dipping in the water.

I said, 'Look there's a swallow,' as a bird plunged down to his hat and rose on the instant to fly upwards and away into the trees.

He, lazily turning his head, replied, 'Nonsense, girl, more likely a sand martin,' and lay back again.

I could not argue with him because, though I spent a great deal of time in the woods and considered myself a naturalist, I never truly knew one bird from another. Harriet with passion collected ferns and leaves and wrote down migration months in her scrap book, referring to flowers by dear latinic names, but I never remembered.

'What's your school like?' he said, 'not too bad?'

'Not bad. I've got used to it.'

'Being away from your parents will do you a power of good in the end. Develops your sense of identity.'

'It's jolly expensive.'

'Quite.'

He asked how long were the holidays and spoke conventional platitudes about my missing Harriet, and the mischief we would get up to on her return. I said, Yes, I did miss her, and Yes, no doubt we would get up to one or two larks. I was filled with distaste as I spoke; not at my sentiments but at the restraint that made me couch them so childishly. While I talked uneasily I watched the bird's skull of his head nestle a space for itself in the sand. The time might come I felt when I would be moved to stretch out a hand and cradle his head

13

against my palm. Soft-blown hair drifted over his skull, so vulnerable in its fragility. My hand in the pool opened and curled upwards. After an hour he sat up and said, 'I'd better be going.' But he did not move, only peered upwards at the sky. 'She'll be wondering where I am. It's not easy to fool someone you've lived with for so long. It's difficult for me to face her sometimes.'

I had to ask him questions. It was too good a chance to miss. Harriet would be delighted when I told her.

'What do you mean, fool her?'

'Oh, you know . . . don't disappoint me, child. Fancy me going home and telling the wife I had been in the woods with you.' I said nothing and he continued, 'Will you tell your father you've been talking to me? No, of course not.'

I said for him, 'It doesn't do to tell them too much.'

'Quite.'

He began to shake the sand from his clothes, swishing his trilby hat about in the air to dry it.

'They always know there's something up,' I said. 'They know there's something, but if you don't tell them they can't be sure. But they do know. What will you tell her?'

'Oh, I don't know. She has such a dull life somehow. She belittles my coming down here to the shore, says I'm too old for that sort of thing any more. She doesn't know what sort of thing she means. Neither do I. I do no harm. I just walk down here and back again.'

'That's all Harriet and I do,' I said, not quite truthfully.

He was straightening the strands of his hair now, passing his hand restlessly over his skull. 'She'll be sitting in the dark listening to the wireless when I get in. I'll just pause in the hall, just for a moment to get my face right, even though she's in the dark. When I open the door she'll say, "It's a wonderful invention this you know, me sitting here with Max Jaffa playing just for me . . ." and I'll see how empty the room is except for her sitting on the sofa in her cardigan and sandals and the room in darkness but for the orange dial on the wireless. And you see,' he looked at me now, 'she'll know I've been talking

14

to someone. I won't be able to hide it. It will put her out.'

'Quite,' I said, thinking how feeble he was worrying about what she thought and what she might think. It was all right me and Harriet having such qualms about our parents, we did have to pretend to conform, but at his age it was awfully flabby. I wished I could convince him of his weakness but he was already standing up, holding his hat in both hands ready to go, if not eager then anxious to get back to her. I knew he had to walk home on his own, I knew that. My father might come to meet me; she might be at her gate; but it was soft of him not daring to. I said good night and we shook hands and he began to climb the hill slope to the pines. He stumbled, nearly fell, as I watched him. I wondered if he were old. He had never looked any different even when we were children. Was he old? I lay flat in case he turned to wave to me, covering my face with my hands. I shut my eyes tight and tried to see his face in the darkness. But I could not see him clearly. I saw his head and his trilby hat, but the face was blank and smooth as glass.

3

I DID not go down to the shore again for several days. Instead I stayed at home and tried to be nice to my sister Frances. She was younger than I and quarrelsome because I had betrayed her. I had loved her dreadfully when she was very little but when she grew older and I went away to school I found my love faded. It was still there but the delight in her had gone. She had red hair and pale blue eyes and two front teeth were missing. If I teased her she cried annihilatingly; if I was gentle with her she drew back, tears of uneasy happiness in her eyes. I had to push her from me for her own sake, because of Harriet and me. I did not want her to be like us. God willing she would grow up normally and be like everyone else. But I read her some stories and praised her little crayon drawings; I helped her make clothes for her doll out of scraps of material.

Every Friday Father stayed off work to help clean out the house. He wore his old A.R.P. uniform complete with black beret and got down on his knees to scrub out the kitchen. Harriet said he was manic and that he looked like a cross between Old Mother Riley and General Montgomery. He was very dedicated; Frances and I were moved from room to room as he dusted and scoured and polished. My mother walked to the village to do a load of shopping and when Father had finished the house-work he drove off in the car to fetch her. They came back laden with cabbages and carrots, apples and toilet rolls, fresh eggs from the farm, she looking pale and exhausted, he grumbling and swearing and carrying on

16

shouting he did too much and it wasn't right for a man to do what she expected of him. Which she didn't. She said she wished to hell he'd go out, and he said he would get out of this hell-hole once and for all one of these days. But after lunch he got the car out meekly enough and drove us to Southport for tea and cakes at Thoms'.

On the way back I shut my eyes and pretended I was out for a spin with Charles Boyer. He talked to me in his broken French and told me how lovely I was. 'O my darling you and I must nevair be parted.' We drove through Birkdale along the coast road to Hillside. When I saw the long stretch of beach I begged them to stop and let me walk home.

'Please,' I pleaded. 'You don't know how I feel at school shut away from the sea.'

They were worried for me but they could never argue with conviction. 'Don't be long,' they cried. 'Walk straight home, don't talk to strangers, don't get your feet wet,' and I was out of the car with Frances still whining to be allowed to come with me, and scrambling down the bank on to the shore.

I had to take my shoes off but I left on my stockings. My legs were so large and white. I liked it best when the wind blew strongly. I whistled and ran with my arms spread out like a bird. All the time I kept looking for interesting objects left stranded by the tide. There were no end of things Harriet and I had found. Whole crates of rotten fruit, melons and oranges and grapefruit, swollen up and bursting with salt water, lumps of meat wrapped in stained cotton sheets through which the maggots tunnelled if the weather was warm, and stranded jelly fish, purple things, obscene and mindless. Harriet drove sticks of wood into them but they were dead. Several times we found bad things, half a horse and two small dogs. They were full of water, garlanded with seaweed, snouts encrusted in salt, and teeth exposed. Their necks were tied with wire. 'They buy them for their children,' Harriet told me, 'and when they muddy up the house they bring them down here and drown them.'

17

At Ainsdale the shore narrowed and I went inland to the golf-course. There were more pines to walk through, growing in ragged grass beside the smooth green turf of the course. Nearby was a college for Catholic priests and I hoped one day I might meet someone from there and have a chat about religion. Harriet met a priest once but she said he was awful, his fingers stained up to the knuckles with nicotine and obviously he hadn't got a vocation because the body was a framework to the soul and his frame was dreadful.

But I met nobody.

At Freshfield, the small estuary was fouled up with mud and refuse. There were cans and bottles and paper smeared with excrement, petrol tins and ammunition containers. 'One day,' Harriet warned, 'we shall find a unborn baby still in a bag of skin on its side in the mud.' The thought both thrilled and horrified us.

Without her I did not look too closely; I did not know what I should do if the presentiment became actuality. There were two shabby boats stuck fast, never used. Nobody had the money any more.

Once on the Freshfield side of the estuary the beach ran straight to Formby and I jogged along with my shoes in my hand, thinking all the time about Harriet, about the Tsar, and a little about Charles Boyer. The tide was a long way out, the sea lay motionless; at the rim of the sky an oil tanker stayed still.

When I cut away from the seashore over the dunes to the woods, I was praying, 'Please God, oh please God,' ducking under the barbed wire and on to the cinder path, praying to God as I turned a bend in the road. I was not religious but I had a crucifix in my room and I often called on God when I was at school or away from Harriet. I just wanted something to happen.

At the gate of the Canon's house stood a group of men, standing in a circle with legs like misshapen tulips, trousers tied at the knee with string. Jimmy Demon, the Canon's gardener, was leaning against the fence and laughing.

'It's old Perjer,' he explained. 'Had a drop too much by the look of him.'

Perjer was the village recluse who lived in the sandhills with his dog, in a home made of odd planks and boxes. Harriet said he was a pederast, but I didn't really believe she knew, so I bent over him confidently and helpfully, saying to Jimmy Demon, 'I'm sure he's ill, Jimmy, he's a funny colour.'

'Dirt,' he said callously, touching the body in the dust with the toe of his boot. The men sniggered and looked sideways at me, and laughed again.

Perjer's dog sat apart, nose sniffing the air, waiting till his master should move. He turned his head suddenly with ears well forward and the Canon came out from the garden at the back of the vicarage with the Tsar. We had called the Canon senile years ago; now he seemed less so, but dribbling from the mouth and lisping as he spoke.

'Dear me, Jimmy, what is it, a meeting?'

The Tsar, with hat in hand, came nearer and looked at Jimmy.

'Drunk,' he said.

'I think he looks ill.' I turned to the Tsar. 'He almost looks as if he might be dying.'

'Rubbish.'

The dog settled down in the dust and went to sleep.

'I really think I'd better phone for the Constable to remove him . . . he can't stay here.' The canon was already purposefully moving up the path to the house. His legs were very bowed. Harriet always said to my father to annoy him 'O the canon, decent fella, been on a horse all his life'. But my father never knew what she meant.

The Tsar stood irresolute in the road. He looked at the circle of onlookers and back to the Canon fast disappearing out of sight. He passed his hand wearily over his head and said finally, 'Move him into the woods, Jimmy. He'll sleep it off. They'll only fine him at the station.'

'Reckon the Canon won't like it,' said Jimmy Demon.

Eager to show I didn't care about that, I bent too swiftly to tug at Perjer's feet. The dog swivelled in the dust and nearly caught my wrist in his teeth.

'Aaaah,' I wailed, genuinely shocked.

'O God,' the Tsar said, with disgust in his voice. 'Come on lads, get him into the trees.'

The men looked knowingly at the Tsar, picked Perjer up from the road, a welter of trousers and flapping jacket, and bundled him over the wire netting into the trees. The Tsar and I stood in the road and watched the men climb the fence and drag Perjer deeper among the pines till he was hidden. They returned and the Tsar said, 'Good, lads. We'd better be moving. Canon might not like it.'

I thought while the men were about I had better be seen going away alone, though I wanted to stay with the Tsar.

But he seemed unable to make a move. He stood, turned away from me, watching Perjer's dog run agitatedly among the trees.

Without looking at me he said, 'Let's have a look at the old fraud to see if he's comfortable.'

When I ducked quickly under the netting and waited for him I thought again he must be old. He laboured over the fence, his feet betrayed him as he alighted on the sand; he gave a little delicate sideways skip to regain his balance.

Perjer lay in a trench, one of the many left by the soldiers during the war, his head in the sand, his large hands moving frettishly over his mouth. I knelt at the side of the pit, turning my face upwards slightly so that the Tsar would see my kind expression.

'Are you feeling all right, Mr Perjer?'

There was no reply; the man's dirty face lay against the sand, the pale mouth slack.

The Tsar looked down at me. 'The police are coming,' he warned.

There were voices now in the road; we could hear the

Canon lisping out the story and the high voice of a woman, recognisable as that of the Canon's sister. We crouched down in the trench, Perjer's dog lying across the Tsar's legs.

'The Canon's sister has got wind of us.' The Tsar peeped cautiously out. Elsie stood, one capable hand on the wire netting, peering into the woods.

'O fat white woman whom nobody loves,' whispered the Tsar, and giggled nervously as he knelt in the sand.

Perjer moved his head restlessly and opened his eyes.

'He wants something,' I said, turning round awkwardly and putting my head close to the recluse.

'What is it, Mr Perjer? . . . What do you want?'

There were no voices from the road now, and the Tsar swung himself up to sit on the side of the trench, legs dangling over the edge.

'I got to piss,' said Mr Perjer very firmly, and the peevish hands struggled with his fly.

I wanted to laugh. I thought how Harriet would have stood on one leg and screamed, 'Aye, Yah! I gloat, hear me gloat!' but I pretended to be shocked, scrambling out of the trench and turning my back on the crude Mr Perjer.

The Tsar said, 'Well, there's nothing much wrong with him,' and placed his hand under my elbow and steered me away through the trees.

Sometimes late in summer Harriet and I carried what we called divining twigs, to hold before us and brush aside the webs of spiders, slung invisible from bark to bark. Now it was the Tsar who waved his hand, bestowing blessings, keeping a way clear for us. The contact of his hand on my arm was so delightful that I walked very fast, talking inarticulately and not noticing the path we travelled, till we were in the Rhododendron Lands. The Lands were private gardens and alone I should have kept to the grass verge, ready for the gardener or the squire himself, not walking in the centre of the path as I did now, alone with the Tsar. Great flowering

21

bushes three times my height rustled on either side of us and hid the sky.

'I remember,' I began, and paused to prod the purple flowers that bounced the air and showered petals at our feet. The Tsar stood still, waving an eloquent hand to encompass the garden and the sky, and brought the movement back to his heart again.

'Never remember,' he bade me. 'It's too boring. Think of the future and the places you'll visit. Athens, child, think of Athens. I'm going to Bordeaux in the winter to bring back a barrel of wine to sweeten the dark days.'

I thought of Athens and watched his face; the lines at the corner of his mouth, the dryness of his skin as if the moisture had run out with his youth, the droop to his eyelids as if he were tired. I tried to look right inside him but nothing stayed fixed. I could only see clearly the shape of his skull and the hand placed on his heart. I sat down on the grass. I had walked a long way.

'I'll be leaving school soon.'

'What will you do then?'

'I might go to art school . . . if my Dad lets me.'

I knew I wouldn't. It was Harriet who drew well, not me. It was Harriet who was educated; she told me what to read, explained to me the things I read, told me what painters I should admire and why. I listened, I did as she said, but I did not feel much interest, at least not on my own, only when she was directing me.

'Why not come to Bordeaux with me?'

I wanted to shout with laughter. I sang wildly to myself, 'Here we go again Sister Jane.' It was just it was so marvellous to be asked by a nearly old man, thirty inches round the belly-o, to go to Bordeaux to collect a barrel of wine for the winter.

Aloud I said, 'Oh, I couldn't, I haven't any money. Thank you very much for asking though.'

Then we could not talk any more because I had been out hours and they would be worried at home and perhaps having

22

a row over me, spoiling their supper with words. All the way home I kept repeating to myself, 'O I couldn't, God, surely I couldn't'.

But I felt I could.

4

ON Sunday morning I went to church. My mother nearly spoilt it by making me wear a hat, but I took it off in the road and carried it. I knew very well what I should look like if I wore it, because Harriet had told me on previous occasions: like an old maid at a flower show. I met the retired postman in the lane who tried to delay me. He balanced dubiously on his bicycle, feet splayed out to steady himself. 'Hallo, hallo, hallo.' He was able to go on like this for ever, like a small child knowing simple words. 'Hallo, hallo, fancy seeing you! What a bonny girl you're growing . . . fancy . . .'

I said, 'Hallo, hallo', and thought it daring, but then Harriet was not with me.

'I've had an upset,' the postman said confidingly. 'Mother, you know. Yes, I heard a bump, thought she'd dropped something, she's always dropping things, but when I went to look I couldn't open the door. She was flat out. I had to push the door, I can tell you. She's a big woman, and there she was with a great crack in her head.'

'How awful.'

A woman passed on a small bicycle, engulfing it ponderously. 'Hallo, hallo,' cried the postman, but there was no reply. 'Mrs Biggs,' he said, turning round on his seat and nearly toppling over.

It wasn't till after lunch when my mother asked me if I had seen anyone I knew in church that I remembered Mrs Biggs. The woman on the bike that the postman had called out to, was the wife of the Tsar. I went to my room and lay down on the bed, trying to think what she looked like. Big, taller than he was and grey haired; that meant she was old. And a tweed coat with a belt on. Big legs. That was all. Mrs Biggs was the one who had told my mother about me and Harriet being on the shore with Italian prisoners.

'Mother!' I opened the door and stood on the landing. I could hear her saying something to Frances in the room below.

'Mother!'

The kitchen door opened. The door knob rattled as my mother leant her weight on it. I imagined her bland face peering inquiringly into the hall.

'Yes, dear.'

'Was it Mrs Biggs from Timothy Street who said we were meeting Italian prisoners?'

I felt very brave mentioning it. Of course Harriet had lied so convincingly that my father had said Mrs Biggs was a dangerous woman, but Mother had seemed very cool with me for weeks afterwards.

'Yes, I think so. Why?' At once my mother was curious. If I wasn't quick she would be upstairs to have a little chat with me. 'Oh nothing. I thought I saw her this morning, that's all.'

I waited a moment then went back to my bedroom and shut the door. So that was her. She had seen Harriet a year ago in the arms of an Italian prisoner. I was behind a sandhill with another one and she only heard my voice. She told my mother that Harriet was a bad influence but she never went to Harriet's parents. Harriet had met her in the street and told her to mind her own business. She was so angry that the woman recoiled from her. But if Mrs Biggs spotted me with the Tsar she would come round right away and there would be no Harriet to defend me.

I felt despair. I could not bear it when my mother was angry. When I had been little it had been different. Small sins expiated by flurried scoldings and smacked bottoms. I was not frightened of her anger, just distressed by the futility of her emotions.

I waited anxiously till tea was over and walked to the

church knowing I would meet the Tsar. It was raining again and we sat in the church porch, our feet resting on the tomb of a Norman soldier, arguing listlessly about the importance of things. I said that the historic body beneath us was a thing of reverence. After all, he had gone on about the ruins of Greece but all he said was, 'Nonsense, just a heap of bones.'

'It's romantic.'

He looked gloomily out at the green-drenched world and said, 'Do you think so, do you really think so?'

When I had nearly found the words to tell him about Mrs Biggs and that it would be better if we did not meet again, he said, 'I was married here. Held the wedding breakfast where you're sitting.' How harsh, I thought, listening in the porch to an old man's recollections.

'I put on my dark suit,' began the Tsar, blowing cigarette smoke before his face, 'and she had a coffee-coloured dress, very short, and pointed shoes with straps. We walked here from Timothy Street and her mother and the Canon sat in the back of the church while we were married. A friend of mine, Arthur, performed the ceremony, gliding and cavorting up the altar steps. Those days,' he said, looking out at the poplars blowing wetly by the Canon's fence, 'they hadn't got graves all round the church. Instead there were trees, great tall elms that shut out the light. There were protests about cutting them down but the arguments were sound enough. Had to cut them down, there were too many dead to bury. I could hardly see Arthur but for the white smock he wore; he looked like a moth in the darkness. Then we came outside and her mother unwrapped the cake she had made, and she and the Canon and the wife ate most of it sitting where you are now. I didn't have any. I wasn't hungry.'

He fell silent. I could not move. I stared at the ground expecting to see crumbs dropped effortlessly from the Canon's mouth, but there was nothing.

I felt sleepy; a great heaviness filled me. He was old.

All those years we had known him and never once was he young. We had smiled fleetingly, nodded our heads; he had raised his trilby hat and waved to us as we wandered down the lane towards the sea and all the time we grew and he stayed motionless. Twenty years before we were born, at random almost, he had married Mrs Biggs.

The Tsar said, 'She was pretty, you know,' and I waited. His voice had grown small, he was talking out loud to himself.

'No, not pretty. Big, full, her throat was . . . her hair smelled . . . those lovely kisses . . .'

I coughed, it was too embarrassing listening to him. He turned and said, 'We did our courting here you know. We met under the lamp under the tree.'

'Indeed.' Primly I swung my legs above the tomb and hunched my shoulders.

'Lots of evenings in the rain . . . the struggling under the beech leaves . . . the talking we did . . . the promises we made . . . you do, you know, and you mean it . . . the smell of the grass . . . I thought . . .'

I had to lean forward to hear him. I did not want to hear but I had to.

'I thought her legs were made of pearl, dappled under the trees . . . when we heard a rustle in the grass I would know it was a bird or an animal, not a man prying and I would lean back tenderly, saying, "*Keine mensch*, my love, *keine mensch*" . . . and now our dancing days are over.'

He cleared his throat, looked at me speculatively and turned away. I wished with all my might that he had never been. My eyes seemed so wide open in the rain; I felt I would never be happy again. The woman cycling down the road, all her promises turned to fat, the vast legs obscenely dappled under the beech leaves thirty years ago, the marionette doll on the bench, head dangling, eyes filled with sentimental tears, they walked the graveyard together.

The thought came to me that if I touched his mouth with mine it would taste salt from all the years he had walked up and down, up and down the lane to the sea.

'I will walk away now,' I told myself fiercely. 'I will walk away now.'

The Tsar said musingly, 'It must be getting late. We'd better go our separate ways.'

I said good night. I said it so normally I surprised myself. We parted at the cross-roads near the Canon's house; the Tsar to go down the avenue of pines towards the railway crossing, and I across the fields to the station. I waited under the lamp until he turned and waved his trilby hat in farewell, a dark figure whose dancing days were over. Then I began to run home, shouting out loudly in the empty field, 'God bless me, Harriet . . . come home.'

5

Harriet came home two days later. She whistled outside our house and sat on the wall farther down the road. I was so pleased to see her I did not notice how withdrawn she was. I looked at her clever face with joy and told her about the Tsar, and she listened kicking the wall with thin legs and rubbing her arms all the time.

They were sunburned and the skin was peeling. I waited for her shout of surprise, expecting her to jump off the wall and hop about the lane, but she just sat there rubbing her arms.

'He said' – surely she would look at me now – 'he said that he and I should go to Bordeaux to fetch a barrel of wine for the winter.'

Harriet said 'Oh' politely and looked down at her body complacently. I was silent.

A man was mowing the lawn opposite; he walked neatly up and down. The blossom on the mock-almond trees behind the wall drooped a little and fluttered in the breeze. A petal fell curled tight on Harriet's neck, and she shook herself quickly.

'I met a boy in Wales,' she said. 'He's nineteen.'

I was embarrassed; yet I wanted to ask her questions. It was only fair; I had told her everything about the Tsar, though of course that was funny. It was meant to be comic, so I laughed.

Harriet got down from the wall very carefully, and began to walk up the lane to her house.

'Please, Harriet.' I tried to catch hold of her arm. 'Please, Harriet, what's wrong?'

'I just want to be quiet . . . It's so hot.'

I stopped helpless, watching her walk away, and climbed back on the wall again. If she looked round she would see how hurt I was, so I hung my head dejectedly, but when I finally looked up she had gone. After tea I went upstairs and washed my face, and dabbed some of Mother's powder on my cheeks; but it made my face look grey almost, so I rubbed it off on the towel.

I looked so different from the frail way I felt. A noble nose and a pale bold mouth, robust limbs and crinkly hair. My mother had it permanently waved every year, and because I ran about energetically it hung messily over my forehead making me look sullen. It also smelled when it rained. I thought I looked lumpy and middle-aged, but I smiled resourcefully and said, 'God bless me and make me beautiful,' and combed my hair with care.

Harriet was in her bedroom; she saw me from the window and came down to open the front door.

'Hallo, you.' She smiled. The small irregular teeth showed. She was all pleasantness.

'Come on up.' She led the way upstairs to the small dark bedroom. We sat on the floor, Harriet leaning against the bed and rubbing her sunburned arms.

'What's all this about the Tsar?' she asked.

I told her the story all over again, but left out the bit about the wine. It was too good a thing to risk telling Harriet in her present state.

Now Harriet understood the importance of my news; she lay on the floor encouragingly, kicking her legs in the air. I was so triumphant I forgot her earlier mood and described the sallow neck beneath the collar.

Harriet's voice rose higher. 'It's probably dead white after that bit. Like something under a stone. You see it in the summer always when men open their shirts, and they're grey underneath.'

We both shuddered and Harriet raised her arms victoriously. 'That's the colour to be, burnt all over,' and she sat up and rubbed them. I wished she had not said that. She knew I was never anything but white. Even when the sun was so hot, Harriet was a deep brown, I stayed white.

Harriet knelt upright, drew out a box from under the dresser, opened it and handed me the diary. 'We've neglected it,' she said as I took it. 'I've lots to write about.'

While she found a pencil I looked at the last entry. 'We have both read D. H. Lawrence's *Lost Girl*,' I had written. 'We find it very fine and imagine Italians make good lovers.'

Harriet gave me the pencil and lay on the floor again.

'Put, "She has been away in Wales".'

I began to write and kept my face averted, trying to be neat and quick at the same time.

'She has been away in Wales. What next?'

'Put, "I have been here alone".' Harriet's voice was muffled against the carpet. 'And that you have become more intimate with the Tsar.' It was always Harriet who dictated the diary, but it was in my writing in case her mother discovered it. 'She might read something of mine,' Harriet had explained, 'but not if it was strange handwriting.' We never mentioned names and everyone had a pseudonym, to be the more safe.

'She,' Harriet said, 'has made an illuminating discovery. She has met a boy of nineteen . . . no.' Harriet sat up. 'Put "a man" instead, don't put the age. "He has yellow hair and is devoid of humour, but she found him very interesting".'

She stood up and combed her hair at the dressing table, peering at her face and leaning her elbows on the dresser top to get a closer view.

'Look,' she bade me. 'Look at my bottom lip, it's bruised.'

Before I could look she turned hurriedly away and began to dictate with her back to me.

'Her lip is bruised. It is a queer brown colour and swollen from underneath where he kissed her. He made her face rough too.'

I wrote it all down and felt dismayed at the sentences. Not

31

that the diary contained no other such passages, but Harriet was taking pleasure in dictating and telling me simultaneously. Always before we had both discussed things to go in the diary, analysed emotions, looked in the dictionary for suitable words, and fashioned the paragraphs sentence by sentence.

'We've got to be scientific,' Harriet had said. 'Otherwise we'll find it merely smutty on reading.'

'Go on,' I said, anxious to hear more.

'We lay down in a field near a farmhouse one day . . .'

I could not look up, I held the pencil so tight my fingers ached.

'Yes,' I said.

'He kissed me and hurt my mouth, then he put his hand on my neck and . . .' She broke off quickly and turned. 'Oh, give it to me, I'll write it.'

I could only sit there watching her scribble across the page, a deep frown of concentration on her face, her bottom lip slightly swollen. When she had finished she shut the book, placed it in the box and thrust it under the dresser. Seeing my face she said kindly, 'You can read it next time. Don't worry, it's nothing really. Let's go down to the sea.'

'Yes,' I said miserably, and waited for her to apply lipstick.

Harriet was a year older than I but looked much younger, with plaits fastened round her head. I was thirteen but I looked ancient beside Harriet, with my permed hair and plump body. Harriet never wore hats except sometimes an old straw panama when it rained. My spirits returned as we walked down the lane. I clutched at Harriet and laughed nervously. 'Don't laugh, he'll be there, he always is, just you see. Oh, don't laugh.'

Harriet haughtily turned her face to the sky and said in her special society voice, 'I'm sure I don't know what you mean, dear.'

And while we laughed and swayed down the lane we caught sight of the Tsar leaning against the lamp by the Canon's fence, head craned forward on the thin discoloured neck, hat in hand.

32

'Now, now,' said Harriet busily approaching him. 'What's all this. Can't have followers, you know.'

'Oh Harriet, really,' I said watching the Tsar's amused contemptuous face.

Harriet and the Tsar walked together, and I followed a little way behind them through the trees. Now and then I heard the Tsar say, 'And you think so?', and saw Harriet shake her head vehemently. I hoped they were talking about me but suddenly Harriet broke away from the path and jumped to swing on a branch, and shouted, red in the face, 'He's nineteen.'

I stopped and looked up at her in disbelief. Her feet clear of the ground threatened to kick me over.

'Move,' she ordered. 'Go on, move.'

She pushed at my chest with both feet and I stumbled and fell backward. Harriet let go of the branch and stood over me, her dress rumpled, one plait beginning to slide from its position, her face defiant.

'I told you to move, I did warn you.' She held out her hand but I just lay there refusing to look at her.

'Well, all right, sulk.' She stood undecided. 'When you feel more sensible I'll be near the tadpole pools.'

I sat up then and watched her go, brushing pine-needles from my frock dejectedly.

'She's a hot-tempered girl.' The Tsar squatted on his haunches a little distance from me, and swung his hat between his knees.

I wanted to tell him he didn't know what he was talking about; that he ought to have learnt more about people than to say she was hot-tempered.

Instead I stood up and rubbed the side of my leg patterned with pine-needles, and looked down at him balanced on his heels like a dancer. Perhaps not so old after all, even if he wasn't nineteen like the boy in Wales.

'Come on, Tsar,' I said. 'Let's find Harriet.'

But he only rocked a little where he crouched and looked at me with light eyes.

'I want to tell you something.'

'What? I want to find Harriet.'

The Tsar stood up and came close to me, and I turned in the direction Harriet had gone and saw the sun had drawn level with the trees and circled them with flames.

Please God (I could feel the Tsar's hand on my shoulder) please God send Harriet. Then I turned to face the tiger. So dingy he was with his sallow skin and thin hair brushed carefully back. For all his elegance, and graceful walk, the delicate way he moved his head, indefinably he lacked youth. Later I was to remember the stillness in the woods, the evening in an avenue of light between the tree trunks, and the Tsar with his hand on my shoulder. I did not know I loved him then, because as Harriet wrote later in the diary, we had a long way to go before we reached the point of love.

The Tsar moved himself worriedly and took my fingers between his own. 'No, no,' he said under the pines, as if he had read my thoughts, 'No, child, no,' and with a sudden clumsy movement pulled my head against his shoulder. I stood there awkwardly straddled, not daring to ease myself away, but turning my face gently to gaze alone the avenue of light. He stood back so suddenly I almost stumbled, and he walked away shouting in his high amused voice, 'Harriet, where art thou?'

Harriet told me afterwards she had seen it all, and that I looked most uncomfortable, but when we reached the edge of the trees she was sitting a long way down the slope with her back to us. Her plaits hung about her ears, she sat without shoes, the bony feet curled under the sand. She looked cold all over.

I sat down beside her and nudged her arm but she would not look at me. The Tsar stood above us; we could hear him breathing heavily from the effort of the climb. I wanted to shout, to laugh, to roll in the sand; anything to throw off the awful weighty responsibility I felt. Always before the feeling had been occasioned by Harriet, by something she had made me do. The time she had borrowed the hand-cart from Mr

34

Redman and wheeled me up and down the lane crying, 'Bring out your dead,' I had lain crushed and embarrassed with pain. I had smiled and shown my splendid teeth, clutching tight to the side of the barrow and wishing to die. But that had come to an end when we put the cart back in the garage. The Tsar would not be so easily disposed of; and the putting away in the end would be up to me, not Harriet.

When we wrote in the diary later that night, Harriet told me to use a new page so that I should not see what she had written earlier about the boy in the field. What she had dictated about the Tsar seemed to both of us inarticulate. But it was so difficult.

I wrote . . .

The Tsar tried to kiss me, I think; but nothing happened. She hid behind the sandhills and thought I looked very uncomfortable. I should have stood closer, then I would not have felt so foolish.

Then Harriet told me to write the bit about love, and how we had not tasted everything yet. Before she shut me out in the garden I held the door open, whispering in case her mother overheard.

'What haven't we tasted yet?'

'Oh many things. You wait.'

Then her mother joined us on the step, talking pleasantly and emptily. Harriet put an arm round her waist and looked fondly at her, but it was unconvincing. We both tried very hard to give our parents love, and security, but they were too demanding.

I said good night, and walked home down the lane pointing my feet at every step, craning my neck the better to see the stars.

6

'I ASK you dear,' said Harriet rolling over on to her
stomach, holding her plait up to the sunlight. 'Is it likely
that a woman would admit to being jealous of a girl of
thirteen?'

'I suppose not.' I sounded unconvinced. 'But supposing she
did admit it and came round to our house to see Mother.
Think of the row there'd be.'

Harriet lay still and serious. 'You could always say Mrs
Biggs was perverted. After all, it's a nasty thing to imply.'

'But Mother,' I insisted. 'She's hardly forgotten the Italians
yet.'

'Good Lord,' Harriet sat up amazed. 'That was years ago.
We may have been precocious but it was innocent enough.'
She looked round the field. 'Wasn't it?'

I tried to think what innocence meant and failed.

'I don't know if we were ever innocent.' I hoped I sounded
casual in case we became embarrassed and pedantic.

'Well, we felt daring the time we met the prisoners.' Harriet
was annoyed. 'We were awfully scared. That's innocence.
Why, you said you didn't want to go the second time, and I
went alone and said you were ill. What happened to you?'

I stared at the poppies by the fence, the stiff hairy stems
that wavered when the flower burst. In bud they stood fierce
and firm; once wanton in the sun they flowered and grew
weak. I nearly told Harriet I felt like that but it seemed too
vague and sentimental. 'I just went for a walk along the shore.'
I lay back in the grass.

36

'You should have come,' said Harriet. 'It was interesting.'

I had read the diary so I knew it was interesting. Instead I had walked along the edge of the sea, picking up shells and rolling burst melons soggily over the sand.

The first time we had met the prisoners I had been uneasy but not frightened. Harriet had asked them questions about their families and country, and they had shown us photographs. Sedate images of brothers and mothers, and one of a girl with a cross on a chain around her neck. 'Anna-Maria,' the younger one pointed at the photograph. 'Very beautiful girl . . . like you.' And he smiled at Harriet. The older man was plump and short with a neat nose and tiny ears that lay flat against his head. The last time we had gone to meet them, the time Mrs Biggs saw us, Harriet told me to take the plump man away somewhere on my own.

Walking in the sun along the sand, shirt torn open, arms spread high, feet wet and cold in the sea. Sliding damp skinned over green moss, alive and moving on the rocks by the concrete hangers. Walking behind the sandhills and sitting with bare feet beside the plump Italian. He called me 'a dirty little angel'. Adolescent tremblings, swirls of nerves gone gold. The pain of the moment, the awful uncontrolled joy; that was innocence.

I sat up in the field and said loudly, 'Remember, Harriet, he called me a dirty little angel.'

'Mmmm.' Harriet face downwards in the grass was in a private dream of her own.

We were in the field behind my house, screened from the garden where Mother sat reading a library book, by a row of tattered poplars that stood close to the fence. As the wind lifted them lightly I could see my mother's deck-chair, and the problem of Mrs Biggs came uneasily to my mind.

'Harriet. Harriet . . . Listen.'

'What?'

'We shall have to be very careful,' I said, lying down beside her. She turned and her breath came sweetly against my face.

37

'We shall have to drop a hint now and then of seeing the Tsar on our walks, so that if Mrs Biggs does arrive our lies will seem more plausible.'

'Very well,' said Harriet. 'But discreetly, just in general conversation. "Oh, I saw Mr Biggs last night, he does look ill," or something like that.'

'And you tell him not to speak to us in the lane.' I warned her.

'It does seem a little unnecessary.' Harriet lay on her back and covered her face with her arm. 'You've got nothing out of it so far.' I felt angry with her. He had told me all his fragile history; told me of his wedding day, and his summer evenings. He had said by the tadpole pools . . . She'll know I've been happy tonight . . . I could not forget that he trusted me. Aloud I said:

'It might be best to finish the whole adventure, just not follow it up.'

But I knew I could not do that, even if Harriet allowed me. A year ago, to be called a Dirty Little Angel would have kept us going for months. Now it was not enough; more elaborate things had to be said; each new experience had to leave a more complicated tracery of sensations; to satisfy us every memory must be more desperate than the last.

In the beginning we had never searched for experience. True we didn't follow the usual childish pursuits. We never played games or behaved like playmates, we never verbally abused each other except on occasions deliberately, to reassure our parents. It was Dodie who began it, telling us of the gay times she had known in her youth, without Papa guessing. 'Making the friendly gesture' she had called it. And we liked her stories, we were fascinated. We took to going for long walks over the shore, looking for people who by their chosen solitariness must have something to hide. We learnt early it was the gently resigned ones who had the most to tell; the voluble and frantic were no use. They seldom got beyond pity for themselves and at the end mouthed soft obscenities. At first Harriet was interrogator and I spectator. When she questioned adults

38

and probed their lives I was content to listen. She said we were not to become involved, we were too young, only to learn. She said our information was a kind of training course for later life; living at second hand was our objective until we were old enough. But of late, even at school and away from Harriet's influence, the process of analysis went on. It had become a habit: the steady search to discover the background of teachers; the singling out of girls older than myself who might add something to what I already knew.

Progressively it became less of a joy when the girl would say, as one had, 'It's so hard to be good now, isn't it? Mummy says it will be much easier when I'm grown up.' I thought of the sins of my childhood; the hats lost on train journeys, the gloves left behind in church, the refusal to go on a message. I thought of the things I had done since, things that Harriet and I did not consider strange, but that would rank as enormities to this girl . . . and my mother. Harriet told me that in other lands, in other cultures, in other times, both past and in the future, we would not be thought abnormal, but it did not help. I was separated from my mother by an invisible wall, a wall of amyl, that had become no longer hypothetical. Never again to share little jokes with her, to sit in the garden peacefully waiting for the apples to ripen and summer to bloom.

Harriet stood up in the field and stretched her body, arms above her head.

'Your mother's calling . . . tea I think.'

'Coming, Mother,' I shouted.

We climbed the fence and walked down the garden towards my smiling mother. She told me to fetch deck-chairs from the green-house. Through the glass I spied on them both, Harriet at my mother's feet, looking up winningly into her face. The smell in the green-house assumed shape and colour; the stuffy green of the tomato plants, the bursting splitting red of the fruit, the pale grey odour of last year's mint hanging from a nail above the door. I was too warm, too indolent to bother any more about Mrs Biggs. If she came and told my mother stories and Mother suffered, it was not I that was to blame.

But when I looked through the glass and saw her sitting there so happy on her scarlet deck-chair, she was my best beloved and I wished she need not suffer.

'Hurry up!' she called.

She asked me to sit on the deck-chair but I wouldn't. I sat on the grass and drank my tea. Harriet did as she was asked and chatted eagerly for my benefit. To cover my silence.

'Yes, I'm specialising in maths now.' She looked fully into my mother's eyes. 'Of course, it's only a means to an end, I'm more interested in science you know.'

A wasp hovered erratically above the lupins, turned suspended in the air, and spun buzzing to the fallen apples beneath the flower.

Harriet was saying, 'We saw Mr Biggs last night. He looked ill, we thought. Didn't we?'

'Oh, I don't know, perhaps a little pale . . . but I hardly know him.'

'I thought you used to be great pals.' My mother refilled my cup, her eyes kind and loving. 'You got a card from him once.'

'Did I?' I looked at Harriet but she avoided my gaze.

Sometimes in a mood of contentment and affection I confided things to my mother. Usually I had reason to regret it.

Harriet was carefully putting her tea-leaves in the grass. She looked up and said slowly, 'You never told me . . . you must have quite a collection by now.'

'A collection of what?'

'Cards, dear,' she said.

'From Mr Biggs?' My mother was puzzled.

'Oh, don't be daft, Harriet.' Crossly I pinched her leg and scowled at her.

'I always remember,' Harriet continued, 'the ones you received from Rome and Naples and all points north.'

My mother was looking at her and then at me.

'I do think you should shut up, I do think you might.'

'Perhaps I got it wrong,' said Harriet contritely. 'Perhaps it was someone else.'

After a little pause she went on, 'I do remember you got one once from Mrs Biggs.'

I very nearly laughed at the absurdity of the lie.

'I met her at the station the day she was posting it,' Harriet spoke severely, 'and she said – was it *Berks* or *Barks*?'

'I shouldn't have thought' – Mother was thinking of the Italians – 'that Mrs Biggs would send you a card.'

It was beyond me now. I relaxed and let Harriet extricate me as best she could, seeing my mother's face as if through a curtain of gauze. I saw her opening her small mouth primly and beautifully, but I heard no sound in the garden. A cloud began to roll softly towards the sun; the lupin beds already were cold and shut off from the light; the grass a little way down the garden faded while I watched.

The shadow crept steadily up the lawn, extinguishing the roses, the holly bush, the apple tree beside the fence. Only Mother and Harriet lingered, glowing in a corner of light; then they too wavered, struggled with invisible shutters, and turned grey. I waited. The cloud disintegrated in the sky, the grass brightened and Harriet enveloped herself in the warmth again.

The back gate loudly closed; the small figure of Frances pushed its way through the privet hedge.

'Don't,' called Mother. 'Walk round, dear.'

But Frances was already coming sideways up the lawn, trailing her coat along the ground.

'Hallo, Harriet,' she said politely, and stood leaning against my mother's knees.

I could see the next-door neighbour looking through the kitchen window into our garden. We must have made a charming group. Tea on the lawn, the mother surrounded by children, the clear voices. At least we looked real. Even if Harriet and I were alien it could not show.

'Let's take a photograph,' my mother said. 'I've a new film in the dining-room drawer.'

'I'll get it.' Frances was running down the garden.

At the privet hedge she swerved and ran along the rockery

to the concrete path. Her face appeared at the kitchen window. 'Thought I was going through the hedge, didn't you, Mummy?'

My mother smiled indulgently and Harriet and I smiled too with relief.

When we sat on the grass, Frances between us, I hoped for a moment the camera would not work.

'Look up, Frances.' My mother waited and the shutter clicked.

What if the film exposed not three children in the sun, but one between two spectres, wearing childish smiles. Faces that crumbled like bread in the fingers, and showed a fearful disintegration. Harriet wanted to take a photograph of mother and myself, but I said no, so she placed Frances between my mother's knees and looked professionally at the group.

'Put your arm round her neck,' she told Frances.

Here at least would be a record of all that was true and good and beautiful.

When the photographing was finished Frances knelt on the grass beside me, putting her arms round my neck, and rubbing her face against mine.

'There's a fair on at Bumpy field tomorrow, isn't there? There's roundabouts and a menagerie, isn't there? Please take me, please.'

My mother looked pleadingly at me and then at Harriet.

'Do take her with you, she does so want to go. It will only be for half an hour.'

'And then I shall have to leave and bring her back I suppose.'

I was angry too quickly. A fierce irritation caused me to shake Frances away from me.

The more kindly and generously my mother looked at me, the more irritated I grew.

'It's so stupid. Just because you won't take her yourself, I have to. Why can't she be more self-contained. I don't beg always to be with other people.'

'But you've Harriet.' Frances began to cry desperately, sobbing terribly on the grass, her whole body given to sudden grief.

Harriet said, 'Thank you for the tea, I must be going now. We'll take you to the fair, don't cry, Frances.'

My mother looked gratefully at her, but still she didn't reproach me.

At the gate Harriet watched me almost with distaste.

'Why do you get so illogical? It's so ugly when you allow them to disturb you.'

I must have looked very close to despair at this, for she added in her society voice, 'Rise above it, dear . . . rise above it.'

'Are we going to the shore tonight?' I asked.

Three high-bosomed women in hard bowler hats, sitting penguin-shaped on three fleshy horses, appeared at the corner of the lane. Massive and leisurely they passed our gate, filling the lane with tweed jackets and cello thighs.

Harriet looked at the group thoughtfully. 'No, I've something special to do tonight. I'll tell you tomorrow.'

She began to walk unhurriedly away from me, her sandals making no sound on the road; in the garden at the back of the house, Frances, her grief forgotten, could be heard screaming with laughter.

43

7

HARRIET went directly home to her father.
He was a tall man, very morose, possessing a fierce
sense of justice and great sentimentality. To hear *Roses of
Picardy* or *Silver Threads Among the Gold* filled him with
emotion. He would talk constantly to Harriet with immense
nostalgia of his youth and his brother William. His childhood
it would seem had been a hard one. 'The cruelty of those days,'
he was fond of saying, 'the ignorance.' It was therefore sur-
prising to us that any misdemeanour on Harriet's part, however slight, brought instant physical chastisement.

She liked to do helpful jobs for him. Filling the watering
can when he ill-humouredly worked in the garden, finding his
cigarettes for him when he mislaid them; taking a certain
satisfaction in thus soothing his irritable mind.

Though he was strict about her school work, and displeased
if she fell back a place in her form, he was relaxed in other
respects. She could in summer stay out long after it was dark,
go swimming in the salt sea off the Point, where the soldiers
splashed every morning and the nuns from the convent shyly
billowed out over the sheeted water of an evening, and he even
allowed her to go without breakfast if she so wished.

Harriet had made tea for her father, her mother being in
town that afternoon, and told him about Frances wanting me
to take her to the fair. She said I had shouted at my mother
and quite lost control. Her father said, nodding his head
wisely, 'I used to be the same myself; it's all part of the process
of wanting to do without guidance and control. I remember

44

I told my mother once, and she was a very hasty woman, that she ought not to rely on me to entertain William. "Mother," I said, "Willam must realise I'm almost a man and learn to stay with you." I was eighteen and been out working for four years, but she gave me a blow across the head with her hand that made me shout. I can feel it now. But she was right you know.'

Harriet pretended to agree with him, and waited till he had come to the end of his reminiscences. Then she said casually she had heard Mr Biggs was ill.

Her father was immediately alarmed, fearing that his Saturday round of golf was in jeopardy.

'Run round and see if it's anything serious,' he told her. 'And find out if he'll be well enough for Saturday.'

Harriet, pleased with her strategy, wheeled her mother's bicycle out of the shed, and rode to Timothy Street.

The Tsar's house was a large Victorian-fronted building, with overgrown gardens back and front. The front gate was large and solid, painted black and so tall it was impossible to see over. Though it was summer and not yet six o'clock there was a light in the front room, and one curtain was drawn a quarter of the way across the large windows; this and the row of thick holly bushes made the light necessary. It was such a neglected house, dark and well made, unlike the houses we lived in, strung like cherry-stones along the lane, that Harriet expected the door to swing open on its hinges without human help. While she was waiting curiously for this to happen, voices were raised in argument somewhere in the house. For a moment she thought her lie had become truth, that Mrs Biggs was quarrelling with the Tsar come home ill from work. Then she realised it was the wireless and lifting the knocker firmly rapped it against the door.

Mrs Biggs, in fawn cardigan and sandals, like those we wore, opened the door, heaving it backwards and staring full at Harriet.

She led her with one hand down the hall, the other to her lips. 'Silence,' she whispered. 'It's such a good play.'

Like characters before the Tabs in a pantomime, tiptoeing

45

across the stage to fill in a difficult transformation scene, they entered the front-room.

Harriet sat on the sofa, knees close together, Mrs Biggs in an armchair by the fire leaning forward, giving her whole attention to the radio. The clock on the mantelpiece said half past five, and listening for a moment to the sense of the words spoken, Harriet realised it was Children's Hour.

The room as she later described it, was heavy and cumbersome with furniture. A huge Welsh dresser against the wall, with a mirror panel partly screened by plates in blue and gold; a sideboard near the window with a statue on its top, brandishing a sword and with one feminine breast rakishly exposed. What made the statue command attention, said Harriet, was not its size which was formidable, but the statue's nipple which was tipped with scarlet. The rest of the room was dark and very warm. Gradually, as Harriet later described it, between Mrs Biggs and herself grew a hedge of green ivy. She saw through the leaves the mouth of the Tsar's wife open giddily as she sat listening to a children's entertainment. Her hands in her lap closed idly and heavily, in and out, sleep-laden like a red-rusted weed in the sea.

The face of Mrs Biggs was large and dry; light-coloured eyes set flat in her head, grey thick hair rolled up above her ears and neck.

'Have you had tea, dear?' she asked when the programme came to an end.

'Yes, thank you.'

Mrs Biggs stood up and poked the fire with a brass curtain rod; as she leant forward Harriet could see on the calves of her legs strong black hairs. She was watching Harriet through the mirror above the fireplace.

Harriet who was fond of assuming the character expected of her in certain different houses, now became the large girl at the Christmas party, arms crossed over a growing chest, her eyes wide open and greedy.

'Father sent me to ask if Mr Biggs will be calling for him as usual this Saturday. He'd heard that he wasn't well.'

46

Mrs Biggs received this last piece of news with less surprise than expected.

'Oh, he'll be able to play golf all right. There's nothing wrong with him that I know of.'

Her eyes strayed to the small table by the lamp, with its array of bottles and syphon.

'A little self-control would be a help.'

Harriet began to hate Mrs Biggs, sitting there untidily in a stained cardigan, talking of self-control.

'He's weak,' said Mrs Biggs, as if to excuse herself. 'His mother told me as much years ago, but somehow you don't pay attention to that sort of thing when you're young.'

She reached up and took a silver-framed photograph down from the mantelpiece and handed it to Harriet.

'Look at that!'

It was a young face, rather smooth and old-fashioned, with oiled hair brushed well back.

'It's Mr Biggs,' said Harriet. 'I never knew he wore spectacles.'

'He became vainer as he grew older. Strains his eyes all the time, but won't wear glasses.' Her face began to change in expression; she wanted Harriet to go now. Her eyes darkened with impatience, her hands fidgeted in her lap. But Harriet would not go. She told me, 'I knew she wanted me to go, and that made it so that I couldn't.'

Stubbornly she held the photograph and tried to see some faint trace in it of the Tsar we knew. She was aware of Mrs Biggs, restless and suddenly tired in her armchair by the fire; voices in the lane outside made the room isolated and withdrawn.

Looking up suddenly at Mrs Biggs, she was aware of an expression half formed in the woman's light eyes, something of cunning or sadness that was wholly unconscious.

'How's that little friend of yours?' Mrs Biggs asked. 'The stout one. Getting on all right at that school?'

'Yes, thank you. I think so.'

Harriet stood up, placed the young Tsar on the mantelpiece

and turned to go. In the hall it was cool; the door into the garden opened to show the pale washed sky; the holly bush near the porch quivered, stabbing green leaves upwards in the warm air. Mrs Biggs waited till Harriet had successfully manoeuvred her bicycle out into the road; she gave a small, not unfriendly smile, and stepped into the house. Then she shut the door.

It was the following night when, Frances between us, we walked to Bumpy field, that Harriet told me of her visit to the house of the Tsar.

We had to be very careful in case Frances repeated what she heard but, as she ran ahead every few moments in her excitement to reach the fair, we felt there was little danger of her understanding such disjointed conversation as ours.

'I wish,' I said kindly to Harriet, 'I had seen the photograph.'

I did not mean it, for though I considered Harriet brave and clever I almost hated her for prising Mrs Biggs open in that way. I imagined the woman's heart laid bare, the cancerous growth of bitterness dissected coldly; as for the photograph, why that was no more the Tsar than I was the frail golden girl I dreamed of being.

Harriet laughed suddenly. 'She called you stout, you know. "Your stout friend" she said.'

I was suddenly afraid lest Mrs Biggs should describe me so to the Tsar. He may not have noticed it before, and then aware of his wife's remark turn slowly to me one day under the church porch, saying, 'You are stout, aren't you?'

Frances ran back again to meet us, hopping on one leg and holding with both hands to my arm.

'You can hear the music,' she said.

A little way past the paper shop and between a row of cottages lay Bumpy field, circled with noise and military bands.

Above the loudspeaker music and the excited cries of Frances I heard Harriet say, 'I kept thinking of Wales when I was sitting with her. Not the boy with the yellow hair, but the country. I kept seeing it.'

48

'Perhaps he'll be here,' I said, thinking of the Tsar, as we turned along the path to the field.

A man in shirt-sleeves sat heedlessly in the rain on a three-legged stool in the grass, before a small table. He gave us tickets without looking up from the paper he was reading, making a small flapping movement with it when Harriet leaned too heavily against the table.

'Don't,' I admonished her, hoping he would look up, and I would be able to tell instantly if he thought me stout. But he paid no attention, just sat there head down, the rain moulding his black hair like a cap about his ears, and read his paper.

Small gusts of wind eddied down the field; the air was filled with sharp intakes of breath; children and girls screamed uniformly, clinging to the striped poles of the roundabouts, spinning round and round on painted horses.

The field seemed small, bounded by trees and cottages and the red brick paper shop; a handkerchief of grass laid out under the wet sky, dragged in the centre by two machines that stamped and whirled and flung fragile boats above the earth.

In the light nothing was exciting; even Frances felt this as she climbed slowly on to the roundabout, gazing flatly about her, waiting for the horses to move. When they did, causing her to lurch forward and cling tightly to the pole, she did not scream, only made a little soft 'Oh!' of surprise.

Harriet and I did not want to do anything yet, meaning to save our money till we had taken Frances home and it was almost dark in the field. It was irritating to have to stand there and be seen bedraggled in the rain.

I had tried to explain to my mother that it was awful to go so early; that one looked so silly when the field was full of small children. I could not explain that when it was dark a new dignity would transform the fair into an oasis of excitement, so that it became a place of mystery and delight; peopled with soldiers from the camp and orange-faced girls wearing head scarves, who in strange regimented lines would sway back and forth across the field, facing each other defiantly, exchanging no words, bright-eyed under the needle stars. I

49

could not explain how all at once the lines would meet and mingle performing a complicated rite of selection; orange girls and soldier boys pairing off slowly to drift to the far end of the field and struggle under the hedges filled with blackberries.

It was then that Harriet and I would ride the roundabouts, whirling in the middle of the field and scattering screams into distant corners of the fairground, hearing in our voices the exhausted cries of those others, smearing mouths together in the rain.

Frances climbed politely down and stood unsteadily on the grass. She waved her arms windmill fashion in exaggeration. 'I feel so dizzy.'

'What would you like to do now?' Harriet asked her. 'The same thing again or those dive-bombers?'

Frances looked reflectively at the yellow boats, tethered on steel rods one above the other. They rose slowly crabwise, plunged sickeningly, spun above the grass and climbed again.

'I don't think so.' She moved her shoe in the damp soil and turned her face away from us.

'I'll come with you.' I held out my hand and led her to the pay stool. I felt sad for her disappointment, her inability to enjoy herself after all. The excitement of the fair she had imagined, had not materialised; she was thrown in on herself, politely going through the motions of wonder.

I clutched her arm tightly in the dive-bomber, enacting fear, screaming as we heeled to the ground, heads hanging above the blurred field.

She began to laugh now and when it was all over begged me to stay for another turn, excitedly jumping in her seat, saying, 'Do let's have another ride. Isn't it awful?'

The machine quivered, the tune of *Soldiers of the Queen* marched strongly out from the loudspeaker and lifted us into the sky. I could not be sure that Frances was really excited, or whether, just as I pretended for her sake, so she too laughed and struggled in an effort to please. Perhaps I had spoilt her joy the day before in the garden, when I had said I did not wish to take her.

50

So together in mutual deceit we plummeted and screamed, breathless at the end, and stumbling a little in the field.

It was growing darker above the spread-eagled trees; multi-coloured lights began to flicker along the Hoop-la stall. A string of pearls, slung from the top of the dynamo van to the roof of the roundabouts, glowed palely against the sky.

I wished for Frances she should go home laden with presents such as one read about in books; traditional prizes of dolls with real golden hair, and little dogs, and a box of chocolates for Mother. But we won nothing, and if we had, the prizes were of such a practical, utility nature we would have been ashamed to carry them. Finally, we bought her a stick of candy floss, that waved loosely before her mouth like fine mist, and took her home.

Mother opened wide arms to Frances, making little sounds of disapproval when she felt the damp hair, fetching a towel immediately from the bathroom to rub protectively the child's head.

It was warm in the front-room with the curtains drawn, and the flowers cast spiked shadows on the tablecloth. My father leaned backwards in his chair, gazing at us through spectacles bandaged firmly at the bridge with sticking plaster.

Almost I wanted to stay with them, not go out riotously into the fairground with Harriet.

I bent to kiss my father on the forehead. I turned to embrace my mother but she was locked in love with Frances so I was embarrassed.

'I won't be late,' I promised them all, opening the door thankfully and walking down the hall.

'Put this on.' My father stood behind me holding a scarf in his hands. He wrapped it round my neck, searching my face with pathetic eyes. He too was afraid and uncertain how to guide me. His face in his inability to pass on experience was crumpled and pompous. I ran out to join Harriet at the gate, the scarf chafing my neck.

It was very cold now; the wind that blew from the sea swept away the fairground music in confusion, so that sometimes we heard it loudly almost in our faces, and then far away and small above the houses.

The field was dark with people; clusters of soldiers like worker-bees rose and fell on the undulating floor of the round-about. The girls linked arm-in-arm, mouths like purple flowers in the artificial light, walked a sedate palais glide for attention. A voice magnified by a loudspeaker sang, 'Your mother was crying, your father was crying and I was crying too'. It should have been funny to hear, but there was such a soaring swooning constancy in the voice, and such a surge of power flooded into the field and overwhelmed the wind, that it assumed tragic proportions.

We rode the roundabouts, shrieking among the painted horses, riding endlessly round and round, waiting for the Tsar to come. When he did come and Harriet shouted to me, 'He's here, Sister Ann,' I did not recognise him, so strangely the light distorted his face.

I stared at the hunch-backed dwarf he had become, his brow like a pale dome, the smile that twisted the black mouth utterly mocking and changed. When he moved to meet us, he bulged hideously under the chain of pearls, his raincoat flapping shroudlike in the wind.

'Hallo,' he said, the cold eyes watching my face carefully.

Harriet wandered away leaving me alone with him.

We both felt it was all so unusual, to be walking together so dangerously in a merry-go-round world, and nothing must be missed. The Tsar won a glass butter-dish at the Hoop-la stall, and put it in his pocket with great satisfaction, smiling at me complacently.

We walked down the field, further into the darkness; at our feet in the wet grass, among the old tins and rubbish, lay the reflections of lights, fragments of glass in blue and yellow and orange, not big enough or tangible enough to take home and look through later, turning the world to gold.

A row of girls went gaily by, heads bent against the rain, flower mouths slightly parted, delicate legs prancing over the puddles. Then there was no one in the whole field but ourselves, walking away down the avenue of bold little lights, walking in desolation. Going over the grass with no one to call us securely in to supper, we became abstracted. No great voice called out terribly, 'Come back, stop!' No great wind came behind us and tore us apart. In a silence bordered by the sad whine of the voice singing wearily now above the soughing trees, the old man kissed my lips, laying them against his own quite flatly and coldly.

Then we walked back towards all the noise and confusion; neither lingeringly nor tenderly, but briskly.

I did not know what to make of it. I had not been kissed many times, but Paul Ricotti had almost swallowed me in his mouth, and the lorry driver Harriet and I had met once when on a picnic had bent me over backwards in his emotion. Both occasions had been funny; the dry calculated embrace of the Tsar might almost have been given by my father, except that it was so sad.

I looked for Harriet among the crowd and found her near the Hoop-la stall, swaying on her feet, her arm round the waist of a soldier.

'Harriet, it's awfully late, please come home.' I felt tired and cold now. The face she turned to me was so wild under the coloured lights I was unable to return her gaze.

Once a long time ago we had met the gardener in the Rhododendron Lands; he had told us we were trespassing and demanded our names and addresses. Harriet, her face illuminated from within by an almost diabolic emotion, had cursed him terribly, walking away a little between the bushes as if to avoid contact with him, white-faced with passion, shouting out insults. The man, appalled by her mood, had turned to me pitifully.

'I'm only doing my job, missie. It's only what's expected of me.'

Harriet trembled on the path and shouted harshly, 'Don't talk to him. Don't talk to the swine.'

Going home she was perfectly controlled and seemed to have forgotten the whole incident.

53

So now I stood hesitatingly, unable to plead with her, fearing her inner exultation. Though she seemed younger than I, it was never my part to be responsible for her; she it was who always decided our actions, and told me what to write in the diary.

I turned and walked out of the field, hoping she would follow.

The Tsar was nowhere in the lane, and though I loitered for a while by the paper shop neither he nor Harriet came.

All the enjoyment had receded from me; I walked miserably down the lane, struggling with a feeling of guilt. There was nothing tangible I had done that was wrong, no sin that I had not committed many times before. I had not even told lies to my parents. I had gone out with their blessing; the scarf now damp and heavy about my neck was proof of this. Still the niggling feeling of uneasiness persisted. I quickened my steps half expecting my father to be at the bend of the road, flurried and harsh with worry at my returning so late.

But there was no one in the lane and, once indoors out of the darkness, my mother and father received me kindly and absent-mindedly, only frowning a little at my wet clothes and exhausted face.

I sat drinking hot milk by the kitchen fire, thinking of Harriet and the Tsar still whirling in infinite darkness outside the window.

8

THE next morning, almost as soon as I had finished break-fast, I heard Harriet whistling outside in the lane.

My mother said firmly, as I dried the dishes, 'You're not going out till I've been helped a little first. She is a nuisance.' I felt disloyal to both of them. 'She's always calling. I've hardly seen you at all this holiday.'

As soon as I could I ran to the door and looked into the garden. Harriet was patiently leaning against the gate, resting her head on its wooden top, swaying backwards and forwards.

'Harriet,' I shouted, 'I'll see you at the library in an hour. Go away now.'

The day was clear and calm, showing no trace of the wild-ness of last night; between sedate gardens hedged with blossom Harriet went her quiet way, clad in a blue dress and cardigan.

All along the street of shops people called out to me enquir-ingly, expressing their opinions on my height and weight. I was extremely polite, voice like a bell ringing the changes, weaving my ponderous papal way to the library.

Harriet said in surprise, 'You're so horribly nice and well-mannered. Fancy even speaking to that awful Heatherlee woman after what she said about the Jews.'

'It's all right.' I felt embarrassed. 'It makes things easier in the long run. Diplomacy, you know.'

It was not true; though I spoke graciously to everyone it was Harriet they genuinely liked. Even Mrs Heatherlee, who in conversation called her 'That Dreadful Child', had given her chocolate in the grocer's.

Harriet had once told the station porter Disraeli that on Victory Day Mrs Heatherlee had seven loose women in the backyard; she had heard them gambolling round the coal shed shouting, 'Dear ole Freddie.' Mrs Heatherlee's daughter Margaret had been standing on the platform a few yards away; but even she lent Harriet a book called 'The Dimsie Omnibus'.

'What happened to the Dimsie Omnibus?' said Harriet suddenly, linking up logically that occasion with the smart Mrs Heatherlee now burrowing mole-like into her little black car.

'You burnt it,' I said crossly and entered the library.

'Guess who I met last night?'

'Charlie Chester.'

'Seriously,' said Harriet. 'I came out of the field with the soldier shortly after you left, and Mrs Biggs was standing on the pavement. Dreadfully wet, with no hat and grey hair to her shoulders, waiting for the Tsar.'

'What did she say?' I remembered that Harriet did not yet know he had kissed me.

'Oh, Hallo, almost as if she were at the races. Trying to pretend she always stood on the pavement on rainy evenings. I felt sorry for her so I told her I had seen the Tsar a moment ago in the field. And she said, "Yes I know, he's forgotten something." I nearly said, "You", but walked away with my soldier instead. Do you know he wanted me to take his pay book and address if only I'd go into the bushes with him. In all that rain. They are funny.'

'Harriet!' A feeling of panic and despair had abruptly taken hold of me. 'Please.'

She looked at my face in bewilderment, unable to comprehend immediately.

'Don't,' she said softly, thrusting a book into my hand, standing huddled against me, screening my body.

Tears ran weakly down my cheeks; I ached with the suppressed desire to howl like an animal in pain, deep alleviating moans that would ease me. I stood there mutely, crying endlessly in distress, without knowing why.

Harriet looked down the avenue of shelves. 'Try to stop. Someone might come in.'

I did not care but I tried to stop for her sake, rubbing my hand convulsively across my eyes.

We walked out of the library, Harriet shielding my ravaged face, talking loudly and quickly. We did not stop till we reached the deserted park; until we sat down in the long grass by the public lavatories.

'Why,' said Harriet, 'what happened last night?'

'He kissed me.' My voice was thick and muffled; it sounded very serious and impressive, but what I said seemed trite.

'Well!'

'I just felt sad suddenly, that's all. Her standing in the rain, and you with a soldier, and me in bed, and the Tsar lost without any of us.'

'Oh!' Harriet sounded aggrieved, pulling the grass with irritated fingers, stabbing the dry soil beneath.

'I don't see what there is to cry about,' she added. 'Unless you just feel emotional.'

Though it was not true, I almost felt that this time she had failed to understand; that her experience and mine had not advanced to the same point.

'It's sad,' said Harriet, 'but not as sad as all that. If he likes to amuse himself with you and she likes to follow him and make herself miserable, that's their stupidity. It's sad too, of course, but it's better than nothing for both of them.'

The word 'amuse' caused me intense sorrow. Tears of self-pity welled in my eyes, the park swam in a huge bubble of moisture; I began to cry noisily.

'Don't be illogical,' Harriet spoke sharply.

'It never has been easy, you ought to know by now. In Wales . . .' She was silent suddenly.

'If you really loved him, really and truly.' I sat up angrily, remembering the page in the diary I had not been allowed to read. 'You couldn't possibly go off with anyone else. That's sad too.'

Harriet turned to me in amazement and disbelief.

'I didn't love him. I never said I did. You are a fool. And that's sadder than anything else I've ever known.'

Face scornful, she stood up and folded her arms, looking down at me with derision.

I began to feel better. Anger bestowed by Harriet was always more exhilarating than sympathy, and the fact that she had not after all loved the boy in Wales was a thing of happiness in itself. I wiped my face with the hem of my dress and said cheerfully, 'You are quite right, I was just feeling emotional. I feel fine now.'

She was thoughtful going home; she spoke little, a frown of concentration puckered her eyes. I might have thought the sun too strong the way she frowned, but I knew her too well to be so easily mistaken. Outside my gate she paused. Her fingers exploring the blistered paintwork, she said, 'Could you be outside my house a little after nine? I have a plan.'

I felt it was rather late to be going adventuring, and told her so.

'Please yourself,' she said, opening wide eyes with apparent lack of interest.

That evening, some minutes to nine, I was waiting outside her house, sitting on the kerb of the pavement, feeling quite warm and comfortable, not wondering or even curious, just waiting for Harriet. Everything in the lane was so quiet, and similar, so conducive to calmness; the row of red-bricked, identical little houses; a toy-town line of chimney stacks bobbing blackened corks into the colourless sky. A Sunday decorum enveloped the lane in silence and respectability. Behind lace curtains, families sat in mettlesome companionship, shut securely in their boxes on the squares of lawn.

When Harriet appeared the peace of the evening seemed destroyed; she danced with fearful energy on the pavement, eyes bemused and restless, a figure that jerked and pranced with impatience before me.

'It's not quite dark enough yet,' she said, still for a moment looking up at the sky.

Undecided, she waited, then pulled me to my feet, shaking

58

me till I cried protestingly, 'Stop it, Harriet, you're hurting me.'

She held tight to my arm, face close to mine, the light eyes full-irised, speckled with brown, mouth moistly parted, pellet teeth strained together; then abruptly she released me and walked rapidly down the road. I had to run to keep up with her, for she strode out manfully past the green painted gates and the rubber green hedges, the hem of her dress swinging high above her knees casting shadows on the brittle legs beneath.

She slackened her pace as we turned into Timothy Street and we walked slowly down the road. A confused image of leaf-dappled kerb-stone and diamond-paned windows reflecting light; high ragged fences of yellowed privet and a long avenue of grey houses with tall trees rustling against their walls.

Outside the high black gate Harriet paused, reflected, and walked on to the path that ran beside the house. There was a ditch on one side, the wooden fence of the Tsar's house on the other, and a field at the end. In the field we moved silently along the back of the garden, and paused again outside a smaller gate. Harriet pushed it open cautiously, stepped inside, and turned unsmiling to watch me. I could not move; all was quiet in the field, the back fences of the Timothy Street houses stretched in an unending stockade across the grass. Grey walls rose up behind the enclosure, curtains like eyelids drooped across blackened windows.

Already it was growing darker as I entered the garden, leaving the gate open for a quick return. Narrow and long lay the garden behind the house, spotted with fruit trees and blackcurrant bushes. A bed of flowering cabbages reared monstrous heads, swollen and decayed above the yellow soil. No sound anywhere, the house motionless at the end of the garden, kitchen window small and clouded.

If we're caught, I told myself, we'll say that we kicked a ball into here; if we're caught, we'll say that. If we're caught.

Lights began to glow along the faces of the houses. We cast

huge shadows on the grass, moving nearer and nearer to the Tsar's house. Harriet's shadow stretched further, bent double and dissolved into the wall. We were on a concrete strip before the back door now, and still there was no sound.

'We'll go along the side path to the front garden when it's dark,' whispered Harriet.

We stayed huddled against the wall, breathing softly; my throat felt constricted, I was afraid I would laugh. We waited for a long time. The darkness settled on the field and garden, rolled towards us along an avenue of trees and grass; we waited at the end of the tunnel, hands spread out against the walls patiently.

Harriet moved in the darkness and touched my arm.

'Now,' she said, and on tip-toe we crept along the side wall to the front of the house. Light shone into the garden, voices murmured in the front-room and we waited outside the triangle of orange light. They ought to pull the curtains, I thought. They ought to pull the curtains. We heard distinctly the Tsar say, 'No, thank you,' and the sound of dishes moved.

Then the curtains were drawn across the windows, a thin ribbon of light raddled the grass, a long pinpoint splitting the darkness. Harriet moved to the far window, breaking the knife-edge of light as she crossed the lawn.

I stayed where I was, hoping Harriet would hurry and tell me we could go home. I heard a low hissing noise that seemed to fill the garden, and moved towards her contorted with fear.

'Be quiet, they'll hear you.'

She stood face to the window, peering through a slit in the join of the curtain. I looked through the glass. Directly opposite sat Mrs Biggs, her eyes turned towards me, mouth opening and closing soundlessly. I ducked quickly, dragging Harriet down by the waist.

'She saw me. She saw me.'

'She couldn't have.'

Harriet pulled herself away and looked through the glass once more. I pressed my head against the rough wall, shaken by the image of Mrs Biggs behind the window, heavy body upright in her chair, eyebrows raised questioningly, staring at me. Oh God please, Harriet, hurry, oh God please. Harriet bent towards me.

'Do look. It's perfectly safe.'

'Please, Harriet, come away.'

'Fool! Look at them.'

Reluctantly I took her position, and searched the room. Mrs Biggs leaned over the radio, hips encased in grey tweed. The Tsar was on the sofa, his face hidden behind a newspaper, legs crossed elegantly, small foot swinging. He put down the paper and shook his head. The face was tired and worn, mouth drooping petulantly, skin puckered despairingly beneath his eyes.

I felt Harriet's breath sweep warmly over my neck. She leaned on me heavily, holding my arm. Mrs Biggs crossed the room and sat on the sofa with the Tsar. Suspended in an arc of light, as if posing for posterity, they sat on the sofa staring into the garden; the Tsar jogged one foot up and down gently, hands slack on his thighs. I wondered at the serenity of them both, the relationship that set them a little apart, among furniture they had chosen together. Mrs Biggs moved closer to the Tsar, eyes still turned to the fire, and leaned her grey head on his shoulder. He seemed to wither, the body slumped down, he raised an expressionless face to the ceiling, the fold of skin tightening under his jaw.

Mrs Biggs in time to the music began to stroke his knee with her plump white hand, her head sinking lower on his arm, eyes closed against the light. She opened her mouth but we could not hear what she said, and the Tsar shifted in his seat and spoke to her. Mrs Biggs stood up suddenly, and Harriet pulled me down on to the flower-bed beneath the window. We breathed deeply in fear, kneeling on damp soil.

When we looked again the room was lit by firelight alone. It flickered on the brown wall opposite; the brass fender shone at one point like a star, but the sofa was in deep shadow.

'What's happened?' whispered Harriet. 'Can you see them?'

At that moment a black confused mass heaved and bulged

into the firelight. A grey head snuffed itself against the arm of the couch. Two legs thrashed the air. A hand, round and full, clutched at the edge of the carpet.

I felt huge and bloated with excitement; legs, arms, stomach, mind, ballooned out into the darkness.

The fire blazed up suddenly in the grate; flames thrust outwards into the dark room, illuminating the couch. Under the monstrous flesh of Mrs Biggs, the Tsar lay pinned like a moth on the sofa, bony knees splitting the air, thighs splayed out to take her awful weight. I could not breath. Wave upon wave of fear and joy swept over me.

Like an oiled snake, deep delving and twisting, Mrs Biggs poisoned him slowly, rearing and stabbing him convulsively. Her body writhed gently and was still. Ignoring the woman above him the grey Tsar lay as if dead, pinioned limply, eyes wide and staring, speared in an act of contrition. Full-blown love eddied from the woman, blowzy hips sunk in weariness, litmus flesh soaking up virtue from the body beneath.

Never never never, beat my heart in the garden, never never; battering against invisible doors that sent agonised pains along my wrists, unshed tears dissolving in my head, I crouched against the window helplessly, unable to move.

After a long, long time the light was switched on in the room; the Tsar poured himself a drink, standing with his back to the window. Mrs Biggs in the armchair by the fire held a magazine on her lap, moving her lips as she read, sandalled feet planted firmly on the carpet. Everything was the same; fire burning steadily, light in a pool about the sofa and table, flowers on the mantelpiece. No change in the woman's sensible face, no transfiguration of joy or bliss, and the eyes the Tsar turned to the window as he moved to the fireside were empty and dry.

'It won't do,' said Harriet.

Her voice was too loud in the garden. I turned in fear.

'Let's go now, Harriet.'

Even as I spoke she raised her hand and rapped on the pane of glass. I ran quickly over the lawn and down the path alongside the house. I felt envy as I stumbled through the long grass. I was envious because, though I had felt sickened by what I had seen, I had not dared to voice a protest. No matter how moved or desperate I became I could never do what she had done. My mind could flood with dreams of fighting against stupidity and evil, but it was Harriet who would realise them.

Behind me feet sped down the garden, voices cried out as Harriet lunged against me, light opened up the lawn. As she ran ahead she made strange stifled sounds in her throat; uncontrolled laughter shattered the darkness. It was like a nightmare, the panic-stricken flight into the field, the commanding voice of Mrs Biggs behind us, the swift rush of night air, the fruit trees looming large and formidable in the flood of light, and the sound of laughter far ahead. I whimpered as I ran, breathing promises to God to let me go. Just this once, I promised, oh just this once.

It was no use escaping by the side path into the street, the Tsar would be standing there ready for me. I had to run on into the darkness of the field. I could no longer hear Harriet, for all I knew she had deliberately gone to meet the Tsar.

My body arched and thundered over the ground, excitement carrying me further into the darkness. Each step jarred my body painfully, my heart thudded in my breast till I thought it would break in consequence. Exhausted I fell face downwards in the grass.

Gradually it became quiet and still in the field, my breath ceased to fill the world with noise. I was aware of rustlings in the grass, ringed ploplets of water circling in the ditch; the soft rush of a bird in alarm as it left the dark hedgerow. I knelt upright and looked back towards Timothy Street. Two trees that grew thinly in the earth midway between the houses and the hollow where I lay, splintered the light that shone from the windows, dividing and subdividing each pane of orange glass, so that the whole row of houses moved and shimmered with myriad points of light. A precise clapping sound began behind my head, and turning, I saw a train flickering along the horizon, compartments sending a small glow into the darkness, illuminating the wooden posts beside the railway line. Though it was so late and I knew my parents would be anxious and angry, I could not feel alarmed. The train moved compactly on; a red rear light trailed into the night; the sound of wheels grew fainter in the distance and dissolved away.

If I never went home again, but stayed here in the grass till I died of starvation, that would solve everything. I felt this sincerely and felt unhappy, but I still wanted to laugh. The humour of the situation grew. I dreamed a scene between the doctor and myself.

'But you were very close to death, my dear. Why did you just lie there?'

'Because I saw Mrs Biggs and the Tsar on the couch.'

The doctor turned a critical face to my mother suffering at the end of the bed.

'She is still delirious. A severe shock you know.'

The fantasy unfolded in my brain, tentative shoots probed crabwise into the recesses of the night; figures with lanterns stumbled over my body, the child's chest rising shallowly, body slender at last in near death, lips murmuring in delirium . . . I saw Mrs Biggs and the Tsar on the couch.

When Harriet all but trod on me I screamed sharply with shock. 'It's me,' she said. 'It's terribly late.'

'It would be better not to go home at all now,' I said unable to see her face in the darkness. Harriet thought about it.

'It would be lovely in the woods. Quite warm too. But we'd have to go home in the morning, and then what would we say?' I imagined sleeping on the floor of warm leaf mould under the branches, wind blowing in from the sea, a murmur of incoming tide more vast than by day. A sinister insidious sound of water stretching along the coast, enveloping slowly the broad sands.

'We'll have to go now,' said Harriet.

The nearer we came to the lane the slower we walked. Even Harriet was alarmed at the lateness of the hour, afraid of her predictable father. At the gate of my house Mother waited in a flurry of anger. Inside the house my fear evaporated as she spoke sharply to me.

'What do you mean by staying out till this time? How dare you cause us so much worry. Where have you been?'

Each question dissipated a little of her anger. Head bent humbly I did not answer. It was not expected of me. My father had gone to bed very worried. My mother had stopped him phoning the police to say we were missing. Harriet's father had been on the phone twice to see if she was here. It was almost half past eleven . . . Did I know that?

'I'm sorry,' I murmured.

I could go to bed now. In the morning my mother would be cold and distant with me but by afternoon friendly and loving once more. My father would look sullenly at me and bring back sweets when he returned from work. Everything would be the same, tomorrow.

9

I COULD not find my notebook.

We each had a book in which to write down our impressions of people we might meet. I had carried it in the pocket of my school blazer when we visited Timothy Street. I sat helplessly in my bedroom, feeling ill at the implications of such a loss. If I had dropped it in the garden and Mrs Biggs found it, nothing could save me. There was nothing in it because we tore out each page on completion and placed it in the box with the diary. But my address was on the cover for all to read: No. 4 Sea Lane, Formby, Lancs, England, Europe, The World.

Harriet looked grave when I told her, but for once was unable to advise how to act. She sat moodily on the bed, forbidden to go out. Her judicious father had hit her about the head the night before. She said he laid strong palms about her ears, measuring each blow, swearing all the time. 'I shouldn't wonder if I have a father-complex later,' she said. I went with stealth down the stairs to the front door, avoiding her parents successfully, and let myself out into the garden.

I had not missed the notebook till after tea; Mrs Biggs, should she have searched the garden after last night's intrusion, had already had nine hours in which to find it. It was now a little after six, and the Tsar would be home from work. Either I walked to the shore in the hope of a chance meeting, and there appealed to him to find the notebook, or I went alone now to Timothy Street, and searched the garden. Since the night of the fair we had not met, at least to his knowledge, and it was probable he might go out in the hope of seeing me. I could tell him we were playing a joke, that Harriet and I had been in the garden for fun – he need not know we had watched through the curtain – and that I was afraid I had dropped the notebook when we ran away.

The fear that seized me at the thought of Mrs Biggs calling on my mother, left no room for embarrassment at seeing the Tsar. Besides, the scene on the couch had shown the unimaginable to be pitiful; a function as empty of dignity and significance as brushing one's teeth. The darkness had heightened the tension and mystery, but it was Mrs Biggs who had put out the lights. It was her I hated, not the Tsar. Henceforth I could wait, without tarantella nerves, for the Tsar to lay his lips on mine, remembering he had loved Mrs Biggs, times without number, long before I was born.

My mother had said I was to be out for no more than an hour. Supposing they had thought us thieves last night, and Mrs Biggs, nervous, asked the Tsar to stay indoors in deference to her fears. I would only waste time going to the shore. Still I hovered there, outside Harriet's house, unable to make a decision. A figure turned the corner beyond the cottage hospital, walking close to the lemon wall, head bent, hands in pockets. Though I could not see his face I recognised the elegant walk, the fastidious feet pacing the lane. I ran into the garden, consumed with excitement, and whistled under Harriet's window.

'Harriet, Harriet, he's here, he's coming down the lane.'

Harriet disappeared from the open window immediately, and I ran backwards and forwards over the lawn, not daring to peer into the lane in case he saw me, but unable to be calm. When Harriet opened the door I almost knocked her over in my excitement, thrusting her backwards into the hall.

'Harriet, what shall we do? He's in the lane.'

'Shut the door.' She pushed her head under the frilled curtain to watch through the glass. A bird hopped warily over the grass, wings folded close, bright eyes searching the soil.

67

'Are you sure you saw him?' Harriet turned her bridal veiled head and touched my cheeks with her hand.

'Are you sure you just didn't feel emotional again?'

The bird flew swiftly up into the trees as the Tsar entered the gate. Harriet held my hand firmly and led me into the back room where her parents sat.

'Father,' she said, 'Mr Biggs is coming up the path.'

A neighbourly expression transfused her father's face. A jovial smile softened the mouth habitually severe; he cleared his throat self-consciously.

'Oh, good. I expect he wants to see me. Better put the kettle on, Mother.' Importantly he went out into the hall.

Harriet's mother placed coquettish hands to her hair, patting the waves more securely above her forehead. She was never deliberate in her flirtatiousness, it was more a habit than anything else. Her husband called her his 'little woman', and with all men she was bright and coy. So now she preened herself for the task in hand, bending and plumping the cushions adroitly, straightening the drab table runner, hiding the newspaper behind the wireless. She spoke worriedly to Harriet before going into the kitchen.

'Just sit quiet on the sofa, and don't interrupt your father more than you can help.'

Voices were loud in the hall. The Tsar laughed. I felt there was very little in his life to laugh at, and sat clenching my hands behind my back; nostrils and throat were constricted, a sweet spasm of shuddering gripped and as abruptly left my body, leaving me inert on the sofa. Harriet's mother came out of the kitchen, and greeted the Tsar profusely. He stood in the doorway, bowing slightly, hidden by her body, surrounded by friendliness. Then he straightened and saw Harriet and me on the couch under the window. A moment of indecision, eyes meeting briefly; then he walked boldly to us. Harriet pressed her arm hard against my side; there was a soft rush of air as her mouth opened widely to smile; the pressure of her arm strengthened as if she sensed my growing thoughtlessness. I cared nothing for her warning, nothing for the tableau before me. The man of justice poised by the door, the woman in the act of placing a saucer on the table, seemed to swivel round in the room and become unfocused. I stared with wonder at the Tsar. I felt quite safe. I was there by intent, not accident. I had been put on the sofa by Harriet's mother. None could stop me looking at him, not even Harriet.

She said, 'Hallo, Mr Biggs.'

He sat on the chair beside the table, white shirt against dark suit, city shoes of black leather beating a tattoo against the leg of the table. A thin hand splayed out on his knee, the middle finger stained with nicotine; handkerchief tipping his breast pocket, eyes small in his sallow face. No longer the Tsar of the night of the fair and the father kiss, nor the puppet Tsar on the couch behind curtained windows. A new Tsar of offices and daily work, one who talked business with other men, and carried a brief-case to the city. I watched the adults talking pleasantly and felt marooned with Harriet on the sofa, almost a feeling that I was indeed a child.

Why didn't he have children? Why didn't they make a child out of the nights spent under the beech leaves?

The Tsar was saying, 'So I'm afraid I won't, regrettably, be able to play golf on Saturday.'

'Oh, too bad.' Harriet father's mouth drooped in disappointment at a routine violated. His pleasure at the Tsar's visit soured. He drummed petulant fingers on the arm of the chair. Brightly his wife poured out tea, little finger crooked genteelly, wrist arched with the weight of the pot.

'What a shame, dear, but there's always another day.'

Another day. The notebook lost in the vengeful Mrs Biggs's garden; the impending visit to my mother, face righteous, voice gravely telling the awful story. Childhood fled from me, I sat upright and watched the clock. I would have to leave very soon, my mother would be waiting.

Harriet leaned forward and rested her elbows on her knees, staring at the Tsar with interest.

'Mr Biggs, why did you stop wearing glasses?'

Her mother looked at her and then at the Tsar, her

face expressing the hope that Harriet was not being rude.

The Tsar said, 'I broke so many pairs I just gave up wearing them.'

I felt he was ashamed in front of me at the admission. I wished I knew if I only imagined he cared for me, it seemed so strange the things I attributed to him. I did not know where the dream and the reality merged, I did not know anything.

'I may have to wear glasses soon,' I lied. What was the point of it? What did I mean him to understand? It was seven o'clock and I dare not stay any longer. I hated the bulk of me standing up in the room, clumsily moving to the door, self-consciously saying good night, avoiding their eyes. He stood up when I did, and for a moment I thought he too was taking his departure, but it was only a blessed politeness. Did he stand up for me because he thought me a woman? I beseeched Harriet silently to come to the door with me, but she only rocked gently on the sofa and said casually, 'Good night dear,' and left it to her mother to accompany me into the hall.

For two evenings and two days I waited for Mrs Biggs to ring the bell, and disturb the credulous mind of my mother.

Harriet told me to write in the diary, 'I am waiting now only for Mrs B. to call with the notebook. All the hours pass waiting for the fulfilment of this. I can neither eat nor sleep . . .' I felt this was a little dramatic, but it was true, and no other words seemed to evoke clearly what I was suffering.

On the third day, when still Mrs Biggs had not called, a faint hope filled me. She had found the notebook, but would feel foolish telling my mother, and she was not going to tell her. Harriet agreed this might be so, and told me not to worry.

'It's a closed incident, dear. You must forget it.'

While we still could not go walking in the evening and were restricted to one hour after tea, we spent the time writing in the diary. One passage in particular puzzled me. Harriet dictated, 'If two people commit a sin, it is a bad thing. If one person commits a sin with another, it is worse. The passive one is the person most guilty, and should be punished for betraying himself . . .' Then she made me write, 'Events must be

70

logically concluded. We must be tidy.' When I questioned her about it she was only evasive.

'I'm right,' was all she would say. 'Really I am, trust me.'

'But, Harriet, I feel funny about him.' There was no reply. She lay on her bed and would not look at me.

'Harriet, you know the way you would not let me see what you had written about the boy in Wales?' I tried to sound at ease but it was an appeal.

'Yes.' She was looking at me now.

'Well, I feel that way about the Tsar.'

'What way? What way is that?'

Dare I say it? Even the relationship between us was changing. I ought not to have to explain.

'What on earth are you going on about?'

I spoke self-consciously, running the words together in embarrassment.

> Shall my heart remain my own?
> Oh the tears upon his cheeks;
> Do I dare to walk alone?
>
> How the beech leaves pale and whiten,
> How still the little churchyard lies.
> Let compassion shut my eyes.

'What's that got to do with it?' asked Harriet, but not crossly. 'I wrote that after we met those boys from the remand home when I took my clothes off and you wouldn't because your knickers were filthy.'

'They weren't filthy,' I protested. 'I told you, they were my mum's and they were pink with awful lace.'

'Well, so what?'

'I love Mr Biggs,' I said, and wondered instantly why I had called him that. It sounded so funny – 'I love Mr Biggs'.

Harriet sat up. 'In that case we better hurry. There's not much of the holidays left.'

71

I resented the 'we'. It wasn't we who loved the Tsar, it was I alone.

'But I don't know that I want it to be an experience,' I said miserably. 'I don't think I want it to be something for the diary.'

Harriet spoke in the same reasonable way she talked to her mother.

'At thirteen there is very little you can expect to salvage from loving someone but experience. You'll go back to school for years, you'll wear a gym tunic long after all this is over. What do you expect? No one will let you love yet. You're not expected to. They don't even know how to do it themselves. And all he'll feel for you is a sort of gentle nostalgia. No – bring it to a logical conclusion. If you don't you'll feel emotional for ages over something that was pretty trivial.'

'But what if we find it's not trivial?' I was appalled by the wisdom of us both. It seemed unnatural. Why had I not noticed it before?

'Don't let's suppose,' Harriet said efficiently. 'Now write in the diary what I tell you. "This man is a very complex one. He seems to like to suffer. It is a very great weakness and one that she (the wife) has helped to cultivate. We saw him on the couch in an attitude of resignation, and we thought the wife was to blame. But now we are not so sure of this. We caught a glimpse of their life through the window and we found it disgusting and abasing. He should not submit to a woman like that. Obviously he is a victim and likes to be punished." '

'But we don't know, Harriet, we can't be sure.'

Harriet went on firmly, 'We must work quickly to punish him in a way he will not like.' I wrote it down in my best handwriting and felt uneasy.

Voices could be heard bouncing in a tight ball against the ceiling. I stopped writing and listened.

'Are they quarrelling?'

'Yes,' said Harriet.

I was interested. Harriet said they often quarrelled and that it was terrible when they did because the little woman began

72

to cry, and the father grew more bullying to protect himself.

'Open the door,' said Harriet, and placed her hands palm downwards against the floorboards, as if to brace herself for an inevitable shock. I did as I was told. Two voices were raised and both were angry and I looked at Harriet inquiringly because I knew the little woman was not given to argument. Harriet shook her head and whispered, 'They can't be quarrelling . . . unless they're both angry about the same thing.'

We tried hard to hear what it was they said, tried to piece words together but it was difficult, until suddenly the father clearly said, 'Right!', and the door below opened and his voice shouted fearfully loud, 'Harriet, come here!'

Harriet did not move. She stared at me with wide eyes, mouth open, unable to breathe.

'Harriet, do you hear?'

Harriet got to her feet and crept over to the window. She cupped her hand over her mouth and called, 'What is it?'

The hand over her mouth made it seem as if the bedroom door was shut and she had not heard properly. She motioned me frantically with extravagant hands to close the door. The father below called once more.

'Come down!'

All was quiet; the parents waited in the silence. Harriet leaned against the window, she pressed her nose to the glass.

'You'll have to go.'

I was frightened that the father would come upstairs and fetch her.

'All right, all right,' said Harriet sullenly. She kicked with her foot at the skirting-board and hunched her shoulders. Moving to the door, her face in shadow, she passed me humilated. Before she had reached the bottom of the narrow stairs the voice called,

'Both of you, please.'

Harriet looked up at me to where I stood on the landing and stared at me. I could not be sure whether she wanted me to walk downstairs and out of the house and defy her father, slamming the door loudly and whistling easily as I shut the gate behind me. I just followed her down the steps and entered the living-room.

Her father sat with deception in his chair by the fire, pushing his feet against the fender, easing his toes more surely into his brown slippers. The little woman with despairing face stood with her back to the fire, and touched her cheek with one hand as if to reassure herself.

'Now,' said her father, smiling pleasantly at me, 'I'm just going to ask a plain question and I want a plain answer. None of your clever talk, Harriet, do you understand?'

He gave a vicious little toss of his head and turned to her. If Harriet understood she gave no sign, but stood looking out of the window into the dark shrouded garden. Her mother leaned forward to poke the fire unnecessarily and a live coal fell into the brown-tiled hearth. He looked at her with distaste at this and pouted his lips bad-temperedly. The noise irritated his already inflamed nerves.

'What were you doing round at Mr Biggs's house the other night?'

At once my mind turned and spun out intricate patterns of invention. I had felt faint as we passed the Tsar's house and Harriet had dragged me on to the grass. We had banged the window to get help . . . because I needed help. I was always feeling faint; I was ill. I had not felt well for a long time now; the doctor thought I was growing too fast. Harriet was saying, 'We went a walk. We felt like an apple so we went into the garden.'

She bent down over the back of the empty rocking chair, swaying forward with it, letting her plaits hang down to brush against the green cushion. Her mother swept industriously at the ash in the hearth, flushed with the heat from the fire. She tightened her grip on the brittle brass rod of the ornamental brush, waiting for the blow to fall.

'I see. You went to pick apples.' Her father leaned back, smiling now, his hands touching only at the tips of his fingers, as if in delicate prayer. 'And what else did you do beside picking apples?'

74

'What do you mean? We ate the apples . . . why?'

'Perhaps you remember what else you did, eh?' He looked at me over his hands and waited.

'Well we just . . . I mean we looked at the window. We didn't do much, honestly.'

I had betrayed myself and Harriet. I had appealed to the man. I had defended myself involuntarily by the use of the word 'honestly'. Harriet stopped rocking the chair and hung motionless, head down.

'Well, I won't have it, do you hear. I won't have it.' Blood suffused his face; an angry vein throbbed in his temple.

'Your mother had a visit from Mrs Biggs today. She said you spied on them through the window. She doesn't like it, do you hear?'

Harriet stared at her father. 'How did she know we looked through the window?'

'Because she did. I'm asking the questions.' His voice strengthened. He seemed to be filling himself with air, ready to blast us from the room.

He began to bully Harriet in earnest. He shouted with eyes dark with emotion. Her mother and I stayed as grieved onlookers, relieved to be watching. As Harriet remained silent, he became threatening. The more he shouted and lost control, the more difficult became his position, and as yet he could not say why it was so wrong of us to spy through the window. Naughty, yes, but not wicked.

He was afraid of what Harriet might say in reply. He was afraid even now she would ask him, and he shouted rather to drown her question should it come, than because he was righteously angry. I began to feel sorry for him. Harriet was so strong in battle; even I was strong. He had not the courage to tell her what worried him, that we were young girls, that the Tsar was a funny fellow, wandering down to the shore on his own, that there had been incidents in the past never properly explained, involving Harriet and men. Instead he said that we mustn't go round to the house any more, that we had to be indoors earlier, that it was about time we realised we were

75

growing up. At this Harriet permitted herself a small smile, and looked down at the carpet with pretended amusement. Finally she said:

'But what is so awful about peeping through Mr Biggs's window, Father?'

It was very cruel. He threw himself forward in his seat and glared at her. His hands gripped the arms of his chair furiously and impotently. He was choking with the hurt and fear he felt, and his round blue eyes stared for a moment at Harriet as if she were a landscape utterly barren, distorted by lightning and unknown. Then he said brokenly, 'Good God, girl!' He got up and stood broadly over her as if to make her fall down, overpowered by the bulk of him, but Harriet mercilessly looked up at him, eyebrows arched inquiringly.

'You talk to her.' He turned to her mother. 'I'm through, blast her. Let her go to the devil.'

He went to the door, and as he moved his slipper came off his left foot, and rather than return and struggle into it he kicked it away from him and slammed the door. He shouted all the way upstairs; we could hear him repeating endlessly that he was through, through, until the bedroom door closed on him. The slipper stood on end against the far wall, shabby and badly out of shape.

While her father was in the room, Harriet had seemed the victor. Now that he lay muttering on his bed upstairs, chanting that he was through, all through, we felt guilty and deflated. Harriet leaned her head dejectedly against the mantelpiece. She said to her white-faced mother:

'What have we done wrong, little woman? Why did he go on like that?'

I knew that Harriet was upset because the little woman had been exposed to the scene, that she wanted to comfort her.

'I think you're extremely unkind, Harriet.'

Her mother spoke formally in front of me.

'You know why you shouldn't go round to Mr Biggs's house, especially not in their garden, looking through their window. It's not nice behaviour . . . He just doesn't want you to do anything you'll regret . . . He's so proud of you and you do everything you can to antagonise him.'

'Well, you shouldn't have told him. You know how stupid he is.'

The muttering upstairs broke out afresh.

'Put the wireless on, dear.'

Her mother was so resigned and kind it was awful. Harriet turned on the wireless to drown the sound of her father's voice, in case the neighbours should hear. I knew this because Harriet had told me that when she came home from school and the wireless was on, she knew there had been trouble and her father was in a temper. I wondered if along the whole row of houses and back rooms the wireless hummed out its message. Her mother hated the wireless at other times and refused to have it switched on. Cheerful dance-music filled the room. It might have been a holiday the way the tune spun and spiralled among us.

Her mother continued, 'For Heaven's sake, dear, try to see it from his point of view for a change.' The little woman warmed to her task and became almost coherent. 'If you don't mind about him at least consider me a little. It's not you that bears the brunt of it. He'll be in a mood for days. I can't stand it. You know how low it makes me.'

'All right, all right.' Harriet sounded desperate.

After a pause her mother said, 'I did say to Mrs Biggs that she could not expect me to believe such an extraordinary tale without some sort of proof. I did say that.'

It was strange. The little woman sought to justify herself to us.

'What extraordinary tale?' asked Harriet gently, as if dealing with a child unable to tell right from wrong. 'What did she tell you?'

'She said you were in her garden the other night, the front garden, and that you knocked on the window and swore at them, and ran away. Were you in the garden?'

I waited for Harriet to answer. I would have denied it utterly but, as I expected, she said in the same gentle tone,

77

'Yes, we were. I did knock on the window. I said damn you, but I wasn't swearing.'

Harriet's mother sat in the armchair, not knowing what to say.

'But why?' she asked finally. 'What on earth possessed you to do such a wicked thing?'

Harriet smiled indulgently. 'It wasn't wicked, little woman, it was a joke.'

I felt admiration for the way she spoke, the calm refusal to be blackmailed into submissiveness by parental grief. Where I would have broken down and begged for forgiveness, Harriet reasoned sensibly.

'Who told Mrs Biggs it was us?' she asked. 'Did she recognise my voice?'

'Mr Biggs caught a glimpse of your face, and persuaded Mrs Biggs not to inform the police. He also found this in the garden next morning.'

The notebook lay on the sideboard face down.

'I see,' said Harriet, picking up the book and handing it to me.

I took it, and held it to me guiltily.

Harriet's mother looked at me. 'I don't suppose,' she said cruelly, 'your mother would be very proud of the episode.'

Only the fact that Harriet was in the room stopped me from going down on my knees and begging her to be lenient.

'No,' I stammered wretchedly, 'I'm sorry.'

Disgusted, Harriet turned away, and there I might have stayed for ever, unable to move from the room, dejected and at a loss in front of her mother, if she had not said to me, 'You'd better run along home, dear.' She hesitated. 'I should be glad, dear, if you didn't say anything at home about tonight – he's not been well you know, dear. He has a lot of trouble with his stomach.'

Harriet cried impatiently, 'Oh stop making excuses. She wouldn't dare mention tonight, and if she did, what does it matter? It's so absurd.'

78

'You don't think he'll come round to our house do you?' I could not help myself.

Harriet flung her arms above her head despairingly.

'You two – you're a pair, aren't you? He's not been well you know – it's his stomach – you don't think he'll come to our house?' She mimicked us cruelly, looking down on us with disgust.

I had so much in common with her mother; but she would be comforted by Harriet – after I had gone. Harriet would sit at her feet and put her arms round her and tell her not to take it so hard. I felt ashamed at my selfishness. Poor little woman. How would she go to bed? How could she go into the sulky bedroom and lie down beside the muttering man with his face swollen with anger? Perhaps she would stay by the fire all night with Harriet, discussing me, saying how cowardly and deceitful I was, how stout, how I could never tell the truth. I resolved to go away, not just away to school in a few weeks' time, but away for ever, so that Harriet would be sorry.

'Good night.'

'Good night,' said Harriet grudgingly. 'Better leave it for a day or two. I'll see you on the shore some time.'

'All right.'

I went out of the back door and ran down the path in the dark almost sobbing. I leaned on the cherry tree that grew against the garage and listened to the loud beating of my heart. I rubbed my cheek across the slender trunk of the tree and whispered over and over, 'I can't bear it, I can't, I can't bear it.'

I wanted to see Harriet just once more before I went away. I walked on tip-toe along the path and stood at the side of the window. I was reminded of the night we had spied on the Tsar; it was another thing to remember this long summer by, an endless peering through secret windows.

Harriet's mother sat on her chair by the fire reading the evening paper. The wireless was quite loud and she had put fresh coal in the grate. Her face was screwed up in concen-

79

tration over the newsprint. Her mouth bulged slightly as she chewed a sweet. Harriet was not there.

I leaned against the wall and thought it over. If you were very unhappy you could not possibly eat sweets. I felt sure I could not. And if Harriet really loved her mother she would be with her; if her mother needed her.

I went round the house to Harriet's room at the front. Her light was on, but the curtains were drawn across the windows. Three people of one flesh, all alone in separate rooms, one chewing sweets and reading the evening paper, one chanting out his tom-tom message of doom, and the third motionless on her bed, dry eyes wide open under the electric light.

It began to rain as I stood there keeping watch over Harriet. That was it, I would stay here all night and never move.

Harriet pulled back the curtains and opened the window. She leaned on the sill and stared out into the garden. I did not know what to do. She wanted to be alone, she was glad I had gone home. I could sense in the shadowed inclination of her head and neck that she fancied herself unseen and solitary. Greatly daring, I whispered, 'Harriet . . . it's me . . . Harriet.'

'What are you doing?'

'I'm going away, Harriet.

'I should hope so. You'll catch your death there . . . it's raining.'

So miserable was I that I had forgotten the rain. How could she be so cruel as to misunderstand?

'I mean I'm going away for good, Harriet.'

In my anxiety to make her understand I stepped on to the flower-bed under her window and peered up at her.

'Oh, you fool,' Harriet half said, half cried. 'And mind the plants. He'll be furious. You're trampling all over them.'

She withdrew into the room and shut the window. The curtains with finality closed once more.

I stood in the rain and wished her in hell.

Victor Sylvester was still conducting foxtrots on the wireless. Bending my neck I stretched out my arm and went quick, quick, slow across the lawn. Then I got down on my knees in the grass and brushed the top soil of the flower-bed in case her father should be furious. I wished I could erase my love for Harriet as easily as my footprints. I spoke seriously to myself on the way home, resolving to be more adult in my emotions. I felt exhausted, as if I had run for miles in a high wind.

10

On Sunday evening I met Harriet outside the Cottage Hospital. I had said nothing to my parents who, working laboriously in the garden, hardly seemed to notice when I fetched my coat and walked out of the gate. Harriet had telephoned me after tea, and told me she had thought of a good plan to help me get over my love for the Tsar. I felt that I did not want to get over it, such a strange mixture of pain and pleasure it gave me, but I could not tell her so.

As we walked to the woods she told me what she had decided. First, I must put my meetings with the Tsar on a more regular basis. No more going down to the sea, as we did now, in the hope of meeting. I must arrange times and places with him.

'But, Harriet,' I protested weakly, 'he may not want it.' The fields along the cinder path swayed in rhythm, as the wind moved over the tops of grasses. Trees, fields, and hedges fluttered in one circular regular spasm, and were still.

'Also you must get him to kiss you again,' said Harriet, walking steadily, paying no attention to my interruption. It sounded very simple. I was not afraid of the Tsar any more, but there was a difference between that and actually thrusting myself on him. I shook my head and wondered what was wrong. The woods seemed smaller and blacker, the church tower breaking through the pines, tiny and ineffectual. Time was when the whole earth lay buried beneath the blue trees, and the tower split the clouds with a fist of iron.

'Mrs Biggs usually goes away for a few days in the summer to see her sister,' Harriet was saying. 'You must find out when, and we'll call on the Tsar at his house.'

She had told me before that Mrs Biggs's sister had a backward child. The sister took drugs to stop the child from growing in her, and it tore her body when it slid with monstrous head on to the rubber sheet. That was what Harriet said. Would Mrs Biggs sit listening to Children's Hour, idiot child on her lap?

But Harriet was too serious. It was different from the first evening she had come home from Wales, when we swayed giddily to meet the Tsar waiting under the silver-painted lamppost.

The lane was empty as we turned the corner by the Canon's house; high tunnel of broad elms motionless beneath the sky, the light filtering white and radiant between the still leaves. We climbed the wall into the graveyard and stood ankle deep in the black ivy, creeper stems of wine-red coursing the earth like veins. Pale shoots of beech fluttered against the fence, small leaves fanned out precisely.

'What if he doesn't come?' I asked Harriet, walking away through the tangle of grass and ivy towards the church. She tossed her head, jerking the colourless plaits of hair about her ears, and shouted:

'He will, dear. He must.'

She was always so sure now. As if returned from Wales surging with power and knowledge, she straddled the summer days like a colossus, carrying me with her.

The Canon kept the key of the church under the hair mat in the porch. We used it whenever we liked; sometimes we had picnics when it rained and sat in the pews eating sandwiches, and other times we took refuge there from the streams of city children that screamed and ran about the woods on holidays. The Canon had surprised us once delivering loud sermons from the pulpit, but Harriet had charmed him with her ambition, newly discovered for his benefit, of becoming a missionary and carrying the word of God to foreign lands. He

called her the Constant Nymph, lisping the words in his baby-
ish voice honeyed with sentimentality.

Harriet bent down and felt for the key under the mat. A
fine cloud of white sand puffed out across the stones as the mat
flapped back into place. She turned the key in the lock, and
pushed the massive door inwards, and stepped inside. Dust
spiralled upwards in the sunlight that shone through the
stained windows. Harriet stood beside the stone christening
font, holding an imaginary baby in her arms.

'I baptize thee in the name of the Father, the Mother, the
Tsar,' she chanted, looking to the doorway where I stood,
watching my face curiously. I smiled uneasily, feeling unbearably hot in my school coat of navy blue.

'Are we going to wait here? It's so hot, Harriet.'

She joined me at the door, folding brown arms across her
chest, and peered into the lane. A man rode by on his bicycle,
trilby hat bobbing grotesquely above the church wall. It looked
like a distorted bird limping horizontally among the trees.
'Hallo!' he shouted, to someone in the lane.

'It's him,' said Harriet, holding my arm with fierce fingers.
'I'm sure it's him.'

I thought of how Thomas Becket had run into some
church, and flung himself across the altar in order to escape
the hired assassins, and wanted to do the same; but Harriet
held tight to my arm and I could not move. It was awful just
to stand there, smiling widely while he walked up the path,
anchored together against him. He smiled too from the gate,
hands fumbling on the catch, gazing with awkward intensity
at the graves bordering the path. He had to smile at us twice,
and look away, before he finally reached us.

'Hallo?'

'Hallo, Tsar?'

He whirled his hat between his fingers, avoiding our eyes.
I thought he must feel ashamed, creeping away down the lane
to meet such cruel friends. It was very difficult to know what
to do now. Harriet just stood there in the porch, eyes turned
to the sky, ignoring us both.

I said, 'I'm sorry about the other night. It was only a joke.' I wished I hadn't mentioned it. He might wonder how long we had watched through the window.

'She was a bit difficult,' he said, watching Harriet almost humbly. 'I had to tell her it was you. She would have called the police.'

For a moment I wondered if it was Harriet he loved, the way he looked at her over my head.

Then he said :

'Harriet, I want to talk to you.'

She turned to look at him, tongue curling out a little beneath her lips.

'All right.' She spoke to me commandingly. 'Go away, I'll call you later when we've finished.'

I hoped he would tell me I might remain, but he hardly glanced at me, hat twirling relentlessly in his hands.

I walked a little way between the graves, and sat down under the trees with my back to the porch. It was very quiet. He was telling her he thought me stout and large. He wanted to tell her what happened on the couch was meaningless. He was saying, 'She's unintelligent, but you understand,' placing thankful arms about her neck.

In despair I stood up, trying to be brave. I would stand behind them mutely. Just this once I would not be afraid. My eyes would not betray dislike or pain, only a gentle sadness that would for once outweigh the solid cheerfulness of my body.

Suddenly Harriet ran out on to the path in front of me. I stopped in surprise, so quick was the movement. Then I was filled with disproportionate fear, as if I had lit a match and dropped it in the grass, seeing in the small flame a whole world afire before I trod it underfoot. There was such fury in the headlong flight of her body over the grass that I could not call out. Astride the wall she turned and faced me accusingly, then dropped into the lane. I could not be sure whether she was in earnest or not. It could be that it was an elaborate way of leaving me alone with the Tsar, and that even now she was walking calmly and with great satisfaction over the fields towards home.

The porch was empty, the huge door half closed against me. I called softly, 'Mr Biggs,' pausing for a moment outside. 'Are you there?' I had to call him Mr Biggs, though it sounded comical. 'Mr Biggs, Mr Biggs! Is it true that your ribs, are as thin as the bark on the trees?' Harriet's rhyme jingled senselessly up and down in my brain. The Tsar sat facing the altar, back bent, head sunk forward on his chest. It would be so easy to slip out silently into the graveyard, and run thankfully over the fields. Only the thought of Harriet's anger made me move hesitatingly towards him. It was like a play I had seen, where a man had failed terribly in business. The daughter, home from expensive school, stood helplessly beside him, wishing to touch his arm and tell him she did not care about leaving school, but frightened of the hopeless face he would turn to her.

'Mr Biggs.'

The face of the Tsar, when he did look at me, was so normal and ordinarily thoughtful, that I stared at him with disbelief. I fought the desire to call him Father, and said nervously, 'What was the matter with Harriet?'

'I'm not sure, child. I think I told her the truth.'

'What do you mean?'

'I said she had an evil mind.'

I was appalled. I wanted to shout, 'I love Harriet. She's brave and true and beautiful,' but the words stuck in my throat. Instead, I said:

'I don't understand you.'

'I know. You haven't an evil mind.'

It was all so unlike what I had imagined. He was telling me that I was the good, the wonderful one. Harriet so thin, so brown in the sun, so like I wanted to be, was the outcast. I could not love him after all if he hated Harriet. If I loved him when he thought Harriet evil, then I could not love her. How could one be evil who walked every day the lane to the sea, and breathed the air from the pines? And if Harriet was in truth evil, then I was, and so was the Tsar.

86

'Why is she evil?'

'She'll perhaps tell you herself.'

The sun had gone behind the trees, leaving the church dark and no longer warm; the rows of pews rose up out of the stone floor like the headstones in the graveyard outside. The Tsar made no move, but sat there gently rubbing his hands, warming himself.

I began to grow tired of the scene.

'I had better go now,' I said, staring down the church to the altar now in shadow. He did not move in his seat, only bowed his head as if in acquiescence, and then suddenly, belatedly,

'Don't go.'

I fidgeted unhappily, scraping my nails along the polished wood by his head, unsure of what I should do.

'Why?' I said. I meant it to be knowledgable and flirtatious, the way Harriet's mother used it, but it sounded childish, a cry in the dark.

'Why?' he said, mimicking my voice unkindly, petulantly mouthing the word. My eyes filled with tears. I swallowed quickly, wondering if he disliked me. The tears were not for that reason; it was the darkness and the lost echoes of our voices in the darkness, and the black shapes of trees outside the high windows, that made me want to cry. If I creased my face upwards in a grief-stricken smile, and wailed between clenched teeth a long-drawn-out wail of sadness down the church, then I could cry. As it was I could only stand there silently, the tears unshed and almost gone. If he did not want me to go, why did he not talk to me, or at least look at me? In this dim light shadows would create wonders in my round, full face. I imagined I looked pale and ethereal, hair smudged about my head, eyes shining with faint tears.

When he did look at me, and said softly in his amused dry voice, 'What a tragic little Muse,' it was almost as if I sat bare-footed in the sand, hearing the Italian say 'Dirty little Angel'.

What was a Muse? A thoughtful person, or a Greek god-

87

dess singing siren songs on the rocks above the sea? It was a beautiful, beautiful word. 'What a tragic little Muse,' I told Harriet tenderly, in my mind.

It was so clumsy an action when he stood up and placed his arms round me, that I had to close my eyes tight and cling to the words to keep the beauty there.

'Please,' I said unhappily, hating the sour smell of skin against my cheek. 'Please let me go.'

He dropped his arms at once, standing back and smoothing his hair in a gesture of weariness. It was so dark I could not see his face clearly, only the outline of his hand placating the thin hair. I began to feel light-hearted and sure of myself, saying over and over again, 'I'm sure it's terribly late. I'm sure it is. It must be terribly late, Tsar.'

Anxious and relieved to be going I pulled at the big door, now closed against the churchyard. I could not open it.

'The door won't open, Mr Biggs.' I felt afraid, conscious now that it really was late.

He turned the iron ring beneath the lock, and pulled backwards strongly, then placed his shoulder to the dark wood and heaved outward. But it would not open. Speechless I waited, praying desperately that it would move. The thought that Harriet might have come silently back and locked the door, gathered strength in my mind.

'It's locked,' I cried, 'I know it's locked.'

I clung to him with fear, holding his hand to my cheek, trying to ease the terror that stormed in me. It seemed as if the whole summer had been lived between the two extremes of joy and fear, and both were unbearable. I was not angry with Harriet, for I might some time, for some explicable reason, act in the same way. But I was angry, within my fear, at the circumstances that turned such simple natural things – like doors locking or time passing – into events of magnitude and worry. I could not imagine what peace the Tsar must feel at not always having to think of the hour or the place, of being answerable only to himself. I forgot until he spoke, that Mrs Biggs for him took the place of my mother.

'She'll give me half an hour more,' he said, 'assuming that it's ten o'clock. Then she'll come down the lane in search of me.'

'What about the windows?' I said carefully, unable to see his expression, but knowing that it must be weak and despairing. At least my fear was real, I had cause to be afraid; at thirteen it was natural my parents should be angry and upset if I returned late home. I was not a grown man, married thirty years, who had taken the initiative under the beech leaves. I felt elated and superior to him grown so flabby in his relationship with Mrs Biggs, and wondered if this were part of Harriet's plan.

'They're too high,' said the Tsar, looking up into the darkness. 'Besides, they only open at the top.' He moved his hands along the wall beside the door, his nails making a tiny scratching sound as they grated against the stone.

'The light switches are all outside in the porch,' I said, sounding almost gleeful in the darkness.

It was a very good plan of Harriet's, and I was sure now it was a plan.

Only she could have thought of something so exquisitely subtle, so calculated to show the Tsar as a frail creature, limited by relationships such as we knew. I had only to tell the truth at home, and most of the anger would be mitigated. 'Someone locked me in the church,' I would say, or 'A ghost shut the door. I was terrified.'

The Tsar was gliding down the church, striking matches every yard, to enable him to see better. I followed him, feeling my way with hands on the pew rows, stamping my feet down firmly so that he would know I was following. He opened a door and light flooded out across the altar steps, from the vestry. A row of white cassocks hung on pegs, frilled out and lay back again on the cream wall.

'Good,' said the Tsar, moving round the room hopefully looking for keys, face wrinkled under the bulb of electricity. We crossed eagerly from corner to corner, buoyed up with expectancy, pulling aside the cassocks and the verger's black

gown, searching for keys, enjoying throwing the garments untidily to the floor. The one cupboard was bare save for an old
hat of the Canon's, and a pair of small football boots. The
desk under the window contained only some sticky-backed
pictures issued to the Sunday school, and one woollen glove
knitted in green. Everything reminscent of white-clouded Sunday afternoons – the picture on the wall that used to be in the
Children's corner, the special plate for us to put our pennies
in – conspired to make the night more strange, and fringed it
with a lunatic delight, the delight of searching the Canon's
vestry without stealth. How lovely, in spite of the lateness of
the hour and the trouble no doubt to come, the situation was.

'Damn,' said the Tsar worriedly, standing in the middle of
the room. There were no keys to find.

I tried to think what Harriet would do in such an extremity.
Break the stained-glass windows or burn down the door with
the Tsar's futile little matches? Both measures seemed equally
awe-inspiring in their finality.

'Mr Biggs,' I said politely, 'we could break one of the
windows.'

The Tsar was too worried to reply; he stood like a man
might who had been hunted for days, and was now trapped
with his back to the wall. I thought that any tender shoot of
love that was to have flourished between us, was now cruelly
underfoot. He must be tired and bitter at all the trouble
Harriet and I had caused him. I didn't think Harriet had
meant that to happen.

The Tsar leaned against the cream wall and studied the
windowless room. The vestry door, though smaller than the
main door into the churchyard, was as thick and sturdy, and
he could never hope to force it open. He looked up at the
vaulted ceiling and shook his head hopelessly.

'I'm sorry, child, God knows what time it is.'

I allowed my face to become tragic and upset.

'Don't worry.' He patted my arm bravely. 'We'll get out
somehow.'

I did not feel I could convincingly remain the helpless little

90

girl, at least not for very long. If it were left to him we might possibly die here and be found helpless and skeleton-ribbed on the vestry floor when the Canon eventually opened the church next Sunday. I said, 'Mr Biggs, I'm going to break one of the windows if I can.'

'No,' he said petulantly, 'no, be sensible. You can't do that.'

With noble face and eagle heart, remembering Mrs Biggs had called him weak, I said in my determined voice, walking to the open door, 'You'd better help me for I mean to do it.'

The church was huge and black with darkness; I had to tell myself that trees in winter looked different from those in summer, that it was only a seasonal difference. The church by day was the same as now, I had nothing to fear.

I spread my hands in front of me, coaxing the wall to come nearer, feet splayed out cautiously like a matador. In the corner near the side altar the Canon kept a window pole. I had only to feel along the brass rail and remember him Sunday upon Sunday advancing to the corner, luscious mouth parted a little, hand outstretched, and I would find it. 'God's pure air, children,' he had said as he opened the window. Triumphantly I shouted. 'It's here, Mr Biggs, come and help me.'

His voice in the darkness was low and upset. I felt sorry for him then.

'What do you want me to do?'

How often had Harriet made me feel dominated and ineffectual, so that I answered her repeated orders in just such a voice of self pity and suffering.

'Here is the window pole' – I spoke briskly to cover the giggle in my voice – 'we must put the hook in the window ring and haul ourselves up on to the sill. There's only one window we can break, the third one. You can tell it by feel. It's the only one that got damaged in the war and they replaced it with coloured glass. We have to stand against the pane and smash hard at the bottom and when it gives jump on to the grass. We both run to the gate into the woods, so that if anyone hears us we'll have plenty of cover under the trees. You run up the dunes above the tadpole ponds and I'll go over the fields near the barracks. We will be much safer if we separate.' I felt Harriet would be proud of me.

The Tsar said 'Yes' in an expressionless way, and struck a match, holding it between cupped hands till it burned more fiercely, and held it out. His eyes in the small glow of light were arched wide as he looked at length of pole I held. The expression of immense surprise faded and died as the match went out.

'Give it to me,' he said. 'You go and put off the light in the vestry.'

His hands as they circled my fingers felt dry and cold. I let go of the pole and stepped back quickly.

It took me a long time to reach the vestry, because the small light that seeped from the doorway did little to alleviate the darkness. I could look fixedly at it and make for its goal, but my feet and body moved heavily in the blackness. When I reached the door and put up my hand to the light switch I paused and thought there might be something else Harriet would wish me to do. I opened the drawer and pulled out the sticky-backed pictures and looked at them. On all of them a fair angelic Jesus stared out blindly with eyes of cobalt blue. If I had a pencil, I told myself, I would draw moustaches on them all, honestly I would. I was glad I had no pencil. I switched the light off and closed the door and stood with my back to it. I shouted, 'Where are you?'

'Here.'

I started to move cautiously back along the way I had come, moving in the direction of his voice. His breathing, agitated with effort, filled the church. 'Here,' he shouted, 'here.' When I reached him he told me to keep on striking matches to give him light to find the ring at the top of the window. Endlessly I did as he instructed. There never seemed to have been a time when we had not been imprisoned in the church among the trees. Beyond the pines the tide must have ebbed and flowed for generations without number, while we struggled to hook the pole on to the window. Then it was done. The Tsar said nothing but gave a grunt of relief. He stopped struggling and stood still, hand upstretched.

'Well done,' I said, bolstering him, although now it hardly mattered. I waited a moment before telling him what I wanted him to do because I did not like to bully.

He laughed suddenly and said, 'What an impossible position to be in,' and laughed again, this time more loudly.

'When you're ready you'd better climb on to the pew behind you and jump against the wall, both feet out to meet it. Put your hands as high up the pole as you can, so that it won't unhook as you jump.' Bravely the Tsar scrambled upright on the back of the pew. I struck a match to help him to estimate his leap but it died almost at once. He launched himself at the wall and a groan of pain rose softly out of the church.

'What's wrong?'

There was no reply, only a sound of hurried breathing and feet slithering on the stone wall. A noise of laborious crawling, as if some strange primeval crab moved towards the window sill above my head. Then I could see the dark outline of the Tsar in a tortured mass against the glass, the pole held tight to his head.

'There's nothing to hold on to.' His voice was high-pitched and distressed. 'I can't let go of the pole.'

'It's all right. Hold the pole in your left hand and move as far along the sill as you can.' It was easy to tell him, 'There's a cord round a hook on the wall. Feel for that but don't jerk the pole.' The Tsar did not move. Angrily I shouted, 'Go on, it'll be all right.'

He must have felt abandoned and furious now as he was forced to move along the thin sloping sill, seeing confused shadows of trees swaying outside in the churchyard.

I was conscious of being very tired. The effort of moving the Tsar into position, the strain of compelling him to carry out my plan made me realise the power and drive Harriet needed to be always manipulating and coaxing me along the lines she desired.

'I've found it.'

The Tsar seemed to be spreadeagled in a starfish of arms and legs against the window. The pole jutted out like a third elongated limb. I stood on the end of the pew and felt for the end of it.

'Let go,' I ordered. 'You hang on to the hook and move further over.'

He nearly fell. His body ballooned outwards, invisible hands clawing at the glass. Then he folded inwards breathing heavily. I wanted to laugh at the fuss he was making. He was so awfully bad at this sort of thing even though he had lived for years.

'Are you all right?'

'Yes. When you jump mind you don't knock your face.' I showed my teeth in the darkness and tilted out towards the wall on raised feet and hauled on the pole, pulling myself slowly up to the sill, keeping my eyes to the window, to the faint greyness that was not light but was not total darkness.

'Mr Biggs,' I said feverishly, 'Mr Biggs, I can't get any higher.' He began to edge along the sill, one hand clutching the hook in the wall, the other groping for me.

'Can you get hold of my arm?' His voice was stronger now that he was in a position to help me.

It was very difficult; the Tsar balanced on a narrow ledge grasping a pole that might slip free of its hook, and I pulling frantically at his raincoat to lever myself upright. When finally I lay along his back, crucified against him like one of the saints in the window he leaned his cheek upon, we both stayed there helpless, unable to move. If after all Harriet had come back and unlocked the door, I would not have stirred.

'You're a heavy girl,' said the Tsar at last. I hated him. I hadn't remembered that I was stout, I had thought how fragile and childlike I must seem clinging to his superior strength. I tried to ease away from him and nearly fell, clutching at him convulsively so that he groaned.

'I'm sorry. I nearly lost my balance.' He did not reply, he did not seem to breathe.

At last he asked me, 'What am I supposed to do?' He meant

94

more possibly than the words conveyed. A question of the future and what it was Harriet and I expected of him.

'Mr Biggs, is the pole very heavy?'

'It's an awkward length, that's all. It's too damn short to rest on the floor and too long to hold easily.'

'Well, swing it inwards and lean on the glass. If it doesn't break, let go of the pole at once.'

Secretly I doubted if the glass would even crack, so thick and hard it felt. I waited a long time, then the Tsar said, 'I'm going to try now. Are you ready?'

'Yes,' I said bravely, voice thin in the darkness.

There was a sound like ice breaking, a sharp clean noise, and then a slithering free as the pane fell out. I heard the pole fall behind me as the night air rushed to meet my face and I landed heavily on the grass. The soil was so cool and the ground so firm that I wanted just to lie there, but I stood up and ran along the path to the gate into the woods. The gate was difficult to open, jammed tight by the heap of dead flowers and wreaths that littered the path. Harriet had a collection of memoriam cards edged with black that she had salvaged from the pile. She kept them in a special folder and wrote little postscripts to each one.

'Mr Biggs!' I shouted. 'Mr Biggs!'

Such an escape we had made, how cleverly I had freed us. The trees distilled a sweet smell of beech and pine; the fragrance of summer days cradled the woods and rose up from the cinnamon brown earth. The thought that I had achieved so much without Harriet to guide me filled me with exhilaration. What mattered if I was only thirteen and my parents liked me in bed by ten o'clock. I did not care if they called the police and locked me finally in my room. The round dark wound in the side of the church, the window splattered among the graves could easily be remedied by the Tsar sending some money, without his name, to the Canon.

I was hurrying across the field that lay in front of the army camp, making for the station. When I climbed the wall into the road I saw the figure of a man crouched under the lamp at the foot of the hill. He was holding a handkerchief to his face.

'What is it, did you cut yourself?'

He looked so pale and hurt, thick blood running into his mouth. 'I banged my nose as I fell,' he said with difficulty, dabbing at his nostrils with the stained cloth. What a petty injury to have. He had smashed a window, leaped into the grass but he had only managed to bang his nose.

'How did you do that? I landed on my feet on the grass.'

'You were lucky. There's a concrete verge right round the walls.'

'Look, I must go. My parents probably have the police looking for me.'

I ran on up the hill strongly, leaving him huddled under the lamp. A car breasted the hill, fierce headlights swept my face as it slowed to the kerb.

'Dad, I'm so glad.'

I opened the door and fell inside and started to cry. 'It's been dreadful, I've been so frightened.' He was quite silent, slumped over the wheel in massive reproach.

'I was in the woods and I saw a woman running through the trees, wearing a cloak. She had blood all over her face.'

He started the engine and turned the car, driving back over the hill.

'Just before I saw her I heard a crash from the church, like a window breaking . . . it was dreadful, Dad.'

I let myself sink into the waves of grief that tore over me, spurred on by his silence, convinced he knew I was lying. We stopped outside the house and he helped me out, still not speaking. A light shone in the hall; the door was open and Mother stood on the step, small and defenceless.

'What is it, George? Is she all right?'

'God knows what the hell happened. It's beyond me.'

I was led into the kitchen. The light was so harsh I had to shut my eyes against it.

'Mother, I couldn't help it, I couldn't, it was the lady in the woods.' I clung to her unable to bear her credulous face.

96

'She shouldn't go into those damn woods with all those blighters from the camp roaming the blasted place.'

Throughout my story Dad's face seemed about to smile. I felt the absurdity of the story irritated him though he could not prove I was lying. My mother asked me questions sharply and coldly, but when I broke down she folded me in her arms and rocked me, big as I was, on her knee.

At last I was able to go to bed. I lay in the dark wide-eyed. I had avoided real displeasure, I had been kissed, I had explained the broken window. They would never trace it to me, the more so as Harriet had been home early. I had lied very well and cried effortlessly; I would look white and ill in the morning. I thought of the beautiful night and my god-like strength in the church and I began to smile when I remembered the Tsar's banged nose under the lamp. Harriet could not have managed better.

11

ARRIET'S father saw the Tsar in the city with his arm in
a sling. Harriet said perhaps he had only sprained it when
he jumped from the window, and it was probably not a serious
injury. She offered to call on Mrs Biggs but I said it was unwise to go so soon after the adventure in the garden.

We talked at length about the evening I had been locked
in the church with the Tsar, but she did not say she had closed
the door. We wrote in the diary that we had been mysteriously
imprisoned by persons unknown, but I knew it was Harriet.
I wanted to ask her if it was part of the plan but I was afraid
she might call me stupid. She told me her father had said the
Tsar usually crossed the river on the ferry boat on a Wednesday to visit the firm's other factory.

'We'll go tomorrow,' she said. 'We'll tell them we're going
to the museum and they'll be delighted.'

'He mightn't go after all, not if his arm is bad.'

'We'll go anyway.'

We travelled on a morning train. I was made to wear my
school uniform but Harriet said it slimmed me down anyway.
We went on a tram to the docks, bouncing up and down on
the wooden seats. The landing stage was littered with papers
and refuse and old men in white mufflers sat on benches and
stared out to sea. We sat beside them for a time waiting for
the boat to come in, trying to adopt just such an attitude of
forgetfulness and isolation, but we were too alive. They did
not look directly at anything, not even at the gulls that circled
and screamed above the oily stretch of water. Harriet said

they had the view imprinted on their eyes long ago, and only thought of distant things connected with the landscape.

An old man on a bench further along began to whistle between his teeth, tapping his stick on the ground. When the red-red-robin goes bob-bob-bobbing a-long . . . A row of thin knees jerked up and down, a row of polished boots clumped in time to the tune. Any moment now, I thought, Harriet would fling arms wide and sing the words at the top of her voice. She was probably only waiting for a tired chorus of old women in shawls and tattered skirts to dance over the stones, massive bosoms a-bobbing, before she began. Seagulls flashed white wings in the sun, flying across the tin roof of the pier. The hands of the clocks that indicated the time of arrival of boats from Birkenhead and Wallasey moved jerkily into place. A woman with a pink face and yellow cardigan leaned against the rail. 'Red-red-robin,' sang Harriet loudly, stamping both feet and leaning out over the bench to smile at the row of old men. The whistling stopped, knees stiffened, boots rested heavily on the stones; the row of small eyes stared unresisting into the sun.

We sat there for two hours, waiting for the Tsar, watching each passenger patiently and carefully. I was not quite sure what we were to do or say if we did see him, and when I asked Harriet, she said, 'It doesn't really matter. The important thing is that he should see us all the time, not only on the shore or in the woods. I want him to feel hemmed in.'

I wondered if he had to feel hemmed in because he had called her evil. The love affair of the Tsar and me seemed to be forgotten. She had not even remembered to ask me if I had come to a more definite arrangement with him. She had not even asked me with great eagerness what he had said to me in the church.

When we did see the Tsar, he was with a dark handsome little man with a black moustache. They alighted from the Wallasey boat talking quickly, placing tentative hands on the rail of the gangway, the Tsar turning sideways to look at the man's face.

99

'Hallo, Mr Biggs,' said Harriet, screwing her face up fiendishly, standing before him with legs wide apart and hands behind her back. 'Fancy seeing you here.'

The Tsar raised his hat to her uncertainly, and Harriet said, 'We were just looking at the boats you know. We didn't know you would be here. What have you been doing?'

She smiled openly and with immense innocence at the dark little man beside the Tsar. He, like so many others, wanted immediately to confide in her. He leaned forward with a smile that was meant to be dashing, and said, 'I don't think I've had the pleasure.'

The Tsar hesitated; he seemed to shrink in the sunlight at the man's awful vulgarity.

'Two young friends of mine from Formby,' he said. 'This is Mr Douglas Hind.'

Harriet and Mr Hind embarked on one of her long cere-monial conversations.

'And what do you do with yourself these long summer days, dear?'

'Isn't that rather impertinent?'

'Oh come now . . .' the moustached man laughed de-lightedly.

'Harriet's father said you had your arm in a sling, Mr Biggs.'

The Tsar rubbed his wrist at the thought.

'Yes, I did, child. A bit of a sprain I think, nothing serious.'

'Was she in the road when you got home?'

He seemed to be searching the crowds on the landing stage for a familiar face. He half turned and touched his jaw with his fingers.

'No, she wasn't,' he said abstractedly.

Mr Hind laughed again, little moustache moving like a cork on the ocean of his lip.

'How did you explain your wrist?' I asked, wanting him to look at me.

'I said a boy ran into me on his bicycle,' said the Tsar.

He did not smile. He looked unhappy. I wanted to make

him happy again if Harriet would let me. Mr Hind touched the Tsar's arm. 'Peter, this young lady suggests a cup of coffee. Good idea, eh?'

He smiled frankly at the Tsar and then at Harriet.

'Yes, of course.'

The Tsar seemed to think anything would be preferable to standing in the open like this where anyone might see. Harriet and Mr Hind led the way into the snack-bar. It was all wrong, I knew that. We ought never to have spoken to him away from the shore. The trees and the church and the lane to the sea were the right borders for our relationship. It was a mistake to think we could function outside these boundaries.

The Tsar stirred his coffee and looked out of the window, stretching his neck like a boy whose pride had been hurt. He swallowed repeatedly, his Adam's apple moving unbeautifully in the thin discoloured throat.

Flies circled lightly above a plate of iced cakes on the next table; a workman in overalls and peaked cap yawned vastly, showing white gums, and blew cigarette smoke at the flies.

'Actually,' said Harriet in a sweet childish voice, 'I shall be fourteen in a few months' time. Mummy says I can cut my hair then.'

'Aaah . . . no.' Mr Hind was unbearably shaken. He stretched forth a swarthy hand and lightly touched the plait that lay on Harriet's shoulder.

'No,' he said sadly and foolishly, 'don't have it cut off.'

The Tsar gave him a swift guilty look and turned away to the window not trusting himself to speak.

'I don't think,' said Harriet, looking sorrowfully at Mr Hind, 'that Mr Biggs cares for me very much.'

Mr Hind leaned back in his chair and placed his hands behind his head, elbows spread upward like a kite.

'Surely not. You're a lucky fellow, Peter.'

He dipped his body and dug at the Tsar's shoulder with one sharp elbow.

'I believe I am.' The Tsar relaxed, sprawling a little over the table, eyes of friendship twinkling at Mr Hind.

101

They were friends and confidants, I was sure. Even friends such as Harriet and I were, but separated by different ways of life. The Tsar had probably told him about the night in the church, but vulgarly, to match the mood of the moustached man. He had said, 'Locked in – imagine, Douglas. Had me scampering over a window ledge with a damn big window pole.' 'What happened before that, eh?' Mr Hind had asked with sly insinuation. 'Oh, I tried to kiss the girl, but she wasn't having any.' Then they had both laughed loudly.

Fascinated I watched the charred moustache springing above the moist mouth. The Tsar was so frail and yellow-skinned beside this man. He seemed to be made of hair. It waved crisply over his round head, growing down to the tips of his ears. Eyebrows, lashes, cheek-bones, lip, all dark and quivering with black hair. Hands, throat and neck shadowed with its profusion, Mr Hind spun and glowed in the sunlight. Under the table two legs brown and hard were covered too with a pelt of fur. It was as if a bumble bee hovered with three moths and the Tsar was the palest of the three.

Harriet kicked my ankle with her shoe. I supposed Mr Hind was pressing her knee under the table, so I looked at her with a sympathetic excitement that conveyed something of envy too, and she glowed at me across the table, mouth curved at the corner in a pleased small smile of satisfaction. My envy was real because no one ever pressed my knee so quickly or so daringly, and though it was quite likely that Harriet had pressed his knee first I could not be so definite with the Tsar. I comforted myself with the thought that I was the more feminine and refined. The Tsar said, 'Were your parents very worried about you the other night?'

I might truthfully have replied that they were very worried but it was always more romantic to be the neglected child.

'No, they were out drinking with friends. They never seem to notice whether I'm there or not.'

In another situation I would have said my parents had cried and phoned the police in their worry, and even that would have sounded a lie, so long ago had Harriet and I forgotten how to tell the truth. The clock on the wall of the building opposite chimed the hour. The Tsar consulted his watch for accuracy and put his hand on the edge of the table in preparation to rise.

'Tsar.' I had to speak very quietly in case Harriet overheard. 'Tsar, will you be going to the woods tonight?'

He looked at me startled, the hand braced against the table edge relaxed slowly, his body leaned forward once more over the coffee cups. Quick, quick, I thought, before Harriet stops talking, say something, Mr Biggs. His eyes narrowed suddenly as I watched him, his expression was almost of distaste. I blinked rapidly and moved my lips to change my own expression. How often had Harriet recoiled from me, telling me I was ugly, that I must modify and govern the muscles of my face. It was not that my feelings illuminated and transformed me, as Harriet became transformed in diabolical anger or joy, it was more a dreadful eagerness and vulnerability that made my face like an open wound, with all the nerves exposed and raw.

Weakly the Tsar said, 'I expect so . . .' The little boy swallowed nervously, blinking back the tears of self-pity, red eyelids fluttering.

'Not in the road though. Behind the church.'

He spoke very quickly, as if Mrs Biggs might be within earshot. The hand pushed against the table, this time with decision, and he rose to his feet. Mr Hind regretfully removed his hand from Harriet's leg and stood beside him.

When they had gone Harriet sat well back in her chair and smiled warmly at me. I wanted to tell her at once about my arrangement with the Tsar, but I knew she wanted to be quiet. The man in overalls pushed his plate away noisily and stretched himself, lifting his cap for a moment to ease his hot forehead. Harriet said, 'Mrs Biggs is going away next week for two days, and Mr Hind is coming to keep the Tsar company.'

'Oh.'

How clever Harriet was to find out something so important from a stranger. All the satisfaction I had felt at my mumbled

103

request to the Tsar dissolved away, and left me humble.

'How clever you are, Harriet. How did you ask him?'

'I didn't.' She looked at me in surprise. 'He told me himself. I just led the conversation along certain lines and he told me all I wanted to know. Mrs Biggs leaves early Tuesday morning and Mr Hind and the Tsar will be alone till Thursday.'

'Oh.'

'Mr Hind suggested we might call round Tuesday evening and drink coffee.'

Even Harriet was impressed by this. Drinking coffee was part of a way of life alien to us; it went with concert and theatre going, and people who played bridge of an evening. Seeing a man on the train in the summer, wearing a neat little suit of small check and shoes of honey-coloured suede, one could say with contempt that he drank coffee after his meal. But oh the stylish little panel in the back of his jacket, that flared out like a skirt frill as he alighted on the platform. Anyone who called in the evening to the homes we knew wore gun-metal trousers and green jackets, and at nine o'clock they were given tea and fancy cakes. They were always invited, never unexpected. People who arrived unheralded were rare indeed and Harriet's mother, had such an occasion arisen, would have talked about it for days with a mixture of pride and bravado. 'No,' she would say, 'we didn't expect them, they just dropped in. Strange, wasn't it?' And a small baffled smile of pleasure would gently curve her mouth.

We both sat silent, imagining the scene at the house of the Tsar, drinking coffee out of thin white cups, locked together in the lamplight with the two men: the delicious secrecy of the night, the unfamiliar bitter taste of the dark liquid, the fearful danger, footsteps coming up the path, the Tsar crumpling paper-pale against the window as Mrs Biggs returned before time and fitted her key in the locked door. It was a lovely fearful thing to imagine, and we kept the image of it all the way to the station.

On the train I told Harriet casually that I had asked the Tsar to meet me in the woods behind the church, but she said

104

nothing, merely nodding her head and staring out at the flying hedges and fields.

In the evening I almost hoped my mother would tell me I ought to stay indoors, but when I put my coat on in the back kitchen she smiled and told me merely to be in before it grew dark. So I had to go out. I felt excited as I turned the bend of the road and saw the church, remembering the broken window and the helplessness of the Tsar. I climbed the low wall demurely in case he was watching me, and stood among the cold ivy with thoughtful face. Everything seemed damp and sallow, the horizon was flushed green, so that there was no longer a division between earth and sky. The whole world looked sickly and weak; tombstones, slate church and pebbled path tinged with a green unhealthy light. It was as if the churchyard had been modelled with wax and placed under an enormous dome of glass, causing tiny particles of moisture to ooze and dribble along its inner surface. I could not move, so heavy had my limbs become; if I raised my foot only a little it might grow slack and slide away from me. All the time I kept the thoughtful sad look on my face in case the Tsar should see me. A small wind bustled along the pines and crept over the grass. The leaves of ivy trembled against my legs and my hair swayed and hung over my face, freeing me. I walked over the grass and the Tsar and the Canon came out suddenly and stood in the porch talking together. The Canon moved an arm up and down constantly, like a broken wing on a black crow, and the Tsar stared out into the graveyard and nodded his head. I was quite near them if I measured nearness by the relation of my body to the porch, but they looked tiny and distant, creatures under a microscope. The Canon's bulk seemed curiously whittled down and the Tsar stood a motionless yellow doll, with limp head and face of wax. I must not imagine things, I told myself. I must not imagine things. Even if my nose and ears seemed filled with cottonwool and I was moving in and out, out and in like a child's fist, I must not imagine things. A foolish smile formed on my face for the benefit of the two men.

'Why should anyone do that, Mr Biggs, do you think? Such a big expensive pane of glass.'

The Canon's voice seemed full of tears. He lisped his vowels firmly and loudly and pointed with showmanship at the piece of hardboard that had been wedged into the aperture, a blind eye among healthy ones. The Tsar hung his head and swung his hat between his fingers.

'Who did it?' I asked bravely, gazing at the Canon's petulant face and the brown eyes so filled with love. It was his eyes first and then his voice that Harriet said made you know he was senile. He shook his head ponderously from side to side, admitting, 'We do not know, we do not know.'

I could not bear the gaze of those luminous eyes, the tiny flecks of yellow light that pitted the brownness. I looked down at my feet in embarrassment and saw against my shoe a piece of glass stained dull red.

'May I keep it?'

'Of course.'

A mandarin smile narrowed his eyes, and a network of wrinkles spread out joyously across his face as the heavy mouth thinned to a line of pure sweetness. It was a terrible smile. Harriet had said he was like the witch in Hansel and Gretel who had a house made of sweets and candy, only instead of a house it was he himself who was made of sugar.

'If we broke a piece off him,' she said, 'even a bit of his little finger, it would be sweet through and through.'

And now when he smiled I felt against my tongue a fearful cloying stickiness, as if I had bitten his fingers.

'Thank you.'

I stood there uncertainly, holding the fragment of glass in my palm. The Canon wished me good night with beautiful courtesy and the Tsar smiled gravely as he was led away. I watched them go through the gap in the fence into the Canon's garden and along the path to the vicarage. The Tsar did not even signal with his hand behind the Canon's back, he just swayed delicately towards the house and turned the corner, leaving me in the porch.

He would make extravagant gestures with his hands, bring the quick tears to his eyes, and not once remember me. But I wanted him to talk to me tonight, I wanted to wait breathlessly and painfully for him to kiss me, I wanted to tell Harriet how powerfully I had questioned him. I willed him with all my strength to come back, but moments passed and I was plump and foolish in the darkening porch. Appalled, I walked round to the other side of the church and sat with my back to the fence, hunching up my knees about my face. Each time I looked up and thought, Now surely he must come, the yard was deserted. Once I heard a rustling in the woods behind me and looked half fearfully over my shoulder expecting him, but all was still, '*Keine mensch*, my love,' I whispered deeply into my folded arms and smiled knowingly to myself. I felt such an ache, as if I was yawning deep inside my chest, and when the tears came I sat astonished because I did not feel unhappy. I'm just emotional, I told myself between sobs, and buried my face in my arms. If he came now he would grow pale and very gentle with me, he would . . . but I did not know what he would do. Then I remembered Mrs Biggs on the couch and the darkened room, the death's head against the leather back, and I shut my eyes so tight that the tears stopped abruptly.

'I'm going home,' I said loudly, 'I'm going home.'

I had to sit a long while in the field at the bottom of the hill for my face to become less swollen. And I really had not felt so very unhappy.

12

HARRIET arranged that we should go separately to Timothy Street. She was to walk an elaborate detour round the village and approach the house over the fields. I was to come by the usual route and meet her at the house of the Tsar. On no account were we to enter the door together; singly we might go unrecognised and if one of us was caught then the other would be safe. Harriet was to arrive ten minutes ahead of me and leave the high gate open. If the gate was shut I was to walk past and walk straight home. 'Don't turn round,' she warned me as if afraid Mrs Biggs would turn me into a pillar of salt. 'I promise,' I said.

'And don't you dare say your mother wouldn't let you out. If you don't turn up I won't speak to you ever.'

My mother was busy making a dress for Frances when I left. I kissed her cheek, avoiding the row of pins caught between her lips. The high gate was open but I walked on, turning back at the end of the road and approaching it as a runner might a difficult hurdle, very fast and not looking to right or left. I rang the bell firmly, patted my hair smooth, rubbed my hand roughly across my mouth to make it red, performing these actions with feverish haste so as not to be caught when the door opened.

It was Harriet who let me in, face flushed, her plaits loose and the colourless hair hanging about her ears.

'Yes, it's her,' she called into the house and whispered quickly to me, 'don't refuse a drink but sip it slowly.' Harriet shut the front door behind us. I stood there wondering why she thought I might refuse the coffee and why I should only sip it. Perhaps there was not enough to go round. There was a grandfather clock in an alcove; it shivered and jangled its brass weights as we trod past.

It was not the dreaded front-room, it was a smaller one at the rear of the house overlooking the garden and the fields beyond. The relief at not having to sit on the blue leather couch was overwhelming. Mr Hind sat on the arm of a chair, swinging his muscular leg; the Tsar stood with shrivelled face, smiling shakily.

'Well, well, come on in, dear,' he said loudly.

Mr Hind continued to balance on the arm of the chair, watching his brown shoe as it rose and fell. He wore a blue striped suit and a waistcoat of brown felt with a watch chain across it. They were awfully like our fathers, both of them.

'Well, well,' echoed Harriet, placing her hands childishly behind her back, staring unblinkingly at the Tsar.

They were both very nervous; we had thrived and matured on such situations and had the advantage.

'Oh Harriet,' I cried, 'look, a piano!'

I sat down, perched on a velvet-topped stool, placing my hands on the keys. The only tune I knew was 'The Fairy Wedding Waltz' and I played one bar.

'Do go on,' said Mr Hind.

'I couldn't possibly,' I said truthfully. 'I'm not a bit musical.'

Harriet laughed, an easy relaxed sound of amusement, and Mr Hind coughed.

The Tsar poured a drink out of a decanter and came across the room to me, holding his glass like a flower. He sat on the stool beside me and swirled the mixture in the bowl of the glass, looking over his shoulder at Harriet and Mr Hind. I folded my hands together and stared down at the keyboard. The Tsar leaned his elbow carefully on the notes, so carefully there was no sound at all, and crossed his legs. I had only to turn sideways a little and we would face each other. Instead I sat apparently lost in thought, slack hands cupped in my lap.

'Do you think you ought not to have come?' he asked

quietly, shading his eyes with his hand, arching his palm about his brow as if to shut out a too bright light.

'Oh no, it's just, it's just . . .'

'Well, what?' He paused kindly, anxious to help me. Try as I might I could not be sincere, I could not begin to be truthful.

'It seems wrong to be here in your house, when she is away. She would suffer so if she knew.'

The skin puckered round his shadowed eyes. He massaged his forehead, kneading it unhappily, mouth drawn down in misery.

'She won't know, God willing.'

God willing was like when my father at Christmas picked up his glass of port and raised it high, saying good-humouredly, 'To absent and sea-faring friends!' There were no absent and sea-faring friends, just as the Tsar knew there was no God willing to keep our visit from Mrs Biggs. Still, it had to be said, to preserve the formalities.

'Why have you come?'

The question was so sudden and so unlike him that for a moment I was almost shocked into telling the truth.

'I wanted to see what it would be like. I mean I only know you on the shore and in the lane. It's . . . it's interesting to see where people live.'

The mouth twitched uncontrollably. The word 'interesting' had hurt him.

'I see.'

He did not see, but it was again a game and the rule was not to enlighten him; Harriet would appreciate that later when I retold the conversation. I did not want him to be hurt, though.

'I mean I like seeing you and I wanted to know how you looked inside a house.'

Mr Hind rose to his feet energetically and went to the table and its decanter. Harriet said gaily, 'Only a very little one, honest.'

The word 'honest', recalling school, seemed out of place in the room. I imagined her arm lifted in mock reproach, her bright eyes smiling at Mr Hind. The Tsar looked at her between his fingers and away again, and now I knew her arm had dropped into her lap, and the bold eyes no longer laughing were staring at him curiously. Mr Hind stood in front of the Tsar.

'You haven't offered the young lady a drink yet.'

He shook a finger roguishly at the man on the stool and asked me, 'What will it be, my dear? Sherry or a little whisky?'

Such a confiding smile, the moist mouth very red and lively beneath the thick moustache.

'Whisky, I think.'

I turned on the stool, away from the Tsar and towards Harriet, but she sipped at her drink demurely and would not look up.

'Right you are.'

Mr Hind turned his muscular back to me and stooped over the decanter. The Tsar sat heavily and in silence, one hand almost obscuring his face. The blurred edge of his jaw and the fold of skin above his collar seemed to express reproach.

'Is whisky all right?' I asked, sounding timid.

'Whisky's very much all right.' Mr Hind stood on the carpet, swaying from the waist, offering me the small glass half-filled with brown liquid. I had a confused image of him sharing a room at night with the Tsar, unbuttoning his city shirt to expose his virile chest, and the Tsar turning his back to thrust withered white arms into his pyjama jacket.

Mr Hind returned to Harriet.

I sipped experimentally at the drink I held, and shuddered at the bitter taste. I had tasted it before, when I had been ill in bed with a chill, and once when I had a period pain. It did not seem possible that one drank it for enjoyment.

'It's very warm once it's inside,' I told the Tsar.

'Do your parents go out drinking a lot?' He looked down at his glass.

'Not all that often. It's a relaxation.'

'Just as well they do, eh?' He gave me a gentle smile and rubbed at his cheek. 'You wouldn't be allowed out so often.'

111

'They don't bother about me. I've always run wild, that's why I was sent away to school.' I felt very wronged suddenly. 'They don't understand me.'

I realised at once I had said a silly thing; it was such an obvious remark. Why, if the Tsar understood the game he had even been waiting for me to say it.

The Tsar gazed at Harriet and Mr Hind in the far corner under the window, the light fading now in the garden outside, and said:

'When you are young you think the tragedy of life is not being understood – not having the chances or the right books to read. When you are a few years wiser you know that nothing is so sad as the injustices of old age.'

'But you're not old, Tsar, not nearly old.'

I knew what he meant. I knew that my saying he was not old would make him sure I had misunderstood, but perversely I did not care.

'Why, you're quite young you know.'

'I was twenty-six when I married.' His eyes grew red-rimmed as if he was about to cry. 'I did not want to marry, I just drifted into it. I don't really regret it.' He sounded surprised, his eyes opened wider.

I fidgeted on the stool, rubbing my hands along the soft velvet, enjoying the soft touch of my frizzed hair as it fell against my cheeks when I hung my head. I could not possibly this evening make him say he loved me, even if Harriet and Mr Hind left us alone. He was not in the mood; he was all sorrow for himself and surprise that he did not regret marrying Mrs Biggs. He oozed astonishment and self-pity; a kind word would stretch him sobbing across the piano in a wild welter of discordant notes. Mrs Biggs had said he was weak, that a little more self control would help. Doubtless she was right; she might be the one who was the more sinned against.

'Why did you marry if you did not really want to marry?'

There was no answer. Helplessly I felt Harriet's eyes on my back, ears strained to catch the conversation. I forgot she had told me to sip at the drink; I shut my eyes and swallowed quickly, and placed the empty glass on the piano top.

The room was very warm, I was aware of a wetness on my palms. Harriet began to laugh. It was her exhibitionist laugh and very realistic. I looked over my shoulder and saw Mr Hind with his hand on her hair, and Harriet, half hidden by him and the breadth of his shoulders, leaning back in the chair with her head right back and her mouth wide open. Mr Hind any moment was meant to kiss the open mouth to stop her laughing, and even as I watched his head bent suddenly and Harriet became quiet. I turned away and looked at my miserable Tsar.

The Tsar uncovered his eyes and glanced quickly at the empty glass. He frowned at it.

'I forgot I had to sip at it,' I said. 'Will I be drunk now?'

'You know how we got this house?' He sounded angry with me, as if I had prompted the question. I wondered if he were drunk, and if he was would it be easier to make him kiss me.

'No, how?'

'She won it in a raffle. Yes, she did; that's how we got it.'

'Really.' For all the world I sounded like Harriet's mother indulging in a slightly risky conversation and handling it in a ladylike way.

'Someone had a bazaar down at the church . . . before the Canon's time. They had tickets for this house, and she bought one. That's why we got married, because she won the raffle. Seemed the only sensible thing to do.'

'Yes, but . . .' Supposing they had won a ship, not a house, would he have gone to sea? Or a horse . . . he might have been a jockey.

'You could have sold the house.'

'Oh no, you had to live in it or forfeit it. You had to play fair.' He was quite right, I could see that now. You had to play fair.

Mr Hind and Harriet were opening the door. I sat motionless on the piano stool, unable to call for help. 'Harriet,' I

113

might have said loudly, 'Harriet, it's getting out of hand. He's crying.' But the door shut and we were alone.

The Tsar appeared not to notice. He stood up and went to the decanter to fill his glass.

'It's funny you know, how things happen . . .' He swung round to stare at me, one hand holding the decanter by the neck. 'Just a little ticket . . . a little ticket and you get married and settle down.'

The whisky poured steadily into his glass; he stood, one leg bent at the knee, his eyes watching, his hand pouring. I hoped he would not realise how like a bad poem he sounded. Harriet would say it was because most people had unoriginal minds, but I could not think just then how else he could paraphrase his existence.

Darkness settled along the neglected garden; leaves rustled frantically in a sudden small wind.

'What number was the ticket?'

Something so important must remain for ever engraved upon the memory.

'The number?' He became irritated. 'Lord, how would I know. Thirteen most likely.'

He sat down beside me on the piano stool. His elbow this time struck with elation on the notes, making ugly musical sounds. 'All I know is, she won the raffle.'

If he was not drunk he was being very clever. Perhaps he thought it would be easier to kiss me if I thought he was drunk. I wondered what Harriet was doing to Mr Hind. Now was the time to start saying the Lord's Prayer; I had waited long enough. If he did not kiss me before Thine is the Kingdom, he would not kiss me tonight.

The Tsar crossed one thin leg over the other, and drank a little of the whisky.

Our Father which art in heaven . . .

'I go into her room now and then, once in perhaps six months. Usually it's after a night out with Douglas Hind. She never says a word.'

But what about the evening on the couch. He wasn't telling

114

the truth. Hallowed be Thy name, Thy Kingdom come . . .

'Other times she tries to sit on my knee . . . It's dreadful, she's too heavy. I get cramp. Wouldn't do to let her know though.'

Thy will be done, as it is in Heaven. That was wrong surely.

'Sometimes she comes into my room in a blue nightdress she had when we first got married. I lie there with my eyes shut, praying she'll go away.'

It was horrible. I could not listen to such words. Harriet must be wrong. He was far too old, far too sad to be helped or turned into an experience. He put a hand on my shoulder, and I leant sideways under his weight. He placed his glass carefully on the piano top, shut his eyes, and laid his forehead against my cheek.

'I should like,' he said formally, 'to kiss you, my dear.' But he just remained folded against me, almost as if he slept. Please, please, I thought, I'm sorry, I'm sorry, bring it to an end. Two tears rolled off his cheeks and down my face. He smelled like an invalid who had been too long out of the sun. He sat back blindly on the stool, took me by the shoulders as if to steady a moving target, and brought his tear-stained face closer.

Dryness on my lips, a sour smell of drink, his knee with its too sharp bone pressing into my leg; such clumsiness in his whole gesture. I felt so weary I wanted to lean back and pretend to be ill. It was terrible to be kissed by him. I closed my eyes and thought what I should say when he had finished. I must look long and wonderingly at him and say presently, 'You make me feel funny.' He did not make me feel funny, not as the Italian had when he called me a Dirty Little Angel, but I would have to say so, otherwise he would feel hurt. Besides I did not know what else to say. All the time I kept wondering why I had felt I loved him, why I had loved him on the shore and when I was with Harriet, and why I did not love him now when he kissed me. His mouth relaxed its pressure, a flat little sound of air escaped as his face drew away from mine. I had no time to look long and wonderingly at him, no time to say anything; he pushed at me fiercely so that I slipped and lay along the stool, and all the time he kept his eyes closed.

'Please don't,' I said politely. 'It's awfully uncomfortable.'

On his knees beside the stool the Tsar shuffled to hold my hands in his. He laid his head on my hip and said :

'You're so young. You're so young. I love you. I love you.'

I looked at the chair by the fireplace, and the framed picture on the wall above it, memorising positions so nothing should be lost when I told Harriet. I did not dare smile though, in case he opened his eyes.

I touched the thin skull with my hand, and stroked the hair to soothe him, remembering as I did so the evening by the tadpole ponds when I dreamed of this moment. Tears ran down his face, making him ridiculous. I could not forget my conventional upbringing, my instilled belief that it was not right for a man to cry. His hands moved, they spread out over my knee and he bent his head and cried through his fingers. I pushed at his wrists with all my strength, and he looked up quickly and stared in astonishment, a look of bewilderment in the distressed eyes, as if he could not believe I was unwilling to comfort him. Then with cunning he pressed his face against my leg and held on to me, the tears spilling on to my skin.

The room was almost dark, the house quite silent; Harriet and Mr Hind were lost somewhere in the upstairs rooms.

'Please don't,' I whispered. 'Please don't, Mr Biggs.'

Twilight flutterings, peevish struggling; fingers like goldfish squirmed and flickered to be free. Back and forth in a dim aquarium the Tsar and I threshed with our hands. He fought desperately to find a reservoir for his grief, and suddenly the strength and the will left me. I lay still and turned my face away from him because I did not want him to see my expression should he look up.

I knew I could comfort him; I could be kind and good and heal him; but I would not. I imagined his sobs must be more from shame and self-pity than from sadness, so I just sat there and stored up the experience inside me.

I looked down unsmiling at the top of his head, at the soft

116

skin showing beneath the crown of his hair, at the taut neck stretched over my knee. It was happening so differently from the way I had imagined, even if he had said he loved me. He had not demanded that I love him in return, that I should give myself to him. He had not told me that I was not fat but thin and golden. So I would not be kind to him, I would not lift a finger to show my sympathy. And then it was he slipped away from me and lay face downwards on the carpet at my feet. He lay so abjectly, shoulders lifting a little as he wept, that I stood up in embarrassment, not knowing what to do. I touched him gently with the toe of my shoe, and he moved convulsively and clutched at my foot with his hands. And while I stood there helplessly, the Tsar with my foot in his two hands, and his head buried in the carpet, the light was switched on, and I heard Harriet laugh. She stood in the doorway, arms folded over her chest, and laughed her exhibitionist laugh. She did not look at me, but kept her eyes fixed on the Tsar, to punish him. He had looked up into the light and stared at her in the doorway. I was glad she did not point at the door and tell me to go home and not turn round. I looked curiously at the Tsar. He lay quite still, face of grief yellow in the harsh light, small head straining upward. I did not understand why Harriet was laughing. The Tsar looked comical enough, but the plan after all was to make him fall in love with me.

After this last indignity he would never wish to see me again. Mr Hind, furry mouth apart in surprise, pulled at Harriet's arm worriedly.

'Steady on,' he said, not looking at the Tsar. He pulled more harshly at her, dragging her backwards into the dark hall, and closed the door. Slowly the Tsar bent his head and got to his knees. He got up on to his feet neatly and turned to the window, staring thoughtfully out into the garden. Harriet's voice rose loudly in anger beyond the door; Mr Hind was silent, speechless before her unaccountable rage.

Moments passed as the harsh light penetrated deeper into the room. The carpet under my feet became a lighter grey, drab flowers struggled outward in a tangled pattern across its surface; the piano, which in the darkness had filled the room, shrivelled at my back and was unimportant.

'I think,' said the Tsar, 'we had better all have some coffee.'

He stood still, arms slack against his sides, thin hands idle. Finally he coughed, a small dry sound that reassured him, and went out into the hall leaving the door open. When the light was first switched on and the Tsar exposed so foolishly, I had not dared smile. Now, alone, I did not want to smile. It did not seem very funny.

If he had scrambled at once to his feet, face comic in dismay, I would have laughed. But to lie there quite still in front of Harriet, head rearing like a tortoise, lined face so grieved and sad, had spoiled the scene. I felt I should have comforted him so that he need not have lain on the floor for Harriet to laugh at him. It was my fault and I felt guilty.

Harriet came into the room with Mr Hind. Her anger was gone; she smiled kindly at me and leaned against the mantel-piece.

'You should see upstairs,' she told me. 'Why, there's two rooms full of boxes filled with postcards and things, all scattered over the floors.'

'Two rooms . . . how wonderful. Are there really, Mr Hind?' I did not look at him and he did not reply.

'It's true, isn't it, Douglas?'

Evidently Harriet had been very harsh with Mr Hind, and was now willing to forgive him. He drooped in his armchair by the grate, face sullen. All his charm had deserted him, his moustache lay heavily and without life across his lip.

'Yes,' he said shortly.

Harriet said, 'And we found a telegram sent to Mrs Biggs on her wedding day. "Wishing you every happiness today and always, Meg and Wilfred." Didn't we, Douglas?'

'Yes,' said Mr Hind.

He seemed suddenly to be very sorry for Mrs Biggs. He crossed his legs and swung a resentful foot.

'I read the other day,' said Harriet, looking at me seriously, 'about a woman who collected elephants. She only managed twelve, but think how fortunate we are that it's only postcards for Mrs Biggs.'

She looked at Mr Hind innocently. If Mr Hind did not respond soon the evening would be a farce.

'I also read somewhere,' she continued, 'about a man who had a passion for collecting egg shells. He planted things in them.'

'What things?' I asked, feeling smothered by the laughter inside me.

'Just things,' said Harriet sternly, and added, 'mostly herbs, I gather.'

Mr Hind looked at her without understanding. He relented and laughed briefly. He thought no doubt that Harriet was an odd girl, pale with anger one moment and talking nonsense the next. Mr Hind did not matter, however; he was a shallow man and insensitive. It was the Tsar who must be amused and won over.

'I'll just see if I can help Mr Biggs with the coffee.' I walked quickly out into the hall and shut the door. The Tsar stood smoking a cigarette in the kitchen. He looked tidy, clean, and matter-of-fact. He had brushed his hair carefully and I thought he had washed his face. Pale smoke drifted across his eyes as he exhaled, so that I could not see his expression.

'I don't think Harriet meant to laugh.'

I stopped, not knowing how to make it sound convincing. 'I don't think she laughed because it was funny, Mr Biggs. It's just she gets angry sometimes.'

The Tsar took two blue cups from a shelf above my head, then another two, and found saucers for them. He arranged them neatly on a black tray painted with golden dragons, and opened a cupboard by the door.

'Don't worry about my feelings, my dear.' His back was to me as he said it, and his voice sounded cold, as if the light, that had so savagely been switched on, had in some way hardened him and drained away his weakness.

'It's you I'm concerned about. You and Harriet.'

119

He lifted down a green bowl carefully and turned and placed it on the Chinese tray.

'There . . . all ready I think.'

In the sitting-room he poured coffee and handed cups to Harriet and Mr Hind without embarrassment. I thought it strange that he was so at ease until I remembered the night Harriet and I had seen him on the couch, and all the other nights there must have been that I did not know about but could imagine. Harriet sat up straight in her chair, her eyes bright, two round dabs of colour on her pale cheeks. She did not look at the Tsar.

And he, unsmiling, talked a little to Mr Hind about business, and did not look directly at any of us.

Harriet tried to salvage something from the evening, but she sounded dispirited and I could only lean back in my chair and balance the coffee cup on my knee and feel hopeless.

When Harriet finally stood up in the small room and, raising her arms above her head in an unconscious gesture of surrender, said, 'We must go, it's very late,' Mr Hind sprang to his feet almost with relief and said he would see us to the door.

The two men were now alert once more; they were impatient for us to leave them. They had both drawn away from us and it was not only the scene of an hour earlier that had caused the withdrawal. Even if Harriet had not switched on the light and stood laughing in the doorway they would have been anxious for us to leave. The effort of appearing young and in sympathy with us was beginning to show.

The Tsar said good night to me at the door. He did not wait to see us go through the gate. The door shut and they must have turned the hall light off immediately because I stumbled a little in the darkness and jostled against Harriet.

'Be careful,' she snapped.

'You shouldn't have laughed at him like that.'

'I know. It was that stupid bugger Hind. I can't bear –'

'What was wrong with him then?'

' – men like that. Honest, when you think he's married and bringing up children it makes you despair. He's a cretin.'

'I thought you liked him.'

At the corner of the lane she said briskly, 'I'll see you to-morrow. Good night.'

Nothing more, no chat, no questions.

I began to wonder if it was deliberate, the way she no longer discussed things with me. Maybe she was letting me go. She still had to point me in the required direction but she was no longer holding my hand. I did not think I liked it.

13

In the morning my mother asked me to go over the line for a loaf of bread. Harriet was leaning on her gate. 'Come in,' she said. 'There's a lot I want you to write in the diary. I've been thinking all night.'

Seeing the expression on my face, she added, 'It's all right. The little woman's gone to have her hair done.'

'What have you been thinking about?'

'Lots of things.'

In her room I opened the diary and she said, 'We have been to have coffee with the man and his friend, and he deliberately made himself an object of pity and ridicule. He lay weeping on the floor and did not try to hide himself. When she laughed at him to punish him he became strong and gratified. This is not good.' The words were in ink; they could not be rubbed out, unless I tore a page from the book and burnt it. I felt ashamed.

Weakly I tried to argue with her. 'It seems so cruel, Harriet. I'm sure he wasn't glad to be laughed at. We can't be sure. You've said often and often that there are dozens of reasons for people behaving in a certain way, and that one person dare not presume to know which reason is the most likely. You've said that, haven't you?' Harriet closed her eyes and leaned her head against the side of the bed. For a moment I feared she was not going to talk to me, that she was in one of her superior moods. But quite soon she opened her eyes and looked at my worried face.

'Yes,' she said, 'I have. But just sometimes I know what the real reason is. You'll just have to accept that.'

'But, Harriet, it doesn't sound right.'

I rubbed the back of my hand over the page I had written and shook my head hopelessly: 'It sounds all wrong. It's not what I felt.'

I felt warm suddenly and almost happy. Harriet and I were talking together again as we had last summer and all the summers before. She was not racing on ahead making me feel heavy and stupid. She said kindly, seriously:

'If it sounds all wrong it's because of the way it's written, not what it means. All the best parts in the book were written years ago when we didn't know the proper names for things. We are limited now by knowing how to express ourselves. It sounds worse perhaps, but we can't go back.'

'If we put "There was a piano in the room",' I said, 'and that we drank whisky, it would sound more real.'

'But the whisky and the piano wasn't real,' cried Harriet. She sat up and stared at me fiercely, her under lip thrust outward. She clenched her hands so tight the knuckles whitened.

'Don't you see – only the Tsar was real and his weeping at your feet.'

I kept silent and nodded my head. She was wrong, she must be. All very well to say the piano wasn't real when she had not lain across it. Perhaps she had not understood what I meant. I tried to think of other instances in the book, experiences we had written about that sounded real, but I couldn't.

I looked at Harriet's hands as they lay in her lap and saw thankfully they were loose and inert.

'I often think,' she said quietly, looking at her idle hands, 'that we've passed the best bit in ourselves.'

She looked at me almost pleadingly.

'I mean we'll never be as good or clever as we have been. We start going back again now.'

I wished Harriet would not tell me such things. I had such belief in her and faith, that whatever she told me I accepted utterly, and most of the things she made me believe nowadays were painful. It seemed dreadful that at thirteen I had reached my best, that I could never be any better.

'But you said it would be wonderful when we were older. You promised that we'd be full of truth with all the experiences, and see beautiful things. You promised, Harriet.'

But all the time I felt it was true. I would never be better than I had been, all my life.

Harriet began to laugh, but affectionately.

'You look so sad, as if you hadn't known it all the time. Who's going to have a pony after the war?'

I had to laugh. That was a great joke. During the war our parents had told us, 'After the war I'll buy you a pony.' The war had been over a long time now and the ponies had never been mentioned again. It was because our parents wanted to believe everything was going to be all right that they had promised such a thing. And now, whenever we yearned, half-unbelievingly, after the unattainable, we teased ourselves and used the mythical pony as a symbol of all impossible things.

'Go home,' said Harriet, closing the diary. 'Your mum will only carry on if you don't get the loaf.'

After all the rain, the little square of grass in front of the house was green; the poor sandy soil in the borders appeared healthily black and moist. It was good for roses and lupins and Sweet Williams as long as my father bought tons of manure from the farm. During the war we had grown potatoes at the back, carrots too, and he had made an air-raid shelter where now the roses climbed. Harriet said it was pathetic, a hole in the ground with a lid of tin. Like going to sea in a matchbox. There was a shelter in the back field for all the houses, but my mother said not very nice people went there, so in the end we stayed under the mahogany table in the front-room. Everyone went to the farm for manure to grow their roses in the sand. Even so if my father heard a horse going down the lane he would run out with a bucket and spade and scrape up the dung. All the gardens sprouted flowers ringed with black droppings, alive with flies. My mother in her gardening gloves hovered over the blooms, bare legs blue-veined in the calf and wasted. Sometimes she wore an old straw hat, but this afternoon the sun shone on her dry hair and burnt her neck.

124

I lay on the front porch, stretched out on the red-brick tiles. Frances swung on the gate and sang loudly. A small dog from the house opposite trotted over the road and sniffed at her feet. She stooped down to touch him and he leapt sideways and padded back to his side of the road, nose to the hot surface, tail quivering and agitated. He climbed the low bank into the copse of elms before the farm, and crashed noisily down into the darkness and coolness of the foxgloves and nettles. Frances sang on, stomach pressed to the top of the gate, riding the structure like a wooden horse, patting an imaginary nose as she galloped across the deserted plains.

Behind my closed eyes I relived the evening spent with the Tsar. I led up to it carefully, deliberately postponing the moment I most wanted to remember. I waited for Harriet to get up from her chair and leave the room; in slow motion I slid sideways along the piano stool and offered my mouth to the Tsar. And just as I felt I was remembering most vividly, and the feeling of warmth was just within my reach, I opened my eyes and saw my mother sitting back on her heels in the grass, wiping her hot face with a clumsy glove.

'It's so hot,' she told me, satisfied. For a moment her eyes looked coldly at me as if she read my thoughts, and in my confusion I buried my head in my arms and mumbled it was too hot.

'Why don't you read a book?' she asked me relentlessly. 'Get a deck-chair from the greenhouse and sit in the shade.'

'No, I'm all right here.'

'You're too big to be lying about like that. I do wish you'd sit up properly.'

She meant I was too fat to loll about in the sun like a white worm. I wondered what she would say if I told her this. I sat up and folded my heavy legs under me and avoided her gaze. 'That's better, dear.'

She was pleased and surprised that I had half done as she wished. To appease me she asked, 'Don't you think my pinks have done wonderfully this year?'

I looked at the flowers and said enthusiastically, 'Yes, wonderfully.'

When she turned away I should lie down again. She turned her attention to Frances. 'Don't make such a noise, dear.'

But her tone was friendly this time. Love welled up in her voice, and though I could not see her face I knew it would be calm and relaxed, not hard and held in check, the lines dragging her mouth down, as when she spoke to me. Frances obediently stopped singing and smiled a charming smile at her mother. 'You've made your face dirty,' she said.

She fingered her own cheek to show better where the dirty mark was. 'Just there,' she said helpfully, and climbing down from the gate came on to the green lawn and, stooping, rubbed my mother's face with her hand. My mother put her arms about her and they knelt as if in ritual, forehead to forehead. I shut my eyes so as not to see them. And while I sat in darkness I could still see them swaying a little on the grass, a small undignified pyramid of love. I felt irritated; Frances after all was not such a very young child. It was affectation to be so trusting. When I opened my eyes it was because Frances was singing : 'Harry-i-et is coming up the road.'

I sat very still, pretending not to have heard, hoping a miracle would take place and Harriet who was coming up the road would dissolve into the warm air and spare me the embarrassment of seeing her.

'Hallo, Harriet, isn't it hot?'

My mother spoke in her coldest voice. Had I been spoken to in this way I would have burst into tears of distress. Cheerfully Harriet said, 'Hallo. I say, your garden looks beautiful.'

She saw me sitting in the porch and waved one hand casually, continuing, 'I believe you must have green fingers.'

She walked along the path and studied the earth, face serious.

'Father has a terrible time with the soil round here, but you seem to have no difficulty.'

My mother struggled bitterly to preserve her displeasure. Her mouth fluttered in distress as she said, 'My pinks have

126

done particularly well this year I must admit.' She capitulated utterly. 'We haven't seen much of you this holiday, dear. You've grown taller I think.'

I made an enormous effort to say something.

'She's not, you know. How high are you, Harriet?'

My mother did not turn her head, and Harriet, pretending not to have heard me, bent low and dug at the soil with her fingers.

'It's the same consistency as ours. I just don't understand it.' She crouched over the flowers, fish-bone-thin vertebrae of her spine showing through her dress, and, humming to herself in a slow sleepy way, touched the plants with her hand, not with the fingers but with the whole palm brushing lightly across the surface of the leaves, as if she were blind. My mother gazed down at her wonderingly. A fluted giggle escaped my lips. In another moment my mother would be down on her knees amongst the pinks. The quick tears came even as I giggled. Their eyes turned to look at me, and I opened my own as wide as possible to stop the tears from falling on to my cheeks, shaming me.

'I was just thinking of something I heard on the wireless,' I explained, seeing them blur and run together in the moisture of my eye.

We had tea on the porch. Mother wanted to sit more respectably in the back garden among the lupins and the roses, but Frances pleaded to be able to have hers in the front.

'It's full of bumblebees in the back,' she argued, screwing up her face desperately, as if already one of the creatures hummed and worried about her head. She was terrified of bees and wasps, and at this time of the year the garden behind the house lay like a golden bowl heaped full of flowers shimmering and quivering with minute fragile life.

So we all had tea in the front as she wished. Mother had a deck-chair. There was no room for more chairs, so we were allowed to sit on cushions at her feet. Frances, a piece of currant bread in one hand, wandered back and forth from porch to gate and gate to porch, to drink from a cup that left her mouth pale and milk-filmed. Harriet and my mother talked intimately about a book they had both read, and did little to draw me into the conversation. I was surprised that my mother had chosen from the library a book such as Harriet would like, and surprised too that my mother did not think it a strange thing for a child of thirteen to understand. Harriet said :

'You see I've read so many books now which just tell a story that I begin more and more to go after style, rather than dramatic content.'

'Really,' said my mother. Her eyes looked at Harriet with wonder and admiration. The beautiful smooth skin of her cheeks and brow, roughened a little by the sun, glowed rosily as she held out her hand for Harriet's cup.

'You see,' the wonder child continued wickedly, 'in this book you had style and content very finely mixed, but I could have done with less.'

'Stuff,' I wanted to shout rudely. It distressed me that Harriet was baiting my mother so. I was pleased to hear in Harriet's voice the slightly flat vowels and nasal intonations of the neighbourhood. It made her a little less perfect, a little more common-seeming. I studied her minutely to find more flaws, this time physical ones. But the bland face with its arched brows and small dry mouth was so dear and familiar to me that I no longer saw it clearly, however much I tried.

Even as I looked at the thin child's body with its bony hips and spine, so oddly at variance with the clever meticulous mind that flourished plump and powerful within, Harriet looked at me and smiled. She seemed to say, 'Yes, you know and I know, but no one else.'

Frances, who was leaning on the gate, suddenly cowered sideways and put her arms up helplessly as if to avoid a blow. A sound as of a cat mewing came from her lips as she spun round to face us, head grotesquely on one side. She screamed once, sharply. Mother ran down the path making small sounds of distress, arms held wide. Frances backed away from her, screaming thinly and uniformly; arms stuck out in front of her

128

as if in supplication, she crouched against the gate, evading the passionate circlet of arms that my mother held out like a garland for her head. It seemed an age before Frances was aware of anything but her pain. Through her own tears my mother asked, 'But what is it, darling . . . tell Mummy what it is.'

It was difficult to distinguish the words through the sharp intakes of breath.

'A thing in my ear . . . in my head.'

'It must have been a wasp,' said Harriet. 'It must have stung her.'

We took her indoors and my mother telephoned the doctor. She sat with Frances on her knee, cradling the shocked child in her arms, till he should come.

Harriet and I went out into the field at the back of the house. I felt I was choking. It had been so sudden, so violent. We climbed the bank that led to the Trail. The Trail was a long mound of earth built to separate the field in half, planted with trees and thorn bushes. On one side were the rows of houses with their ordered unremarkable gardens, on the other the wire netted compounds spread with sand, belonging to the farm. They housed pigs, hens and rabbits. When we were younger, too small to go to the shore, we had struggled along the Trail every evening after tea, making believe that we were escaping across the frontier, leading a line of grateful soldiers. Harriet led the way, and as before I had become aware how small in reality the Norman church was in the blurred woods, so now the trail dwindled and shrank into a trivial line of twisted trees. We came out among the blackberry bushes at the far end of the field and Harriet lay down in the yellow grass and shut her eyes. I sat a little way off and looked for ants in the soil. Poplars swayed elegantly with insect tattered leaves under the high white sky; a blade of grass swung in the breeze and filled the world. Presently Harriet said, 'That was horrible. That was so degrading.'

She sat up and leaned on one elbow to look at me. The park-keeper nearby rode his electric mowing machine over the already prim grass. The noise of the engine was like a bee humming with purpose.

'It's something as tiny and devastating as an insect that we need to humble the Tsar,' Harriet said. She sat up and crossed her legs. On her cheek, where her fist had pressed, was a red mark. It looked like a blow that had been dealt in anger.

'To humble the Tsar,' I repeated stupidly. 'I thought you had forgotten all about that.'

There was a long silence in the field. In the silence there was a warning. It was in the air and the poplars and the earth beneath me, and it was swollen out by the steady insistent note of the grass mower as it turned in a wide circle and rode in our direction. Nearer and nearer it came until I was deafened by the sound of it. And just as it seemed as if I would cry out, the mower wheeled and started back up the park, the noise of its engine receding and dying away, and Harriet, the mark on her face faded now, bent her head on its thin neck and looked at the earth.

'Something really subtle,' she said, 'if you understand me.'

How could I not understand her. I would have given all the power of my too imaginative mind and all the beauty of the fields and woods, not to understand her. And at last I gave in to Harriet, finally and without reservation. I wanted the Tsar to be humiliated, to cower sideways with his bird's head held stiffly in pain and fear, so that I might finish what I had begun, return to school forgetting the summer, and think only of the next holidays that might be as they had always been.

14

THE Tsar and I strolled together under the pine trees. At first when I had met him at the bend of the lane to the sea, he had been sulky with me, withdrawn. There were, it seemed, too many memories in the woods around us for him to be anything but resentful. The blind window in the church nearby, the tadpole pools, dry now, where first we had spoken together, the sand dunes that Harriet had filled with echoes of derision – all served to accentuate his misery and render him inarticulate.

Then it was I had the idea to go right away from our usual paths.

'Let's walk somewhere we don't usually go,' I told him gently, and he straightened his shoulders and said, 'Right you are, but where?'

'Through the Rhododendron Lands and up behind the rifle range.'

For a moment he hesitated. The rifle range was out of bounds to civilians and dangerous, and it might have occurred to him that it was another trap set by Harriet. Then because even walking into a trap was preferable to this feeling of emptiness, he said :

'Good, shall we start?'

Under the trees he told me with difficulty, 'I want you to know I regret the other night more than I can say. It's not a question of shame, it's more a question of shabbiness. And it wasn't the drink.' He faltered and looked at me quickly and away again, moistening his dry lips with his tongue.

I wondered what part of the evening he regretted, the time when he tried to pull down my knickers or when he lay on the floor and cried. I wanted to say he need not feel shabby, that such things happened in the best-regulated families, but it seemed too light-hearted. Instead I said, 'I know how you feel . . . as if something was spoilt.' I turned my face from him and smiled, showing all my teeth. It was quite easy to bring myself to hurt him, he was such a fool.

The smell of beech and pine mingled in the woods. We inhaled its sweetness with every breath we took. It did not seem to matter that every breath I exhaled poured forth poison and evil.

The Tsar said, 'As if something were spoilt . . . I think not. There was nothing to spoil. Harriet saw to that.'

Always Harriet. No matter if he had told me he loved me, it was Harriet who engrossed him.

'When my wife came back,' continued the Tsar, 'she knew you had been in the house. God knows how she knew, but she did. She stood in the dorway and looked at me and she knew. She said, "They've been here they have, those terrible children, they have, haven't they?" ' He stumbled and nearly fell into one of the potholes. His voice shook with shock, 'I didn't tell her, but she knew.'

'Why has Mrs Biggs's sister got an idiot child?' I asked.

'Something to do with brain damage at birth,' he said.

'Has it really got a big head?'

'I've never seen it. We're not a close family. The birth went normally to begin with.'

I held my breath because though I knew all about that sort of thing, I'd only read it; no one had ever spoken of it to me before. Long before Harriet and I knew about things I had read in a book the word 'pregnant'. My mother said it meant being very ill and though I knew she was stupid, I still half believed her.

'She was given gas and air to make her sleepy. In the middle of her sleepiness she heard herself singing verse after verse of "There is a Green Hill Far Away". And when she reached the

132

line "O dearly, dearly, has He loved," she began to laugh.' He looked at me to see how I was taking it.

'When did they tell her the baby was funny?' I asked. I felt pale and sick, frightened of something. No wonder the sister of Mrs Biggs laughed when she thought how dearly, dearly had He loved.

'Later on, when they realised the child was hardy enough to survive.'

'Why?' I was shouting. 'Why didn't they kill it?'

'Now, why indeed?' He looked up at the sky above the trees. His eyes were bloodshot as if he had cried too much or smoked too much. He said, 'I don't know why. Some people are born blind, or deaf, or with minds warped in some way. But you can't kill them all . . . you wait for famine or flood or war. After that, you believe in a Divine wisdom.'

'I didn't know you believed in God. I thought for you it was Greece and all those ancient ruins.'

He laughed at me. He stopped walking and felt in his pocket for cigarettes. He stood with hunched shoulders while he lit one, and as he blew out smoke his thin neck reared up like a tortoise emerging from its shell.

I had noticed before that he felt more sure of himself when he smoked. I thought it might be one of the things that hurt Mrs Biggs beyond endurance, goading her to call him weak and in need of discipline. It was a habit that would seem after years without love to epitomise the selfishness she ascribed to him. Just when she felt he was sorry that he had hurt her by his self-preoccupation, and that this once he understood and would make an effort to feel some part of what she suffered, she would turn and find him standing perhaps by the window, his hand already creeping insidiously into his jacket to reach his cigarettes, and she would know again how selfish he was, isolated behind his cloud of smoke.

We walked on and passed the line of warning noticeboards at the edge of the dunes. Rifle shots came spasmodically like twigs breaking underfoot, but the Tsar seemed not to notice, relaxed now, talking charmingly and breathing out smoke into

133

the evening air. The sky that had been infinitely wide and white began to darken; the light squeezed out; everything began to fade. A seagull cried out and the wind dragged its note forlornly across the beach as we dipped and rose like birds among the hillocks of sand. On a sandhill, a red flag on the end of a stick fanned out across the sky, stayed for an instant blood red, rolled slowly in the breeze and blackened.

'It must be getting late,' I shouted.

The Tsar was already climbing the little hill and did not hear. He went on all fours up the face of the dune, his hands reaching out to grasp wildly at the tufts of grass that grew in the sand and whose dry harsh blades were like knives to the touch. I shouted again and he turned, his face small and white, the scanty hair blowing about his ears. 'Come on,' he shouted back. The world was so desolate and darkening that it seemed swept by violence. The sea behind me yawned, a gigantic yawn that never reached its climax. The mouth of the world opened and the rough tongue of the sea licked the shore and tried to suck us down into the depths. Above, the triumphant Tsar held the flag aloft. He shouted something, but it sounded like a moan of protest in the huge land. Firing broke out behind him. I wondered if unwittingly I had outdone Harriet in subtlety, if the ending would be the Tsar shot dead with a red flag for danger clutched in the hand.

'Take care,' I called.

My voice sounded girlish and remote, belonging to Sunday mornings after church when we ran about under the trees and mimicked the Canon, crying, 'Blessed are the meek for they shall inherit the earth.'

I climbed laboriously up to the Tsar. It was lighter here; plainly I could see the row of target boards behind him.

'Let's go down there and rest.'

He pointed below to a small valley between the targets and the dunes. His eyes watched my face for some sign of protest.

'Yes,' I said, and slid downwards into the near darkness. A shot whined somewhere above us. I was glad the Tsar could not see my face or its expression. We lay in the sand and he

134

smoked. It was cold and damp but curiosity kept me there. It was completely dark now, too dark to see my own hands, only the end of the Tsar's cigarette sweeping in an arc from his side to his lips. I thought how I would be careful to shake the sand out of my hair before I saw my parents, how I would wake tomorrow and it would all be over.

'Now,' said the Tsar finally, as if he had been preparing all along for this moment, and flinging his dying cigarette into the night, he turned to me. He sought me in the darkness as if I was a bundle of rags, unwrapping me in layers. I thought of a picture I had seen in a book of an Egyptian king with an arched painted face of repose, and pursed my mouth primly in imitation. Minute grains of sand slid through my hair. The hard collar of his shirt hurt my chin. He did not kiss my mouth, he said nothing. There was no strength in his arms, no pressure of sand beneath me, no swinging meteorite and swift along the orbit of the moon. Pinned there raptureless, a visit to the doctor, nothing more, and a distant uneasy discomfort of mind and body as if both had been caught in a door that had shut too quickly. 'Gerroff,' I wanted to shout, 'Gerroff.' But I did not want to hurt his feelings.

Mrs Biggs, in her sandals and her groping search after love, came alive. She breathed heavily in the darkness, whispering softly, rapidly in my ear, 'He's selfish, he's so selfish. I told you so.' And when the Tsar had completed his own uncomplicated ritual accompanied as it was by low whimpers of distress, I did not know what to do. Harriet I knew would have sworn at him and made him cry, but I could not. The truth was that I was fond of him. He was part of the small group of souls that I was responsible for, who depended on me not to hurt them : my mother, my father, Frances. It did not occur to me till later that the Tsar should feel responsible for me.

'We had better go,' I said as gently as I was able.

He got to his feet and shrugged sand free from his clothes, not speaking. He followed me up the dune and in my mind I knew what he must look like, shambling red-eyed and slack-limbed up the shifting sand.

I was surprised how little discomfort I felt, apart from a kind of interior bruising, and how cheerful I was. I swung my arms vigorously, rejoicing that I was young and not out of condition like he was. I almost ran in the darkness and he stumbled in my wake, breathing harshly. Once he said, 'Stop,' and then, 'Not so fast,' but I went even quicker. It would have been better I thought, with amusement, if he had been shot on the sand dune and avoided all this. It was delicious to be in the position that Harriet alone had enjoyed – to have someone meekly follow wherever I chose to go. I wanted to shout commands, to have the Tsar do tricks to satisfy my vanity. 'Sit up and beg,' I wanted to cry; 'balance on your head.' How often in the past had Harriet with imperious voice and sweetly smiling face, bidden me fasten her shoe-lace in the street. And I, scarce knowing what lay behind the innocent-seeming request, had knelt before her in the road, only to look up in the middle of my task and see her expression of gratified power. Each time she made me kneel to fasten her shoe I expected her to kick me from her, disgusted at my servility.

I no longer cared if we were seen together, the Tsar and I. If Mrs Biggs herself had confronted us on the shore I would have wished her a pleasant good evening and continued on my way. Half-way along the shore we met Perjer, a dim shape at the edge of the water. Seeing him standing there and not knowing who he was I walked slower to allow the Tsar to catch up with me. The Tsar said in a low voice as we drew level, 'Good night,' and Perjer turned and thrust his face close to mine in the darkness.

'Good evening. Calm evening now.'

There was a moment of silence as if both men could not make up their minds.

'It is Mr Biggs, isn't it?'

'We've been miles along the shore, Mr Perjer. It's so beautiful at this time of the evening.'

Perjer said nothing to this. He moved closer to the Tsar. 'I haven't seen you and your good lady in a long time. Keeping well, is she?'

It seemed comical to hear Mrs Biggs referred to as a good lady.

'Oh yes, well enough, thank you . . . you all right?'

The Tsar had tried to be formal but Perjer was a lost soul like himself. I sensed his face relaxed in the darkness. He said almost jovially:

'Still on the water wagon?'

Perjer grunted. 'Now and then,' he said, and grunted again.

The conversation seemed ended. The Tsar jerked my arm with his elbow and I cleared my throat in preparation for a polite farewell.

He said with exasperation: 'Damn, I've run out of matches – got a light, Perjer?'

'In my hut.' He moved away and called into the wind, 'Mind how you go! Careful of the wire!'

They disappeared into the blackness. Far out to sea squares of light twinkled beneath the starless sky. The wind blew steadily above the dull breathing of the sea, as it covered the sand. The Tsar called remotely, 'Come on, what's the matter?'

I walked slowly in the direction of the sound, burying my hands deep in the pockets of my coat.

The hut was below a sandhill that hung out over it forming a second roof. Coming into the light, I blinked my eyes and heard the hum of the paraffin lamp swinging from a hook in the ceiling. There was a wood fire and a black kettle without a lid, in the embers. Perjer's dog raised a tired head from the sand-covered floor and lay flat again. The Tsar went and sat with his back to the far wall, stretching his legs out in front of him. He dug at the dog's ribs with his foot and sank his head lower on to his chest. I was annoyed that the Tsar was so evidently at home, that he had been here before.

There was an upturned box behind the door, so I sat on that and kept watching Perjer. There was nothing of him in the black clothes that hung in folds on his body. The hands and wrists seemed without arms, the neck waved stemlike to support his oval head. Only the full mouth in the dark face was alive, pouting and grimacing continually. He tore a strip from a newspaper on the floor, and lighting it at the fire held it out to the Tsar who waited cigarette in hand. No one spoke in the hut; sand slithered down from somewhere above us, and a little of it poured in a fine stream through a crack in the roof. It fell on the dog's head, who moved in his sleep and a spasm shook his ears free of it.

Perjer got more wood from a pile in the corner of the hut, and removing the black kettle from the embers and placing it with a neat house-proud precision on a rough shelf above the door, he returned and kicked the wood into place and rubbed his hands together.

The Tsar said, 'It's not too warm is it?' His eyes took in the worn black suit. 'I expect that's wearing a bit thin now.'

It sounded personal and in my ignorance I feared Perjer would be offended.

'I wore it on my wedding day,' said the Tsar.

He looked at me and away again. Perjer squatted by the dog; placing his palms on his knees, he looked down contemplatively at the black cloth across his breast.

'We all come to it,' he said, as if comforting a child.

Perjer cradled the dog's paw in his. 'I sat on the wall outside and wished you luck. The Canon tried to get rid of me.'

'Yes, so he did.'

The two men smiled at the recollection and gazed into the fire.

Perjer had been there that day too. Mrs Biggs in her bridal gown, the Canon dropping crumbs from his baby mouth. There on the floor of the hut sat Perjer in the wedding suit the Tsar had worn thirty years ago.

'It was a grand day for it,' said Perjer.

Going home I was silent. The Tsar told me that Perjer was the son of a doctor in London. 'He started out to be a lawyer but he never took his finals. Upset the old man. No staying power at all . . . he just wasn't interested. He said he was born tired.'

'Lazy sod.'

'Quite.'

The lamps were lit in the lane. The windows in the church shone gold; the Canon's sister whom nobody loved was playing the organ. Like the broken window I too had been violated. As Perjer had said this evening . . . we all come to it in the end.

15

THERE were but two weeks left of the holidays. As before at school I had counted the days to the end of term, willing the hours to pass quicker, so now I waited for summer to finish. Shadows of fatigue darkened my face though I went to bed early and slept late each morning. My mother said twice I looked poorly and hoped I was not going to be ill.

I tried to talk to Harriet but there was a barrier between us. She did not mention the diary and we were not allowed out at night. It would have been nice to mention casually that I had been inside Perjer's hut, that he was the son of a doctor in London. And but for Harriet's mother it could have ended then, it need not have gone further.

Harriet was sitting at the kitchen table writing her nature diary. The little woman and I sat twined in cosy intimacy together winding wool.

She said, 'I met Mrs Biggs this morning on her way to the station. Her sister's child has been taken to hospital.'

She looked up, suddenly aware of whom she spoke. I kept my arms held wide and looked at the wool strung across them as if they were strands of gold. Harriet said nothing. I let the silence develop. Then I said, 'What a shame,' and, moving my arms from side to side, 'Why don't they invent a machine to do all this?'

Relieved, the little woman continued winding her ball of wool. The small head bent low was vulnerable. For no reason I thought how easy it would be to crush the skull beneath the

soft hair. All the time I was really thinking of Mrs Biggs, looking at the little woman's feet half expecting to see the square
brown sandals planted firmly on the grey carpet. I knew
Harriet was watching me and I felt afraid. She said in a bright
exultant voice :

'What a bit of luck ! I say, little woman, how do you spell
fauna?' It was our old strategy, evolved to cheat the adults at
their own game. The first sentence was for me, the second a
blind to cover the real message. I waited. When the Little
Woman had spelt the word, Harriet said, 'I never expected
that . . . Thank you.'

'We must go there as soon as possible . . . I need another
leaf for my collection.'

If she had said, 'scalp' it would have been more appropriate.

'No, no we can't.' I heard my voice incredulously.

Surprised, the Little Woman stared at me, a frown pucker-
ing her forehead. Harriet pushed her chair back noisily behind
me and came over to her mother.

'Do you like my drawing?'

She sat on the arm of the chair and put an arm round her
mother's shoulders. She looked at me as she said, 'It's a little
uncontrolled, isn't it?'

Her mother said delightedly, 'It's a lovely drawing, darling
. . . and your writing is so much better.'

I sat holding the wool in my hands and looked down at the
floor. 'Very well,' I said, 'but this is the last time.'

I did not mind if her mother was puzzled, it was all one
now. 'Then that's settled. We'll go tomorrow.'

Harriet bent and kissed her mother on the cheek with
fondness. She stood up yawning with satisfaction, stretching her arms high above her head, her eyes closed against her
thoughts.

As before, we met in the lane; but this time nothing was said
about arriving separately at the house of the Tsar. Nor did we
pause in Timothy Street, for fear people should see which way
we went. It was dark when we opened the high gate. It was a

pitifully short path to the front door and the holly bush beside the porch. Some of the light from the lamp in the street spilled through the hedge and lay on the dark lawn.

I told myself, as I lifted the heavy knocker to summon the Tsar, that I should remember all my life the smell of the paint that had blistered in the sun, the sound of Harriet breathing in the blackness, the dry rustle of the coarse hair-mat beneath our feet, as if we stood on fallen leaves.

The Tsar stood as if at the end of a long tunnel, a small figure with hands outstretched.

'Well, invite us in,' said Harriet.

The face of the Tsar was old. He smiled hectically, waggling a reproving finger.

'Naughty, naughty. You shouldn't have come.'

'Well, we have,' she said.

'I could say it's a great pleasure, a deep pleasure. I could indeed say that.' He swayed a little on his feet.

Harriet fell silent. She had not anticipated that he would be drunk. For myself our meeting was mist bound after a lapse of eternity.

Last holidays I had seen Papa, the husband of Dodie, after a period of several months. He was so old all at once, standing in his garden, tottering over the lawn when I called his name. 'Papa,' I had said, 'it's me, don't you remember?'

Behind the hedge he peered at me, holding on to his walking cane, the breeze moving his white hair. A handsome face, still, thick waves of hair on his temples. A long while ago we had been the best of friends – Harriet and Dodie and Papa and I – sharing little jokes, sitting in his garden waiting for the strawberries to ripen, the plums to fall.

So gallant, Papa, in his blazer and boater among the flowers. He stood there, ill and almost blind, and I too sure facing him, watching his groping expression in the sunlight as he fought to thrust aside the years' corrosion and recognise my voice, eyes clouded like milk spilt.

Looking at the Tsar I felt now that he, unlike Papa, was thrusting life away from him with all his power, pushing backward all that might yet keep him nearly young. I said quickly, 'We came to say good-bye. We go back to school at the end of the week, there's no more time.'

'Ah now, that's a blow.'

The Tsar began to laugh immoderately. He shrugged his shoulders in a spasm of mirth and tapped the grandfather clock on its glass middle.

'No more time left,' he recited lovingly, and a deep boom of protest came from the clock as he leaned heavily against it. Harriet opened the door into the front-room.

'I'm tired,' she said and walked in. Beyond the doorway I could see the sofa glimpsed through the window an age ago. As we stood in the hall with the shrivelled Tsar, it assumed its proper importance, no longer an altar of sacrifice on which he had lain, but a comfortable piece of furniture, its design repeated and echoed in a hundred other rooms in a hundred other houses. I followed Harriet and sat deliberately on the sofa. Harriet began to enjoy herself. She hugged her knees with enjoyment so that the two lank ropes of her hair touched gently the faded carpet.

'Hark at him,' she said with mock severity as the Tsar struck at the grandfather clock in the hall. She rolled her eyes comically as the Tsar half sang, half shouted, 'Ding-Dong, Ding-Dong.'

'He's mad drunk, that's what he is,' I whispered. 'Stark raving drunk.'

I leaned backwards on the sofa to see the Tsar laboriously winding the aged clock.

'Trying to make more time,' he shouted, and broke into laughter. We laughed too, though it was sad what he said. He came sideways into the room and shut the door with elegance, pivoting round on his toes to face us with one hand raised in blessing.

'So be it,' he said gently to Harriet and walked to the small table with the bottles stacked on it.

'Is the child very ill?' asked Harriet sitting bolt upright on one of the chairs by the hearth.

'The child? . . . Oh did she say that?' He poured liquid into a glass and held it up to the light.

'She's gone for a rest. That's what she said. She said I was making her ill. That's what she said.' His voice lifted the last words as if he was reciting a poem.

'It's as good as a play,' said Harriet eyeing him with delight. 'The stage husband deserted by his wife steadily drinking himself into oblivion. The part's made for you.' She curled herself deeper into the massive armchair and looked thoughtful.

'But what are we?' she asked the Tsar.

'Ah now, that's more difficult.' He propped himself against the mantelpiece and pointed the toe of his shoe upwards. 'Angels of light,' he said giving Harriet a sly glance, 'come to show me a way out of it all.'

Delighted with each other's wit they laughed together. It became clearer in my mind. What I had known in the hut on the shore had not been false. Harriet, who had schemed and planned the summer long for this, and who finally believed there was not enough time, could not realise she no longer controlled events. Every breath we took spun the wheel faster and faster, and neither she nor I nor God could stop it. Had I believed God would, I might have prayed, but this too Harriet had perhaps foreseen, for how many times over the years had she taught me that God was powerless without innocence?

Harriet said, 'This place needs brightening up, Tsar. Let's rearrange the furniture.'

She stood and surveyed the room.

'Now this would look much better here.' She seized the armchair with strong hands and pulled it into the centre of the room. 'There.' Head tilted on her thin neck so that the lamplight fell full on to her smooth pale face, she looked at the room. The Tsar stared stupidly at the large armchair in its unfamiliar place.

'It won't do, you know,' he said finally, and moved on precise feet to rescue the chair, but Harriet was already moving swiftly about the room like an uneasy whirlwind, dragging the

144

table from its accustomed place under the window, so that it reared out into the already cluttered room.

The Tsar let go his hold of the isolated chair and tried to push the table into place, but it was too heavy for him and he sprawled breathlessly against it, watching Harriet with disbelief. She, standing on tiptoe, stretched up a violating arm and snatched the statue with its exposed breast from its niche on the sideboard. Holding it aloft she faced him triumphantly.

'This,' she cried, 'ought by rights to be on a raised dais so that Mrs Biggs can pray to the vulgar thing.'

The minute sword brandished in the figure's hand tilted slightly and cast a huge shadow across the curtains.

'No, no, put it down.' The Tsar giggled in a weak fashion and placed his hand on his heart. 'You'll break it . . . Take care.'

He seemed to slip downwards into his neat city clothes, so that they hung on his thin body and fluttered as he moved towards her. 'Put it down,' he repeated in a high fluted voice without control. Harriet darted to the mantelpiece and stood the statue directly in the middle. It leered at the room, its red-tipped breast pointing upwards, its sword rakishly spearing the blue lupins that lolled in their cream vase.

'That's better,' she cried. 'Now Mrs Biggs can get down on her knees to it.'

I kept my eyes fixed on the Tsar so that I should see the exact moment at which he broke under the strain. His face as he looked at the disordered room was almost hopeful. It was as if by changing the position of the furniture Harriet had minutely struck at his life with Mrs Biggs. Each new arrangement of a familiar object blurred and unfocused the years and moments of their existence together, so that he felt in this new catastrophe that the memory of Mrs Biggs was being edged slowly, little by little, out of the room. He wanted to complete the dismissal. He turned to the Welsh dresser and took down the blue and gold plates one by one from their places. His hands moved so clumsily and so eagerly that one fell from his

145

grasp and dropped to the carpet. It did not break but lay reproachfully face down at his feet. All the time I sat upright on the blue sofa, while Harriet and he moved like birds of prey around the stricken room.

Harriet found a match and lit the virgin candles in their brass holders on either side of the hearth. She turned off the electric light and, as the wax melted and the wicks burned, the room was nearly beautiful. Mrs Biggs, had she returned, might have been pleased with the improvements. She might have appreciated the soft leaping shadows on the dull cream walls.

Back and forth in the candlelight the Tsar and Harriet went their destructive way. Now, I told myself, now. Surely she must come back now. And as I said it, the Tsar lifted his foot and kicked at the glass dial of the radio. Harriet, appalled, looked at the wrecked instrument and said slowly, as if returning from a long journey through dangerous places. 'That was stupid . . . You shouldn't have done it.' The face she turned to me was bewildered.

'Let's go home now,' she said, and the childish mouth remained open in fear.

The Tsar stood in the expensive glass, swaying on his feet. 'Why, why?' his voice was accusing. 'You wanted me to do it. You did, didn't you?'

Harriet stood motionless, defenceless in the centre of the room, her mouth quivering.

'Oh come now,' the Tsar spoke to her tenderly, stretching out a hand to her with beguilement, 'I thought it would be a gesture after your own heart.' He looked wonderingly round the shadowed room, taking strength from the new unfamiliarity, and said with gaiety, 'Let's enjoy ourselves while we can. Let's all have a cigarette.'

He patted his pocket hopefully and felt with eager fingers for his case. Harriet said nothing, keeping her eyes fixed on him as one hypnotised by something terrible.

'I'll have to run out and get some.'

He showed us his empty cigarette case with despair. 'Can't possibly be without a cigarette.'

146

He waited as if half expecting Harriet would stop him, and then seeing she only watched him, he moved gladly to the door.

'I won't be long. Just you sit back and enjoy the décor.'

We heard him go down the hall and out of the door. His footsteps went softly down the path, the gate creaked as he opened it and left us alone in the house.

I wondered if the Tsar would ever return in our lifetime. I would have liked to tell Harriet this but her face was so white and mute I left her to her own thoughts. She stood uneasily in the middle of the room not knowing what to do, then because there was nowhere to go sat down on the sofa beside me. In the candlelight the tables and chairs jostled for position; the figure on the mantelshelf flickered and thrust its tiny sword deeper into the flowers. Harriet said, 'He shouldn't have done that.'

She looked fearfully at the broken glass that lapped the carpet.

'It was stupid.'

I could not agree, so I kept silent.

'What's the matter with you?' Her voice was petulant.

'Nothing.' I enjoyed my calmness, my ability to puzzle Harriet, above all the knowledge that she was frightened. She sat up and caught hold of my arm fiercely.

'Why are you so calm all of a sudden . . . tell me?' She pinched my flesh viciously so that I squirmed. Go on, tell me.'

'Nothing. I just don't mind any more.'

Harriet let go of my arm and lay back defeated. The candle nearest the window lurched in its holder and dripped grease on to the carpet, a round globe of wax among the shattered glass. Kindly, I told her: 'You see, dear, we've done what you wanted. We've humbled him like you said.'

Slowly she turned her face to me, the eyes widening, 'What do you mean?'

I almost hesitated but there did not seem any reason now why I should not tell her.

147

'Well, it happened . . . the other night on the shore. I mean he . . . he . . .' I could not say it.

'He had you?'

Her voice was weak with incredulity. She watched my mouth for a denial, and seeing none came, flung herself back against the arm of the sofa, looking at me as if she had not known me before. Then as the full realisation struck her: 'My God, he had you!'

She stood up and stared wildly round the lunatic room. My mouth twitched in the beginnings of a smile because she embarrassed me. I dug my teeth into my lip in an act of suppression. The phrase she used was comical, it reminded me too much of the sentences we had written with infinite labour in the diary.

I said, 'But I thought that's what you meant me to do. You said we had to bring it to a conclusion. You said so.'

'I didn't say to do that, I never – '

'You said humble him.'

'I never said to do that.' Her shoulders jerked in a spasm of distress. 'Why do a thing like that? We're not ready. You had no right.'

'I don't know what you are fussing about. It was nothing really. I hardly noticed. Just a bit like going to the dentist. Not even as bad.'

I thought she was going to hit me. Instead she spun round and ran from the room. I was left sitting on the blue sofa with the candles burning on the walls. I really couldn't see what she was so angry about. Stifled by a desire to laugh I walked to the door and called her name. I thought for one moment she was not in the house and then in the darkness I heard her whisper, 'She's come back . . . it's Mrs Biggs.'

In the night the dull capable footsteps came up the path. There was nowhere to go, nowhere to hide; my heart beat so loudly I was afraid Mrs Biggs must hear it. I stood beside Harriet behind the door and she pressed against me and clenched my hand reassuringly. I struggled to preserve my independence as Mrs Biggs stood in the porch, battled my will against Harriet's, and as the key fitted in the lock and the wife of the Tsar leaned her weight against the door, Harriet pushed something into my hand.

'Hit her,' she said softly, 'hit her.'

The door opened inward and I stepped out into the centre of the hall raising my arm high above my head. She was huge and menacing in the porch and I meant to push her down the steps so that Harriet and I might run away. When I hit her she swayed on her feet, unaccountably facing the dark garden, and did not fall. I struck at her again with desperation and boldness because she could not see my face, and when she fell softly away from me and drifted into the darkness like some great leaf, the Tsar was standing in the open gateway looking at me.

I could not move, I could not lower my arm. Harriet switched the hall light on behind me and I felt the night air sweeping over the plot of grass to cool my face. I wept inside and loved my mother and my father with all my being, but I could not move.

The Tsar came along the path slowly as if he were very tired. I wanted him to hurry so that I might be released from my inertia and he could tell me that nothing after all was wrong. I hoped Mrs Biggs would stay with her face on the steps till Harriet and I had run home. I could not bear the weight of the stick in my hand and I hoped too that the Tsar would take it from me and put it back in its stand behind the door with Mrs Biggs's red and green umbrella.

'Go inside,' the Tsar said. 'Go inside and don't come out.'

I was frightened but I did what he told me. I had done something wrong and he and Mrs Biggs united would talk to me severely. This time for sure Mrs Biggs would come and visit my mother. I was glad they would all be angry with me now because I had felt so strangely vindictive when I struck at Mrs Biggs; I should be punished and purged, could kiss Harriet on the cheek and return to school never more to think of the Tsar and this dreadful summer. Harriet had blown out the candles and put on the electric light, reducing the room to shabby disorder. I was surprised she just stood there and did not rush frantically putting the furniture to rights so that Mrs Biggs would not be further shocked.

'I didn't hit her very hard, Harriet. I only meant to push her.'

Harriet said 'Yes' absently and rubbed at her cheek.

'What if she has to go to hospital?' With fear beginning I looked at her for reassurance.

'She won't.'

The front door closed loudly and the Tsar came into the room. He stood in the doorway looking at the glass on the carpet and felt in his pocket for cigarettes. He hunched his shoulders and thrust his jaw forward so that I could see the faint perspiration on his face when the match flared up. The smoke from his cigarette wreathed his head familiarly, clouding the sparse hair. Harriet at the mantelshelf raised her hand and brushed the lupins with her palm, shaking the loaded stems gently. 'She's dead,' said the Tsar.

Someone was crying, sobbing as if their heart would break, making ugly sounds in the otherwise silent room. My face puckered up, though inside I was calm. My father was saying I had done it now, I had really done it this time, and I was arguing with him rationally, telling him that Mr Biggs did rude things to me in the sandhills, that it was not my fault, I had been corrupted. More sinned against than sinning. I was shouting but he would not listen and Mrs Biggs was straddling over me, shaking me furiously in giant hands, stamping on my feet with her great sandals and I was telling her to get off, get off me you big fat sow, but I could not get my breath and my tongue would not shape the words. Then she shook me so violently the room slid headlong past me and receded. Harriet was pushing the small of my back with a rough hand, forcing my head between my knees and when I sat up I was on the blue sofa. The Tsar was not in the room. There was a stale smell of sickness all over me; my hair was sticky.

I could not make out what Harriet was telling me. Something about time and the fact that the Tsar had got his cigarettes from the slot machine at the station.

'Nobody saw him at the station; he says it was completely deserted.' She spoke urgently into my ear, her warm breath fanning my cheek. 'And nobody saw him in the street either, he's sure of it.'

In just a few days I could go back to school. In just a few days. Today my father would have bought the train ticket. It would be lying on the hall table when I went in. I held on to the thought of the train ticket while Harriet's voice went on and on . . .

'Nobody saw us come here. We'll go out through the back garden and along the ditch. We'll come quickly up the side lane into the street again and I will scream. Then we will run all the way to my house and when they ask us what is wrong we'll say we saw the Tsar hit Mrs Biggs.'

She leant over me powerfully and took me by the shoulders. 'We'll say we saw the Tsar hit Mrs Biggs . . . do you hear?'

I did love Harriet then. She was so wise, so good, so sweetly clever and able to cope with the situation. I would say we saw Mrs Biggs fall down the steps, and the Tsar behind her with a stick in his hand.

'Yes, Harriet, I'll say that.'

Now that Mrs Biggs was truly dead I would do whatever Harriet wanted. I would never doubt her again but acknowledge she was more beautiful than me.

She stood up and looked quickly at the room. She searched in the pocket of her dress for her handkerchief and began to wipe the mantelpiece. The Tsar came into the room and closed the door behind him. He watched Harriet thoughtfully for a moment and then said:

'What are you doing?'

I was glad he asked her that because I wanted to know too.

'There'll be fingerprints,' said Harriet, 'and we don't want that. If we're thorough no one will guess we've been here.'

She took down the statue from above the fireplace and wiped it carefully.

151

'I see.'

There was a long silence while Harriet finished what she had to do. She even rubbed the door knob and the edge of the table.

'Now we'll go,' she said with authority. She eyed him carefully to see if he was equal to the situation, and having satisfied herself, continued :

'You must wait at least an hour for us to get home and tell our story.'

I waited fearfully for the Tsar to ask what our story was, but he stood by the window and said nothing.

'Then you must phone the police and tell them Mrs Biggs is dead. Do you understand?'

The old man nodded his head and fingered the material of the curtain.

'It's important you wait that hour. You do see that, don't you?'

'Quite.'

'Good.' She looked at me and made a slight upward gesture with her hand. I stood up obediently and followed her out of the room.

She closed the door behind me and leaned against it, her eyes searching the hall. 'The stick,' she said, but not to me.

It was in its stand along with the red umbrella with green stripes. She lifted it out carefully and wiped at it with the grey lining of her coat.

Above the clock was a shelf with a blue plate. There was one like it at home. Outside in the porch Mrs Biggs slept on. The clock ticked on.

Then we walked out of the back door into the garden.

THE DRESSMAKER

O

AFTERWARDS she went through into the little front room, the tape measure still dangling about her neck, and allowed herself a glass of port. And in the dark she wiped at the surface of the polished sideboard with the edge of her flowered pinny in case the bottle had left a ring. She could hear Marge at the sink in the scullery, washing her hands. That tin bowl made a deafening noise. She nearly shouted for her to stop it, but instead she sat down on mother's old sofa, re-upholstered in L.M.S. material bought at a sale, and immediately, in spite of the desperate cold of the unused room, the Christmas drink went to her head. She had to bite on her lip to keep from smiling. The light from the hallway shone on the carpet, red and brown and good as new from all the years she had spent caring for it. Here at least everything was ordered, secure. The removal of the rosewood table had been a terrible mistake, but it was foolish to blame herself for what had happened. There was nothing mother could take umbrage at in the whole room – not even the little mirror bordered in green velvet with the red roses painted on the glass – because the crack across one corner, as she could prove, was war damage, not neglect or carelessness. The blast from a bomb dropped in Priory Road had knocked it off the wall, killing twelve people, including Mrs Eccles's fancy man at the corner shop, and cracked mother's mirror.

'Are you alright then, Nellie?'

Margo was in the doorway watching her. Mother had

155

always warned her to keep an eye on Marge. Such a foolish girl. The way she had carried on about Mr Aveyard. He hadn't been a well man, nor young, and she would have lost her widow's pension into the bargain. Fancy throwing away her independence just for the honour of siding his table and darning his combs. It had taken a lot to persuade her, but in the end she'd seen the sense in it – sent Mr Aveyard packing into the bright blue yonder; but her face, the look in her eyes for all to see – there was something indecent in the explicitness of her expression.

She'd said: 'You would only have been a drudge for him, Marge.' And Marge said: 'Yes, I know, Nellie.' But her eyes, then as now, burned with the secrets of experience.

'Let me be,' said Nellie. 'I'll be through in a moment.'

Valerie had been right about a belt for the engagement dress. It would add the final touch. She let her eyes close and dozed as if she were sitting in the sun, her two stout legs thrust out across Mother's carpet, threads of green cotton clinging to her stockings.

She was awakened by voices coming from the kitchen. She listened for a moment before getting to her feet. Rita had come in and was weeping again. She was at the age for it, but it was trying for all concerned.

'Oh, Auntie, I wish I was dead.' She didn't mean it of course.

Marge was saying, 'Shh, shh,' trying to keep her quiet.

Beyond the lace curtains something glittered. Jack had pasted strips of asbestos to protect the glass, sticky to the touch, but she could just make out a square of red brick wall and the little dusty clump of privet stuck in the patch of dirt beneath the window, all pale and gleaming like a bush in flower, frozen in moonlight. She smoothed the folds of the lace curtains, re-arranging the milky fragments of privet, distracted by the sounds from the next room. If that girl didn't stop her wingeing, the neighbours would be banging on the wall, God knows, there'd been enough disturbance for one night.

She went into the hall, hiding the wine glass in the pocket of her apron. She swept broken glass into a heap and wrapped the pieces in newspaper; knelt to pick out between finger and thumb fragments embedded in the dust mat at the front door. She found an imitation pearl that Marge had overlooked, lying like a peppermint on the stair. She went into the kitchen with her parcel and laid it on the table.

'Valerie Mander says her Chuck hasn't seen him in over a week,' wailed Rita.

'Ssh,' Margo said again, putting her arms about the girl to calm her, looking up at Nellie with entreaty in her eyes, no colour at all in her thin cheeks.

'That's enough, Rita. It's no use crying over spilt milk,' said Nellie. ' You're better off without him.' Which was the truth, surely, though she had not meant to shout so loud.

'Turn that gas off, Marge,' she ordered and not waiting went into the scullery to turn off the ring under the kettle.

'But we always have a cup of tea before bed,' said Rita, lifting an exhausted face in protest, and Margo said for the umpteenth time, 'Sssh, ssshh,' in that daft way.

The girl washed in the scullery while the two women prepared for bed. The reflection of her bony face, pale with loss, flittered across the surface of the tarnished mirror above the sink. She bent her head and moaned, quite worn out by the depths of her emotion. A shadow leapt against the pane of glass high on the wall among the frying pans. She looked up startled, a piece of frayed towel held to her mouth, and opened the back door to let the cat in.

She called : 'Come on Nigger, come on Nigger !'

'Shut that door!' Her aunt's voice was harsh with irritation.

'Can't the cat come in then, Auntie?'

'No, leave it out.' But Nigger was in, streaking across the lino into the kitchen, up in one bound on to the sofa, eyes gleaming.

Rita went into the hall to put away her shoes in the space

under the stairs. When she came back, Auntie Marge was standing on the table, reaching up to the gasolier with its pink fluted shades, showing a portion of leg where her nightie rode up. Nellie held her firmly by the ankle, in case she should turn dizzy.

'Where's the other half of the curtain under the stairs, Auntie Nellie?' asked Rita.

Nellie had her hair net on and her teeth out. When the gas died, her face looked bruised in the firelight. She didn't answer. She tugged at Marge's gown and told her to come down, which she did, teetering wildly for a moment on the edge of the chair before reaching the floor and going at once to the sideboard. She fiddled about among the knives and forks, bringing out a packet of American cigarettes. At the sight of them the girl's face crumpled. She flung herself on her knees and buried her head in her aunt's lap as she sat down by the fire.

'Oh Auntie,' she cried, muffled in flannel, 'I do love him.'

Nellie could see Marge's hand with the thin band of gold encircling her finger, stroking the girl's bent head. The packet of cigarettes slithered to the rug. With a puritanical flick of her wrist, Nellie flung them clear to the back of the grate.

'You daft beggar, it was a full packet.'

Margo was outraged, looking up with hatred at her sister. But she quailed before the fury of the older woman.

'Shhh,' she said over and over to the girl at her knee, gazing sullenly at the cigarettes consumed by flame.

Nellie took the newspaper parcel into the scullery. She returned and stood at the mantelpiece holding her clenched fist out over the fire. The eyes of the cat flicked wide. The flames spat. Wax melted over the coals.

Rita said, startled: 'What's that?'

'Someone knocked over the little wax man in the hall. It's broken.'

The girl sat upright, the tear-stained oblong of her face full of accusation.

158

'The little wax man?'

'Don't look like that, Miss. It couldn't be helped.'

Nellie sucked the pad of her finger where a splinter of glass had penetrated, adding, so that the girl would know where to apportion blame : 'Your Dad knocked it over.'

'Uncle Jack? Has Uncle Jack been, then?'

She looked from one aunt to the other, but there was no reply. Nellie bolted the back door and brought a jug of water to pour on the coals. The smoke billowed outwards. The cat sprang from its place on the sofa and went with disgust to lie on the heap of newspapers behind the door.

Auntie Margo said : 'Poor old Nigger, he doesn't like that,' beginning to laugh deep in her throat and bringing her hand up to her mouth to smother the sound. Turning her face to the grate, she stared into the dampened fire.

Rita was puzzled about Uncle Jack coming. He only came round on a Saturday with the Sunday joint.

'Did Uncle Jack come about the engagement party, then?' she wanted to know. 'Is he getting Valerie Mander a cut of meat?'

'Bed,' said Nellie, but not unkindly. By now Jack would be on the dock road, heading towards Bootle. She waited in the hallway while Rita and Marge went upstairs. She let them get settled before leaning over the stair rail to extinguish the gas light.

'Are you in?' she called after a moment.

Rita could hear the banister creaking as Nellie hauled herself up the stairs. On the dark landing her bare feet smacked against the lino.

'Are you cold, Rita?'

'Yes, auntie.'

'You best come in with us.'

She didn't want the girl having that nightmare. She hadn't had it for several weeks, but she was obviously upset, fretting herself. It was best to have her near. They'd all catch their death of cold shenanniging about in the middle of the night.

159

Rita climbed on to the bed and slid down between the two women, putting her head under the starched sheets to shut out the cruel night air and the heart-beat of the alarm clock set for six, thinking it absurd that she should even attempt to close her eyes when her mind wandered so restlessly back and forth in search of the happiness she had lost, and falling asleep even while her head nuzzled more comfortably into the stiff linen cover of the bolster. From time to time she whimpered; and Margo snored, curled up against Rita, with one arm flung out across the green silk counterpane, cold as glass, joined to the girl by a strand of hair caught on her dry upper lip.

Nellie dreamed she was following mother down a country garden, severing with sharp scissors the heads of roses.

1

I T WAS late August when Valerie Mander asked Rita to the party.

'Well, it's more of a sing-song, really,' she amended. 'But you'll enjoy yourself. Tell your Uncle Jack you're a big girl now.' And off she went up the street, swinging her hand-bag and tilting her head slightly to catch the warmth of the sun.

Rita had first seen her on the tram coming home from work, but she hadn't let on. She had been travelling since the Pier Head, wedged hard against the window near the platform. When the tram stopped opposite the bomb site that had been Blackler's store, she hadn't noticed the people boarding, only moved her feet to avoid being trampled, gazing out at the rumpled meadow on the corner of the city street; thinking of Nellie working there at the beginning of the war, on the material counter facing millinery, shearing with her sharp steel scissors through the yards of silk and satin and velveteen, taking such pride in the great bales of cloth, smoothing them with her hands, plucking with disapproval at the minute frayed ends. To no avail. When the roof split open, the prams and bedding spilled from the top floor to the next, mingling with Auntie Nellie's rolls of dress material, snaking out wantonly into the burning night, flying outwards higgledy piggledy, with the smart hats hurled from their stands, the frail gauze veils spotted with sequins shrivelling like cobwebs, tumbling down through the air to be buried under the bricks and the

161

iron girders – covered now by the grass and the great clumps of weed that sprouted flowers, rusty red and purple, their heads swinging like fox-gloves as the tram lurched round the corner and began the steep ascent to Everton Brow. Only then did she glance up and see Valerie standing with one white-gloved hand raised to clutch the leather strap for support, her head swathed in a cream turban and a diamante button clipped to the hidden lobe of her ear.

Rita hung her head to avoid involvement, hoping that Valerie would not look in her direction, ready to spring to her feet and be off when her stop came. But outside the Cabbage Hall cinema, a horse pulling its coal cart took fright at an army lorry passing too close. Feet sliding on the cobblestones, it shied sideways into the traffic. Rita hesitated, was too afraid to run in front of its hooves and heard Valerie calling her name. She was forced to walk the length of Priory Road with her, dreadfully inadequate and cheeks pink with resentment. It wasn't that she felt herself to be inferior, it was more that the overwhelming ripeness and confidence of the older girl caused her acute embarrassment. Valerie was larger than life, prancing along the pavement with her heavy body clothed in a green and white frock made by Auntie Nellie, arching her plucked brows, fluttering her eyelashes shiny with vaseline, opening and closing her moist mouth, the colour of plums. It was the glossiness of her.

'Your Auntie Nellie said you were working in Dale Street now.'

'Yes, since April.'

'What's it like, then? Alright is it, Rita?'

'Yes, it's very nice, thank you.'

'What do you do, then?' Persistent. Trying to communicate. Trotting in her wedge-heeled shoes past the red-brick houses and the small shops and the ragged plane trees, windswept on every corner.

'Not much, really. I run messages for Mr Betts sometimes.'

'Well, that's not much, is it?' A kind of criticism in her voice. 'I thought you were good at English?'

'Me Auntie Margo was getting me a job with her in the factory at Speke.'

'Oh yes.'

In sight now, the tin hoarding high on the wall at the corner of Bingley Road, advertising Gold Flake.

'Auntie Nellie said they weren't a nice class of girl.'

They walked under the lettering, bright yellow and two-foot high, set against a sea of deepest blue, one corner eaten by rust. It was Valerie that had told Aunt Nellie that she was too pale to wear bright colours... 'Your Rita hasn't the complexion for it'... and Nellie took notice of her. Until then she had felt like a pillar-box every winter, decked out in a scarlet coat with a hat and handbag to match.

They crossed the road and went into the shadow of the air-raid shelter in the middle of the street, its concrete roof blotched by rain and a black and white cat prowling its length.

It was then Valerie asked her what she did on a Saturday night, though she knew, she must have done. She knew what Valerie did. Mrs Mander told Nellie all about her daughter's opportunities and what young man was courting her and how she'd been to a tea-dance at Reece's Ballroom and an evening do at the Locarno and what the fellow at the Ladies' Hot Pot Supper night had said about her. Nellie discussed it often with Margo, and neither of them seemed to think it strange that what was alright for Valerie was all wrong for other girls living in the street. Just fast, they were. But then Valerie, as Auntie Nellie never tired of reiterating, was a lovely girl and she did know how to take care of herself.

*　　*　　*

Aunt Nellie had just sent the man from the Pru on his way, richer by her sixpence a week, when Rita got home. It was for her funeral, so that Jack wouldn't have the expense. Around her neck she wore her tape measure like a scarf and a row of pins stuck in the bodice of her black dress. On Sundays she exchanged the white measure for a fox fur, holding the thin little paws in her hand as she went on her own to the church. She stood at her pastry board in the scullery, coating three pieces of fish with flour. She told Rita to set the table, adding : 'Get a move on, chuck. I've Mrs Lyons coming for a fitting after tea.'

'I met Valerie Mander on the tram,' said Rita, collecting plates from the shelf above the cooker. 'They're having a party on Saturday.'

She took the plates into the kitchen and left them on the sideboard, while she removed the table runner and the yellow vase full of dressmaking pins.

'I know,' Nellie said. 'Well, it's more of a sing-song, really. What was she wearing?'

'She asked me.'

Rita unfolded the white cloth and smoothed it flat on the table. Aunt Nellie was so surprised she came through from the scullery with the frying pan in her hand.

'What did you say to her?'

'I said thank you very much.'

'Oh dear, I don't know that it's wise. I'm not at all sure.'

She shook her head and went to put the pan back on the stove. Rita arranged the plates, the knives and forks, the china salt cellar, a memento from Blackpool, the water jug, the pudding spoons and the three Woolworth glasses. Still Nellie kept silent. Only the fat hissing in the pan as the fish cooked. Rita sat on a chair sideways to the table, fingering the edge of the cloth embroidered with daisies, staring at the wall with her pale eyes patient. There was a picture of a landscape above the sewing machine : a blue lake and a swan sitting on the water and the green grass fading into a cloudy sky. There was also the window framed in blackout curtains showing a brick wall and a wooden door that opened on to the alleyway, through which Auntie Margo would come presently to persuade Nellie. She watched Nigger the cat crawl silently along the wall of the roof of the out-house where her aunt kept the dolly tub and the mangle.

Nellie called: 'What about your Uncle Jack coming?'

'Valerie Mander said to tell him I was a big girl now.'

She looked at her aunt and saw she was smiling. She was all admiration for the lovely girl, so outspoken. She nodded her head wonderingly, jiggling the frying pan about to stop the fish from sticking. 'That Valerie,' she observed, 'she's a card.'

* * *

As soon as Margo came in, the food was put on the table. She sat at the edge of the hearth like a man, splaying her knees wide and rolling a cigarette.

'Sit decent,' said Auntie Nellie, scraping margarine from a dish and covering her bread sparingly.

It was one of Marge's irritating habits to ignore what was on her plate till it had gone like ice and then she would say, 'By heck, Nellie, this is blooming cold.' Some nights she was quite dry about her day at the factory, telling them in accurate detail the remarks screamed by her fellow-workers above the noise of the machines. She said she couldn't repeat everything they said because she had to be guarded as careless talk cost lives. Nellie got all exasperated and said that was foolishness, it was more like some of those women needed their mouths washing out with carbolic soap. Marge said that ten minutes before the whistle blew for the end of the day shift, the disabled left by the side gate, two hundred of them, in chairs, on crutches, limping and lurching down the invalid ramp on to the pavement – like a hospital evacuating at the start of a fire. Shortly afterwards came the speed merchants on bicycles, streams of them, ringing the little bells on their handlebars, wheeling in formation out of the main gates and swooping

165

away down the hill to the town. How rough they were, how quick to take offence and come to blows. The women were worse than the men. Mr Newall, the foreman of her section, was given the glad eye by a different girl each week. But tonight Margo had nothing to tell them. She sat gloomily at the side of the empty grate, rubbing the tips of her fingers through her sparse sand-coloured hair, jerking her neck from side to side as if she were keeping time to some tune in her head. She listened to the six o'clock news before joining them at the table. She stirred her tea so savagely that some spilled into the saucer.

'What's up with you, then?' asked Nellie aggressively, as if it were a personal affront to her that Marge was out of sorts.

'It's the machines, they get on my nerves. Everyone complains of their nerves.'

'Well, it's your own fault,' Nellie said with satisfaction. 'You had no need to go into munitions in the first place.'

'Get away. I was requisitioned.'

'That job at Belmont Road Hospital was quite good enough.'

They stared at each other with hostility, their mouths munching food.

Rita said: 'Was that where those naughty girls were?' They both turned and looked at her, sitting in her pink frock with the white cotton collar that could be removed and washed separately. 'The girls with the shaved heads – to stop them running away?'

She had a picture in her head of a green tiled hall and a long corridor with its floor shining with beeswax and two figures walking towards her in dressing-gowns and slippers. Above the thin stalks of their necks two naked heads with lidless eyes and sunken mouths and on each fragile curve of skull nothing but a faint down that quivered as they moved. Like birds fallen from a nest.

'Who told her that?' Margo demanded, though she knew.

Nellie held her to one side as if she were listening to the wireless.

'Who told her a daft thing like that?' persisted Marge.

'Auntie Nellie said they had things in their hair.' She wished she had not spoken.

'You don't go to hospital for nits, Rita.'

Auntie Nellie stiffened in disgust.

'You're so common, Marge. That factory has coarsened you beyond belief.'

A shred of potato dropped from her lips to the plate. Mortified, she dabbed at her chin with a serviette, shaking her head sorrowfully.

'You're a foolish girl. I thank God, mother has been spared from seeing the way you've turned out.'

It was as if she were talking about a cake that hadn't risen properly. Rita could tell Auntie Margo was giddy with indignation. It wasn't a tactful remark to make to someone who had spent ten hours on the factory floor, clad in cumbersome protective clothing, grease daubed on her face and a white cloth bound about her head. It was alright for Auntie Nellie to live grimly through each day, doing the washing, trying to find enough nourishment to give them, sewing her dresses – she was only marking time for the singing to come in the next world and her reunion with Mother. It was different for Margo, a foolish girl of fifty years of age; she needed to come home, now, and find that somebody waited. How colourless were her lips, how dark the shadows beneath her eyes.

'Rita,' cried her aunt, looking at her across the table severely, 'those naughty girls, as your Auntie Nellie saw fit to call them, had a flipping sight more wrong with them than nits. It wasn't only their heads they shaved neither.'

And she broke into a cackle of laughter, eyes growing moist, leaning back in her chair at the joke. She was silent then, having gone as far as she dared, contenting herself with a mocking grin worn for the benefit of Nellie, tears of amusement at the corners of her glittering eyes.

167

When the meal was finished Nellie said: 'Rita, tell your Auntie Marge about Valerie Mander.'

She spoke coldly, on her dignity, making a great show of siding the table before taking the dishes to the sink. Margo half-rose to help, because Nellie, when put out, could appear to be suffering, her white hair plastered to her head in waves and a kirby grip to keep it neat, and that disappointed droop to her mouth. But she sat down again at this.

'What about Valerie Mander?'

'She asked me to a party.'

'She never,' said her aunt, looking at her in astonishment.

'She did. On Saturday.'

'What does your Auntie Nellie say?'

'She doesn't know if it's wise.'

They both looked down at the surface of the white table-cloth, thinking it over. On the beige wall the eight-day clock chimed the half-hour. In the kitchen they could hear Nellie swishing her hands about in the water to make it seem she was above listening.

'Do you want to go, then?'

'I don't know.'

'Won't you be shy?'

'I'm not shy.'

She met her aunt's eye briefly, and away again, looking at the dull black sewing machine with its iron treadle still tilted from the pressure of the dressmaker's foot.

'She's not got anything to wear,' Nellie said, coming to stand in the doorway, twisting her hands about in her apron to dry them.

'If that doesn't beat the band! You put dresses on the backs of half the women in the street and you say our Rita's got nothing to wear.'

Nellie had to see the fairness of that. She was never unreasonable. She supposed she could alter something in time if the child was really keen. Neither of them looked at Rita to see what she felt. Or they could pool their clothing coupons and go to George Henry Lees' for a new frock. That might be best.

They were interrupted by the arrival of Mrs Lyons, come for her fitting. Rita curled herself up on the sofa with a library book and the cat. She murmured 'Good-evening' to Mrs Lyons, keeping her eyes down to the printed page as the stout lady stepped out of her skirt and stood in her slip on the rug.

Nellie put a match to the fire so that Mrs Lyons wouldn't catch her death. She grudged every morsel of coal burned in summer time, but she couldn't afford to lose her customers. Even so, the room took some time to warm, and it wasn't till Mrs Lyons had left that the benefit could be felt. Nellie made a pot of tea before getting ready for bed, spooning the sugar into Marge's cup and hiding the basin before Marge could help herself. The aunts put on their flannel nightgowns over their clothes and then undressed, poking up the fire to make a blaze before removing their corsets. The girl sat withdrawn on the sofa, stroking the spine of the cat, while the two women grunted and twisted on the hearth rug, struggling to undo the numerous hooks that confined them, until, panting and triumphant, they tore free the great pink garments and dropped them to the floor, where they lay like cricket pads, still holding the shape of their owners, and the little dangling suspenders sparkling in the firelight. Dull then after such exertions, mesmerised by the heat of the fire, the aunts stood rubbing the flannel nightgowns to and fro across their stomachs, breathing slow and deep. After a while they sat down on either side of the fender and removed their stockings. Out on the woollen rug, lastly, came their strange yellow feet, the toes curled inwards against the warmth.

'Rita,' said Nellie, picking up the half-furled corsets, rolling them tidily like schoolroom maps, 'what sort of dress shall it be for the party?'

'It's not a party,' said Rita. 'It's just a bit of a sing-song.'

She said she didn't know what the fuss was about. She

169

didn't want anything altered nor did she need a new frock. She knew she would have to go, if only for the sake of Margo. Left to herself, she mightn't have bothered. But at some point on Saturday Margo would start to apply rouge and powder, saying she was thinking of popping along to the Manders to keep the child company. And Nellie would say she was pushing herself, and they would start to argue, until turning to her they would remind each other of the time, telling her she must hurry, comb her hair, change her frock.

'Don't you want to look nice?' cried Nellie.

But Rita wouldn't discuss it any further. She went upstairs on her own to bed, leaving them muttering by the fire.

2

J ACK came promptly at four-thirty. He parked his van in the back alley and carried the Sunday joint wrapped in newspaper. He wore his Homburg hat and his overcoat.

'Have you got a cold, then?' asked Nellie, for it was a warm afternoon and the sun was shining somewhere beyond the dark little houses.

He had brought a piece of pork and some dripping and he put them on a plate high on the shelf so that the cat would leave it alone.

'Where's Rita?' he asked, removing his coat and going into the hall to hang it over the banisters.

At the foot of the stairs he cracked his ankle bone against the little iron stand set in the floor.

'That blooming thing,' he said, hobbling into the kitchen. 'God knows why they put the damn thing where you can trip over it.'

'What thing?' said Nellie, not understanding him.

'That umbrella stand. One of these days I'll break me blooming neck.'

'I never trip over it,' she said.

He lay down on the sofa with his feet on a newspaper and his hat still on his head. He always lay down when he came to Nellie's; she was forever telling him to rest and he mostly felt tired as soon as he set eyes on her. He didn't say much when Nellie told him Rita had gone with Marge to have her hair set for a party. But then it wasn't his province any more.

171

When his wife had died leaving him with Rita not five years old he had suggested that Nellie pack up the house in Bingley Road and come to live with him in Allerton. But she wouldn't. She said Mother would never have approved and where would she put the furniture? She was right of course – she was too old to be uprooted. Nellie knew about death – she was his right hand man, so to speak. Three sisters in infancy; Sally with the consumption, though Marge insisted it was a broken heart; Mother, Uncle Wilf, and George Bickerton, Marge's husband, dying with influenza within six months of returning from France. The last four had passed away in the little back bedroom upstairs. It was not as if Nellie cared to leave a house that held so many memories of departure. Grieved as she had been to say good-bye to mother, it was only in the nature of a temporary farewell. She had merely sent Mother ahead on a journey and would catch up with her later. It would never do to leave her post till her call came. So he sold his own home and moved with Rita into the two rooms above his butcher's shop in Anfield. Nellie was a wonderful woman. She came every morning and did for them and took the child out for an airing and put her to bed at night. But several times she took her back to Bingley Road, because she couldn't neglect the dressmaking, and it didn't seem sensible to troop out after tea, in winter, on the tram, all that way. It became a regular thing. After a time the child copied her aunts and called him Uncle Jack. He tried sleeping in the little boxroom at weekends to see more of her, but it wasn't convenient. And Nellie looked after her beautifully, making her little dresses, and always seeing she had clean white socks, and putting her hair in rags every night to make it curl. And later Nellie was very strict about her education and her homework – only the bombing was at its worst and the child was in the shelters at night, and then the school she attended had a direct hit and a lot of her friends were evacuated. Marge used to say it was all wrong for the child to live with them, they were too old, they hadn't the patience. But that was nonsense. Nellie had

172

never raised her voice to the girl, never said a bad thing to her. Marge had gone on about the nightmare Rita had from time to time. She said it wasn't natural for a young girl to have such nasty dreams, at least not the same one every time. Nellie said it was growing pains. Dr Bogle said the same. Nellie was livid with Marge for taking the child to the doctor behind her back. Most of the time he too forgot that Rita was not Nellie's daughter, but his. And she did favour the aunts in appearance. She was in their mould – nothing of his dead wife that he could see : like Marge in feature, with a mouth so pale that the upper lip seemed outlined in brown pencil, making it prominent, and with Marge's slightly frantic eyes, startled, owing to the width between brow and lid. But she was Nellie's creation. It was as if the dressmaker had cut out a pattern and pinned it exactly, placing it under the sewing machine and sewing it straight as a die, over and over, so that there was no chance of a gap in the seams.

Even more like Nellie, he thought, when Rita came in with Marge, face flushed red from the dryer and her hair stuck dry as a bone to her small head.

'My word,' he said, 'we do look a bobby dazzler!' though secretly he wondered what had happened to her nice brown hair – so little of it left and that all curled up.

'Have you had it cut then?' he asked. But she had gone out into the back yard to look for the cat. 'How much did it cost?' he wanted to know, half sitting up and putting his hand in his pocket.

'Never you mind,' said Margo, 'it's my treat.'

There was something restless about her, agitated. She strode about the room picking things up and putting them down, forgetting about the cigarette she held between her fingers. She was forever going into the scullery to bend down and re-light it at the gas jet under the kettle.

'You'll not have a hair left on your head one of these days,' warned Nellie, putting the Saturday tea on the table.

He ate his tea lying down. Nellie propped his head up

173

with pillows and balanced his plate on his chest. They had a tin of salmon that a customer had given him in return for a favour. He couldn't tell Nellie how he got it because she didn't approve of the black market. Instead he said he'd had it in the cupboard since the beginning of the war. They listened to Toy Town on the wireless and Marge stood at the mantelpiece, covering her mouth with her hand, her eyes all screwed up as if she were in pain, pretending it was Ernest the policeman she found comic, though he knew it was him.

'What's so funny, Marge?' he demanded, offended.

And she said : '*Rigor mortis* will set in if you stay like that much longer.'

He had to smile at that even though Nellie was tut-tutting. He struggled to sit upright on the sofa and put his dish down on the table. Marge had always had a sense of humour – dry, bitter at times – but she was good company. Sometimes it was as if Nellie was a damn sight too worthy for this world, making him feel he was perpetually in church, or remembering mother who had died when he was seven, all lowered voices and pious talk. He looked at Rita, but she was stolidly eating – not a trace of a smile, the colour quite faded from her cheeks.

At seven Marge went upstairs and came down in a peach crêpe dress with a necklace round her neck that had belonged to his wife. He'd offered it to Nellie, but she said she had no need of such fripperies, and it was hardly suitable for Rita.

'What's all this, then?' asked Nellie, and Marge said she was just popping round to the Manders' with Rita, to keep an eye on her.

'You weren't asked,' said Nellie.

'Get away,' Margo said, and proceeded to put powder on her cheeks.

He could tell Nellie was put out about something.

'Do you want to go?' he asked. 'Don't worry about me. I'll put me feet up and listen to Saturday Night Theatre.'

At this she made a funny little gesture of contempt with her

174

elbows, flapping them like a hen rising from its perch in alarm.

'Not me,' she said.

So he lay down again and placed the Saturday Echo over his eyes to be out of it. He could hear them talking in whispers out of deference to him, trying to get Rita to hurry up and change. 'In a minute,' she kept saying, 'I'll go in a minute.' And before she went upstairs he distinctly heard her say, 'That was my mam's, wasn't it?' and he opened his eyes and she was at the fireplace staring at Marge's neck, half reaching up her hand to touch the necklace about Marge's throat. God knows how she knew that. He was quite startled, screwing up the side of the newspaper and damaging the Curly Wee cartoon with his clenched fist. But she didn't touch Marge; she peered as if she were short-sighted, leaving Marge standing there with her own hand up to the cheap link of pearls and her mouth all red and bold with lipstick.

He closed his eyes again, and soon Nellie sat down at the sewing machine and spun the wheel, pressing the treadle up and down rapidly, running material under the stabbing needle, settling into the rhythm of it, in her element. As long as he could remember, Nellie had played the machine, for that's how he thought of it. Like the great organ at the Palladium cinema before the war, rising up out of the floor and the organist with his head bowed, riddled with coloured lights, swaying on his seat in time to the opening number. Nellie sat down with just such a flourish, almost as if she expected a storm of applause to break out behind her back. And it was her instrument, the black Singer with the handpainted yellow flowers. She had been apprenticed when she was twelve to a woman who lived next door to Emmanuel Church School: hand sewing, basting, cutting cloth, learning her trade. When she was thirteen Uncle Wilf gave her a silver thimble. She wasn't like some, plying her needle for the sake of the money, though that was important: it was the security the dressmaking gave her – a feeling that she knew something, that

175

she was skilled, handling her materials with knowledge; she wasn't a flibbitygibbet like some she could mention. For all that she lifted the tailor's dummy out from its position under the stairs coquettishly, holding it in her arms like a dancing partner, circling the arm-holes with chalk, stroking the material down over the stuffed breast, standing back to admire her work with her mouth clamped full of little pins, tape measure about her neck.

When the knock came at the front door he was almost asleep. He opened his eyes in bewilderment and saw Marge on her chair by the grate, and Nellie, her foot arrested in mid-air trying to recognise the hand at the door. He rubbed his eyes and stood upright, smoothing his clothes to be respectable. They all listened. Rita opened the front door. A strange voice, like on the films, drawling. She brought him into the kitchen. He was well-fed, dressed in uniform and he had been drinking. A great healthy face, with two enquiring eyes, bright blue, and a mouth which when he spoke showed a long row of teeth, white and protruding. It was one of those Yanks. Jack was shocked. Till now he had never been that close. They were so privileged, so foreign; he had never dreamt to see one at close quarters in Nellie's kitchen, taking Rita and Marge, one on each arm and bouncing them out of the house. He ran to the door to watch them go, linking arms, heads bowed, like they were doing the Palais Glide.

'I didn't know there would be Yanks,' he said.

'There's no harm,' said Nellie. 'Valerie Mander knows how to conduct herself.'

But he was bothered. He couldn't lie down and compose himself; the sheer fleshiness of the young American disturbed him – the steak they consumed, the prime pork chops, the volume of butter and bacon. He remembered all the things he had read : the money they earned, the food they digested, the equipment they possessed. He'd seen them down by Exchange Station, pressing young girls up against the wall, mouth to mouth as if eating them, and jeeps racing up

Stanley Street full of military police and great dogs on metal chains with their jaws open and their pink gums exposed.

'I didn't know there'd be Yanks,' he said again, walking up and down the room in his green waistcoat that Nellie had made and his gun metal trousers.

'Did you notice what our Rita said about that necklace?' he asked in astonishment.

But Nellie was placing the top half of Mrs Lyons' grey costume under the steel clamp, her head bent and all her concentration on the lovely width of serge beneath her fingers.

3

I N THE circumstances Margo couldn't help feeling that she was superfluous. The party was not a knees-up for the neighbours with a few of Cyril Mander's business acquaintances on show to make a bit of a splash. She didn't suppose there would be any political talk or views on how the war was going. Nor would there be fancy cakes and a few bottles of beer on the sideboard. The house was swarming with American soldiers and young women in their gladrags. The three-piece suite was quite submerged. On the hall table there was a pile of mustard-coloured caps, one upon the other, like a plate of sandwiches. She was struck, as usual, by the dazzling display of lights, in the hall, the front room, the kitchen. She stood blinking, helped out of her duster coat by the young man who had escorted them the few yards up the street. 'Thank you,' she said, and repeated it for Rita, who said nothing at all, allowing the pink cardigan to be removed from her shoulders. Valerie was wearing a black skirt with a patent-leather belt about her waist. She was bubbling over with excitement and generosity, explaining that she thought Rita would never have come if Chuck hadn't fetched her. Chuck nodded his head lazily, and she put her arm through his and pressed close to him.

It occurred to Margo that it was a funny name for a grown man. Surely the whites of his eyes were a shade too milky and the curve of his eyeball somewhat extreme. She remembered all the stories circulated about English girls marrying GIs and having black children. You could never be sure until it was too late. Jack said all the decent Americans had left the country before D-Day, ready for the thrust into Europe; only the riff-raff remained – canteen staff and garage mechanics. Mrs Mander couldn't wait to tell her all about him. Valerie had met him at a dance a week ago and he'd taken her out nearly every night since, to the State Restaurant, the Bear's Paw, to the repertory company, to some hotel over on the Wirral, very posh by all accounts.

'The repertory company?' said Marge, bewildered.

'To a play,' said Mrs Mander, 'with actors.'

'He must have money to burn.'

'Well, there's no harm in that, and he does seem keen, doesn't he?'

She peered at Marge, trying to gauge what she was thinking, scrutinising her mouth as if she were deaf and needed to lip-read.

'They certainly seem very thick,' Margo said, watching the young man at the fireplace with his hand dangling over the white shoulder of Valerie Mander. On his wrist, strong black hairs and a watch of solid gold.

'Oh, they are,' cried Mrs Mander gaily, putting a glass of whisky into her hand and leaving her, waddling out of the doorway in her midnight blue dress with the enormous skirt.

Cyril Mander was playing the piano very slowly as if he weren't sure of the tune. He was in his best blue suit, showing a lot of white cuff, his silver links catching the light. On the top of the piano was a jug full of lupins and a photograph of son George in his sailor's uniform. Every time Cyril struck a chord, the flowers trembled and showered petals on the keys. None of the young couples heeded his playing. Valerie was looking through the gramophone cabinet for records.

Marge wondered whether the Manders were wise, filling the house with strangers and letting them behave any way they pleased. There was a war on, of course, and she knew attitudes were different, but there was such a thing as a

179

responsibility. It would serve Mrs Mander right if she became the proud grandmother of a bouncing piccaninny.

Sipping her drink and shuddering at its strength, she went out into the hall to look for Rita. The coats on the banisters had slid to the floor. She could see Rita's cardigan lying all crumpled. As she bent to retrieve the clothing, Cyril Mander came behind her and seized her by the hips. She was quite embarrassed. He told her she must come and meet people – she mustn't be a spoil sport. He took the coats from her, spilling them carelessly on the stairs. Clutching the cardigan, she was propelled into the living room. Jack detested him – said he was a profiteer and a swine, which was a bit unkind. Margo rather liked him, though not at such close quarters. He'd made a lot of money out of scrap metal and he did tend to be showy; but that was preferable to being moody like Jack, or martyred like Nellie.

'What do you think of our Valerie's latest acquisition?' he whispered, crumpling her shoulder in his big hand and shaking her like a doll.

The heat from the fire was unbearable. Such a reckless use of coal, and summer not yet ended.

'I like the new grate,' she said.

But he wasn't listening. There was no mantelpiece: nowhere to stand her glass. Just a thin little ledge of cream tiles, and above it a fancy mirror with scalloped edges. She could see her own face reflected – damp, as if she were rising up out of the sea, with staring eyes, and behind her head young couples dancing cheek to cheek, circling and gliding out of the mirror.

'This is my girl from up the street,' said Cyril, thrusting her forward at an angle, yet still retaining a grip on her shoulder.

'How d'you do,' Margo said to the two young men who stood on the hearthrug, shaking hands with one, who smiled at her with his beautifully rounded cheeks dimpling in welcome and went away to refill her glass, while she held Cyril upright and was ready to save him if he toppled forwards.

She sweated under the combined heat of Cyril and the fierce flames that roared up the chimney. She took her replenished glass when it came, endeavouring to stand a little straighter, sipping the drink rapidly before Cyril should spill it for her. She had last tasted whisky four years ago at the height of the blitz when an A.R.P. warden had given her some to steady her nerves. She remembered the occasion with bitterness, having slipped on the kerbstone in the blackout on her way home, raising a bump on her chin. Nellie said she was drunk.

'This little lady,' Cyril was saying, 'is a soldier's wife, through and through.'

Seized by an abrupt melancholy, he released Marge and stared down at the carpet.

'Where is your husband stationed, mam?' The American looked at her with his head tilted deferentially to one side.

She was convulsed, choking on her drink. How richly oiled was the hair on his head, how smooth the skin beneath his eyes. Her chest heaved with the effort of suppressing laughter.

'Up there,' she wheezed, rolling her eyes in the direction of the ceiling.

'Dear God,' said Cyril, shaking his head and yawning.

Deserting the three-piece suite, the couples rose to Ambrose and his Orchestra, clutching each other in the centre of the room. Standing on the leather settee with legs bent, as if to take an unlikely leap into the dark, Cyril struggled to open the window. Exhausted, he sank to his knees and leaned his forehead peacefully against the cushions, back turned on his jostling guests, the yellow curtains shifting gently in the draught.

'Dear me!' remarked Margo. 'Mr Mander is well away and no mistake.'

The young man with the dimples in his cheeks asked her to dance. She went with streaming eyes, fox-trotting across the carpet in his arms. Silly really, in such a tiny room — bumping into the sideboard, tripping over the rug. She was breathless before she had completed one turn of the floor.

181

'Are you alright, mam?' he asked her, mistaking the marks on her cheeks for tears of distress.

'Yes, yes,' she assured him, and turned her head away for fear she should laugh again. It was no use explaining how she felt about her dead husband from another war, it was so long ago. She hardy knew him to begin with, let alone remembered him now, so many years on. She had always felt he was more Nellie's relation than hers, seeing Nellie had nursed him toward death. Whenever she had tiptoed upstairs, Nellie had told her to go away, he was resting; and even at the funeral it was Nellie that did enough crying for both of them.

It was a relief when the record ended and the young man took his hand from her wrist. Wiping her eyes, she left him to look for her glass and refill it from the bottle on the sideboard. She didn't feel guilty; it hadn't been come by honestly, so why shouldn't she have the benefit of it? Years ago Jack had given her a pad of cottonwool soaked in whisky for the toothache. 'Get rid of them,' said Nellie contemptuously. 'You don't want any truck with those. Get yourself some nice new teeth.' And she did, though it took her six years to pay for them. Rita went to the dentist regularly – but then times had changed. Rita? She went into the hall to search for her. The door was open on to the street. Mrs Evans at No. 9 was leaning out of her bedroom window to get a shuftie at the goings on. Margo caught a glimpse of a green velvet dress and a tall soldier with his hands in his pockets lounging against the privet hedge.

She hesitated, and at that moment Mrs Mander called from the kitchen: 'Marge, Marge, give us a hand with the eats!'

She couldn't refuse, not being an invited guest in the first place.

'Our Rita's on the step,' she said, 'with a soldier. There's no harm, is there?'

'Get away,' said Mrs Mander. 'She's seventeen.'

182

The display of food on the table was quite pre-war in style : a whole ham lying in a bed of brown jelly, a bowl of real butter, like a slab of dripping, white as milk; on a dinner plate, piled high, a pyramid of oranges. Margo sat down on a chair and looked.

'It's Chuck,' said Mrs Mander. 'He insisted.'

'I was never in the limelight, was I?' asked Margo.

'You what?' Mrs Mander paused from slicing bread.

'You could never say I was made much of?'

'You've been drinking, Marge,' said Mrs Mander, relieved.

'I've never felt,' continued Margo, picking at the ham with her fingers, 'that people took enough notice. I have got thoughts.'

'Oh yes,' said Mrs Mander.

'You've got Cyril and George and your Valerie . . .'

'Well, you've Rita.'

'She's not easy, you know. We've got her and we haven't.'

At that moment Chuck came into the room and asked for an orange.

'We're going to play games,' he said; 'I want an orange,' taking one from the dinner plate and beginning to tear the peel from it.

'That's nice,' said Mrs Mander. 'What sort of a game?'

'Napoleon's eye,' said Chuck. 'Valerie knows it.' And he went out with the fruit clamped in his sharp wolfish teeth.

After a time there was a lot of activity in the hall. Girls sat down giggling in the kitchen alongside Margo. She held her head up and tried to concentrate. Shrieks came from the front room. A young woman in a grey costume appeared, wringing her right hand and moaning with mock terror. 'It's awful,' she cried, 'it's really awful.'

One by one the girls were taken into the other room. At last they came for Margo.

'Get off,' she protested. But they blindfolded her and led her away. She was aware of men's hands holding her, spinning her round in a circle.

183

'You are now on the flag ship,' drawled an unfamiliar voice, and she was lifted in the air and rocked like a baby.

'Oh, oh, oh,' she screamed, little flecks of light dancing before her eyes.

'It is a rough and stormy night. You are about to meet Napoleon, greatest of British admirals.'

Her hand was held in a dry palm. She sat down on something soft and yielding.

'How do you do! Pleased to meet you.'

'How do you do,' repeated Marge, her hand pumping up and down.

'Feel his head,' said the voice, and she stroked at something slippery, like satin – quilted like a tea cosy.

'Get away,' she screeched, 'it's a cosy.'

'This is his good arm – this is his bad arm.'

She felt a bandaged wrist, a bulky object. All around, the air was filled with whispers, instructions, smothered bursts of merriment. She was like a dog, pointing her nose to scent the wind, sitting there in her best crêpe dress, helpless.

'This is Napoleon's good eye,' said a girl's voice, and her nails flicked skin. She could feel the quivering eyeball beneath the lid.

'And this is Napoleon's bad eye –'

All at once her finger was seized firmly by the root and stabbed fiercely downward. Into moist juicy flesh. She screamed thinly, over and over, shaking with revulsion while the cloth was torn from her eyes and she saw Chuck grinning at her with the obscenely fingered orange lying in his palm. Woken by the commotion, Cyril stirred by her side. He pulled her down across him and she lay with beating heart against his white shirt.

'It's not Napoleon,' she protested, 'it's Nelson,' and closed her eyes.

When she awoke, the room was in darkness save for firelight. There was a couple in the armchair against the wall

184

and a young man dozing on the floor. She struggled upright, disentangling herself from the still-slumbering Cyril, thinking of Rita. Mrs Mander was in the kitchen amidst a debris of food.

'Feeling better, are you?' she asked. 'I saved you some ham.' And she handed her a plate lined with pink meat and a slice of bread and butter.

'I must find our Rita.'

There was a sour taste in Margo's throat and she felt as if she'd been up all night working.

'She's most like upstairs,' said Mrs Mander. 'They're playing sardines.'

'Sardines?'

'Somebody hides and whoever finds them like, hides with them. You know – girls and boys.' She winked a mascaraed eye. 'Didn't you ever play it?'

'They got the last game wrong,' said Margo crossly. 'It was never Napoleon.'

She resolutely put down her plate of ham and went into the hall. The trouble with the Manders' house was that it pretended to be different from hers and Nellie's. No landmarks anywhere. Everything old had been ripped out and replaced by something modern, unfamiliar. A recess lit by a lamp where the cupboard under the stairs would have been; a whole window of glass put in the hall at the side of the front door. To give more light, Mrs Mander said. Light was meant to be outside – that was the point of living inside. And anyway it was sheer foolishness, considering the bombing could start up again. There might even be doodlebugs, and they'd be sorry they hadn't kept the bricks.

On the bottom stair there was a couple courting.

'Excuse me,' she said. 'I want to get up there.'

They made themselves small, squeezing against the rail. The war had made everyone lax, openly immodest. It wasn't only the Yanks. There were all the jokes she heard at work about the girls in the Land Army getting in the hay with the Italian

185

prisoners of war, and Up with the Lark and To Bed with a Wren.

Upstairs the place was in darkness. She tried putting the light on in the front bedroom, but there were bodies everywhere – on the bed, on the floor – so she turned it off quick. But not before she had caught a glimpse of Valerie lying on her mother's bed, dazed in Chuck's military arms.

'Valerie,' she said loudly, 'where's our Rita?' And Valerie replied in a funny strangled voice: 'She's hiding, Auntie Marge.'

'Rita!' called Margo, thoroughly alarmed.

The back bedroom was empty. No breathing, no sounds. She put the light on. There was a small bed and a big wardrobe. She stood not knowing what to do; it was not in her nature to make a scene in someone else's house. Nellie would look under the bed and into the wardrobe, but this was Valerie's room, private, full of her belongings and her secret jars of face cream. It was a shock to find the room so plainly furnished – oil cloth on the floor and a cheap little square of carpet bought at Birkenhead market. It was not as she expected. Where was the flamboyancy, the style that showed in the clothes she wore? She opened the wardrobe and looked inside. There was Rita among the dresses and the pin-striped suits, staring out, not touching the young man with the long bony face.

After a moment of surprise Rita said: 'This is Ira. He's an American.'

'How do you do?' said Margo, and Rita stepped out of the wardrobe and he followed.

They walked ahead of her down the stairs: casually, not hurrying. In the kitchen she saw his face plainly; pale eyes, pale mouth, colourless hair. They were like brother and sister. Not at all threatening, no bulk to him, thin as a whippet, with big hands dangling and feet like an elephant. Rita was perfectly composed, sitting down at the table and sipping thoughtfully at a glass of dandelion and burdock. He said nothing,

186

leaning against the wall as if he was sleepy, looking at the girl.

'Do you want to go now, Auntie? Have you had enough?'

'Well, I think we better. I haven't brought the key . . .'

'And Auntie Nellie will be waiting up,' said Rita, finishing the sentence for her, thanking Mrs Mander very much for a lovely party, not looking at the young man, going out into the hall. Mrs Mander gave Marge a serviette full of ham for Nellie and a pickled onion – to placate her, though she didn't say so.

'Tarrah, Valerie!' called Rita up the stairs. 'Thank you very much for having me.'

It was warm in the street, dark and sheltered. From two roads away the sound of a tram.

'It's not that late, then,' said Margo wonderingly.

*   *   *

'You look a fair sight,' said Nellie, eyeing Margo's washed out face and the lipstick smeared at the corners of her mouth.

Mrs Lyons' costume, inside out and lined with grey taffeta, shimmered on the padded torso of the dressmaking dummy.

'Did you enjoy yourself, love?' asked Jack, of Rita.

'Yes, thank you.' And she was off upstairs to bed, not even bothering to wipe her face or clean her teeth.

'What happened?' asked Nellie. 'Who was there?'

'We played games,' Margo told her.

'Games?'

'You know, party games. Hide and seek – and dancing –'

'Hide and seek?'

'Upstairs in the wardrobes.' She fidgeted on her chair, aware that she had told a part but not the whole. 'I'm tired Nellie. I'll tell you in the morning.'

'You'll tell us now,' retorted Nellie firmly. 'It seems to have been a rum do. What about the sing-song?'

'They had none of the neighbours in,' said Margo.

'Who played the piano?'

187

'We didn't have a sing-song. There were just Yanks from the camp and friends of Valerie's.'

'Did Mrs Evans do "Bless This House"?'

'I told you, none of the neighbours were asked.' She tried hard to keep the irritation out of her voice. 'Mrs Mander saved you some ham.'

She reached in her handbag and brought out the serviette parcel.

'Very nice of her, I'm sure,' said Nellie, unwrapping it. 'Jack and I had rubber egg and boiled tomatoes.'

There was something troubling Margo, something she wanted to verbalise if she could only find the words. She wanted to get it out because it put her in a good light, made her seem responsible and right-thinking. But how to phrase it? She began : 'I wonder if it's normal for Rita to be so –' and couldn't go on.

Nellie said sharply : 'To be what?'

Margo pondered. 'So – quiet.'

It wasn't right. Jack looked at her without expression.

'I mean, she doesn't let on much, on the surface, how she's feeling.'

'Get away!' said Nellie, remembering the afternoon Jack had told Marge to give up Mr Aveyard. They all remembered it, even Margo whose thoughts were confused. Jack had driven with Rita in the van to meet Marge coming out of work at Belmont Road Hospital. She was a long time, and like all men kept waiting he was in quite a paddy when she finally got into the car. Blurting it out with no finesse, telling her he and Nellie had decided she must give up Mr Aveyard the push. Marge said she didn't see why she should, and he said women of her age got foolish notions; and that made her weep. And the child, leaning her elbows on the front seats, stared at both their faces : Jack white because he was thwarted, and Marge with the tears dripping down her cheeks. At the lights on Priory Road she had leapt out of her seat and run headlong down the street. Jack had followed in

188

the van, bellowing at her out of the window: 'You daft baggage! Learn sense woman!' 'I love him,' screeched Marge, mad with rebellion. 'I won't give him up, I won't!' And an old woman wrapped in a black knitted shawl, with a baby's hand like a brooch clawing at the front of her bosom, stopped and turned to look. Jack jumped out on to the pavement and caught up with Marge, struggled with her, tried to drag her back to the car. Twisting away from him, she ran like a girl down the side street, her hair coming out from under her hat and her heels flying. Jack thought he heard a baby crying as he passed the old woman all in black, but when he climbed into the car it was Rita. When they returned to Bingley Road, Nellie was angry with him. 'You shouldn't have,' she said, 'not in front of the child, you shouldn't have,' taking the little girl in her arms and rocking her. 'I want my Auntie Margo,' wailed the child, running to the door and not tall enough to turn the latch. There was nothing for it but to sit in the best front-room with the chair turned to the window, the lace curtains hitched up, so that she could see down the street. Waiting. Twice Nellie tried to carry the girl upstairs to bed, but she woke and broke out sobbing afresh, so they sat all night on the green plush chair. Now and then Nellie dozed and the little girl slipped on her lap and held her hand up to cover her cheek from the row of pins stuck in the bodice of her aunt's dress – then the light coming in the sky, like war being declared or mother dying, dramatic, till the bow-legged man came with his long pole and snuffed out the lamps in the street.

'I just wondered. I'm not easy in my mind,' said Margo, watching Nellie picking at the ham crushed in the paper napkin, strands of silko adhering to her skirts, and Jack packing shreds of Kardomah tea into the bowl of his pipe.

'How you can smoke that stuff beats me,' said Nellie. She stood up, grasped the dressmaking dummy in her arms, as if she was tossing the caber, and staggered the few steps into the hall. Parting the brown chenille curtains under the stairs with her foot, she trundled the dummy safely into the darkness.

189

4

I F I AM SEEN, thought Rita, I shall deny it. I shall think of
nothing but the house with the cherry trees in the garden
and I won't hear what they say. She looked out of the window
of the bus and resisted the temptation to hide under the seat.
Her companion, wearing a little mustard cap tilted over one
eye, raised his long legs and rested them on the curved rail
before the window. She tried not to be agitated by his lack
of consideration. Auntie Nellie said only louts behaved in
public as if they were in the privacy of their homes. She did
notice he wore nice white socks.

All the way on the tram from Priory Road she didn't think
she would meet him. What if Auntie Nellie had an accident
and they phoned her at work to come home quick? She should
have stayed in her seat till they reached the mouth of the
Mersey Tunnel, but she found herself standing on the platform as the tram swayed past the Empire Theatre, with a
picture of George Formby pasted to the wall; and she jumped
while the tram still moved, running on the pavement with her
handbag clutched to her chest. It surprised her. She didn't
look up, because that way it was more of a dream, walking
through the crowds hurrying in the opposite direction, with
the stone lions crouching on St. George's plateau across the
square and Johnny Walker high on the hoardings above the
Seamen's Hotel. When she was little, Uncle Jack had held her
hand, in the dark, and said, 'Look at his hat', and there he

190

was, all lit up and moving, his hat coming off his head and his legs marching, and the great bottle of whisky emptying as the coloured lights mathematically reduced. It's me, she thought, and it's not me, scurrying along in her macintosh, for it had rained without ceasing all summer.

'It's a helluva place,' said Ira, looking at the scarred streets and the cobblestones worn smooth by the great cart-horses that thundered down the hill to the coal yards behind Lime Street Station.

'The place we're going to,' said Rita, 'is quite nice really. Not like America, but it's nice.'

She felt better once the bus was on the dock road going out of town, past the sugar refinery of Tate and Lyle, and the warehouses, a smell of damp grain coming through the open window and the glimpses beyond the bomb sites of ships in the river.

'Uncle Jack,' she told him, 'says the slaves built the docks. On the wharves they've got posts with rings in where they chained them up.'

'Oh yes,' he said, 'it's a helluva place.'

Maybe she shouldn't have mentioned the slaves, he being American and used to coloured soldiers. She hadn't the knack of conversation; all her life she had been used to being spoken to without the need to respond, of looking at faces without imagining she was being observed. It came hard to her, the business of being alone with him. She sat weighted in her seat, distressed by his silence, her neck aching with the effort of not turning to stare at him. She would have feasted her eyes on him if others had been present, the pale saddle of freckles on the bridge of his nose, the almost invisible line of his blond eyebrow, which she had registered on a previous occasion.

They were leaving the town altogether now, the miles of docks that carried on into Bootle and beyond, winding inland away from the camouflaged depots and goods yards – not entirely countryside yet, but fields here and there separating

191

the groups of houses; allotments growing vegetables; washing hanging on a line strung between two leafy trees. They went over a little hump-backed bridge and there were water lilies floating.

'Oooh,' she went, as the bus accelerated and dipped down sharply.

'It's not far now,' she said, darting a glance at him, seeing his eyes closed as if he slept.

She hoped she had remembered the place rightly, had not mistaken its situation : a corn field and ornamental gates guarding a big estate, a small lodge house with a cherry tree growing against the wall. Uncle Jack had shown it to her when she was a child, on the way to a farmer he knew, to slaughter pigs. And again at the beginning of the war, to a picnic at the side of the corn-field. 'When the Germans come,' he said, 'which they will, mark my words, they'll smash the house down, quick as a flash.' 'How?' she asked, mouth open that such a thing could happen, looking in through the mullioned windows and seeing a potted geranium and a round stuffed hen with stippled breast and legs set wide apart. 'Tanks,' he had said darkly. 'Armoured tanks, drive straight at the gate and through, and Bob's your uncle.' And she saw it all, the bricks giving and the stairway collapsing, one wall with a picture still hanging on a nail, and the hen with its stuffing coming out lying under the cherry tree.

When they came to Ince Blundell and the roundabout planted with pink and mauve flowers, she thought they were near. The bus swung round the curve of the road, hugging the pavement, nudging the branches of a tree that brushed its leaves the length of the windows.

'Jesus,' said Ira, waking in alarm, his eyes filled with a blur of green whipping across the glass.

'You shouldn't say that,' she said, and could have bitten her tongue.

'Are we there?' he asked, yawning, and stretching his long arms above his head.

192

So eager was she not to miss the place that they left the bus a mile too soon, plodding along the main road lined with red-brick bungalows, the sun coming out, not strongly but shining all the same.

'Look,' she said 'at the gardens.'

And he looked, though she couldn't tell what he made of the neat hedges, the shrub roses, the crazy-paving spotted with small rock plants, white, blue and buttercup yellow. Isn't it pretty, she thought; it's so pretty. She remembered the back yard under soot in Bingley Road and the one lump of lupins coming up each year by the wash-house wall.

The road cut clear through the woods. They were forced to walk single-file because the path was so narrow. On the films she had seen women wandering down deserted country roads, dappled by sunshine, about to meet lovers or strangers, and they all swayed with a particular motion of the hips, as if they were bare under their clothes. She herself moved stiffly, she felt, like a nailed up box. She had wanted to wear a thin summer dress under her macintosh, but Auntie Nellie would have commented, and she hadn't known when she dressed that she had intended to meet the American. She wasn't clear in her mind whether it was fear on her part or a belief that he wouldn't be there, at the bus terminal, as they had arranged. She wished it could be hot and dazzling in the heat – walking hand in hand through the green glade and a rush of words because they were so close. At the moment they were strangers, the words waiting to be said, but soon it would be different, she was quite sure of that. She wished he could catch a fragrance from her hair or the folds of her sensible dress, that he would hold her hand as he had done so fleetingly in the wardrobe, that he would look at her searchingly; she was so anxious for the love story to begin. The gates were still there, set back from the road, the carved griffins on their stone posts beside the entrance, the lodge through the iron bars, windows encircled by ivy and a tree growing close to the wall. But when she ran to look through the gates into the

193

house she couldn't see into the room. In some way the lodge had retreated further into the trees.

'There was a stuffed hen,' she cried, 'with a yellow beak.'

'Hens,' he said, 'are cunning birds. Why, we had a hen at home that sat on a chair by the fire and never gave up. Not if you poured water over it.'

'Have you got pets at your house, then?'

'No, we have a dog and a goat and a mare, but we don't have no pets.'

She was mad for the way he said 'dawg', like he was a movie star, larger than life.

'I had a rabbit called Timoshenko. I kept my nightie in it.'

'You what?'

'It was a bag with ears, for me nightie. Auntie Nellie made it me. When I got the measles she sent it to a children's home in case it was infected.'

He shook his head, either in sympathy or because he didn't understand. He stood, scuffing his feet on the gravel, watching the cars as they drove past. After a moment he said, 'What we going to do now – now that we're here?'

'Just walk,' she said. 'We can't get in there, it's private.'

She tried to think where the corn-field grew, in which direction, beyond the woods or up the road. She didn't want to go ahead of him lonely any more, so she ran across the road and scrambled down into the ditch, climbing up on to the far bank with her shoes soaked and her stockings splashed with mud.

'It's a helluva place to go,' he said, looking at her across the ditch.

He stayed on the path, separated from her, as she tore a trail through the puddles of water and patches of bramble. She was amazed at the amount and variety of plants that grew in the woods, quite apart from the trees – the quantity of thorn bush and briar that assailed her on every side. It only made her the more determined; she wasn't put out.

'There's a corn field,' she cried, keeping up with him as he

194

sauntered along the pavement wtih his hands in his pockets. 'My dad took me when I was little for a picnic.'

He stopped quite still to look at her.

'Your dad?'

It had slipped out, it wasn't any part of them. She dragged her feet through the mud and wondered what Auntie Nellie would say about the state of her stockings. I fell off a tram, she thought, and a dog got at me. In spite of the worry, she began to laugh. It was daft to try and get away with it. She could see her aunt's eyebrows slanting upwards like a chinaman, bewildered : 'You fell off a tram?' Her eyebrows, grey like her hair, save at the tips which were tinged with brown, inscrutably raised in disbelief. 'I was pushed from behind, Auntie Nellie, and then this spaniel worried me.' Like in the English lessons at school, finding the most suitable word for the occurrence.

She gave little high-pitched gasps for breath, on her side of the ditch, treading the blackberries underfoot, her hair sliding down out of the brassy kirby grips, and he said : 'You gone crazy or something?'

'I'm thinking of me Auntie Nellie and what she'll make of the state I'm in.'

'You look fine to me.'

He had said it, he had noticed her. The journey on the bus, when he had so cruelly closed his eyes to shut her out, no longer mattered. The trees ended : ahead, splayed out under the weak sunshine, three acres of corn, uncut because of the bad weather, pale brown under a sky filled with frayed white clouds.

* * *

Marge had asked Nellie to call at the corner shop on Breck Road for her ciggies. She was going to have a bite of tea with a girl from work and the shop would be closed by the time she came home. Nellie thought it a foolish thing to do, going off like that to someone's house after a hard day's work, but she couldn't interfere. There were times when Marge was adamant. It was a nuisance, of course, having to keep her dinner warm in the oven. She hated sewing with the smell of food in the air. It lingered, penetrated the fabric of the material; but what was one meal kept on the gas in a lifetime? She didn't seek to be restricting, but she'd always been a leader, even if it was in a purely domestic sense – arranging, decorating, budgeting – and Marge was a follower. She'd do what anyone wanted, provided it was silly enough. Her intentions were good, but she lacked tenacity. She was the big blaze that died down through lack of fuel. All that fuss about fire-watching in spite of her bronchitis, down into town every night to her post, prowling about the roof of the Cunard Building with her bucket of sand and her tin hat, keen as mustard at first, then sloping off home earlier and earlier, making excuses, absent without leave. She couldn't sustain it. When she came home one night with a bruise on her chin and her breath reeking of whisky, she realised herself that that was the end of her little jaunt into battle. The truth was, Nellie thought, stabbing her hat-pin into the back of her brown hat, it wasn't only Marge that found it hard to preserve interest. She too was beginning to retreat from the front line. She was forever peering out into the world, listening for the sound of the bugle, willing reinforcements to arrive. She had confided her worries to Mr Barnes, the minister at St Emmanuel's Church; but though he was a good enough man, he was naturally limited by his own maleness from understanding her problems. She was concerned that when she woke each morning to the alarm clock on the bedside table, her first thoughts were not thankfulness that she had been spared breath, but worry over mother's furniture. Did the damp warp it in winter, the sun expand it in summer? Had it deteriorated in the small hours of the night? There was dry rot, wet rot, woodworm. She lived in dread that she would be taken ill and begin to die. Marge wouldn't bother to wipe

196

with vinegar the sideboard, or draw the blinds against the warmth of a summer afternoon to ensure the carpet wouldn't fade. She was indolent. She had sewn Rita into her vest when the child was small and the winter particularly bitter. She could confide to Mr Barnes her weariness of spirit over the endless making-do with the rations, the queueing at the shops; but to admit her slavery to mahogany and rosewood was difficult, when he continually admonished her from the pulpit to consider the lilies of the field. Had they been her very own lilies she would have spent a lifetime ensuring that they too retained their glory. Brooding, she walked the length of the road, smiling briefly at one or two neighbours who nodded in her direction, clutching her shopping bag to the breast of her black tailored coat. The thought of mother's things in a sale-room, or worse in the junk shop on Breck Road, caused her pain in the region of her heart. She hoped she wasn't about to suffer a decline. She would wake at night with Marge lying beside her and remember quite vividly episodes of the past, unconnected : an outing as a child to the birthplace of Emily Brontë; Father in his broadcloth suit; Mother faded, sepia-coloured against the sky, sitting in the sparse grass on the moors, squinting into sunshine. Or she was at a desk at school with her mouth open watching a fly caught in a spiral of light, beating its wings against the panes of glass. She lay moistening her dry lips with her tongue, staring out into the dark little bedroom.

She had walked the length of Priory Road and turned at the Cabbage Hall into Breck Road and not known it, not recorded one tree or shop or item of traffic. Of course it had changed. There were bomb craters and rubble and old landmarks cleared away, but still it bewildered her that she had come so far in her mind and not been conscious of the route. Inside the corner shop she asked for Marge's ciggies.

'Good afternoon. Lovely day, isn't it?'

The woman said it was a grand day but she only kept cigarettes for her regular customers. She wore a pink turban with some wax grapes pinned to left of centre, and drop ear-rings with purple clusters. Nellie's eyes rounded in wonder. She put her fingers on the counter and explained that Marge was regular, always bought her ciggies here, but she was going to be late home and she'd come instead, 'to fetch them for her.'

'I'm sorry love, I don't know you from Laurel and Hardy.'

'She comes every night. She's thin and she's got a green coat and . . .'

But Nellie couldn't really say what Marge looked like, couldn't for the life of her describe her features. After all those years. Her eyes travelled the rows of glass jars half-filled with sweets, such pretty colours, on shelves rising clear to the ceiling, among advertisements for tobacco, for chocolates, a naval man with sea spray on his cheeks, a dandy in an opera cloak smiling down at her with eyes like Rudolf Valentino. She stood in a circle of light, dazed by the flecks of white at the centre of his eyes and the dust-filled rays of the sun that shone through the topmost window of the shop.

'She always has ten Abdullah. Every night.'

'Sorry, luv. I told you.'

Nellie was deafened by her own heartbeats. She clutched the counter for support, unable to move. There was a jar of liquorice laces on the counter, coiled like snakes. Nellie wanted to pick up the jar and smash it in the woman's face – there, where the edge of her dusty hair caught fire in the sun and the little grapes dangled.

'I'm sorry, luv, but you see how I'm placed.'

Nellie saw her placed – painted like Carmen Miranda on a pantomime backcloth that bulged outwards and wavered as if a gust of wind swept the shop. Faint with anger, Nellie went out of the door and started for home. It was the third time in one month that she had made herself ill with ungovern-able rage over a trivial incident.

* * *

They were sitting at the edge of the cornfield. Apart. He hadn't held her hand or tried to kiss her. He squatted on his haunches above the ground damp from the rain and the narrow ditch that ran beside the field. She had asked him about books, and he said he didn't read much, and when she mentioned poetry he had looked at her curiously, not commenting.

'My Auntie Margo is a great reader.'

'Is that so?'

'She reads all sorts. I found a book once. She hid it in a drawer.'

'She did?'

'It was awful. You know, it was rude.'

'What kind of rude?' he asked, his eyes not quite so sleepy.

'You know, men and women.' She wished she hadn't told him.

'How come you know it was that kind of a book?'

'Don't be daft. You only had to read the first page. You must have seen books like that, you being in the army.'

'I don't have no call to read them kind of books,' he said. 'I seen pictures in magazines, but I ain't read none of them books.'

She felt he was criticising her, blaming her alongside Auntie Margo.

'I only read a bit of it,' she said defensively. 'I don't know where she got it from.'

'She didn't look to me like a woman who would read them sort of books.'

'Oh, she's deep, is Auntie Margo. She was married once to a soldier, but he died from the gas in France.'

He swung his hands between his knees and gazed out across the flat countryside, following the ribbon of highway that wound like a river into the distance.

'She was courting once when I was small, but she gave him up.'

'Courting?'

199

'She didn't care enough, she didn't fight for him.'

He wasn't comfortable with her, she could tell. Every time she looked at him it hurt that she couldn't finger his hair or touch his cheek. She wished he would put down the stick that he dug into the yellow earth, poking the soil, not paying her attention.

'Let's go,' she said. 'The sea's over there.'

'If you like.'

He moved carefully, trying not to dirty his beautifully polished shoes, treading the marshy path alongside a black ploughed field. When they came to a lane she held the strands of barbed wire wide for him so that he wouldn't tear his uniform. She herself would have liked to enter the wire on the opposite side of the road and tramp in a straight line across the grass towards the horizon and the dark row of houses before the sea-shore.

'Jesus,' he said with relief at standing on firm ground, and she stamped her foot at him.

'There's other words to use when you're cross. You don't have to say that.'

'Aw, come on, Rita.'

But she was striding off resentfully down the lane towards the corner where a red barn half-stood with its tin roof sliding into decay amidst a clump of elms. When he caught up with her he put his arm about her shoulders, but without warmth, digging his fingers into her flesh, shaking her. She became very still, waiting.

'What's up?'

'Nothing.'

'I guess your Auntie Margo wouldn't have no qualms about saying "Jesus". You're too sensitive getting all hotted up about a word.'

'Leave off.'

She shook herself free, pained that he had practically praised her aunt in preference to her, hearing the sound of marching feet beyond the barn and voices singing. She pretended she was tying her shoelace, squatting down by the nettles and the ragged blackberry bushes, bowing her head. It was like being caught fraternising with the enemy, alone on a country road with an American. He lounged against the tangled hedge, sucking a blade of grass, watching the squad of soldiers stamping round the bend of the road, feet splayed out like Charlie Chaplin, stub-toed boots black as soot.

> My eyes are dim, I cannot see,
> I have not brought my specs with me...

And a wail, drawn out, sorrowful, as if they howled in protest at walking through the warm afternoon:

> I have not brought
> My specs with me.

Ira whistled shrilly as they strutted past him, but he was ignored.

'Don't,' she hissed, crouching in the wet grass, fiddling with her shoe.

Eyes front, shoulders raised, they swung their arms and went mincing up the lane. The rooks left the elm trees and swooped down to the rusted roof of the empty barn.

'Don't,' she cried again, jumping upright and dragging on his arm as he stood blowing between his fingers in the middle of the lane. She wrenched his hands from his mouth, her face flushed with anger. 'Don't make a show of yourself.'

'What's got into you?' he wanted to know, digging his hands into his pockets and looking at her sullenly. Now that the soldiers had gone, she was sorry she had flared up at him.

'It's just that they don't like you, do they?'

'Who don't like me?' His eyes, grey not blue, reflecting the surface of the road, stared at her coldly.

'Our Tommies. They don't like the Yanks. It's the money you get.'

201

'We don't have no trouble with Tommies. We're allies.'

'Well,' she finished lamely, 'they have fights in Liverpool, down by Exchange Station. Everybody knows.'

'Is that so?' he muttered, turning from her and kicking at the hedgerow.

She didn't know how to remedy the situation. Rather like her Aunt Nellie who could never say she was sorry. She twisted her hands together and gazed helplessly at his hostile back.

'Oh,' she said, 'I didn't mean to speak out of turn.'

To her relief he stepped away from the hedge and shrugged his shoulders. But his face was hard. She looked at him furtively, trying to read his eyes, but they were guarded, revealing nothing.

'I'm sorry, Ira.'

Tears came to her eyes. He gave her a small lenient smile, and she was instantly restored, untroubled. The road led them toward the coast. They went along a cinder path over the railway and across another field.

'We could go home on the train,' she said, 'if we wanted.'

'I'm hungry,' he complained, but she didn't seem to hear him.

The land was level, the sky heaped with white cloud. She raced ahead of him between hedges inclined inwards against the constant wind blowing from the sea. They came to the long waste of foreshore and the row of empty houses heaped about with sand. He looked curiously at the deserted road and the front gardens run wild.

'Was this the blitz?' he asked.

She didn't know. 'It's near the docks and maybe people got scared and left. They don't look bombed.'

'They sure do,' he argued, looking at the windows empty of glass and the debris spilling on to the road.

'I think people are daft. I'd rather live here than Anfield.' And she ran into the nearest house, through the open doorway into a long hall that led into a back room overlooking the beach. 'Come on,' she shouted. 'It's nice in here.'

He followed her without enthusiasm, seeing the dog dirt on the floor and the human excrement and the soiled pieces of newspaper. Outside the window was a short garden with currant bushes and a broken wall tumbling down on to the sand.

Nellie had made her two sandwiches for her lunch and wrapped some biscuits. She took them out of her handbag and showed them to Ira. He held his hand out eagerly, but she put them away again, closing the clasp of her bag with a decisive little click.

'Later,' she said. 'I never have my dinner till one o'clock.'

It was a way she had with her, sticking to routine. They found strawberries in the garden, huddled under grey-green leaves weighted by sand. These at least she didn't own. She watched him as he strolled about the neglected garden, sitting on the faded square of lawn, and wished he would come near her. He leant against the crumbling wall looking at the barbed-wire entanglements rolling torn and rusted along the shore. In rows, the concrete bollards stood, planted to repel the landing craft.

'You don't talk much, do you?' she said, stung by his indifference.

'I guess I'm not much of a talker. Anyrate, I'm too hungry to think of words.'

She opened her handbag and took out the sandwiches and gave them to him. He lay down on his back full length upon the wall, tossing the paper wrapping on to the beach and holding the bread in both hands, his cap slipping sideways on to the grass. There was his ear, neat to his head and an inch of shaved scalp before his bleached hair began.

'Your Auntie Margo make you these?' he munched.

'Never,' she scoffed. 'She wouldn't give you the time of day.'

She felt uncomfortable being mean about Auntie Margo, and she could hardly credit that what she felt was jealousy.

'Auntie Margo isn't much good at shopping and stuff. Nellie does all that.'

'Did you tell your auntie that you were meeting me?'

'I didn't like.'

'Don't they let you date?'

'I don't talk to them very much.'

He didn't comment. He folded his arms behind his head and closed his eyes.

After a while she opened her bag and took out mother's pearl beads and laid them on the grass. She looked round for something to dig in the soil, something sharp. In time, she found the jagged half of a slate fallen from the roof, and she knelt and scooped a hole in the sandy earth. When she was ready, she put the beads in the shallow depression and spooned the sand back into place. Finally, she threw the slate over the wall into the next garden and stamped the ground level with her shoes. She snapped a piece from the flowering currant bush growing by the wall and planted it on the spot where she had buried the necklace. Wiping her hand on her coat, she went and looked down at his face. His eyelids quivered.

'You're shamming,' she said. 'You're never sleeping.'

There was a line of sweat beading his upper lip and the dull gleam of a tooth where his mouth lay slack. She shook him gently and felt his body tense so that he wouldn't fall off the wall.

'What were you putting in the earth?'

'Secret. Mind your own business.'

He sat up then and shook her quite roughly by the shoulders, thrusting his narrow face at her. Suddenly he kissed her. So flat and hard her gums ached. She pulled away from his mouth and buried her face in his jacket to hide her wide smile of delight that it had happened at last. He swung her round and stood holding her by the hips, pushing himself against her. All her bones hurt and the top of her legs where the broken wall caught her. But it didn't matter. Possession

204

blazed up in her, consuming : someone belonged to her. After the war he would take her to the States, and they'd have a long black car and a grand piano with a bowl of flowers on the lid. There'd be a house with a verandah and wooden steps, and she would run down them in a dress with lots of folds in the skirt and peep-toed shoes. Auntie Nellie would tell Mrs Mander how well-off they were, how Ira cared for her, the promotion he kept getting at work.

'What you say?' he asked, flushed in the face.

'What's your work when you're not a soldier?'

He was clutching her hair in two bunches on either side of her head, tilting her neck. Her mouth opened like a fish.

'You're hurting me.'

He let go at once, taking a step backwards, and she followed him blindly, nestling up to him, content to be on a level with his chest, her arms rather awkwardly about him, her head full of dreams.

'What job do you do when you're not in the army?'

'I ain't got no job. Leastways, nothing settled.'

He was bringing his arm up against her chest as if to push her away but his fingers were feeling the fabric of her dress.

'Leave off!' she cried, shocked, butting him with her head so that he stumbled and almost fell.

'You shouldn't do things like that. It's rude doing that.'

Already she was wishing he was different, more to her liking – more chatty, ask her things, tell her about the future, kiss her gently on the lips and not act rude.

He sat down on the wall, defeated, and scratched his head. She felt scorn for him because he didn't know how to behave. And yet she did love him. She went clumsily and put her arms about his neck, pushing his head down against the throat of her dress, stroking the skin behind his ear as if he was the cat.

'I like kissing,' she said primly, 'but I don't want to do anything rude.'

'I can't make you out,' he said. 'I don't see what I done that was rude.'

205

The tide was coming in, the sea invading the beach, trickling through the line of concrete defences. She patted his back, as if he was a child that had fallen over.

'I don't think it was very awful,' she said, helplessly. But he laced his arms slackly about her waist and did not attempt to kiss her again.

They walked to the nearest railway station to catch a train to the town. There was a public house near the ticket office and he wanted to see if he could get a drink, but she said her Auntie Nellie wouldn't like it. She hung on his arm and chattered all the time, filled with confidence, sitting on the upholstered railway seat with her torn stockings and her muddy shoes stretched out for all to see. She covered his hand with both her own, like a little dry animal she was keeping from running away.

5

———

Jack came to take them for a run in the car.

'One of these days,' warned Nellie darkly and left the room to fetch her coat.

'Don't you want a run out?' he asked when she returned, but she drew in her narrow lips and kept silent.

'I'm allowed a certain amount of petrol,' he said mildly.

'It's not right, Jack, and you know it, buying black-market stuff.'

'Good God, woman!' he exploded. 'Anyone would think I was the Gauleiter of Anfield, plundering the poor.' He felt quite nettled and put out.

'Take no notice,' said Margo, and told Rita to get her things on.

Nellie sat on the front seat beside him and he wound a rug about her knees. It was raining and the streets were gloomy; he didn't know where to go.

'Do you fancy anywhere special?' he asked Nellie, driving down Breck Road towards the cemetery and turning into Prescott Avenue. He would have suggested a cup of tea at Winifred's Cottage on the East Lancs road, but it was a fair run and he didn't want another scene over his petrol ration.

'I want to go to the Cathedral,' said Rita, tapping his shoulder.

She was wearing some kind of scent, sweet and powerful.

'My word, someone smells nice. Doesn't she smell nice, Auntie Nellie?'

But Nellie only nodded her head with an air of martydom, and Marge remarked grimly from the back seat: 'You'll not get a word out of her. She's been like Sarah Bernhardt all week.'

He thought maybe that Nellie had been overdoing it, that she needed a holiday. When she put her hat on, he had noticed the pallor of her face and a little blue vein standing out on her forehead. But where could the girls go for a holiday, that was the problem. Most of the seaside boarding houses had been requisitioned, and he doubted if Marge could get off work.

'Nellie, what was that place we went to in Shropshire before the war?'

Rita said: 'I don't want to be late back, Uncle Jack. I'm going out later.'

'What place?' asked Nellie.

'It had a bowling green. When they put a net up it was a tennis court. You remember.'

'Herbert Arms Hotel,' said Margo. 'Where are you going, Rita?'

'Just out.'

'That's right, Marge, the Herbert Arms. Everybody round a big table for meals and there was a yard with a stable.' He hardly saw the familiar streets for the picture in his mind of a grey church and an old car parked near a bridge. They had jam for tea in little bowls, all different kinds – strawberry and plum and blackcurrant jelly.

'It was a cow shed,' said Marge, 'with cows, and a great big hill of muck outside the back door.'

'Trust you to remember that,' said Nellie.

'Get off!' Jack said. 'It was a proper midden, scientific. There was no smell. They put it on the fields.'

They were driving up Princes Road toward the Park, over-taking a solitary tram. The tall trees in the centre of the boulevard were heavy with rain. They swayed and dripped, turning the interior of the van into a green box full of shadows.

Marge was laughing in the back of the car. Jack looked in the mirror and saw her wiping her eyes with her handkerchief.

'What's up with you, Marge?'

'I just thought of that chappie from the Wirral with the short pants.'

'The what?'

'With the bike.'

'It was a tandem,' said Nellie, and her lips curved upward at the corner and she let out a little abrupt snigger.

'By heck,' said Jack delightedly, 'I'd forgotten him. With red hair –'

'And his mam rubbed his legs with goose fat to keep them ready for his bike –'

They were all laughing now, thinking of Marge going off on the tandem with him in little short white socks and a pair of tennis pumps. It was funny, Jack thought, how Marge always attracted the men, even if they were silly beggars. She always had, even when she was getting past her prime. And he darted a quick look into the mirror and saw her there, with tears running down her face and her two cheeks flushed with rouge and her body the same thickness from shoulder to thigh.

They went down hill towards the river. Passing the old black houses built by the shipping owners, four-storeys high with pillars at the front door and steps of granite – occupied now by riff-raff: washing hung sodden on the wrought-iron balconies, a pram with three wheels in the gutter, a running herd of children without shoes. Some of the railings had been taken away to be melted down for the war-effort and there was wire meshing to stop people breaking their necks in the blackout. There was the new Cathedral rising like an ocean liner out of the sunken graveyard, tethered to its dry dock by giant cranes, coloured all over a soft and rusty pink. Rita wouldn't let him take her round to the front entrance. They parked on Hope Street and watched her push her way through a portion of broken fencing into the cemetery.

209

'Why can't she use the proper gate?' asked Margo.

'I wouldn't mind going for a walk down there myself,' Jack said, and he looked sideways at Nellie. 'Do you feel like a blow?'

'It's drizzling. Let the child be on her own. It's natural. She doesn't want you lumbering about after her.'

'Would you like a holiday?' he asked after a while. He opened the window to let out the smoke from Marge's cigarette. She looked at him astonished. 'You've been looking peaky lately,' he said.

'How can I go on a holiday with young Rita to look after?'

'Well, there's Marge –'

She withered him with a glance. 'I wouldn't leave the cat with our Marge,' she said.

'By heck, I'd take a damn sight more care of her than you do.'

There was a silence while the storm gathererd.

Jack looked out of the window and saw the small figure moving along the path that wound round the walls, descending lower into the well of the cemetery. She stopped to pull leaves from a bush. On the sky-line floated one small barrage balloon, idiotic, like something a kiddie had drawn with a blue crayon.

'That would be a fat lot of good,' he said, half to himself. Marge was going on and on in that way she had, stumbling over her words. She had a good voice, throaty – not like Nellie's, strained and shrill. Whatever Nellie said came out like a criticism because of the lack of tone.

Marge said: 'She said she was going out tonight. You never asked her where.'

'I know where, that's why.'

'Well, where is she going?'

'She's going to the moving pictures with Cissie Baines,' Nellie said grudgingly.

'Well, she might say that, but you can't be sure.'

'Get away with you!' Nellie said, twisting round in her

210

seat to look at Marge. 'D'you know what, Miss? I think you're jealous, you're blooming jealous.'

Jack tried to keep out of it. In a way it was easy, for he had heard of it all before, not the same subject, but the bitterness lying beneath the words. Nobody could keep young Rita chained up. If she said she was going out with Cissie Baines he supposed she was. Marge wanted to know if it was Cissie Baines she had gone out with earlier in the week and come home with her stockings in a mess and her shoes all muddy. Jack wondered if the parents of Cissie were arguing about Rita at this moment.

'We don't even know who Cissie Baines is,' cried Margo. 'We've never set eyes on her. We don't know where she lives or if she's rough or anything.'

He could see Rita leaping about the path far below. She wore a macintosh and a spotted scarf wound round her head. Beyond the river he thought he could make out the distant blue swell of the Cheshire hills. The voices went on around him, Marge attacking, Nellie defending. Sooner or later Marge would go too far and Nellie would take umbrage and they'd have a silent drive back and a silent tea of cold meat that he'd brought and half a tomato each. The thought of the little bowls of jam on the white cloth years ago nagged him.

'D'you remember the plum jam,' he said unwisely, 'and the crab apple jelly?' His face was illuminated, his eyes round with longing under the shabby Homburg hat.

'If I told you,' said Margo, rounding on him in fury, 'that your Rita was nicking things, I don't suppose you'd take a blind bit of notice.'

'Steady on!' he said, sobered. 'What d'you mean, Marge?' He looked at Nellie for an explanation.

'Take no notice. She's touched.'

'No, no, steady on.' He was insistent. 'What she mean by that?'

'She's lost that necklace and some book she had in a drawer.'

211

'What necklace?'

'That necklace I put on to go to Valerie Mander's the other night. It's gone,' said Margo dramatically.

'The state you came home in that night it's a wonder you brought your clothes home, never mind a string of beads,' snapped Nellie.

'You grudge my going out, you do. You'd like me locked indoors pedalling away on a sewing machine and me mouth jammed full of pins. You'd like to keep me down –'

'Keep you down!' Nellie gave a little sarcastic laugh. 'Who blacked the grate every morning of their life and who left me to nurse Mother and Uncle Wilf?'

'You wouldn't let me see him,' wailed Margo, her eyes glittering, remembering George Bickerton dying upstairs.

Jack was trying to fathom what it had to do with Rita. They goaded each other with memories of the past and confused him with their bickering.

'You stopped me going to the keep-fit classes,' cried Margo.

'I never –'

'You rang up the fire-post behind me back and told them I was too poorly to fire-watch any more –'

They were spitting at each other like cats, arching their necks and clawing at the leather seating of the car.

Below in the cemetery Rita meandered between laurel and dusty rhododendron and frail spires of mountain ash.

'By God!' began Nellie, and he turned to look at her and watched her eyes open very wide as if she saw something outside on the road that surprised her. Above the little white muffler tucked about her neck her lips were turning a delicate shade of violet.

'Hey-up, Nellie!' he cried in alarm, as she slid downwards in her seat and fluttered her eyes. He couldn't think what to do at first. Marge said it was sheer bad temper that made her go off in a faint. 'Shut your gob!' he shouted, out of his mind with fright, because he knew it was her heart.

He got out of the car and half-laid her across the two front

212

seats, taking his coat off and bundling it under her head. Something about her thick little ankles and the sensible shoes like boots he had worn as a boy caught in his throat. He tried to call Rita to come quickly, but the wind pulled his voice and she didn't look round. He looked for a house so that he could get help, but there was only a row of half-demolished buildings on the far side of the road and he didn't like to leave Nellie alone with Marge, who was crying now.

'It's your heart,' he muttered, kneeling on the running board of the van and patting Nellie's gloved hand so that she would know he was near.

'Go and get Rita,' he ordered Marge, wanting to get the sick woman home and in her bed.

After a moment Nellie opened her eyes and he told her to lie still. He looked back and he could see Marge running along the edge of the fencing waving her arms and shouting 'Rita!' A small girl came with great patches of hair missing from her head and stared into the van without expression.

'It's your heart,' he told Nellie, over and over, for he wanted to reassure her that it wasn't a road accident or a nightmare or something she couldn't understand.

He gritted his teeth and prayed for Rita to hurry up. Marge was still swooping up and down the fence, like some gull crying in the wind. Nellie was conscious now, a little more composed. Struggling to sit up, she tried to ram her hat more securely on to her head.

'Look at your good coat,' she said weakly, and he flapped it straight and put it over her and the rug on top of that.

Rita and he put her to bed when they got home, taking her out of her tight dress and leaving her in her slip and her corsets. Marge went up the road to the Manders to use their telephone to send for Dr Bogle. To Rita, the house was exciting, full of whisperings and sudden knocks at the door.

'She does too much,' said Jack for the umpteenth time, striding back and forth with his hat still on his head, waiting for Dr Bogle to finish his examination.

Nellie was quiet enough when Dr Bogle had gone. She liked him: he was her generation, he never asked too many questions. He told her she should lie up for a day or two and not fret about the house.

'After all,' he said without malice, 'it'll still be here after you're gone.'

He went downstairs to talk to Jack and left her moping in the chill little bedroom with the rain sliding down the window. She decided she would do as she was told, stay in her bed for a day or two and Marge could take time off work and keep house and make her a cup of tea when required. She needed time to think what she was going to do about the future. Marge had been right when she had cried out to Jack in the van that it was bad temper had had made her turn dizzy. It had come on when Marge had accused her of stopping her from attending the keep-fit classes. It was a lie, and the anger she felt at Marge twisting the facts to suit herself had risen in her like bile, choking her. She would have to find some way of detaching herself from such irritations, until she had worked out what to do with the furniture. Rita would have to find a young man and settle down. Jack could find them a house somewhere, nothing fancy, and the sideboard and the sofa and chairs and the bone china could be moved there, into the best front room, away from Marge and her slatternly ways. For the moment she would suggest as quietly as possible that Marge keep her underwear clean until she was up and about again, and pray to God that she wouldn't be run over by a tram before she herself was fit to do the washing.

Margo was very chastened, the fire gone out of her. She didn't even say much when Rita said she was off out if nobody needed her. Jack gave her a ten-shilling note and told her to be a good girl.

'Oh, I wish I hadn't argued with Nellie,' said Margo, when they were alone.

'You've got a vicious tongue in your head, Marge. Mind
214

you, she's not the easiest of women to get on with. She's a good woman, and they're the worst.'

He sat dangling his small hands between his knees, sitting on Nellie's chair beside the grate. Bogle had said there wasn't much to worry about, it was only a little warning that she should take it easy. It would be best in future not to upset her, not to cause scenes likely to bring on an attack.

'How long has she been moody?' he asked Marge; and she replied more or less since the beginning of the week when she'd gone to a friend after work and not come straight home. Nellie said she'd get her ciggies for her, only she forgot; and when Marge spoke out of turn Nellie flew up in a paddy and had hardly uttered a civil word since.

'Ah well,' he said and turned on the wireless to relieve the gloom.

He made Nellie a cup of cocoa, but she didn't want it, and he brought it downstairs and drank it himself. Though there was still daylight outside the window, inside the kitchen it had grown dark. The dimensions of the room were mean, depressing without the glow of a fire. All the good furniture had been removed into the front room – dining-room table, sideboard, the oak chair that father had sat in. Nellie had replaced them with cheap utility stuff bought at Lewis's.

'By heck,' he said, 'I'll get the electric put in before another winter passes.'

'She won't like that,' said Margo. 'You know what she's like about the house being shook up.'

Jack went and lit the oven in the scullery for warmth. Margo sat in her coat feeling sorry for herself; the sausage curls above her ears hung bedraggled from all her running about in the rain. Jack put the tea on the table but neither of them felt up to eating.

'I'm that cold,' he complained, standing up at the table, hugging himself with his arms.

About his brow was a red mark where the band of his hat had bitten too tight. If the calendar said it was summer, even

215

if there was snow on the wash-house roof, Nellie wouldn't light a fire. She said they needed the coal for the winter. In vain he told her that things were going to get better, now the Allies had landed in Europe. She'd read of people being extravagant and having to burn the furniture to stop themselves from freezing to death.

Some lady on the wireless was singing a song about Tomorrow When the World was Free :

> There'll be blue birds over
> The white cliffs of Dover
> Tomorrow just you wait and see . . .

He joined in the chorus, but his voice broke with emotion and he cleared his throat several times to get over it. Margo was watching him with contemptuous eyes.

'It's something to do with the word,' he said. 'It always chokes me up.'

'What word, you soft beggar?'

'Blue.' He emptied his nose vigorously into his handkerchief. 'I remember a bit of poetry at St Emmanuel's, something about the old blue faded flower of day.'

'Oh yes,' she said, mocking him.

'And there's bluebird, bluebell –'

'Blue-bottle,' said Marge, and he had to laugh.

There was a great storm of applause on the wireless to greet the end of the song. They both glanced up at the ceiling, hoping Nellie wouldn't think they were making a holy show of themselves.

When it was quite dark in the kitchen he went again up the stairs and whispered : 'Nellie, Nellie, anything you want?'

She didn't reply. He tip-toed to her bed and she was lying with her hand tucked under her cheek, her body tidy under the counterpane – beneath the bed, half peeping, her shoes with the laces spread.

*　　　*　　　*

There was a row of women standing in front of the long mirror in the ladies' waiting room, spitting into little boxes and stabbing eye-black on their lashes. Uncle Jack said they came from all over England, hitch-hiking, making for the American army bases. He said they were mad for the money the Yanks threw about. 'They're wicked women,' he said, spitting the words out through puritanical lips, and Rita had believed him. But she knew better now : it wasn't the money, it was a search for love, the sort she had found with Ira. The women looked common enough with their bleached hair and their mouths pouting as they put on lipstick, but they weren't wicked.

' 'Scuse me,' she said politely, edging her way in and resting her handbag on the ledge.

Her head scarf was saturated with the rain. Underneath, her hair was limp, crushed to her skull as if oiled. There was a girl with a paper bag full of sand, one leg on the leather seating of the bench. She was rubbing the yellow grains into her skin trying to simulate stockings. The sand fell in a little heap to the floor. Rita wiped her face with a handkerchief and squeezed Creme Simone on to her nose and her cheeks. She had found the cream and a box of orange powder in Auntie Marge's drawer, but there wasn't a powder puff. Carefully she dipped the end of her hankie into the box and dabbed it on her face. When she was finished she didn't know that she liked herself. If her hair would only dry it would give her a softer look, less exposed.

Ira wasn't outside, under the clock, as they had arranged, but then it was raining and he was possibly near the taxi rank or by the barrier, or in the main hall, or the lavatory, combing his hair to look nice for her. She looked everywhere and stood outside the Gentlemen's convenience for almost ten minutes until a sailor came out, with his collar flapping upwards behind his head like a blue sail, and stared at her as if he knew her. He was small and quite old and she didn't want Ira to see her with him – he might think she was man-

217

crazy. She went back into the waiting-room and sat down. There was a different batch of women, newly arrived off the Warrington train. They slumped dishevelled on the black-leather seating, smoking cigarettes, chewing gum. There was a woman that reminded her of Aunt Nellie : the droop to the mouth, the expression in her eyes beneath a tangle of wet black hair. She wore a bow of crumpled white satin, one end hanging forlornly over her plucked eyebrow. She never took her eyes off Rita, not even when children ran in screaming through the open doorway, banging sticks on the oil-cloth of the centre table. When they rolled on the floor, Rita could see the marks of insect bites, pin-points of scarlet clear up the thin legs to the gape of their torn knickers. She could smell the children : a mixture of damp old clothing and dirt, and something sickly like the stored grain in the warehouses; and she sat quite still with one hand curled into a fist as the lavatory lady ran in from the wash-room and ordered them out.

The woman with the bow in her hair made Rita feel uncomfortable. She imagined that it was written all over her face that she had found someone to love her, that she had Ira. She longed for him to come to the door and call her name and she would run to him and all the tired and mucky women on the benches would realise she was different from them. But he didn't come, and after a while she walked out into the station, which was crowded now with soldiers and airman and shrieking women, for the trains ran too and fro between the American base outside Warrington and the army barracks at Freshfield and the aerodrome at Woodvale. The military police patrolled in pairs, swaggering in their white helmets, swinging their truncheons from their wrists on little bands of leather. She went down the steps past the taxi-rank under the arch of the station entrance into Stanley Street. For a time she stood in the doorway of the philately shop, sheltered from the rain, absorbed in a page of German stamps imprinted with Hitler's head. But for him, she thought, she would never have met Ira, never been happy. Uncle Jack

218

said he was a maniac, the monster of the world. She thought he looked rather neat and gentlemanly with his smart black tie and his hair slicked down over one eye. Now and then she popped her head out of the doorway and stared down the road at the station. She went lower down the street to the chemists, looking at all the funny objects in the window : rubber trusses and surgical braces and adverts for pills and lotions. There was a photograph of a man in his combs flexing his muscles like a boxer. There was a great brown nozzle with a ball at one end and holes in the head. 'Whirling Spray,' she read, but there was nothing to say what it was for. It was too big for an ear syringe. She supposed it was for something rude, like the things described in Auntie Marge's hidden book. She didn't like to be seen staring into the window, and there was a tiny sensation of fright just beginning to grow somewhere in her head or her heart. Why hadn't he come yet? Please God, she prayed, don't let him be dead. Make it be the right place and the right day. Bending her head against the gusts of rain she walked back to the station. He was there, lounging against the soot-covered wall under the giant wrought-iron clock.

'Oh,' she cried, laughing with relief, 'I was beginning to think –'

'The train was late. The guard wouldn't shift till some of the guys got out of the carriage.'

He didn't attempt to kiss her cheek, but she was too grateful at his arrival to be discouraged. She did recognise that some part of him resisted her. She saw in his cool untroubled eyes an absence of warmth as if he didn't realise that he had been waiting all his life to find her. He was slow and unaware, locked in the protracted torpor of adolescence.

'We can go to the movies,' he said, looking at her rain-soaked clothes and her face yellow with powder.

'I can't go to the flicks now. It's too late. I can't be late home – me Auntie Nellie's poorly.'

She loved walking with him, holding his arm. She hardly

219

noticed the rain or how cold it had grown. In her head they spoke to one another tenderly, talking about the future, how they loved each other, moving through the town, he with his coat collar turned up against the wind, she with her head scarf trailing about her shoulders – arm in arm, completely silent in the Double Summertime. They walked almost to the Pier Head, sheltering under the black arch of the overhead railway that ran alongside the docks.

'Is it like home?' she wanted to know, listening to the sound of a train rumbling above them, thinking it was like a film she'd seen about America. The municipal gardens in front of the Pier were deserted. The green benches dripped water. Spray rose above the river wall and blew like smoke across the bushes and the grass.

'It ain't nothing like home,' he said.

They walked back to the town, thankful to have the wind behind them.

'Don't you wish we were in the country again?' she asked, but he didn't answer: he wouldn't commit himself. If it had been the aunt's, she would have taken the silence for moodiness. But he, she knew, used words sparingly. When the time came he would know how to talk to her. There were numerous bars and cafés, but she didn't want to share him, nor did she think Auntie Nellie would approve of such places.

'We ought to shelter from the rain,' he said. 'I guess you're soaked right through.'

'I don't mind,' she said truthfully, and he stopped quite still and touched the shoulder of her macintosh. 'You sure feel like a drowned rat.'

She stopped breathing with the hurt, blinking her eyes, not knowing where to look. Everything was suddenly cold and bleak, the black buildings rising into the grey sky, the street filled with strangers wrapped in one another's arms.

'I've got to get my tram now,' she said, and in her head he pleaded with her: Please don't leave me now – you're pretty as a picture, you're lovely as a rose garden.

220

They waited in the tram shelter outside Owen Owen's and she studied the angle of his jaw as he turned to listen to the music of a dance band from the Forces Club across the street. When she boarded the tram he waved his hand in farewell, and she sat stiffly, holding her handbag to her chest, watching him for one brief moment as he sprinted across the street, before the tram clanged its bell and tore her from him.

6

Rita was in the first stage of her nightmare. As yet she had made no sound. She lay perfectly flat with her hands outside the sheets.

She was in the back of the Wolsely car, the green card table in position . . . They were driving down the long road of detached houses. Early evening . . . she looked through the glass at the gardens. The silver lamp post . . . the stretch of fencing . . . now the house. Windows closed to the air . . . the wire basket full of lobelia hanging from the roof of the porch. Inside were the people she cared for . . . never seen . . . they sat somewhere inside on high polished chairs. In the upstairs window a plaster girl patting the ears of a dog with a feathery tail . . . sweet peas cut from the garden in a bowl on the hall table . . . grandfather clock with the hands at eight o'clock . . . a statue in bronze of two men wrestling with an angel . . . a row of tins on the pantry shelf, salmon, soup, pears. A round window cut like a porthole in the front door . . . a little frilly skirt of curtain . . . they passed the house and drove into darkness.

She stirred in the bed, brought her arm up over her face.

She was watching the sky roll down into place at the end of the road. The painted poplars straightened and stood still. The engine of the car ticked over . . . waiting . . . the red

222

penny sun slid into view . . . she tapped the glass partition with a little stick . . . the car drove slowly toward the fence. The house deserted . . . the people gone away on holiday . . . the locks broken on the door . . . the garden gate swinging. Silver gone from the sideboard . . . knives ripped from the green baize box . . . decanters of cut glass torn from the back of the dark cupboard . . . the statue of the naked men toppled from its stand . . . jewellery missing from the upstairs room . . . the good diamond ring, the watch with the platinum bracelet, the glass beads from Venice. And a hat with a pin, speared like a roasting chicken on the banister rail in the hall.

She almost woke now, she tried, she fought to get out of the darkness, opening her mouth and beginning to whimper.

The car crawled to the edge of the kerb . . . slowed to a halt beyond the silver lamp post . . . out on the front lawn among the dahlias the pieces of furniture . . . the polished chairs . . . the grandfather clock . . . the wrestling men flashing fire from the sun . . . a body flung like a doll among the sweet williams . . . a man hanging over the fence with his head dripping blood . . . the people she knew . . . the loved ones . . .

She screamed, trying to get out of the bed, drowning in waves of sleep. A long moment of pressure, heart beating, the blood pounding in her ears, dizzy like a heat wave.

'It's alright our Rita, it's alright Lamb, hush up our Rita, it's alright.'

She woke, trying to focus the dark cold bedroom, seeing the dull cylinders of Margo's curlers touched by a rind of light at the window.

'I can't,' she said. 'It's not my fault.'

*   *   *

When Nellie had recovered, she made one or two adjust-

223

ments to the front room. She moved upstairs to the box-room the little rosewood table and the china figure of a rustic boy resting his chin on his hand. She would have liked to store the sideboard too, but she felt Marge would notice, and it was too heavy to shift without help. She wasn't entirely sure in her mind why it was important to make such a change, to disturb articles of furniture that had taken up their allotted space in the best front room for so many years – whether it was to decrease their chance of decay or to test her reaction to the disappearance of familiar objects. Either way she felt that she had accomplished something. Apart from the truckle bed that had always been there, the box-room, though small, could accommodate other pieces : the shelved mirror with the curved frame, the foot-stool embroidered in faded silks, the bamboo stand which displayed the aspidistra plant. She fully intended to remove all these items – gradually, so as not to cause comment, over a period of months. And to help Rita to find a nice young man and settle down she would make her a whole new wardrobe of clothes, dresses for the winter, a costume, a new coat with a fur collar. She had expected the child to be less than enthusiastic, but she seemed to welcome the suggestion. She spent several evenings poring over pattern books looking for ideas. Jack was astonished when Nellie asked him if he could lay his hands on some extra clothing coupons. Rita said she would go with Nellie to Birkenhead market to choose material, but it would have to be early on the Saturday.

'I suppose you're off out in the evening,' said Margo.

'Yes, I am.'

'With Cissie Baines, I expect,' said Margo sarcastically, but the child only nodded her head passively and went on turning the pages of a book.

They took the mid-day ferry from the Pier Head, leaving Margo at home to do the shopping. She didn't argue. She dreaded lest she should upset Nellie and be forced to spend another few days washing the pots and cooking the meagre scraps of food.

224

Rita went upstairs on deck while Nellie made herself comfortable in the saloon, sinking into the dimpling black leather of the seats that lined the wall, following the curve of the boat. She wriggled herself backwards into position, as if she sat in a dentist's chair, her feet not quite touching the floor, with a clear view of the Pier Head and the gulls gliding outside the glass. She liked the throb of the engines beneath her, the low whine of agony as the boat shuddered and chaffed the rope buffers of the landing stage, the gush of tumbled water as it moved backwards and swung in a wide circle to face the opposite side of the river. There were brave souls marching the deck: a student from the university with his scarf blowing in the air behind him like a woolly streamer, a man clamping his hands to his head as the wind tore at his trilby hat.

It reminded her of the time Jack had sent them to Ireland for a holiday. He'd paid for it. He knew some hotel outside Dublin that he'd been to years ago at the time of the Black and Tans, but he couldn't afford for them to have a cabin and she'd sat up all night on deck under a tarpaulin, with little Rita asleep on her lap – everyone moaning as the ship rolled, for all the world as if they were immigrants on their way to America. They went on a train along the coast and at the station there were some taxis and a funny old-fashioned carriage drawn by horses. And there was Marge, the daft beggar, bustling past the ordinary vehicles and bundling them into the buggy cart, driving through the streets to the hotel, swaying and bouncing, making a right show of themselves. It was a lovely holiday. It was nice to watch Rita running in and out of the waves with her little dress tucked into her knickers. Of course, Marge made a fool of herself, getting off with a commercial traveller from Birmingham, saying she was going off on the bus to Bray, and her and Rita walking past a café in the afternoon and seeing Marge and him sitting in the the window eating egg-and-cress sandwiches: caught red-handed in a yellow straw-hat with red roses on the brim and a piece of watercress stuck to her lip.

Rita searched for Nellie as the bell clanged for the passengers to disembark. Through the window of the saloon she saw her aunt's corpse-like face etched on the darkness of the interior. She was smiling with her eyes closed, as if she was happy, the clasped hands on her lap threaded through the strings of her shopping bag. Rita tapped on the glass. Nellie opened her eyes immediately, stared uncertainly, then came in a little unsteady run to the swing doors, clasping the brass rail for support.

'My word it's rough,' she said. 'You look like the Wreck of the Hesperus.'

She hadn't been to Birkenhead for two years and was appalled at the change: the air of decay and obliteration. The municipal gardens were laid to waste. Gone were the roses and the shrubs, the drinking fountain with its marble basin – nothing now but two slopes of sparse grass; the railings carted away; dogs doing their business where once the tulips had swayed in scarlet ranks.

Rita wanted black worsted for a dress. She didn't care what else, but she wanted the black.

'It's a bit old,' said Nellie.

'I want pleats in the skirt and a white collar and white cuffs.'

'Sure you don't want some lace for a frilly cap and apron?' said Nellie tartly. 'Then we could get you a job in the Kardomah.'

But Rita insisted. Nellie bought four yards of black, five of grey with a stripe in it and a piece of pink velvet.

They had a cup of tea standing up at a stall and Rita wanted to buy a meat pie.

'You won't, Miss,' said Nellie.

'It's me own money.'

'No.'

Nellie had always impressed on both Rita and Marge that there were two things they must never do: never sit down on somebody else's lav and never eat a shop-bought meat pie.

The girl seemed to go into a sulk. On her face a look of suffering as if she had been mortally wounded. She stood there, her face shut to all approaches. Only her eyes were alive, watching the crowd of shoppers in the market square with a peculiar intensity, as if she was searching for someone.

*　　*　　*

Mrs Mander told Margo that things had grown very serious between Chuck and Valerie. There just might be an engagement announcement soon. It would mean a new dress for Valerie if Nellie was up to it. Something romantic, embroidered with sequins to catch the light. She found the ravaged interest of Margo's expression disconcerting: she looked like a woman gutted by fire – she was wearing a dress of a slightly charred texture, several sizes too large for her, with panels of silver let into the bodice. There was a scorch mark at the shoulder and a diamante clasp at the hip. Her fatigued eyes glittered with excitement as she told Mrs Mander how thrilled she was for Valerie. In the fulfilment of the girl's dreams she imagined that she herself moved one step nearer to happiness. Nellie would make the dress, she was sure – why, no one could stop her. She lit a cigarette with trembling fingers and went to fetch the pattern books from under the stairs so that they could begin at once their search for the ideal gown. Forgotten were the preparations for the evening meal, and Mrs Mander was too polite to say it was Nellie's opinion she had come for, even though Marge was younger and could be said to be more modern in her outlook. There were certain indications of hysteria in Marge's appearance, a lack of judgment: the cocktail dress in which she had answered the door, the fur coat she wore to work with white wedge-heeled shoes. There was the occasion, never to be forgotten, when the Dutch seaman billeted on them in the first year of the war had given her a length of cloth from the East and she had gone secretly

227

behind Nellie's back and had it made up into a sarong – wearing it at a Women's Guild night, with a slit right up the leg and all her suspenders showing beneath the baggy edge of her green silk drawers.

'Nellie's gone to get material for Rita from Birkenhead market. She's suddenly taken an interest in clothes,' said Margo.

'Well, she would, wouldn't she?' said Mrs Mander. 'Valerie says she's started courting. She saw them down town last Saturday.'

Margo stared at her. Once her mouth moved perceptibly, as if she was about to say something, but no words came; she wet her dry lips with her tongue. Mrs Mander was busy studying a three-quarter length dress with a little matching bolero.

'It's nice,' she said. 'We could put sequins on the coatee.' She looked up sharply and asked: 'What do you think of him?'

'Well, we hardly know him – she's only been going out with him a short time.' She prayed she was accurate, that Mrs Mander wouldn't catch on.

'Well, you spoke to him at our house.'

'What did you make of him?' asked Margo, stalling for time, trying to remember which young man in particular Rita had sat with. It could only be the fellow in the wardrobe, the long bony lad with the big feet. She felt enormous relief at being able to visualise him – that it wasn't some unknown brutal stranger doing nasty things to Rita.

'Valerie says her Chuck doesn't know him very well. He came along that night because he'd been seeing to Chuck's jeep.'

She implied, Margo felt, that he was in some way inferior to Chuck, less of a catch.

'He's a nice lad,' said Margo. 'Very polite. He knows his manners. His father's got quite a business in the city.'

'What city?' asked Mrs Mander mercilessly and Margo

said it was Washington, near the White House, and was afraid she had made a fool of herself and that the White House was actually in New York.

'That's nice,' said Mrs Mander. 'You know, with the lovely figure our Valerie's got, it's a crying shame to have a jacket.'

'That's true,' Margo said, and wished she would go away quickly before too many things were said. She had known all along that Rita was being secretive, coming home with her stockings ripped to pieces and going down town on a Saturday night and returning drenched to the skin and worn out. That's why she'd had her nightmare. The deceit had preyed on her mind. She herself had tried to keep things from Nellie all her life. She didn't blame Rita, but she was hurt that the girl hadn't confided in her. She felt resentful to be shut out from excitement and intrigue. She had tried in her fashion to shield Rita from Nellie's influence, to add a little gaiety to the narrow years spent in the narrow house.

'I'll take the books back with me,' said Mrs Mander. 'Tell Nellie I called.'

And she was off out through the door rushing back to the lovely Valerie to tell her that Rita hadn't let on at home she was meeting a soldier.

*   *   *

Margo might have told Jack if she had known more herself about the lad in the wardrobe. She longed to be able to tell him that Rita had confided in her. It would make her seem mature in Jack's eyes: it was always to Nellie that he turned for advice.

Jack kept complaining of a stomach ache. Nellie made him a glass of hot water to sip before going up the road to congratulate Valerie.

'Are you going now?' asked Margo, alarmed. She didn't want Mrs Mander blurting it all out to Nellie.

'If I have your permission,' said Nellie sharply, tucking her hair under her hat.

'Don't you think,' said Margo, when Nellie had gone, 'that we had a rum childhood – I mean, thinking about it –'

'Rum,' said Jack, not understanding.

'Restricted. The way Mother was – all them rules, going to church.'

'What rules?'

'Don't you think we were damaged?'

'Don't talk daft.'

He sat up, clutching his belly, filled with irritation at the way she carried on. Whenever Marge started to talk in this fashion it made him angry: he was defending someone, something, but he didn't know what. It was like when Lord Haw Haw had been on the wireless – he wanted to jump to his feet and wave the flag.

'We were never given a chance,' said Margo. 'Never. All that church-going and being respectable – you can never get away from it.'

'Church never did anyone any harm,' he said hotly.

'You haven't been inside a church for donkey's years.'

'It never did any harm,' he repeated doggedly. 'It might have been better if you had listened to what the good book said.'

'I did listen – I did nothing else. Always being told what to do, always being got at. Doing what Mother said was best.'

'Mother was a wonderful woman,' he cried, looking at her with hostility. 'She brought us up never to owe a penny, never to ask anybody for anything.'

'She asked Nellie for plenty. It was Nellie that did all the work. She walked in mother's shadow. She still does.'

'Oh, get off,' he said, hating the sight of her: the naked face with the eyes like an actress on the stage, the mouth spitting rubbish.

'And what about Rita?' She knew she was annoying him – the trick he had of twisting his head sharply as if someone had

230

fired an Ack-ack gun behind his ear – but she had to say it. 'She's just like Nellie, really. Keeping herself to herself, never saying anything important, just being proper.'

She hoped it was true : she couldn't bear to think of Rita getting into trouble – the shame of it, the gossip in the street.

'If our Rita is half the woman Nellie is, she's got nothing to be ashamed of.'

'But it's different times,' Margo cried. 'It's the war. People aren't the same. That sort of person isn't needed any more. The past is gone, Jack. Things are different now.'

'What sort of person?' he asked her, outraged, sensing mother and Nellie relegated to the scrap heap.

'People who had to be told what to do. There's things happening now that nobody can tell you what to do about. You can't act the same. That's why our Nellie gets so bad-tempered – she knows it's not the same.'

'Where would you have been without our Nellie?' he shouted, jumping to his feet.

The small blue indentures on either temple, marks of the forceps at his birth, darkened as blood suffused his face.

'God knows,' she cried, facing him in the unlovely room, 'but I mightn't have been all on me own.'

She trembled, filled with pity for herself and indignation that he thought so little of her. He was marching up and down the floor, twitching his head, struggling to contain his anger.

Margo was spent. She sat down at the table blinking her eyes to stop the tears from falling. She wanted to say : Your Rita, our Rita is going out with a foreigner, meeting him at this moment, going into shop doorways with him. She wanted to reproach him for stopping her belonging to Mr Aveyard, for the chances he had made her miss in the past. It was all his fault – his and Nellie's. All the rubbish he talked about wanting to go and live on a boat after the war, travel, see how the other half lived – his remembrance of poetry, his senti-mentality. It was all me eye and Peggy Martin. He was bound, like Nellie, hand and foot to the old way of life. It mattered

231

to him what the neighbours said, if he caused gossip, if he owed money, if he seemed too much to be alive. He hated to have to look inside himself – the wicked women standing on Lime Street, the immorality, the heart beating raw and exposed like the pigs he slaughtered.

'I'm off,' he said. 'I'm not well. I don't need you blethering on, the way I feel.'

And he went. Tying his muffler about his neck in a paddy, squashing his worn Homburg hat on to his head.

'Why d'you think we're sitting here in the cold?' she shouted, following him up the hall, ashamed she was driving him away. 'All because Nellie won't have a fire in summer! I'm sick of it. Don't you blame me, Jack, if there's trouble.'

Out he went, slamming the door behind him, leaving her exhausted in the hall.

*   *   *

Rita came back before Nellie – like a dog that had been whipped, her face asking for help.

'Oh dear,' said Margo, going through to put on the kettle. 'You silly little twerp, why didn't you tell me?'

'I want to die,' said Rita, dropping her coat to the floor and gazing about the room as if she was demented. He hadn't turned up at the station, he hadn't come to the bus stop, he hadn't said he would see her again. He walked away to the sound of the dance-band and she never saw him again.

'What happened?' asked Margo, wanting a full explanation before Nellie returned home full of talk about Valerie and her glowing secure future.

'He said I was a drowned rat.'

'Oh, he didn't!'

'He said: "Don't you ever wear nothing pretty, no dresses with frills?" '

'Oh, luv.'

'He said I was pretty as a picture, pretty as a rose garden.'

'Oh you are, little lamb, little pet, you are.'

'He never – he said I was a drowned rat.'

There was a storm of weeping, Margo crying with her, recalling other words from other men, time after time, years ago. They clung to each other, voices resonant with grief.

'When we were in the country, in the garden . . . he tried to – touch me. I pushed him away.'

'What did he do to you?'

'He tried to – well, he touched me – here.' She indicated with her hand the small swell of her breast. 'I pushed him away, Auntie.'

'Oh my God!' said Margo, rising to her feet, feeling old and responsible. She made tea and told Rita to wipe her eyes in case Nellie came back. Like something she had heard on the wireless, one of those educational talks late at night, she lectured her : 'Now look here, our Rita,' putting her heart into it, as if there was one more chance, the very last chance. 'You got to be decent, you got to have respect, but if you love him you have to give.'

In her mind a picture of George Bickerton undoing the buttons of his jacket, the drooping moustache painted on the boy's face, the unsure arms encircling her; the way his body trembled, the fear she felt, the stranger she was to her own flesh. She didn't know what to do, and neither did he. Never been talked to, never read any books, never known what it was to take off her clothes without turning away. A mist of ignorance, of guilty fumblings; it didn't matter about the church and that they were allowed to be in bed together. Nellie was in the next room, the blankets over her head. There was no excitement, no joy. It was the doctor tapping her chest, it was an illness.

'You mustn't lose him because you're feared,' she cried. 'You mustn't, Rita. I've read books since – it's natural, you shouldn't listen to Nellie. God knows, girl. Look at me – I'm a casualty.' She held her arms out dramatically as if she was on a cross.

233

And Rita did listen, she did appear to take notice: concentrating on her aunt, the black eyes shining like marble, the mouth grimacing with feeling, the thick body ensnared in the over-large cocktail dress.

* * *

Rita wrote a letter to Ira in her lunch hour.

> Dear Ira,
>   I'm sorry if I annoyed you in any way but I do love you. I waited for you at the station for two hours, but you did not come. Please meet me next Saturday at 6.30 under the clock. I have got my Auntie Nellie to make me some pretty clothes so that you will be proud of me.
> Your loving Rita.

* * *

She wanted to put kisses and even draw a heart, but it seemed common. After work she knocked at the Manders' front door and asked to see Valerie. Mrs Mander was curious to see her and eager to know about her young man.

'Lives in Washington, I believe,' she said, and Rita nodded, because she couldn't admit she didn't know where he lived, or how old he was, whether he had a mother and a father. 'He's got a dog and a goat and a horse,' she said, 'and a hen that sits by the fire.'

'In the city?' said Mrs Mander, taken aback.

Rita went into the front room with Valerie, bent her head shyly, twisted her hands about in their grubby white gloves, standing by the piano with the photograph of George, debonair in his sailor uniform.

'I want you to give a letter to Chuck,' she said.

'Oh yes,' said Valerie.

'Me and Ira had a quarrel.'

'I'm sorry about that.'

'Could you ask your Chuck to give him this letter?'

She took out the letter from her handbag.

'My Chuck doesn't know him very well, you know. I doubt if he sees him much in the camp. They're not buddies.'

It sounded like a tree about to bloom : Chuck and Ira on the same bough.

'I'd be ever so grateful,' Rita said.

She felt close to the older girl, dressed in such good taste, her plump left arm encircled in a bangle of shiny metal, her eyes sympathetic, not quite assured.

'Do you and Chuck have upsets?' she asked, trying to identify herself with them. 'Have you ever fallen out?'

'Everyone does,' Valerie said. 'Don't worry, luv.'

She was curious how Rita had ever gone out with the American in the first place. Rita was so put down, so without passion, living all her life with the old women down the road. As a child she had never played out in the street, never put her dolls to sleep on the step, never hung around the chip shop on Priory Road. In the air-raid shelter she wore a hat belonging to Auntie Nellie as if she was in church.

She stowed the letter away in the pocket of her jacket – not carelessly, with feeling.

*　　　*　　　*

Rita was brighter than she had been for days. Setting the table for tea, humming as Aunt Nellie cooked the spam fritters on the stove. When Margo came in she couldn't wait to tell her what she had done, running into the hall when she heard the key turn in the lock, whispering in her ear that she had written a letter and given it to Valerie.

'That's good,' said Margo, tired from her day and wanting to sit down. Her moment of elation having passed with the night, she had spent the entire day brooding over the advice she had given the girl. She wasn't sure of herself any more, she wanted to share the responsibility. She sat by the grate, and her handbag dropped to the floor and she let it lie.

'Sam, Sam,' said Rita, 'pick up thy musket,' and she and Nellie broke into little trills of laughter, the room filling with the smell of melting dripping.

*   *   *

Jack's shop was in Moss Street on the other side of the Park. When he saw Nellie, his eyes widened with concern at her having made the journey.

'You shouldn't have,' he scolded. 'Bogle told you to take it easy.'

'I wanted the exercise,' she said. 'I'm that busy on Rita's new clothes I had to force meself out of the house. I was straining me back.'

He sat her in the little cubicle at the back of the shop, perched on the stool behind the cash register, while he served his customers. He wore an apron, that Nellie made him, over his suit, with his coat sleeves rolled up. His small hands were always red and chapped from continually being doused under the cold tap in the back – he couldn't bear the contamination of the raw meat. He would have taken Nellie upstairs to rest, but he knew when his back was turned she would be washing his breakfast pots and tidying his bed.

'Was that Ethel Morrisey?' she called, when an old woman wearing carpet slippers had gone shuffling across the sawdust to the door.

'That's right.'

'By gum, she's aged.'

'We all have,' he said, dipping his head, in his Homburg hat, to avoid contact with the two rabbits hanging on a rail above the counter, bending over the marble slab industriously with a wet cloth in his hand.

Outside the window the errand boy balanced his bicycle

236

against the kerbstone and came in whistling. He had red hair and a great bulging forehead over which his cap wouldn't fit.'

'Hello, Tommy,' Nellie called, smiling and nodding at him through the glass of the cubicle. 'How's your mother keeping?'

'Me mam's fine,' he said, keeping his eyes down to his boots, hating to be noticed.

Jack told him to skin one of the rabbits, while he took Nellie upstairs and made her a cup of tea. He thought it would be nice to wrap one up for her and pop it in her shopping bag without her knowing. He had some difficulty bringing her down from the stool; she clutched at him as if she was drowning, leaving a pale dusting of talcum powder on the upper sleeve of his jacket.

She tried to shut her eyes to the state of the living room. She couldn't expect a man to keep it decent, and she supposed he did his best. It made her a little sad, the disarray, the neglect, as if he was homeless, about to move on; there were some things still in boxes and never unwrapped. And he never would move on, not now. It was a funny way to end up – he was a bigoted man in his views, and his surroundings were such a contradiction. He couldn't stand gipsies or Jews, or Catholics for that matter, and here he was in a pig-sty. In his person he was very particular, though: his ears, his nails, the round collars he took himself to be washed and starched at the Chinese laundry over the road.

'Whatever are you doing with that?' she asked, looking in bewilderment at the wind-up gramophone removed from its place behind the door and set in the centre of the hearth-rug.

'I was thinking maybe our Rita could use it. You know, when she's got friends in, now she's of an age.'

It was just an idea he had. He didn't think it would come to anything. He had never met any friends she might have had. Watching Nellie turning over the pile of heavy records, wrinkling her nose as he held one or two to the light to read the labels.

237

'They're a bit old,' he said, 'not very up to date.'

She was touched by his attempt to do something nice for Rita.

'Does it still go?' she wanted to know, wiping her hands together to free them of dust; and he told her it might, when he'd tinkered with it a bit – the spring seemed sound and that was the important part.

He made the tea and she sipped it, holding her cup with her little finger extended, as mother had taught her. She told him about Valerie Mander's imminent engagement, what Cyril Mander thought about it, when they were going to buy the ring, how they would have to celebrate. He nodded his head expressing interest, but she knew he detested Cyril Mander, and he didn't much care for Valerie or for Americans. He was narrow about people from foreign parts. He said they should have joined in the fight in 1939 and not waited so long. He said it was the Russians that were winning the war, not Uncle Sam. She often wondered what his attitude would be if he came face to face with a real live Russian, whether he would be so approving of them in the flesh.

'Chuck's a nice lad,' she said. 'You couldn't take offence at him.'

'It's as they say,' he said dourly. 'There's only three things wrong with them Yanks. They're overpaid, oversexed and over here.'

He got up saying he had to go downstairs to keep an eye on the shop, and left her to finish her tea. She looked at the mahogany cabinet and imagined what Marge would have to say about Jack's gesture and his choice of records: 'Just a Song at Twilight', 'Little Man You've Had a Busy Day'. She could just see the look in her eyes, the way her hands would fly up in a gesture of contempt. She put her cup down on the mantelpiece and peered at the photograph of Jack's wife with baby Rita in her arms – holding the infant wrapped in a shawl, as if she was scared she was going to drop it any moment.

Just then she heard the boy calling 'Eh Missus, come down quick!' And she trotted smartly enough down the uncarpeted stairs, holding her hand to her heart, seeing Jack as pale as death behind the chopping block.

'There's been a mishap,' he said, 'with the cleaver.'

'Where, you daft beggar?' she cried, fierce with shock. 'Where've you cut yourself, Jack?'

'Not me,' he said. 'Him,' looking at young Tommy who was standing at the foot of the stairs with his hands behind his back.

'It's nothing, Missus,' said Tommy. 'It were him that were took bad,' and he went to the back of the shop and put his hand under the tap.

Nellie made him run water over his finger till the cold almost froze him and the bleeding partially stopped. She struggled upstairs and found some sheeting to tear into a bandage. When she had wrapped his wound she told him to get off home and let his mam have a look at it. Already as he went out of the door the rag was darkening with blood. She felt irritated with Jack, slumped there behind the counter, perspiration beading his forehead – like a big soft girl, his face the colour of putty beneath his old black hat.

'Go and wet your face,' she said. 'It will bring you round.'

She couldn't think how he managed his business, feeling the way he did; slaughtering pigs, chopping up lambs, pulling the liver and the lungs out of animals.

The brown rabbit lay on its side, head partially severed, legs stretched out as if it still ran.

7

ALL Saturday morning Nellie stayed at her machine, driving herself to finish one dress or another.

'I just want me black dress,' said Rita, looking in dismay at the grey cloth with the stripe and the pink velvet alternately running under the needle. Margo did the shopping again because she knew how much Rita counted on a new dress for the evening.

In the afternoon Nellie said she had a headache, and with consternation Rita cried: 'Won't you finish me frock then, Auntie Nellie?'

And Nellie said: 'Steady on, Murgatroyd, I'm only human. What's the stampede?'

'I wanted me new frock for tonight. I'm meeting Cissie and I want me new black frock.'

'Well, you can't get blood out of a stone,' said Nellie crossly. 'It's not ready.'

'But you said last night it was nearly finished.'

Nellie couldn't make out what was wrong with the girl, standing there with her face all twisted up with desperation, when only two weeks ago she wouldn't let them buy her a new dress for love nor money.

'You wouldn't let me try it on you,' she said. 'You said you had to wash your hair.'

Rita couldn't bear to be fitted. The touch of the dry tips of her aunt's fingers, as they brushed the circle of her arm or smoothed the material of the shoulder, filled her with

240

revulsion. She had to grit her teeth to stop from crying out her distaste. She had lived in constant intimacy with the elderly woman, soaped her white back in the rusty bath upstairs, nuzzled close to the flannel warmth of her at night. She couldn't understand this sudden aversion, when Aunt Nellie was being so kind, when she was working her fingers to the bone. At half-past four, when she knew it was quite hopeless, she ran upstairs and looked inside her wardrobe : the velvet, the blue satin, two years old, her day dresses, an old skirt – nothing pretty, nothing with frills.

'Oh please God,' she whispered, lying down on the narrow bed and burying her face in the pillow.

She thought with self-disgust of how she had refused a new frock from George Henry Lees, how she had nothing frivolous, no necklaces, no lace hankies, no shiny bangle for her arm. Marge came into her room and said that with a bit of adjustment they could do something with a brown silk dress in Nellie's wardrobe.

'It's old,' she said, 'but it's got a low neckline, it's very flattering.'

'I can't wear Auntie Nellie's dress,' cried Rita. 'I'll just have to make do with what I've got.'

But Margo brought the dress through on a hanger and asked her to try it on.

'Just try it, luv. Give it a chance.'

And it was smooth to the touch : it did make her feel silky and pampered, though it didn't fit.

'Look at the shoulders,' she said. 'Look at the waist.'

'Well, you'll have your coat on over it. I can pin it at the back.'

Marge combed her hair into a bun at the back like Valerie Mander sometimes wore. She took the stiff brown bow from the belt of the dress and pinned it with a kirby grip to cover the little tendrils of hair that wouldn't stay in place. She gathered the slack of the dress into a pleat and secured it with two safety pins. They hadn't any vaseline for her eyebrows,

241

so Margo went downstairs and came back with a small smear of margarine on her little finger and it worked quite as well.

'What if he doesn't come?' said Rita, putting two small circles of lipstick on either cheek and rubbing it in with her finger.

'Oh, he'll come,' Margo reassured her, thinking it would be best in the long run if he didn't, best for Jack and Nellie. As soon as the girl was safely out of the house she was going to tell Nellie and rid herself of the awful weight of responsibility.

'Put some colour on your mouth, girl,' she said; 'you look like a corpse,' and could have bitten her tongue at the stricken expression on Rita's face: the child's forehead wrinkling up, the hair dragged severely back behind her ears, which were small and bloodless. Marge fetched the gold button ear-rings that Jack had given her last Christmas. She wished she could find the pearl necklace, but instead she brought a link of glass beads, orange and green, to clasp about Rita's throat.

'You look older,' she said. 'Look at yourself.'

Rita wanted to be glossy like Valerie, rich and glowing and warm. She saw her face with the dabs of pink on either cheek, the glint of gold at her ears, the green glass beads above the brown dress. In profile the beak of her nose was over-shadowed by her jutting lips, painted purple.

'I'm not pretty, am I?' she said in despair, and Margo said: 'Why, you look lovely, you really are a bonny girl.'

And Rita had to believe her, against her better judgment, because how otherwise could she survive, or go to meet him, or anything? She was dry and faded and slender in the brown dress, with her bold mouth pouting in distress. Being seventeen she couldn't imagine how much to be envied was the childish droop to her shoulders, the tender curve of her throat under the cheap glass beads, the gauche walk she achieved in Marge's best wedge-heeled shoes. It was only a quarter-past five and Jack had come in. She could hear him in the hall shouting to Nellie that someone or other had died. She was hungry, unable to eat, lethargic, unable to sit still. Above all she longed to see Ira and feel that he loved her.

'I'll go,' she said to Margo, pulling on her newly washed white gloves and the macintosh with the flared back. She wanted to have time in the waiting-room at the station to smooth her hair and make sure her dress wasn't hanging down at the back. She said goodbye to Jack and Nellie, flustered by their comments – how smart she looked, quite the young lady. Knowing they weren't the right words, she wanted them to say she was pretty. She wouldn't take the two half-crowns Jack offered her. She said she had money of her own. She hadn't noticed before how old he was, how pinched his face was beneath the familiar hat, as he slid the money into his pocket. At the front door she was compelled to turn back and kiss her Auntie Nellie – the merest brush of her purple lips against the woman's powdered cheek. Even so, she left a mauve imprint to the right of Nellie's nose.

*　　*　　*

She kissed Ira on the lips, standing on tiptoe and screwing her eyes up – out of gratitude and to show she wasn't prudish.

'You got my letter, then?' she said.

'Yeah,' he mumbled. 'That guy gave it to me.'

'Don't you know him, then? Isn't he a friend of yours?'

'I don't reckon I know him that well,' and he looked at her hair and away again and touched her throat with one finger and said, 'You didn't bury this one, then?' and she said 'No,' and was glad for once it was not raining or the wind blowing a gale up the dusty street. He said he wanted to take her to the movies: there was a film in Technicolour about a boy and a horse called 'My Friend Flicka'. She took his hand and after a moment withdrew her own and took off her glove, stuffing it into her pocket, so that she would feel the warm clasp of his fingers.

They had to queue up for the cinema on Lime Street, even

though they weren't going in the one-and-nines. She had never been treated to the pictures before by a boy, never gone in the back row among the courting couples. She was going to canoodle with him – she didn't care if it was common. But she dreaded lest the usherette came and shone a torch on them.

He was so tall, so neat in his clothes, the black tie tucked into his shirt just like Hitler, the crisp edge to his collar; she thought how well her brown frock toned with his uniform. All the same, it was agony to be with him, shuffling nearer and nearer to the entrance of the cinema, trying to make conversation, trying not to ask him why he had failed to come last Saturday. The way he looked at the drunk woman weaving across the road through the traffic, the insolent gaze of his eyes, the pressure of his hand on her shoulder. Every time he spoke to her, colour flooded her cheeks. She wondered how anyone survived being in love, let alone got married – condemned to live for ever in this state of quivering uncertainty. She had never been so aware of herself; she didn't know what to do with her hands, with her feet. There was grit in the corners of her eyes, in her nostrils, she could feel the lipstick caked at the corner of her mouth. How vunerable she felt, how miserable and happy by turns. The pain of being with him was almost as dreadful as living life without him.

*   *   *

Seeing it was such a fine evening, Jack carried the kitchen chairs into the back yard for him and Nellie to sit on. Marge refused; she said it was mutton dressed as lamb to be sitting out there in all that concrete. They'd be asking next for a striped umbrella to sit under. She opened the kitchen window and sat at the table watching them, Nellie with her hands folded piously in her lap, Jack smoking his pipe full of tea-leaves. The tilt of the yard as it sloped down to the back alley gave them a precarious look. Any moment, she thought, they

244

might slide slowly and uncomplaining into the brick wall. She could hear fragments of their conversation.

'. . . in a good way of doing.'

'At the masonic dinner . . . well thought of . . .'

Murmuring together in the evening air and a lone Spitfire, high in the washed-out space of sky, banking in a wide circle before heading out to sea.

'Ah well . . . comes to us all in the . . .'

'God rest his soul.'

Margo shouted through the open window: 'Did Rita say she was meeting Cissie Baines again?'

They both ignored her, placidly arranged in the back yard with little particles of soot floating down from next door's chimney. She thought of Rita meeting her young man. She thought of Mr Aveyard and her old job at the dairy where he was the manager – sneaking out to meet him when Nellie was busy at her dressmaking, making excuses on a Sunday afternoon for not going with her and little Rita to feed the ducks in the park: the time Nellie had given her daffodils to put on mother's grave and she gave them to Mr Aveyard instead. He hadn't known what to do with them, you could tell by his face. He held them upside down at the side of his trouser leg like a sunshade that was partially open. They'd pulled down the byre for the cows in Allsops Lane, and in a way it was a blessing. When they had made her give him up she'd had to leave her job at the dairy, and it was unsettling to hear the sound of the cows mooing in the early morning, waiting to be milked; it reminded her of him. He was getting tired of her long before Jack put the kybosh on things. He couldn't stand the way she had to slip out behind Nellie's back. He used to say, 'Why, you're a grown woman, Margo, what ails you?' and he was so set in his ways, so careful about money – no go in him at all. There was a certain coldness about him, a detachment in his wary brown eyes. Jack said anyone who had survived the trenches in France was bound to be touched – they'd been to hell and back again. In the end she was grateful for Jack's interference, though she would never give him the satisfaction of knowing. When she had run to Mr Aveyard in tears, telling him Jack had said she had to give him up, he had stood like a statue in the little office behind the dairy, as if he didn't know that he should say 'Come to me, you stay by me, Margo.'

There was something very like alarm in his eyes. He never put his arms about her as she clung to him. 'I'm not going back home,' she cried. 'I'm never going back there.' 'It's a bit awkward, Marge,' he said. 'Our Nora's coming next week with the children. You can't stay with me.' So she sat on Lime Street station all night, telling the policeman she had missed her train to London, walking back to Bingley Road in the dawn, seeing Nellie asleep at the front window with Rita on her lap. Nellie said the child had fretted all night, but when Margo held her arms out to her she whimpered and hung back. She wouldn't go to her at all.

She looked out at Jack and Nellie in the yard, silent now, isolated in the little square of brick. Their complacency filled her with a kind of frenzy, the way they had of being content together, shielding each other from the outside world. Out there, over the network of decayed alleyways and the stubby houses, the city had turned into Babel, the clubs and halls filled with foreigners, the Free French and the Americans, the Dutch and the Poles, gliding cheek to cheek with Liverpool girls to the music of the dance bands, while Jack and Nellie sat through their Saturday evening talking about funerals. No wonder Rita had taken a leap in the dark.

She rose and went through to the scullery, standing on the back step, arms folded across her chest.

'Young Rita's courting,' she said. 'She's been meeting him for weeks.' And was rewarded by the turn of Nellie's head, her face shocked as if Margo had just broken something in the front room.

*   *   *

She was watching the boy running through the yellow grasses – a thin boy, bleached by the sun, all the music swelling up, as he ran like a deer under the blue sky to the horse beneath the willow trees.

Ira kissed her. Kirby grips slid from her piled up hair. The boy slowed to a walk and held his hand out; the horse quivered against the green leaves, its coat chestnut-coloured in the sunlight.

The little brown bow slipped sideways from her hair and fell under the seat. He put his hand over her ear and all the sounds became confused, receding beyond his spread fingers, the boy's hoarse voice coaxing the animal, the music of the orchestra, the rustling of their clothes. Her neck ached with the effort of keeping her face turned to his.

When he let her go she touched her mouth curiously with the tips of her fingers. She felt her lips had swollen.

The mother of the boy stood on the verandah of the clapboard house, shielding her eyes from the sun. A dog ran among the scratching hens, and she flapped her apron angrily. The dog grovelled on its belly, its tail sweeping the dust. The hens squawked, dipping their beaks in search of the uncovered grains of corn. At the boundary fence a man in overalls was driving posts into the ground. He raised his sunburnt face and called to the woman : 'Ain't no sign of him yet?' and she shook her head. 'Don't you fret, woman,' he said. There was a close-up of her face, the back of her hand rubbing at her rosy cheek, her eyes on the land and the blue hills beyond the fields.

Ira gathered up the skirt of her dress; he was crumpling it into the palm of his hand like paper. She sat as if she was not aware of what he was doing. The whole cinema was filled with the noise of her rustling dress, drowning the music, the man's voice as he called to the dog.

Ira slid his hand across the top of her stocking and touched her leg. She shivered with apprehension and shame, knowing all the people in the cinema were watching her, waiting for the lady with her torch to catch the glint of her suspender.

There was a finger like a stick, poking at her, scratching her skin. She had to bite her lip to stop from pushing him away.

The blond boy was nuzzling his head against the belly of the horse, stroking its flanks slowly and reassuringly. He slid in his blue overalls over the neck of the animal, holding loosely the beautiful chestnut mane. Now the boy rode the horse towards the hills. Its tail streamed in the wind. The boy's bleached hair blew back from his face and he smiled in the sunshine.

'Stop it,' whispered Rita. 'Just you stop it.' And she gripped the skin of his wrist between finger and thumb and gave a vicious little pinch.

He withdrew his hand and they sat without moving for a long time.

On the screen the boy was crying, standing at a five-barred gate with his knuckles clenched, tears rolling down his cheeks, wood smoke in the air behind him, Mom in her long dress and little tendrils of hair curling about her face.

Ira reached for her hand, clamped in her lap with the nails dug into her palm. He uncurled her fingers one by one, held them loosely in his own.

She watched the boy move with dejected shoulders toward the house – dragging his boots in the dust, passing his mother without looking at her, head hung low.

In her lap she could see Ira's watch, luminous in the dark, feel his little finger move like a snail in the palm of her hand. Round and round. She thought of the girl at school who had told her what it meant, she knew what the signal for acceptance was, she had only to move her thumb back and forth across his. But she could not bring herself to do it. Maybe it meant something else in America, maybe she had misunderstood. She shivered. It was more disturbing to her, this minute sensation in her palm, than anything he had done before.

Face down on his cot the boy lay. His mother sat down on the patchwork counterpane and said: 'Don't fret, son. Reckon it's no use.'

Ira was shifting in his seat, fiddling at his belt to get comfortable. He was lifting her hand in his and guiding it down somewhere in the dark; she felt the edge of a button, a fold of cloth, something cool like putty, adhesive under her touch. She tore free her hand and sat with pounding heart, watching a blur of land with sun shimmering on a field of corn.

* * *

When she got home Uncle Jack was still there – sitting on the edge of the sofa with his hat and coat on as if he had been waiting. Auntie Nellie sat on her chair with her knees bunched together. Margo came to stand in the doorway of the scullery with her flannel in her hand and her eyes red as if she had been crying.

'I've told them,' she said. 'I had to, it was my duty.'

'It's alright,' said Rita, and she meant it. She thought it was outside her control. She stood there waiting, with her hair hanging down and her face composed.

'You've lost an earring,' Nellie said.

'I haven't. It's in me pocket.' She drew out the gold button and laid it on the mantelpiece alongside a reel of grey cotton.

'You shouldn't have been so underhand. You should have told us.'

She kept silent, rustling in her macintosh, looking at the remains of the tripe supper on the table, an inch of brown hem showing beneath her coat.

'Why you had to pick a Yank beats me,' said Jack. And Nellie interrupted fiercely: 'Be quiet, Jack. No need for a song and dance.'

He tossed his head like Flicka, dilating his nostrils as if he was a thoroughbred and offended into the bargain.

'We'll have to meet him,' Nellie said. 'You'll have to ask him here.'

Margo came out of the scullery, her face waxen from her wash. She went out into the hall without speaking and they could hear her footsteps going upstairs. The cat brushed

249

against Rita's ankles. She bent and picked it up in her arms, rubbing her cheek against its fur.

'Don't do that, Rita. You don't know where its been.' But she took no notice.

'Sit down, chickie,' said Uncle Jack. 'We only want to do what's right,' and he patted the sofa for her to sit beside him.

She struggled past the table and sat next to him with Nigger on her knee.

'I believe his father has a business in Washington,' said Nellie. 'What would it be exactly?'

'I don't know,' she said, head down to the beautiful warmth of the cat.

'How old is he?'

She shrugged her shoulders and shut her ears to the questions. Jack said they'd brought her up decent, he was sure she was a good girl. He laid his hand briefly on her knee and patted it. She looked down at Margo's shoes. She thought she was a good girl, but she didn't know for how much longer. He hadn't talked about marriage. He had never said he loved her. The shoes were a size too small. Her toe hurt.

'Are you listening, Rita?'

'Yes, Auntie.'

Uncle Jack reached out his hand; the cat shifted its paw. He patted her knee again, trying to make contact. And she remembered. She had slipped on a piece of soap in Auntie Nellie's bathroom. When she was small. Taken her nail off under the door. Moaning in the big bed that her footie hurt. Auntie Nellie slept and Marge grumbled in her sleep. 'Be quiet, Rita. The sandman will get you.' She clambered out of the bed and stood on the cold lino, wandering up and down the landing, whimpering, screwing up her face in case the sandman should throw his dust in her eyes, until Jack, waking on the sofa in the room below, called: 'What's up? Who's that?' He bathed her foot and wrapped it in a hankie lumpy with Germolene, tucking her up on the sofa with him for comfort. She snuggled close to him and it was as if a spark

250

had leapt from the fire and seared her skin – only it was something damp and cold, like a small animal, that plopped from the front of his combinations and touched her wrist. She recoiled in shock, lying wide-eyed in the dark, and he said, 'Is it still paining, chickie?' And she said it was, holding herself stiffly in case the thing lolling on the sheet should touch her again. She turned her head from the cat and watched his face as he talked to her, the eyes under the hooded lids, the beak of his nose overshadowed by the brim of his black hat, the even curve of his imitation teeth. He was attempting to explain, with Nellie's help, what troubled them.

'All that bothers your Aunt Nellie and me – I think I can speak for Auntie Nellie –'

'All that bothers us –'

'– you don't do anything you'll be sorry for.'

'I don't want you led into temptation.'

She could only stare at him. She tried to make her expression docile, she tried to appear receptive.

'We only want to do what's best for you. You ask him round to the house and we'll have a talk with him.'

'What about?' Rita asked.

'Don't play silly beggars,' Nellie said. 'We only want to be easy in our minds.'

'You must see that,' cried Jack. 'You do, don't you?'

'What's up with Auntie Margo?' said Rita.

'Just as long as he's decent,' Jack said.

He rose to his feet and said he must be away to his bed. He couldn't quite leave – there was something he hadn't made plain. It was as if he hoped miraculously the words he needed would come to him. The habit of speech was lost to him, he could only talk platitudes.

'Alright then, Nellie,' he said, awkwardly touching her shoulder; and she nodded her head at him, her face bleak.

'It never rains but it pours,' he told her, trying to make light of it, and she nodded again, her eyes mournful as if she had known bad weather all her life.

8

U̲N̲C̲L̲E̲ J̲A̲C̲K̲ came into the office at lunchtime to take her out for a sandwich.

'But I've got my sandwiches,' she said, 'in my handbag.'

'Never mind. Give them to one of the other girls.'

She went into the cloakroom to get her coat, upset at his arrival. Ira had promised to telephone her one day at work and she dreaded leaving the building lest he should call while she was gone. She didn't know any of the girls well enough to offer them her sandwiches, so she left them on the ledge under the wall mirror.

'Get in the lift,' said Jack; but she refused, preferring to run down the five flights of stairs to the tiled entrance, watching the lift with its ornamental gates creaking and winding down the well of the building.

'What's all this, then?' she asked, when they were walking to a public house that he knew.

'I was in the town,' he said, 'on business. No harm is there?'

He wanted to get to know her better; he felt he had neglected her in the past. With her new awareness, she recognised the fact and resented him. He had left her alone too much – he hadn't been a good father, or a good uncle. He'd just stuck to the edges like the frieze on the wallpaper.

'I mustn't be late back,' she said, hearing the ring of the telephone in her head. Every step they walked took her further away from his voice.

'Get on,' he said. 'You've a good hour.'

252

They cut across the bomb site beside the Corn Exchange. There was a crowd of people watching a man lying down in the dust, with a lump of rock balanced on his bare chest. He was quite old. He had a piece of string tied about the waist of his trousers. On his arm was tattooed the figure of a woman with a red mouth. His partner was carrying round a trilby hat, shaking it, asking for pennies before he began his act.

'Go on, Uncle Jack,' said Rita. 'Give him some money.'

She was curious to see what the man intended to do. But Jack kept his hands out of his pockets.

'I thought you were in a hurry,' he said.

'I want to watch.'

Stubbornly she pressed forward to take a closer look. The man put down his trilby hat and went towards a mallet lying in the rubble.

'I intend,' he shouted, making a great show of spitting into his palms, 'to break that piece of rock before your very eyes.'

Grasping the handle of the mallet in his hands, he swung it in an arc above his head and brought it down. The man on the ground gave a low groan. He pointed his boots towards the sky and arched his back.

'It's a trick,' said Jack. 'It's all me eye and Peggy Martin.'

'Ssssh,' she said, watching the man's clenched fists as he lay in the dirt.

The man with the mallet gritted his teeth and swung again. Down came the mallet head. The man beneath the rock shuddered. The boulder split into three pieces. The mouth of the tattooed lady opened as the man's fist relaxed.

'Come on,' said Jack, not wanting the hat to be passed round again.

In shop doorways, in windows, Rita sought a glimpse of her reflection. She was constantly on the lookout for herself, to see if she was worthy of Ira. She had taken to wearing her hair brushed back to one side, showing an ear. It made her feel womanly to touch the fine strands of hair that freed themselves and swung across her cheek.

'You might have combed your hair,' Jack said. 'You look as if you've come out of Scotland Road.' She walked sullenly behind him into the Caernarvon Castle.

He kept looking about for people he might know, fellow butchers, men in the meat trade. He sat facing the doors with a look of expectancy in his eyes. It embarrassed her, the eagerness with which he watched each new arrival, the disappointment when he was not recognised. She drank her shandy and thought her nails were growing longer.

He asked her if she'd heard from her young man yet, and she quite bit his head off, snapping at him like Marge. He tried to be patient. He told her he'd noticed the way she looked at the necklace Marge was wearing the night of Valerie Mander's party.

'What necklace?'

'The pearl one your Auntie was wearing.'

'What of it?'

Disturbed by the truculent way the girl spoke to him, he managed to control his bad temper. God knows, he was only trying to be affectionate. She'd gone all sly, twisted inwards away from him, slouching there with her mouth sulky and her hair all over the place.

'I just noticed the way you looked at it. I've got one or two pieces of your mam's tucked away at home. I thought you might want them.'

She almost laughed, the way he put it. It sounded as if he'd cut her into squares and hidden her about the place. After all he was a butcher.

'What pieces?' she said.

'There's an engagement ring and a watch I gave her. A brooch – nothing valuable – but you're getting to an age.'

'I don't want them.'

He couldn't make her out. She had grown all flushed in the face, as if he had said something to annoy her.

'I only thought it would be nice for you,' he said.

'Leave me alone.' She was violent. 'You're always wanting

254

to do what's nice for me just lately – I didn't notice you bothered much before.'

He was stunned. She was a different girl. He had nourished a viper in his bosom.

A man in a black overcoat, a newspaper under his arm, came into the saloon. He stopped when he saw Jack, bent to take a closer look, and put his arm about his shoulder like a brother.

'Well, I never!' he said. 'It's Jack!'

'Walter!' cried Jack, jumping to his feet, his whole face illuminated in welcome. 'Walter Price!'

Rita thought it absurd the fuss he was making, the way he shook hands repeatedly, the way he murmured the man's name, over and over as if they were sweethearts. Walter had a little moustache that had turned grey at the edges. He kept darting glances at her, not sure who she was.

'It's Rita,' said Jack finally. 'You remember young Rita, surely.'

Walter didn't remember, Rita could tell, but he shook hands with her, unbuttoning his grubby leather gloves and holding her fingers tightly. Jack and he had an argument as to who should buy the first drink.

'Let me, Jack.'

'No, Walter, no, no, I insist.'

Off he went to the bar leaving Walter alone with Rita.

She wondered what she should do if Ira had telephoned while she was here. She didn't know where to phone him back. She didn't like to ask Valerie Mander – it would make her look as if she was doing all the running. Walter Price was telling her something, bending forward intently in his seat.

'Why, I remember. You're Nellie's girl!'

She looked at him coldly.

'I last saw you when you were a little lass no bigger than that,' and he held his hand out above the floor on a level with the table edge. She stared at the lino and the space between his spread fingers, gazing at an image of herself when small.

255

'Just a little slip of a thing —'

'I'm not Nellie's girl,' she said. 'I'm Jack's daughter.'

Walter had a lot to tell Jack about his business in Allerton. He'd expanded, done well for himself.

'Three vans!' said Jack. 'My word, you have done well!'

At the back of his mind he was hearing what Rita had said to him about the past. It hurt him, it stuck like a thorn in his flesh, the memory of her words. As soon as Walter went to the bar to buy his round, he said: 'I can't make you out, Rita.'

'What have I done now?'

'What you said before. I'm very hurt.' He drew in his mouth as if to stop his lips from trembling.

'Oh yes,' she said sarcastically. 'I'm sorry about that.'

'What do you know about anything?' he hissed, hating the look on her face. 'What do you know about my life ever since your mam passed on. D'you think I liked being on me own, giving up me house and me family?'

She gazed down at the floor, impressed by his show of emotion.

The presence of the girl inhibited Walter Price. And Jack was not himself. When he mentioned the old days in Allerton, he could swear the man's eyes filled with tears. The girl sat watching them, holding her head disdainfully. After a time the conversation died away. Rita excused herself and went into the lav beyond the bar. She leaned her head against the tiled wall and prayed he hadn't rung — rehearsed what she would say when he did: 'Hello, Ira! Yes luv, it's me — by the way, Auntie Nellie wants you to come to tea — she wants a little talk —'

She was filled with despair; she knew he wouldn't come. What would she tell them at home? It would make her seem despised, as if he wasn't serious about her. He won't come? Why ever not? Auntie Margo would give that laugh of hers, contemptuous, looking at her with pity. For all her chat about giving and the importance of not holding back, she would be the first to sneer, to lash out with her tongue: 'Couldn't you

256

hold him then, Rita? Let him slip through your fingers, did you?' He was telephoning now, the bell was going in the outer office and Alice Wentworth, the one with the big chests, was answering it, talking to Ira, bold as brass, saying no Rita wasn't in, but would she do – making an arrangement to meet him, sitting in the pictures and not bothering to push his hand away. She started to cry, screwing up her eyes to make the tears flow. It eased her. She thought of Uncle Jack, all alone in the rooms above the butcher's shop, wearing his funeral tie, giving his little girl away. She thought of the picnic by the corn field, the way he bandaged her sore foot, the visit to the house in the woods. Before Ira, nothing hurt, nothing saddened to this extent. If there had been less space in her life before his coming, he would not have taken up so much room.

She powdered her nose and went back to the two men. They had been talking about her.

Walter said : 'I believe you're courting. An American, too.'

She blushed, though she liked what he implied. She smiled at him and he wondered what he had done to please. She shook hands with him, told him it had been nice meeting him. Jack went with her to the door. Across the street there was an old woman in a black shawl selling flowers. He wished he could buy Rita some carnations.

'I'm sorry I was nasty,' she said, looking away from him.

'That's alright, chickie.' But his voice was unsteady.

They stood for a time in silence. Jack cleared his throat and asked : 'Is your Aunt Marge behaving herself lately?'

'It's Auntie Nellie you want to watch. She's gone on a vinegar trip.'

His mouth opened in surprise. 'What's up, what's she done?'

'Auntie Margo says she's selling the furniture.'

'She's what?'

'There's things gone from the front room.'

'What things?'

257

'I don't know. Auntie Margo says a table's gone and a bit of china.'

'I don't believe it.'

He slapped his thigh hard and a woman turned to look. He couldn't credit it. Nellie would never part with mother's bits and pieces. Why, that front room was like the British Museum to Nellie.

'There's an explanation,' he said. 'She's having you on.'

She had to go, it was past her dinner break. He kissed the edge of her hair and she brushed her mouth against the collar of his coat and ran across the street away from him – passing the flower-seller all in black, with her shawl wound about her body, and the silver earrings dangling from the pierced lobes of her ears.

*   *   *

Margo knew him as soon as she saw him. It wasn't just fancy. She couldn't claim really to know men – she wasn't sophisticated like Valerie Mander. But as soon as she saw the boy's eyes, blue and incurious, she knew what sort of a man he was. For he was a man, for all his lanky limbs and the smooth cheeks that he obviously didn't shave. The way he entered the kitchen and saw them all standing there, devouring him with their eyes. It was as if he was on a hill-top, lazily watching a distant landscape. He was empty inside, he used no charm, he wasn't out to please; he passed his hand over the pale stubble of his hair and sat where he was placed. Nothing touched him: unlike Marge he had been washed clean of apology and subterfuge – he was wholly himself. At no time while he was among them, answering their questions in his flat laconic way, did she receive the impression that he was stirred by any chord of memory – no longing for mum or dad, for home and country, the things he had left behind. She looked down at the blue table-cloth – not Nellie's best she hadn't gone overboard – at the plates from the sideboard

258

in the front room, each covered with a small portion of tomatoes, lettuce and cucumber. The tomatoes Nellie had grown herself in a seed tray on the back wall – ripened them on the shelf in the hall, above the door. He took it all for granted, he would never be grateful. Suddenly she wanted to gather up the seed cake and the plums and milk and tell him to go away and never come back. Instead she listened to Jack, in his best suit talking about the other war and all the brave young men gone in France.

He didn't flicker a lid; he let his eye slide over Jack as if he was a reflection on the water. He ate his salad and his plums and spooned jam on to his bread. After a time his callousness excited her. She was wearing a plain brown skirt and a cream blouse – Nellie had told her not to overdo it. She leaned her elbow on the table, fingering the buttons at her throat. She wanted him to know that she saw through him, she wanted him to notice her. Jack said he must find it strange being in England after the bigness of America.

'Don't you find the British are insular, being an island race?'

And Margo said quickly: 'Whatever does insular mean, Jack?' because she knew Ira wasn't educated; she could tell by the set of his face that he was untouched by schooling. Nellie always said that the church was an education in itself – the rhetoric, the vocabulary it gave the ordinary working men and women, the hymns with their warlike phrases that expressed so much: 'Onward Christian Soldiers', 'Fight the Good Fight with All Thy Might'. You could tell by his conversation just how lacking in scripture he was, how ungodly – there was no ring to his speech, no cadence. She felt sorry for Rita, fiddling with the remains of her meal, crushed under the weight of her infatuation for him. She was disappointed for herself; it would have been nice if he had been like Chuck, warm and bouncing, bringing whisky into the house and manliness, making life rosy, every day like Christmas.

'Marge,' said Nellie sharply, 'help clear the salad dishes.'

In the scullery she was fierce with her. 'Pull yourself together! What's got into you?'

'He's no good,' Marge said, slapping the best plates into the bowl with gaiety.

'He's a nice enough lad.'

'Get off. He's no good.' And she rammed the tap of the cold water full on, drowning Nellie's protests. Margo felt as if she had been drinking, she found his company so unsettling. She was tired to death of them all being so polite to each other.

'Now Ira,' she said, when she had rinsed the plates and the bowls, 'I'm sure Nellie and Jack are anxious to know how you live in America.' And he smiled at her, slow and casual, lounging back on the settee with Rita huddled beside him, her face solemn with pride and ownership.

Nellie thought he was a nice boy : remote and shy perhaps, but that was better than him being brash as she had feared, flinging his weight about and playing the conqueror. Jack said they were invaders; they followed a long line beginning with the Vikings. Instead of the longboat they used the jeep : roaring about Liverpool as if they were the S.S. But Ira wasn't like that. It would be easy to steer Rita from him. He wasn't a threat to mother's furniture.

'I believe your dad has a business in Washington,' she said; and he said he reckoned he had. He wasn't a show off. He didn't elaborate. God knows how Marge knew, but she said his dad was in real estate.

'That's right, Mam, I guess he's in real estate.'

He helped himself to another round of bread. Jack had always maintained that they fed their army like pigs for the market, but he was wrong. Ira seemed starved of homely food, the sort his mother might put on the table.

'Have you any brothers and sisters, Ira?'

'Two brothers and four sisters.'

Up came Rita's head as if hearing it for the first time.

'Are you Catholics?' asked Jack, and Nellie waited with baited breath because she knew what Jack felt about Romans,

260

but he said no, they weren't anything special, and Jack relaxed and sat back on his chair fumbling for his tobacco.

'My word,' said Margo, 'that's quite a family.'

She had a certain yellowish pallor that irritated Nellie, a melancholy look in her eyes that gave her the air of a tragedy queen. She was always putting herself in the limelight. The young man never took his eyes off her. He kept his hands away from Rita. He never put his arm round her. Nellie had been at the Manders earlier in the week and seen the way Chuck behaved with Valerie. Valerie knew how to take care of herself, of course, but it was dreadful the way he couldn't keep his hands off her – sitting on the sofa, imprisoning her in his arms, with everyone looking, and Mrs Mander smiling and looking through the pattern books as if it was something to shout about.

Jack wavered between hatred and pride – pride in his daughter that she had got herself a young man, and hatred of the blond stranger in his tell-tale uniform, a product of a race of mongrels, the blood of every nation in the world mingling in his veins – nothing aristocratic, nothing pure. It was astonishing he hadn't a touch of the Jew or the black in him. And that drawl of his – bastard English, with its lazy vowels and understatement. Jack didn't care for the way he looked at Marge – familiar, as if they came from the same back yard. He was probably only pretending not to be the least bit interested in Rita, to throw them off the scent. He hated to to think what he was like when he was alone with her. He wished Rita's mam could be here. She would know how to cope with it. He had a dim recollection of her determined sickly face, peppered with freckles, her sharp eyes that missed nothing, watching which way the wind blew.

Marge was telling one of her stories about her experiences in the factory.

'– you wouldn't believe what some of them get up to. In the explosives room behind the main building. It's a regular thing –'

261

They all watched her, drained by her vitality, the tea finished with, all the bread used up and the jam in its bowl.

Rita wanted to be down town with him, kissing in the pictures. He was so far away from her, sitting on the sofa next to her, listening to Aunt Margo. She had been surprised how easy it had been getting him to come home for tea. He hadn't telephoned – she lied, she said he had; she had fled to the station with her heart in her boots in case he should not be there under the clock. The trouble the family had gone to, the tins of food, the polishing of the front-door knocker, the pressing of clothes ready for his arrival. Fancy having all those brothers and sisters. She daydreamed they were married, going up soon to the little back bedroom together with everyone's blessing – no raised eyebrows, or telling them to be back before dark. They wouldn't go up to do anything dirty – just lie there under the eiderdown with Nigger stretched out across her feet. It wouldn't be like it was now. They'd be more like friends. They'd like each other. She hated the way he watched Margo. As if she was something special.

They played cards after tea. He didn't really get the hang of it; he said he'd never played rummy before.

'You just collect one of three and two of three and one of four and so on,' explained Rita.

But he held the cards in his hand as if he was blind. Jack thought it a point in his favour, he wasn't the gambling type.

'Let him keep the score,' said Nellie, fetching pencil and paper.

But he was loath to do it. In the end Jack ruled lines and wrote their names upon the paper in his beautiful copper plate.

Valerie Mander came at nine o'clock, holding her white arm out above the table, fluttering her fingers to show off her engagement ring.

'Oh, how lovely,' cried the aunts, catching her hand and taking a closer look at the small white stones. Rita didn't introduce her to Ira; she wished she hadn't called. She looked so beautiful standing there in a blue costume with her long red nails and her ring that proved Chuck cared for her.

Chuck was going to buy them a fridge.

'A what?' said Nellie.

'For food,' explained Valerie, 'to keep it fresh, like.'

'What food?' said Margo comically; and they all laughed, thinking of the meagre rations inside the coldness of the lovely new machine come all the way from America, sitting round the table, sharing her good fortune, as if it was normal to have a crowd in on a Saturday night – drinking tea, dropping cake crumbs on the carpet with a fine display of carelessness. The light began to fade from the room; the yellow drained out of the beige wallpaper. From next door's yard came the grieved sounds of pigeons calling.

Rita was restless and unhappy again. She took the milk jug and pretended it needed refilling, going away from the voices and the clattering cups into the scullery, leaning her head against the back door. She could hear Marge's voice, full of vivacity and nerve.

'When we were guarding the Cunard Building he said he could never get on with his wife. If you ask me –'

As she ended the story her voice rose in raucous vulgarity : a storm of hilarity, little trills of noise from the women, a man tittering strangely – not Uncle Jack – like a sheep running across a field. With shock she realised it was Ira. She had never heard him laugh before. It wasn't even a conversation, it was a monologue, the demanding tones of a giddy girl being the centre of attraction. And she wasn't a girl any more. Auntie Margo was an old woman with hollow cheeks and little veins that bled under her skin.

Uncle Jack came into the scullery looking for matches. He wore a delighted grin; he was good-humoured with the jokes and the company. He saw Rita against the door, her head on the stained roller towel, her face turned to him with the eyes wounded, like some animal at bay.

'Ah, chickie,' he said softly, 'come on, what's wrong?'

He was distressed by the sight of her. It was easy to comfort her; she was like a little child again.

'I'm not going back in there.'

'Don't be a silly girl. You don't want to be upset by your Auntie Marge.'

The urgency of the situation made him sensitive. He did see in a flash what ailed her.

He unbolted the back door and took her out into the yard, mellow with the last rays of the sun. They might have been in the country, the soft clouds in the sky, the cooing of the pigeons. He put his arm about her shoulder, leading her up and down the slope of the yard. He surprised himself, pacing the slate squares with the lupin plant wilting at the wash-house wall.

'You've got to take into account the fact that your Auntie Marge was a married woman. You're a big girl now, you're not a little lass – you know what I'm getting at –'

His fingers stroked her shoulders in the black dress with the white collar. 'The little maid,' Nellie had called her, but she did suit it. It gave a dignity, a simplicity that you couldn't help noticing. A little collar like a cobweb – cream lace, and cuffs to match. She was like something in a picture frame, an echo of the past. He was moved by her suffering, he wanted to pass on experience. He hadn't lived that long; he hadn't been through much, beyond death, his wife, and the hell of the trenches.

'What's she going on at Ira for?' wailed Rita, tired of his meanderings.

'She's not, our Rita,' he said. 'You don't understand.'

He could see Nellie peeping at them through the lace curtains, her face puzzled, not knowing what he was doing, walking Rita up and down the yard.

'He keeps looking at her.'

'He doesn't. Don't be daft. Listen, your Auntie Marge is a remarkable woman.' Till he said it, he didn't know it himself. 'She's not like Nellie and me; she's a different cross to bear. I can only surmise –'

It was a lovely word, he dwelt on it, turn about turn up the brick yard, till Rita said, 'What do you mean?' plaintive like those damn birds next door.

'When she was little, she wasn't like your Auntie Nellie and me. It was more difficult for her. She had a hell of a time. She never took what mother said for gospel. If mother told her to do anything she had to know why. Nellie and I used to think she was daft. She questioned everything. She made it difficult for herself. You're like her, pet.'

And again with the utterance, he felt it to be true.

'I'm not, I'm not,' she said, shouting the words like someone demented.

God knows what the people next door thought. They'd probably seen the American arrive and thought the very worst. Rita in the family way and he trying to make sense of it.

'You haven't done nothing with him, have you?' he asked, but she didn't seem to hear.

'Why am I like her?'

'Well, she wouldn't accept what was right and proper. I used to think she put it on, just to be awkward. But it's real enough. Nellie understands her, you know. You mustn't take any notice of their upsets. Marge has got more feeling than the rest of us.'

'What feelings?' she asked weakly, like a lamb left out in the snow.

'She always thinks the best is yet to come. It isn't. She never gives up.'

'She does.' Her voice was spiteful, but he continued:

'She doesn't mean to bewitch your Ira. It's just her way.' He stumbled over the phrase; he felt he was echoing what she already feared. Bewitched was such a bold word: it had overtones. 'When we were little she caught on quicker than the rest of us. I don't want to burden you, but I could tell you things about when we were little that would curl your hair.'

'What's up, Jack? What's going on?' Nellie was at the back step.

'Nothing, woman. We're just chatting.'

She went away unconvinced. He knew she would be upset, leaving their guests that way.

'What things?' Rita was puzzled by him. The weight of his arm across her shoulders bore her down.

'It was strict then. It was different those days. Spare the rod and spoil the child. I was beat on me bare flesh with a belt. Marge was beat regular. You don't realise. I didn't.'

He took in the window of the house alongside Nellie's, the fall of a curtain as somebody hid from view. All along the street, the curtains tight drawn across the windows although it wasn't yet dark – a row of boxes bursting with secrets.

'But your Auntie Marge would never learn. She wouldn't give in. She wanted to get married again, you know, when you were little.'

'She gave him up.'

He didn't think she had remembered. 'She didn't want to. We made her. It didn't suit your Auntie Nellie and me. She didn't want to be on her own with you. I didn't want her living with me. Not then. I'd grown used to it.'

'Used to what?'

'Being on me own. When your mam died and your Auntie Nellie took you in, I got used to it. After a bit. It wasn't my fault. I'd been chivvied by women all me life.'

'I want Ira to love me,' she said, as if she hadn't heard one word he'd uttered.

'It's not what it seems,' he said.

'I don't want him looking at Auntie Margo.'

'Talk sense.' It was ridiculous what he was trying to do. She wasn't of an age. She wouldn't understand love was mostly habit later on and escape at the beginning. He couldn't make a silk purse out of a sow's ear. 'Just wait here, our Rita.'

He had got out of his depth. Something in her stubborn face, her sad eyes, had shaken him outside the confines of his relationship with her. He couldn't continue. It wasn't for him to explain; only time could make it plain for her.

'Wait on,' he said, 'wait on, chickie.' He went forcefully into the kitchen, seeing Valerie Mander's white throat flung back in abandon, Nellie smiling like a clown, the young American with his eyes glued to Marge as if he was mesmerised. 'Ira, Rita wants a word with you.'

They went all quiet, but he had to go. He knew that much. He felt powerful when he was alone with the three women – superior, as if he had touched the heights.

'You don't want to encourage him,' started Nellie; and he said: 'Hush up, Nellie, I know what I'm at,' scratching the skin behind his suspenders that held up his green socks. A midge must have bitten him, though God knows it was unlikely, the rotten summer they'd had. It was the bloody cat. Flea-ridden thing.

*　　*　　*

'I thought you said you didn't talk much,' Ira said, 'you and your folks. Seems like they never stop talking.'

'It's my dad,' she said, 'he's gone balmy. I've never known him like that.'

'What he want to talk to you about? He was out here some time.'

He lounged against the wall of the alleyway, watching her push the back gate ajar with her foot.

'I didn't think you noticed.'

'I guess I better go,' he said. 'I got to catch the train.'

She didn't want him sleeping on the settee, not with Auntie Margo and Valerie in the house. It was all spoilt – there seemed nowhere they could be without her feeling miserable.

'It's a lovely ring, isn't it?' she said, seeing the little white diamonds pale above the curved red nails.

'How old are you?' he asked, staring at her in the gloom.

'Seventeen. How old are you?'

'Older.'

'Not much.'

Someone was tapping on the window. She let the yard gate swing back and block them from view.

'Will you telephone me at work?'

'Sure I will.'

'You didn't last week. I waited. If you don't, shall I just come to the station?'

'I guess not. I may have no furlough. I don't have every Saturday.'

He'd turned his back on her. He was pulling at a weed growing in the cracks of the wall.

'But when will I see you?' Her voice was breaking in despair.

'I'll call you. I'll do that. But I guess I won't make next Saturday.'

'Couldn't we go to the country again? I could take time off work. We could go to that place again.'

She was begging and she knew it. She was saying she would go to the empty house on the shore and lie down with him. She might have a baby. It was practically sure she would, but she'd take the risk; she'd do anything as long as he would see her.

'I guess I don't have no furlough next week.'

'Rita, Rita.' It was Nellie calling from the back door. She didn't want them like a couple of cats yowling in the back alley.

Rita had a melancholy feeling she would never see him again, never love him, never be given the chance to show how much she cared. All her life she had been waiting for him, beyond the house in the woods with the stuffed hen in the window. He was the people in her dream that caused her so much fear. He was the loved one who could come to harm. When she screamed in the night it was for him; when she saw the naked statue in the flower-bed it was an image of him wrestling with an angel. He had to love her. Give her time, she would prove to him how much she had to share, beyond

268

the dirtiness, the scrabbling at the elastic of her knickers. She would die for him if he would let her.

'I'll call,' he said. 'Reckon I'll telephone tomorrow.'

He left the house before Valerie Mander, not kissing Rita, sprinting down the road to the Cabbage Hall to catch his tram to the station.

9

A T WORK Margo put her name down on the list for the
Dramatics Society. They wanted extra people for the
Christmas Pantomime. Ever since she was a child, people had
told her she should go on the stage. There was no end to the
facilities in the factory for recreation: football and snooker
for the men and keep-fit for the ladies; lectures in the dinner
break on how to make the food more interesting, how to make
old stockings into novelties for birthdays. She hadn't partici-
pated before, but with the winter coming and the approach
of the festive season it would be nice to be with a lively bunch
of people, larking about and rehearsing songs. She wouldn't
tell Nellie right away, not until she was accepted; there had
been words between them over the way she had behaved to
Rita's young man. She protested indignantly: she said she
wasn't going to sit in silence all evening, not with everyone
else acting as if the cat had got their tongue. It would be a
relief to get out of the house one evening a week. Maybe it
was that summer was ending, the thought of the winter to
be endured, that made the house seem charged with emotion
and tension: Nellie carting bits of furniture up the stairs –
she'd caught her red-handed with the bamboo stand – Rita
going about the house heavy-eyed and dreamy, alternately
singing to herself as she prepared for bed, and sitting on the
sofa with a face like death, unable to speak, not troubling to
turn the pages of her library book. Now and then Margo
caught a glimpse of such vulnerability on her sallow features,

270

such despair, that she was forced to look away. She would not interfere. Rita must come to her. It was almost a week since Ira had been to tea. Once he had gone from the house Margo forgot how threatening she had found him, how unsuitable. She remembered only that he was very young with not much to say for himself. Nellie had been over to visit Jack in the week. Jack said he was afraid Rita was going to get hurt – she was obsessed by her Ira. Nellie seemed to have other things to occupy her mind. She refused to explain why she was storing things in the box-room. Since her turn in the car she had quietened considerably, the sting drawn from her character. She did her housework with an abstracted air as if she was planning something. Between the two of them, Margo felt the house to be depressing. Once or twice she went down the road to the Manders'. Prompt on seven o'clock the jeep came bouncing up the road. Valerie would run to the step. It made Margo laugh the way Chuck leapt from his vehicle almost before the engine had died, propelled into her waiting arms as if he was catapulted across the pavement – flowers in his arms, crushed against her blouse, roses, carnations, little feathery sprays of fern; burying her face in them, her cheeks glowing like the bouquet he had brought her; the two of them always laughing and cuddling, calling each other honey and baby, like on the pictures. He was always bringing them presents – he was a regular Santa Claus: packets of cigarettes, a gold lighter for Valerie, a wrist-watch for the absent George; always whisky on the sideboard, tins of food in the pantry, packets of real butter in the new fridge. Margo could see Jack's point of view – it was a bit like the invasion troops looting the land and the Manders fraternising with the enemy. No wonder the rest of the neighbours looked askance at the jeep swinging up to the door. The contrast between life at Valerie's and the gloom that pervaded Nellie's house was almost too much for Margo to bear. It was as if she ran to shelter from a great black cloud that was gathering in the sky.

On Saturday night Rita didn't get ready to go out. She

271

lay upstairs in her room and told Margo she had a headache.

'But won't Ira be waiting for you?'

'No, he wont. He's training this weekend.'

'Training?' said Margo.

But Rita closed her eyes and wouldn't say another word. All week she had waited for the telephone to ring, though she knew it was useless. She was wallowing in self-pity and withdrawal. She had no friends, no hobbies, no interest beyond Ira. She hated him for being so cruel to her. She dreamed of revenge, of someone in the office telling him, when he did at last ring, that she had left to get married: one of those sudden romances, Alice Wentworth would tell him, a naval officer, a Dutchman. She recalled the seaman billeted on them in the first year of the war, his homely vacant face, the civilian suit he wore, dull and shabby, the little black suitcase he carried with his uniform inside. Auntie Margo had liked him. He bought her some material for a dress once. He took her to look at his ship, though she said she wasn't allowed on board. She saw Ira in his mustard jacket, his black tie; under the jaunty angle of his cap he lowered golden eyelashes to cover eyes that were the colour of the sky. She lay moaning on her bed, wanting to hit at him with her fists.

'She can't go on like this,' said Margo to Nellie, 'lying up there fretting. She's not eaten a thing all day.'

'Give her time,' replied Nellie. 'She'll come round.'

'They've not had a tiff,' Margo said. 'He's just training. There's no call for her to act like this.'

Nellie was cutting out the body of Valerie Mander's engagement dress. The noise the scissors made, as they sheered through the material and scraped the surface of the table irritated Margo.

'How much did that material cost you?' she asked.

'Four shillings a yard,' said Nellie.

'You were done. I saw some just like that in Wharton's window. I swear it was a bob cheaper.'

'What Wharton's?' asked Nellie, not looking up.

272

'That shop near Ethel Freeman's house. Round the corner from where Frisby Dyke's used to be.'

'Ethel Freeman never lived near Frisby Dyke's,' said Nellie. 'You're thinking of someone else.'

'Get away. I went there regular.'

'Not Ethel Freeman,' Nellie said again.

It made Margo mad the way Nellie never gave up, never admitted she could be wrong. She was like a bull terrier with its teeth dug in. She would die rather than let go.

'I've joined the Dramatics,' she said, daring Nellie to make a scathing remark.

But Nellie didn't say it was foolish or wonder how long that little phase would last. 'That's nice,' was all she said, bunched up against the sofa as she snipped at the curve of the arm-hole, the tip of her tongue caught between her teeth with the effort of cutting straight. She wanted to make a lovely job of the dress. She was very fond of Valerie. For all the difference in their attitude to life she could admire the girl. Never underhand, Valerie gave the impression she knew how to deal with living. She was confident. Nellie had thought of giving her the dress as a present, but no one had ever mentioned a wedding or given any indication of how long the engagement might be. They were going to have a party – everyone in the road invited, people from the camp, relatives from Yorkshire, a really big do. No one knew how much longer the war might last, whether Chuck would be sent abroad. It was all indefinite.

'If the war ends,' said Margo, 'will Chuck stay on, or will Valerie rush off to America?'

'How do I know?' Nellie said, 'you see more of them than I do.'

Jack came and they listened to Gilly Potter on the wireless talking about Hogs Norton. Rita stayed upstairs. Jack called her down for a cup of tea and a cream cracker, and she wandered round the kitchen like a stray animal, scattering crumbs from her mouth, slopping tea into her saucer.

'Get away!' cried Nellie, fearing damage to the green taffeta on the table. So she ran upstairs again, tears of affront in her eyes, slamming her bedroom door in a temper.

* * *

On Tuesday Margo was told to come to the Dramatics room the following evening for an audition.

'A what?' she cried appalled. 'I can't do no audition.'

'We only want to hear your voice, girl. We're not asking for bleeding Shakespeare.'

On Wednesday morning when the alarm went for six o'clock she shut her eyes again, tight.

'Get up Marge!' said Nellie, kicking her on the ankle. 'Alarm's gone.'

'I feel terrible,' she moaned. 'I feel that poorly. I think I'll go in later when I feel more myself.'

'Get off, there was nothing wrong with you last night.'

But should couldn't very well drag her out of bed, she couldn't dress her and push her out of the door. Marge stayed where she was till mid-day, waiting till Nellie went out shopping on Breck Road.

'I may pop over and see Jack,' Nellie called, listening to Marge wheezing in the bedroom. Marge didn't reply. She was lying upstairs, right as rain, smoking her cigarettes in bed.

Margo wanted to be really ready for the audition. She washed all over and shook some of Nellie's talcum powder inside her corsets. She was bound to get sweaty, being nervous. She tried singing the chorus of 'I Do Like to Be Beside the Seaside', but she broke into a fit of coughing when the band played 'tum, didly um tum tum'. She put her earrings on, and a bracelet, and pinned a brooch to the front of her dress. Then she unpinned it, because she didn't want to seem to be trying too hard. It was her talent they were after, not the crown jewels. When she was going downstairs, someone knocked at the front door. She saw the outline of a man's

274

head outside the glass. It was Ira. She led him through into the front room. Afterwards she didn't know why. No one ever went into the front room unless the vicar called at Christmas, or in case of extreme illness, like when George Bickerton died. It was typical of him, she thought, that he didn't look at the room, didn't notice the furniture from another age : the good carpet on the floor, the photographs sepia-coloured with eyes black as coal, Mother grimly smiling.

'Whatever brings you here?' she asked. He handed her a packet of cigarettes. She was taken aback : he didn't smoke himself.

'I rang Rita at work,' he told her. 'She said you were sick.'

'I'm not. I've got a —' She stopped because she didn't want to admit anything. He was looking at her opening the packet of cigarettes.

'Just a chill,' she told him. 'I'm off out now to me work. Did you want to see Rita?'

She knew he didn't. He knew damn well Rita was at work. She was scandalised, and yet there was a little bubble of excitement in her, getting bigger and bigger at the thought.

'Now look,' she said, 'let's get one or two things straight.'

But when she looked at his face, she wasn't sure she was right. He looked so innocent, so without guile, boyish with his bony face pale, twisting his cap in his hands. She lit a cigarette. It was no use giving him the packet back — not these days when they were so scarce.

'What have you come for? You know young Rita's at work.'

'I wanted a word with you, Mam, you being more a woman of the world.'

The audacity of the boy! What did she know of the world, cooped up in Bingley Road like a ferret down a hole?

'I reckon I can tell you. I ain't going to see Rita again.'

She didn't know where to flick her ash. Nellie had taken the bamboo stand up to the box-room.

'I can't see her no more.'

'Well, you best tell her yourself. You've no cause to be telling me.'

'I thought you could break it to her. I tried to tell her, but she don't seem to listen. I don't aim to harm no one.'

'Why can't you see her?'

Inside it was doing her the world of good. She hated herself for the joy she got from his words. He didn't want Rita; Rita wasn't going to find the happiness that she herself had missed. She caught Mother's eye, that stern and selfish orb. She stared back boldly. Mother couldn't use the strap any more, not where she was.

'I guess she's too young, Mam. And she's kind of joyless. She don't want no fun, no drinking nor dancing.'

'But she does,' Margo protested. 'It's just she's unsure of herself. We haven't exactly taught her to enjoy herself, her Aunt Nellie and me. I mean I've tried, but it's Nellie that's the power behind the throne.'

She felt ridiculous, telling a complete stranger the intimate details of their life.

'Rita sure sets a store by what you say. You could tell her. I mean, you've known grief, Mam.'

'Grief?'

'Your husband dying. You know about men. The kind of books you read.'

She looked at him, not fully understanding.

'What books?'

'Rita told me about the sort of books you read. She found one in your drawer. You know about men. You could square it for me.'

She couldn't credit Rita had got hold of that book. She'd searched the house from end to end, day after day, trying to find it. She thought she had lost it at work. She went red with shame thinking of Rita reading that filth, Rita reading those dirty words.

'I've got to go,' she said. 'You'll have to excues me. I must be off to my work.'

He stood up, never taking his eyes from hers. He was a bad one, she knew for sure: the cocky way he looked at her, the little tinge of colour in his no-good face. She was devastated by the uselessness of her personality. The kind of men who fancied her – George Bickerton, Mr Aveyard, the chap on the tandem, the Dutch seaman in the box-room. They were attracted to her at first. And it was precisely the glitter that drew them at the start that drove them away in the end. They couldn't stand her at the end. She wished she was Bette Davis, Joan Crawford, languidly sitting in a long dress, calling them darling, sipping her cocktail, loyal and loving always – but cool like a snake, telling them to go before they told her. She threw her cigarette into the hearth, on the virgin tiles that Nellie scrubbed each day though never a fire lit the grate. She walked briskly into the hall and said it had been nice talking to him, but he better go now, she would be late.

'I'll call again, Mam,' he said, very polite, not smiling; and she shut the door after him and put her hand to her heart to catch her breath.

She was so agitated on the tram, in the audition, over Ira and his boldness, that she hardly noticed her voice singing, 'We'll meet again. Don't know where, don't know when'. She clasped her hands together, opened her throat and sang. They accepted her at once; they said she would be an asset. She felt very little satisfaction.

*　　*　　*

Nellie was furious at Marge going out like that. Thinking her safely in bed, she hadn't bothered to take a key. She had to wait for half an hour on the step until Rita came home from work.

'God knows what came over your Auntie Marge,' she said. 'I left her ill in bed. Wait till I see her.'

Rita was so happy she peeled potatoes and made Nellie a cup of coffee.

'Sit down,' she said. 'I'll get the tea.'

All her face was light and curved. Gone the morose set to her mouth, the desperate look in her eyes.

'Ira rang,' she said, unable to keep it to herself. 'He's busy training. He can't see me this week, but he rang me up to see how I was. He's been chosen for some course – they're sending him to Halifax for three days. He's going to write me a letter.'

She was a different girl; it was amazing the effect a man had on a woman. Nellie had seen it before in Marge, the fluctuations of mood, as if the man held the reins and drove as he pleased. It left her cold. She had been too busy nursing mother to experience that sort of thing – blacking the grate, preparing the food, seeing the boys went off to work decent. Time had gone like the pages of a book flipping over.

* * *

When Marge came in she never said she was sorry for gadding off like that. She wasn't contrite about being late home.

'Auntie Nellie was locked out,' said Rita. 'She had to wait on the step.'

'I wasn't to know you didn't have your key,' cried Marge, belligerently.

She tried to get Nellie off to bed early so that she could talk to Rita. But Nellie wouldn't budge – taking her stays off and sitting by the empty grate for an age, yawning, stirring her tea. In the end Margo went up first – she was that worn out – falling asleep without a thought in her head.

* * *

The following night Nellie went to the Manders to give Valerie a fitting. As soon as she was out of the door, Margo asked Rita what Ira had said to her on the telephone.

'How d'you know he phoned?' asked Rita. 'I never told you.'

'I know, he did, that's why.'

'He's been chosen for some course. I'll probably see him on Saturday."

'He's not been chosen for any course,' said Margo. She couldn't put it tactfully – it wasn't the way – it had to be done like a bull in a china shop. She watched Rita's face, like smooth glass, not a line on it.

'He called here yesterday.'

'He what?'

The glass splintered. Furrows appeared on her high forehead, her mouth puckered in surprise.

'He called. He called to ask me to –'

It wasn't that simple. She felt like Jack, slashing the throat of a young pig, letting its life's blood soak into the sawdust.

After a time Rita said : 'Asked you to what?' Her voice was hard like a stone.

'He feels you're too young. He minds about you.'

'Too young?'

'He doesn't want to commit himself.'

'What did he come here for when he knew I was out?'

'He wants to do what's best.'

'I told him you were off work.'

'He's a nice lad.' She felt like Judas, giving the signal for young Rita to be cut down by swords.

'He's going to ring me tomorrow – he said so.'

Margo didn't have the strength. The malice drained out of her. It wasn't competition – it was little Rita, without a mother and father. She wasn't even angry any more about the dirty book gone from her drawer. Jack and Nellie had moulded Rita, cramped her development, as surely as if they had copied the Chinese, binding the feet of infants to keep them small.

'He's been picked for a course,' said Rita stubbornly. 'He's going to write me a letter.'

*　　　*　　　*

On Friday, Rita went straight from work to Uncle Jack –

surprised him in his braces, the shop shuttered, cooking his tea.

'Does your Auntie Nellie know you're here?'

'I just thought I'd come.'

He was cooking kidneys in a white pouch of fat, boiling a whole cabbage in the pan. She was hungry. She sliced the dark brown meat, rare with blood, and shovelled it into her mouth. She told him Marge had said Ira had visited her. She sprinkled pepper on to the cabbage and wiped her bread across the plate. The way she ate disgusted him. He had to put down his knife and fork and turn his head away.

'Who called on Marge?' he said.

'Ira. She said Ira called.'

'He never called to see her,' said Jack. 'It's Marge's way. She's trying to protect you.'

'What from?'

She was looking at him with her mouth filmed with fat.

'Just from getting upset. What's he supposed to have called for?'

'He said he wanted to do what's best.'

'There you are. What did I tell you? It's just Marge's way.'

He walked round the gramophone, still in the centre of the room, and went into the small kitchen, the paper peeling from the walls.

'Don't you mind the mess, Uncle Jack?' Rita asked.

He didn't like her criticising him – it wasn't respectful.

'I don't really see it. It's only temporary, this place. One day I'll buy meself a little boat and retire to the waterways. When the war's over.'

When the war was over, she thought, Ira would go home. Back to his big family and his father in real estate.

'What do you do when you work in real estate?' she asked.

'I'll tell you this,' Jack said. 'You're Ira's dad is never in business. He's a farming lad – you can tell. He's been raised near the soil – it's in his face.'

'He's been sent on a course. He's been chosen.'

Jack was relieved they weren't going to have a scene about

Marge. Whatever the truth of it was, the child didn't seem too upset.

'Do you think he did come round? I said Auntie Marge was off sick when he rang me in the morning.'

'I'm blessed if I know. Don't ask me, ask her.' He made tea and Rita put cups on to the table. 'It's always the same, when you get infatuated. It's like a virus in the blood. A perpetual state of fever. One time, I went on holiday and nearly died of love.'

'With me mam?'

'No, before your mother. I went on holiday to the Isle of Man and we played tennis on the back lawn. And there was this woman there that drove me out of me mind. I've got a photograph somewhere.' And he rummaged through the packing cases on the floor, looking for the image he remembered, finding himself in white trousers sprawled before a net with a young woman with a bandeau round her head and a smirk on her face.

'I loved her,' he said. 'I didn't think I'd survive. But I did. Went back home, caught the number twelve tram and met your mam on the top deck.'

'But why did you leave her on the Isle of Man?'

'She preferred someone else. Went off with him the last week of the holiday.'

He took the photograph from her and stuffed it away among the pictures of Nellie and Marge and Rita as a baby.

'You best be off,' he said. 'I don't want Nellie upset. She's a wonderful woman.'

He was always so anxious about Nellie, afraid she might have another attack. He gave her a piece of meat to take home.

'Passion,' he said, as he let her out of the shop, 'is a strange thing. Why I could have killed the fellow that young woman went off with. I'd have swung for him.'

* * *

281

Rita went down town on Saturday and Ira wasn't there. She came home slowly, dragging her feet along the road, not staying up for a cup of tea, going straight to her room with the pencil and paper she had ready in her handbag. Laboriously she wrote the letter:

Auntie Margo said you came to the house last week. I don't know if you did or not. She said you wanted to do what's best. What's best is that you should see me. You have not written me a letter as you promised. You have not telephoned me. Mr Betts sent me for stamps at the post office on Friday and I didn't like to ask if you had rung. Did you ring me Friday? I keep asking if anyone has telephoned me and it makes me feel foolish. They all look at me in the office. I went to the station tonight to look for you but you weren't there. Are you on your course? I saw all the other women waiting and I thought we were not like them. If you truly don't want to see me, please tell me. Please dear Ira, on my mother's head, please tell me. Your loving Rita.

When she read it again she crossed out the bit about her mother's head. It seemed out of place. She would go tomorrow to Valerie Mander and ask her to give Chuck the letter. It didn't matter any more if Valerie thought she was chasing him. She couldn't live another day waiting for that telephone to ring. She was worn out with waiting for the postman to come, worn out with tossing and turning in her bed trying to work out if Margo was telling the truth or not.

* * *

Rita waited till Monday to give Valerie the letter – in case he telephoned Monday morning. Again she stood in the front room holding her white envelope.

'I know it's a nuisance,' she apologised, 'but I'm desperate, Valerie.'

282

She stared deliberately at the older girl, her lip quivering. She needed to enlist sympathy.

'But what's up now?' asked Valerie, puzzled. 'Your Auntie Nellie said he rang last week.'

'Yes, but he's gone to Halifax on a course and he said he'd write, but he hasn't. And he said he would probably see me on Saturday, but he didn't come.'

'On a course?' said Valerie. 'What sort of a course?'

'In Halifax. He's been chosen.'

'They don't go on courses. He's maintenance. He looks after the boilers and the electricity.'

Rita was insistent. There was a stubborn set to her jaw; she was polite but firm.

'I know it's a lot to ask, but Chuck did give him the other letter.'

'Well, he didn't mind the one about meeting him at the pictures.'

Valerie saw the look on the girl's face. Outside in the hall Mrs Mander was greeting someone from up the road, taking them up the hall, opening the kitchen door. The sound of the wireless was turned lower.

'I didn't want to tell you,' said Valerie, 'but Chuck told me about what was in the letter. He couldn't help it. He had to read it to Ira.'

'What d'you mean?'

Valerie was twisting the engagement ring round and round on her finger, feeling the three white diamonds in their setting of gold.

'Didn't you know?' she said. 'He can't read or write.'

It was too dreadful to take in. It was unbelievable, like Auntie Margo saying he had called at the house. She fled from the Manders', the letter crushed in her fist. She ran up the alleyway behind the houses. Once there had been meadows and trees, cows grazing, ducks on a pond – before they claimed the earth and built the wretched little houses : the industrial revolution, Uncle Jack called it, when they took the green and pleasant land and made it into a rubbish dump, with dwellings fit for pigs, the sky black with smoke from the factories, the houses built back to-back to conserve room – more bricks to the acre : a time when not many went to school, when education was for the few, when only the privileged could read or write. Her mind spun excuses for him : he had been ill as a child, he had been born in a desert far from the city. She saw him lying on a couch like the death of Chatterton with his arms spread wide; she saw him hoeing the sandy earth with a trowel, not a tree in sight. It was like learning he was blind or a cripple or a criminal. She didn't know how to cope with it. He was a dunce, her Ira, thick as a plank, not able to play cards, to read a book; he would never write her a letter. And at this thought hope surged up in her heart, she could have cried aloud with the enormous sense of relief. That was why he hadn't written as he promised ! He couldn't. He had gone to visit Auntie Marge to tell her he wasn't good enough for her. He knew Rita was clever at English, at composition. Nellie had boasted of the fact. He had come to Margo to say he was not worthy. Dear God, she thought, running up the cobbled alleyway, if he was that unschooled, he would need her, he would want to hold her in his life. She kicked the back gate open wide and strode up the sloping yard, not frightened any more.

*　　　*　　　*

Margo was disillusioned with the Dramatics Society. The cast seemed to be mainly workers from the crippled section. Apart from the principal boy and Cinderella, they all had one leg shorter than the other, or withered arms. The Ugly Sisters, two fellows from the explosives department, wouldn't need any make-up. They hadn't offered her a part. She was just one of the chorus. She sat around for hours after work waiting for the pianist to come, wrapped in her fur coat at the back of the hall. They wanted her to come on Thursday as

284

well. Some big mouth had said Margo's sister was a dressmaker and they wanted Margo to give them some idea about costumes.

'It's Nellie that knows about clothes,' she said. 'I don't think I can come.'

But they insisted – they said she must pull her weight. She thought gloomily of staying late one night a week all through the winter, standing in the freezing cold to catch her bus home, her dinner lying shrivelled in the oven.

*   *   *

The feeling of hope inside Rita didn't last very long. He never telephoned. At work she put her fingers in her ears to deaden the sound of the bell that never stopped ringing. Mr Betts spoke to her quite sharply – he said she was slacking, she wanted to pull her socks up.

On the Saturday, hope died entirely. He wasn't under the clock. She waited for hours. She didn't want to go back home.

Nellie had almost finished the beautiful engagement dress; she was sewing the buttonholes by hand. Valerie said she felt the right shoulder was a wee bit out of line. Nellie unpicked the arm-hole and reset it. She wouldn't have taken notice of anyone else, but Valerie had an eye for such things. They were going to have the engagement party next weekend. Cyril Mander was decorating the front room; Mrs Mander had chosen new curtains. George might even be able to get leave. When Rita asked Valerie if Chuck had seen Ira, the older girl hated to tell her there was no sign of the boy.

'Chuck did look.'

'But where is he?' cried Rita.

'It's a big camp, you know, love. It doesn't mean he isn't there.'

Valerie didn't know what to say for the best. Chuck had made a few inquiries – discovered what section he was in – but the boy couldn't be found. Chuck said dozens of the young ones deserted every month – ran off to London with women. He certainly hadn't gone on a course – never to Halifax. She wondered if the girl was confiding in her auntie. Valerie felt responsible – after all Rita had met the young soldier at their house. She disliked the look of despair on Rita's face, the panic. It soured her own happiness. The girl was acting as if she was heart-broken. She hoped she hadn't got herself into trouble. It was just the daft sort of thing that would happen to someone like Rita – damp behind the ears, wrapped up in tissue-paper all her life, never exposed to the wind.

10

NELLIE was tired, but satisfied. She had worked full out on the lovely Valerie's dress. In the afternoon she pressed the skirt and draped the frock over the model. She went down on her hands and knees, crawling round and round the floor to make sure the hem was absolutely even. She had plenty of time. Marge wouldn't be home for a meal – she had gone to her dramatics – and Rita wouldn't want much, not with the poor appetite she had lately. They could have something cold, and she could go round to Valerie's after tea for the final fitting. There was a button not quite in line. She re-sewed it there and then, a little on tip-toe to reach, her eyes screwed up against the light. She sat down to rest and stared critically at the dress. The beauty was in the yards of material in the skirt, the low cut of the bodice. Mrs Mander wanted sequins but Valerie said no, it had to be plain. She saw Valerie whirling round and round like a film star, all her petticoats showing, her plump knees silky in her nylon stockings. She should ask Valerie to get Rita a pair of those nylons. It might cheer her up. It hadn't lasted very long, the courting of the young American. She hadn't needed to show her disapproval – he had simply vanished into thin air. Jack had said something about him calling one afternoon and Marge sitting in the front room with him, but he'd got the wrong end of the stick. Marge would be at her work and she would never dare take him into the front room, not without Nellie's permission. She stood and went through to see that everything was alright;

twitched the lace curtains into line, ran a finger along the mantelshelf. Funny how she didn't miss the rosewood table, the bamboo stand. It was as if they had never been. When Jack was in a good mood she would mention she wanted the sideboard shifting and see what he said. Marge said there were mice in the box-room; she wouldn't be surprised if they ate right through mother's furniture. It was on account of the pigeons they kept next door; there was always vermin. Marge only said it to upset her. She'd told Jack she was selling the furniture. If Jack hadn't known her better he might have believed her; he might have thought she was getting mercenary in her old age. It could have hurt him, after all the money he poured into the house – the bath upstairs, the decorating – and the money he gave each week for Rita. When they had been little, it had been Marge that had been the generous one. Jack was tight, but Marge would give you the shirt off her back. Life did funny things to people, manipulated them. But if you kept faith with God it was alright. She had prayed about Rita and He had listened. She wasn't thinking only of herself, she did know he was not for Rita – the way he held his knife and fork, the way he lounged all over the furniture. Chuck wasn't like that. He called Cyril Mander 'Sir'. He took his hat off when he entered the house.

Valerie popped in on her way home. Her gloves were real leather. She had a little fur tippet about her neck.

'Oh, it's lovely, Auntie Nellie, it really is.'

She stood in wonder in front of the green taffeta dress, touching the material of the shoulder gently with her fingers.

'The shoulder's alright now,' said Nellie anxiously.

'Oh, it's lovely! I didn't want to crush the skirt.'

'I'll come over after tea for the final fitting.'

'Come whenever you like,' said Valerie. 'I'm not seeing Chuck this evening. Our George is home on leave.'

She confided in Nellie that George didn't take to Chuck. Cyril said he was being bloody-minded. Chuck was being very understanding, giving the boy time to get adjusted.

288

George said the Yanks had taken their time coming into the war. Cyril said it was Roosevelt's fault, not Chuck's.

'George is jealous of his money,' said Valerie. 'He's jealous of his jeep – all the time off he gets. He hates Yanks.'

'Well, it's understandable, I suppose,' said Nellie; and Valerie gave her an old-fashioned look. When Rita came in a few moments later Valerie asked her if she would like to see her new shoes.

'They're green,' she said, 'with red soles. They're lovely.'

'I might come along later,' said Rita. She was listless; she had shadows under her eyes as if she hadn't slept. She curled up on the sofa and turned her eyes away from the engagement dress.

'Valerie looks a picture in that dress,' said Nellie, 'a proper picture.'

'I bet she does,' Rita said. But she didn't care if her aunt preferred Valerie to her. She had filled her mind during the week with so many variations, ways of finding him, reconciliations, scenes of the future, that now she was empty. There were no pictures left in her head – just a voice very small and demanding, crying for him to come back.

'You'd suit green,' said Nellie, laying the table for tea.

Rita saw no sense in it – green, blue, it was all one.

Outside it was raining again, the cat cried at the window to come in. All day he had sat in the meagre branches of a sycamore tree at No. 11 waiting for the ginger female to come out into the yard.

Rita wouldn't go to the Manders with Nellie; she said she would come round later.

'You'll be all on your own Rita,' protested Nellie. 'Your auntie won't be home for hours.'

When she had gone, Rita went upstairs into the front bedroom. She opened the drawers of the dressing table and looked inside Margo's old handbag. There was a nail file and an empty carton of cigarettes; a letter from a firm saying her

289

application had been received. She dragged the black suitcase from under the bed: a dress rolled up in mothballs, an empty envelope with a Dutch postmark, Margo's gas mask, a little pen-knife made of ivory, a flat wallet with a birthday card in it and a ten-shilling note. She took the pen-knife and the money. She didn't need it – Nellie wouldn't take any of her wages – but she felt Margo owed her the ten-shilling note. There was nothing personal she could pry into, nothing exciting like the book she had once found. She went downstairs to fetch her coat.

*　　*　　*

Margo was ready for Nellie to be scathing about her coming home early – the remarks about her having no staying power. She was going to say the rehearsal had been cancelled. It had in a way: in her mind at any rate, she had just stopped being interested – sitting about for hour after hour waiting to sing one song. When she let herself into the house she was grateful that no one was in. It was awful sitting with young Rita, watching her waste away for love of Ira. She saw the cat pressed against the window, waiting to be let in. She opened the back door wide and put down a saucer of milk. Outside it was close, the rain coming down softly, spotting the red tiles of the yard. She sat down to rest, spreading her legs to ease them. Reaching out to pull the evening paper from the sideboard, she felt something cool to her touch. It was George Bickerton's pen-knife. She couldn't think what it was doing under the newspaper. She held it in her hand and remembered him peeling an apple for her, long ago on a Sunday afternoon in Newsham Park. It had made her laugh the precise way he loosened the green skin, round and round till it dangled to his lap, exposing the white fruit, the blade of his knife glistening with juice. She went through into the scullery to boil a kettle. She stood at the open door, watching the rain. She heard footsteps coming up the alleyway.

Mrs Mander thought the dress was a perfect fit – for her taste, a trifle plain, but Valerie looked beautiful. Even George was enthusiastic.

'By gum, it looks good,' he said, 'even if it's wasted on a Yank.'

He was putting Brylcreem on his hair, making himself smart to go down to the pub with his father. Cyril thought the world of him – his sailor boy in his bell-bottom trousers, the white bit at his chest showing off his pink skin, the little jaunty hat on the hall-stand.

Valerie stood at the mirror, holding her skirts away from the generous fire, looking at the curve of her shoulders, the plump arms rounded beneath the green straps. She had a tilted nose, brown eyes with full lids, a mouth that perpetually smiled above a slightly weak chin.

'I'm not sure about the waist,' she said. 'What d'you think?'

'What's wrong with the waist?' asked Mrs Mander. She studied her from every angle.

'A belt, you mean,' said Nellie. Valerie was gripping her waist with her two hands, emphasising the fullness of her hips.

'I'm off,' said Cyril. He kissed his wife full on the lips. He was a man that never did anything without gusto.

'What d'you think, Nellie? D'you think a belt would round it off?'

Nellie thought she might be right.

'I could wear me brooch,' said Valerie. 'The one Chuck gave me.'

'Is Rita's young man coming to the party?' asked Mrs Mander. 'He's very welcome.'

Valerie and Nellie avoided looking at one another. When her mother went to put a hot water bottle in George's bed, Valerie said, 'How is Rita, Auntie Nellie? I'm that worried about her.'

But Nellie wasn't forthcoming, she had her pride. She wouldn't discuss young Rita in front of the neighbours. She said she thought Valerie was right about a belt. It would give

291

the finishing touch. She had a piece of material at home that would do.

'Have a cup of tea first,' said Mrs Mander; and Valerie said gaily, 'No mum. Get out the whisky. Give Auntie Nellie a real drink. It'll put hairs on her chest.'

It was a vulgar thing to say, but Nellie took it from her. There wasn't anything Valerie could do to offend, in her opinion. Rita came in but she wouldn't take her coat off.

'I don't think I'll stop,' she said. She was shrunken in her white macintosh, a reproach to the happy Valerie. God forgive you, her face said; here I am, seventeen years old, without hope. She made the little room depressing, refusing to relax or sit by the fire.

'Have a drink,' said Valerie. 'Auntie Nellie won't mind.'

Auntie Nellie, who thought she minded, nodded her head in acceptance, seeing Valerie was in charge. There was something elderly about Rita, despite her youth. As if she was tired, aged beyond her years by her emotion : her eyebrows frozen in an arch like a comedian, the cupid bow of her mouth drooping like a clown.

'Haven't you heard yet?' whispered Valerie, when Nellie was in the kitchen helping Mrs Mander with the tea.

'No,' the girl said coldly, as if it was Valerie's fault. She stood by the yellow sideboard accusingly, her arms held stiffly, taking her drop of whisky in little sips as if it was medicine.

'Sit down, do,' said Nellie, irritated by the sight of her wilting by the door.

'I'm going for a walk,' she said, and off she went up the hall.

'Having trouble?' asked Mrs Mander, genuinely wanting to help. She could have said a lot years ago, when Rita was a little lass; she could have guided Nellie; but she was never consulted. You had to be careful with girls. They were like blotting paper. Boys were devils – they strode away without a backward glance. Girls were different. They lingered, kicking against the pricks, stamped by the mother's authority. When they rebelled in earnest you had to look backwards to find the cause. She herself had only to look at Marge, her looney ways, her mode of dress, that business with the manager of the dairy some years before.

'She's shook up,' admitted Nellie. 'It will blow over.'

Mrs Mander hadn't any business to interfere. She looked at the lovely Valerie in her engagement dress and held her tongue.

*　　　*　　　*

Nellie went home to cut out the belt. She said she would come back when it was finished.

'Rita,' she called up the stairs, hoping she had gone to her bed. She didn't like her wandering about Anfield late at night. Rita had made a show of her, acting so theatrically, not talking to Mrs Mander, never saying 'Thank you very much' for her drink. She thought that Valerie was right about the belt. She cut the material and sat down at her sewing machine, running the piece of cloth under the needle; snapped the thread with her false teeth; took up her scissors and snipped the loose ends free; turned the hem of the taffeta and leaned back in her upright chair to ease her back. She got such pains in her shoulders.

She took her foot off the treadle. She thought she heard something upstairs. The cat was crawling round and round on the newspapers behind the door.

'Give over, Nigger,' she said, turning to the machine.

There was definitely a noise upstairs. She clutched her hands in her lap and stared at the ceiling. She remembered what Marge had said about mice. Something scratched the floor boards, above the door into the hall. Something rustled. It couldn't be mice. The pigeon coops were on the ground floor, outside the scullery door. Mice couldn't be eating mother's furniture. They ate paper and cloth, not wood –

293

like the man in Germany who stowed a fortune away under the bed – bank notes – and found it shredded.

'Nigger,' she said, the scissors still in her hand, 'come on!' picking the cat up awkwardly in her arms, going up the stairs to the box-room. The cat hung over her arm, struggling to be free.

'Give over,' she murmured, anchoring it by the ears, puffing as she climbed.

She opened the door with the cat half over her shoulder, ready to flee down the stairs. It wasn't quite dark. There was a glimmer of light on the landing. Inside the box-room she saw first the bamboo stand; behind it the edge of the truckle bed, and two legs, white in the half light, the knees bunched together, a welter of stockings about the ankles, the feet turned inwards. He was standing up, buttoning his trousers, dressed, apart from his jacket, which was laid across the rosewood table – she could see the metal buttons gleaming. She backed away and stood on the landing. He caught hold of his coat and dragged it along the table. She heard the buttons scratching across the wood – a minute sound like a mouse scampering for safety. She leaned against the wall and the cat leapt from her arms and flowed down the stairs. He came out on to the landing with his jacket over his shoulder. Sheepish. He looked in the dim light as if he was ashamed of himself. He passed her, going to the head of the stairs with his head sunk on his chest. How dare he scratch Mother's furniture? A lifetime of sacrifice, of detailed care. What right had he to drag his clothing across the polished wood? She thought it was safe up here, away from the light of the window, untouchable. He was no good, he was disgusting. She could feel the anger gathering in her breast, the whole house was loud with the beating of her outraged heart. She raised her arm and stabbed him with the scissors – there below the stubble of his hair, at the side of his neck. She was that annoyed. He turned and looked at her, clutching the side of his throat, a quick decisive slap of his hand as if an insect had stung him. He was surprised. He

294

opened his mouth and his foot faltered on the step of the stairs. He flung out his arms to balance himself and he fell sideways, rolling down the turkey carpet, crumpling into a heap, his coat flying to the foot of the front door, and something like a spray of water cascading from his pocket, leaping and bouncing across the lino like sweeties burst from a bag. He bashed his head on the iron curve of the umbrella stand. Flung out a leg and knocked the little wax man from his pedestal. Hurled it from its glass dome. Sent it sliding and snapped in half among the imitation pearls. Opened his mouth in agony. Died before the air left his lungs.

The cat, crouching beneath the stairs, came out and sniffed at the floor. Putting out a paw it slapped a bead playfully and ran to the door like a kitten. Nellie came down the stairs slowly, sat on the bottom step and leaned forward to examine Ira. With her left hand she undid her fingers from the handle of the scissors, and put them away in the pocket of her apron. He lay with his face turned to the hall carpet. She had punctured the skin of his neck. There was blood oozing gently from the wound, staining the cream collar of his shirt. She went into the kitchen and shut him out in the hall, taking the scissors from her pocket and laying them on the table. She felt she had done wrong, but there were mitigating circumstances. He shouldn't have touched the furniture : he had no right to be in the box-room with her – her stockings round about her ankles and her white knees exposed. He had come into their lives and caused nothing but trouble – upsetting Rita, making a liar out of her. She thought of Rita as a little girl, riding a donkey at Blackpool, jogging up and down as she rode across the sand, running in and out of the waves with Jack's handkerchief wound around her head to keep the sun off, kicking her feet in the water. It would be better if children stayed small, never grew up, never knew how deep the sea could be.

'What are we going to do?' said Marge.

She stood in the doorway with her eyes wide open as if she

was standing in a terrible draught. Nellie couldn't look her in the eye. Not yet. The shock had been too great. The sort of things Marge got up to were beyond her. She couldn't have known what she was about. Even though she had been a married woman, she couldn't have understood what she was doing.

'I can't think,' she said. 'I can't get me thoughts.'

'We ought to tell someone,' said Margo.

'Wait on,' Nellie said.

She went out into the hall and looked at Ira again. He was very long and skinny. He lay with his leg buckled up under his buttocks. He hadn't moved.

Marge was looking at her, her hand twisting about at the waist of her dress.

'I've got to do Valerie's belt,' said Nellie. 'I said I would go back.'

'We ought to tell someone,' said Margo again, like a gramophone record – like Jack's records in the upstairs room above the shop, covered with dust.

'If we do,' Nellie said, 'there'll be talk. I don't want there to be talk.'

'But it's wicked,' Margo said, unable to keep her eyes from the man on the floor, with the little pearls scattered about his head.

'We haven't had much of a life,' cried Nellie. 'We haven't done much in the way of proving we're alive. I don't see why we should pay for him.' She thought 'wicked' was a funny word coming from Marge, considering what she'd been doing. She thought of them both being taken into custody and Mother's furniture left with the dust accumulating.

'Think of the scandal,' Nellie said. 'Whatever would Rita do? I only did what was best. He had no right to touch Mother's table.'

They sat on either side of the fireplace listening to the clock ticking. In the hall Nigger rolled beads across the lino.

'Whatever was he doing with that necklace?' asked Nellie.

296

But Margo was moaning, rocking herself back and forwards on her chair as if to ease some private grief.

After a time Nellie stood up and went into the hall. She pulled down the curtain from under the stairs.

'We best wrap him up,' she said.

'What for?' Margo asked.

'We don't want young Rita tripping over him.'

She was very capable, a dressmaker to her bones. She put the chenille curtain under the clamp of the sewing machine and made a bag for Ira. She made Marge drag him by the feet into the kitchen. He pulled the carpet sideways and his head bumped on the lino. At the side of his throat the wound looked as if he had been kissed by a vampire. There was a little bubble of blood about the edges. Nellie said they had to put him inside the curtain.

'What for?' said Margo. She was gormless, all the sense knocked out of her.

'We've got to get Jack,' said Nellie. 'He best come round with the van. We have to cover him up. You know how squeamish Jack is.'

They slid him into the bag. It was like turning a mattress; Nellie made Marge hold Ira in her arms by the sewing machine so that she could sew the bag up over his head. It had to be a proper shroud. Jack mustn't see any part of him. There was no cause to lay pennies on his eyes or cross his hands on his breast. He wasn't one of the family.

'Wait on,' said Margo.

She went into the hall bravely and gathered up the pearls, brought them into the kitchen and slipped them into the curtain with Ira.

'Whatever was he doing with that necklace?' said Nellie once more.

'I don't know,' Margo said, lifting him in her arms again and letting Nellie complete her job. 'He said Rita buried them in the garden and he dug them up when she wasn't looking. He thought I might want them.'

'What garden?' asked Nellie, snapping the thread with her hands, unable to use the scissors. Marge couldn't tell her.

'There wasn't time,' she explained.

She clasped him closer in her arms, felt the curve of his head against her breast, the length of his legs buried in the chenille curtain.

She ran up the road to the Manders' and said Nellie wasn't feeling too good. She wanted to use the phone to contact Jack.

'Shall I go up?' asked Mrs Mander.

But Margo told her not to bother. Nellie wouldn't want a fuss.

'You're to come at once,' she said to Jack. She knew the Manders could hear every word.

'Is Nellie bad?' cried Jack, alarmed. He shouted down the phone as if she was deaf.

'Just bring the van,' said Margo. 'Quick as you can.'

The heels of her shoes as she walked back to the house clicked like knitting needles. It was as if someone was following her.

They dragged Ira through into the wash-house in case Rita should come back. The cat thought it was a game, digging its paws into the material of the curtain, jumping skittishly into the air. Margo got the giggles when they had difficulty getting him through the door. She had to let go of him and lean against the sink.

'Give over,' said Nellie.

She was as white as a sheet, strong as steel. She never paused to gather breath. She pulled Ira down the back step into the dark and told Margo to open the wash-house door. She was used to carrying the dummy about. The screw had gone from the stand – you had to watch the body didn't fall away from the pole. She handled the curtain with skill. When they lumped him on to the concrete they snapped the head of the lupin plant. All its petals blew away down the yard.

298

When Nellie had manoeuvred him into the wash-house she still thought of things to do.

'Straighten the hall,' she bade Marge. 'There's a stair-rod broken. Throw it into the back.'

When Jack knocked at the door, she ran up the hall after Marge and told her not to let him in.

'Tell him to go round the back,' she hissed. 'Tell him to take the van up the alleyway.'

Jack cursed Marge – he thought she was playing silly beggars. He hadn't a collar to his shirt, just a stud. He looked like the vicar.

'Whatever's going on,' he said, coming in through the back door with his face all peaky with bewilderment.

'Sit down,' said Nellie. She told him very little beyond the fact that she had knocked the young American down the stairs. She didn't say what he was doing upstairs. Or why she had stabbed him with the scissors. Something had happened, she hinted, and she'd only done what was best. She knew by his face that he didn't want to ask any questions. He was too frightened. He didn't want to know.

'It was that umbrella stand,' she said, fingering the tape measure that hung about her neck. 'You always said it was a death trap.'

'Oh my God,' said Jack. He clutched the mantelpiece for support. 'Where is he?' he asked, after a moment.

'In the wash-house,' said Margo.

'Oh my God,' he said.

'We'll have to get him in the van,' Nellie told him. 'You'll have to take him down to the docks.'

'Oh my God.'

'You'll have to tip him in the river. That's best.'

'Oh my God,' he moaned again.

He couldn't help them. The two women had to take Ira from the wash-house and slither him down the yard to the van. They could hear Jack retching in the scullery.

'Take him,' said Nellie, when they were done. 'Take him

down to Bootle, Jack.' She held his face in her two hands, shaking him a little to give him courage. 'You're a good boy,' she said.

'Oh my God,' he whispered, going down the yard with his black hat jammed on his head. They waved to him from the back step.

When the gate shut behind him he felt very alone. He knew Nellie couldn't come with him on account of her health. But he hated being in the van with Ira in the back.

Nellie held her hand to her heart. The rain was pattering on the wash-house roof. She stood there for all the world as if she was taking the air.

*   *   *

Afterwards she went through into the little front room, the tape measure still dangling about her neck, and allowed herself a glass of port. And in the dark she wiped at the surface of the polished sideboard with the edge of her flowered pinny in case the bottle had left a ring . . .

300

THE
BOTTLE
FACTORY
OUTING

1

The hearse stood outside the block of flats, waiting for the old lady. Freda was crying. There were some children and a dog running in and out of the line of bare black trees planted in the pavement.

'I don't know why you're crying,' said Brenda. 'You didn't know her.'

Four paid men in black, carrying the coffin on their shoulders, began to walk the length of the top landing. Below, on the first floor, a row of senior citizens in nighties and overcoats stood on their balconies ready to wave the old woman goodbye.

'I like it,' said Freda. 'It's so beautiful.'

Opulent at the window, she leant her beige cheek against the glass and stared out mournfully at the block of flats, moored in concrete like an ocean liner. Behind the rigging of the television aerials, the white clouds blew across the sky. All hands on deck, the aged crew with lowered heads shuffled to the rails to watch the last passenger disembark.

Freda was enjoying herself. She stopped a tear with the tip of her finger and brought it to her mouth.

'I'm very moved,' she observed, as the coffin went at an acute angle down the stairs.

Brenda, who was easily embarrassed, didn't care to be seen gawping at the window. She declined to look at the roof of the hearse, crowned with flowers like a Sunday hat, as the coffin was shoved into place.

'She's going,' cried Freda, and the engine started and the black car slid away from the kerb, the gladioli and the arum lilies trembling in the breeze.

*

'You cry easily,' said Brenda, when they were dressing to go to the factory.

'I like funerals. All those flowers — a full life coming to a close —'

'She didn't look as if she'd had a full life,' said Brenda. 'She only had the cat. There weren't any mourners — no sons or anything.'

'Take a lesson from it then. It could happen to you. When I go I shall have my family about me — daughters — sons — my husband, grey and distinguished, dabbing a handkerchief to his lips —'

'Men always go first,' said Brenda. 'Women live longer.'

'My dear, you ought to participate more. You are too cut off from life.'

When Freda spoke like that Brenda would have run into another room, had there been one. Uneasily she said, 'I do participate. More than you think.'

'You are not flotsam washed up on the shore, without recourse to the sea,' continued Freda. She was lifting one vast leg and polishing the toe of her boot on the hem of the curtains. 'When we go on the Outing you bloody well better participate.'

'I can't promise,' said Brenda rebelliously.

Unlike Freda, whose idea it had been, the thought of the Outing filled her with alarm. It was bound to rain, seeing it was already October, and she could just imagine the dreary procession they would make, forlornly walking in single file across the grass, the men slipping and stumbling under the weight of the wine barrels, and Freda, face

304

distorted with fury at the weather, sinking down on to the muddy ground, unwrapping her cold chicken from its silver foil, wrenching its limbs apart under the dripping branches of the trees. Of course Freda visualised it differently. She was desperately in love with Vittorio, the trainee manager, who was the nephew of Mr Paganotti, and she thought she would have a better chance of seducing him if she could get him out into the open air, away from the bottling plant and his duties in the cellar. What she planned was a visit to a Stately Home and a stroll through Elizabethan gardens, hand in hand if she had her way. The men in the factory, senses reeling at the thought of a day in the country with the English ladies, had sent their Sunday suits to the cleaners and told their wives and children that the Outing was strictly for the workers. Rossi had given Freda permission to order a mini-coach; Mr Paganotti had been persuaded to donate four barrels of wine, two white and two red.

'You should be terribly keen,' said Freda. 'All that fresh air and the green grass blowing. You should be beside yourself at the prospect.'

'Well, I'm not,' said Brenda flatly.

Freda, who longed to be flung into the midst of chaos, was astonished at her attitude. When they had first met in the butcher's shop on the Finchley Road, it had been Brenda's lack of control, her passion, that had been the attraction. Standing directly in front of Freda she had asked for a pork chop, and the butcher, reaching for his cleaver on the wooden slab, had shouted with familiarity 'Giving the old man a treat are you?' at which Brenda had begun to weep, moaning that her husband had left her, that there was no old man in her world. She had trembled in a blue faded coat with a damaged fur collar and let the tears trickle down her face. Freda led her away, leaving the offending cut of meat on the counter, and after a week they found a room together in Hope Street, and Freda learnt it wasn't the husband that had abandoned Brenda, it was she who had left him because she couldn't stand him coming home drunk every night from the Little Legion and peeing on the front step. Also, she had a Mother-in-Law who was obviously deranged, who sneaked out at dawn to lift the eggs from under the hens and drew little faces on the shells with a biro.

It was strange it had happened to Brenda, that particular kind of experience, coming as she did from such a respectable background — private school and music lessons and summer holidays playing tennis — exchanging her semi-detached home for a remote farmhouse in Yorkshire, lying in a great brass bed with that brute of a husband, and outside the wild moors, the geese and ducks in the barn, the sheep flowing through a gap in the wall to huddle for warmth against the sides of the house. She was so unsuited for such a life, with her reddish hair worn shoulder-length and stringy, her long thin face, her short-sighted blue eyes that never looked at you properly, while she, Freda, would have been in her element — there had been white doves on the out-house roof.

It was unfair. She told her so. 'I always wanted to live in a house with a big kitchen. I wanted a mother in a string vest and a pinny who made bread and dumpling stew.'

'A string vest?' said Brenda dubiously, and Freda couldn't explain — it would have been wasted on her.

Since that first outburst in the butcher's shop, Brenda had become withdrawn and unemotional, except for her delusion that men were after her. Freda had hoped working in a factory would enrich Brenda's life. When she had seen the advertisement in the newsagent's shop she had told her it was just the sort of job they needed, even if it paid badly, seeing they could save on tube fares and lunches and wouldn't have to wear their good clothes. Brenda said she'd got no good clothes, which was the truth. Freda had given up her job as a cashier in a nightclub: the hours were too erratic and it meant she could never get up early enough to go for auditions. Every Thursday she bought a copy of *The Stage* and every Friday night she went to a theatrical pub and met people in the business. Nothing ever came of it. Brenda didn't do anything, apart from a little shopping. She got a postal order from her father every week, but it wasn't enough to live on.

'It's not right,' Freda told her. 'At your age you've got to think of the future.'

Brenda, who was thirty-two, was frightened at the implication: she felt she had one foot in the grave. They had gone once to a bureau on the High Street and said they were looking for temporary work in an office. They lied about their speed and things, but the woman behind the desk wasn't encouraging. Secretly Freda thought it was because Brenda looked such a fright — she had toothache that morning and her jaw was swollen. Brenda thought it was because Freda wore her purple cloak and kept flipping ash on the carpet. Freda said they needed to do something more basic, something that brought them into contact with the ordinary people, the workers.

'But a bottle factory,' protested Brenda, who did not have the same needs as her friend.

Patiently Freda explained that it wasn't a bottle factory, it was a wine factory — that they would be working alongside simple peasants who had culture and tradition behind them. Brenda hinted she didn't like foreigners — she found them difficult to get on with. Freda said it proved how puny a person she was, in mind and in body.

'You're bigoted,' she cried. 'And you don't eat enough.'

To which Brenda did not reply. She looked and kept silent, watching Freda's smooth white face and the shining feather of yellow hair that swung to the curve of her jaw. She had large blue eyes with curved lashes, a gentle rosy mouth, a nose perfectly formed. She was five foot ten in height, twenty-six years old, and she weighed sixteen stone.

All her life she had cherished the hope that one day she would become part of a community, a family. She wanted to be adored and protected, she wanted to be called 'little one.'

'Maybe today,' Freda said, 'Vittorio will ask me out for a drink.' She looked at Brenda who was lying down exhausted on the big double bed. 'You look terrible. I've told you, you should take Vitamin B.'

'I don't hold with vitamins. I'm just tired.'

'It's your own fault. You should make the bloody bed properly and get a good night's kip.'

Brenda had fashioned a bolster to put down the middle of the bed and a row of books to ensure that they lay less intimately at night. Freda complained that the books were uncomfortable — but then she had never been married. At night when they prepared for bed Freda removed all her clothes and lay like a great fretful baby, majestically dimpled and curved. Brenda wore her pyjamas and her underwear and a tweed coat — that was the difference between them. Brenda said it was on account of nearly being frozen to death in Ramsbottom, but it wasn't really that. Above the bed Freda had hung a photograph of an old man sitting on a stool with a stern expression on his face. She said it was her grandfather, but it wasn't. Brenda had secretly scratched her initials on the leg of the chair nearest the window, just to prove this one was hers when the other fell apart due to Freda's impressive weight. The cooker was on the first floor, and there was a bathroom up a flight of stairs and a window on the landing bordered with little panes of stained glass. Freda thought it was beautiful. When she chose, the washing on the line, the fragments of tree and brick, were tinted pink and gold. Brenda, avoiding the coloured squares, saw only a back yard grey with soot and a stunted rambling rose that never bloomed sprawled against the crumbling surface of the wall. She felt it was unwise to see things as other than they were. For this reason she disliked the lampshade that hung in the centre of the room: when the wind blew through the gaps in the large double windows, the shade twisted in the draught, the fringing of brown silk spun round and shadows ran across the floor. She kept thinking it was mice.

'Get up,' said Freda curtly. 'I want to smooth the bed.'

It was awkward with all those books sticking up under the blankets. Freda was very houseproud, always polishing and dusting and dragging the hoover up and down the carpet, and she made some terrible dents in the paintwork of the skirting board. She only bothered in case Vittorio suddenly asked to accompany her home. He wasted some part of every afternoon chatting to her at her bench, all about his castle in Italy and his wealthy connections. She told him he had a chip on his shoulder, forever going on about money and position — she called him a 'Bloody Eyetie.' They had quite violent arguments and a lot of the time he spoke to her harshly, but she took it as a good sign, as love was very close to hate. She'd made Brenda promise to go straight out and walk round the streets if ever he looked like coming home with them. Only yesterday he had given her three plums in a paper bag as a present, and she'd kept the stones and put them in her jewel case in the wardrobe.

She told Brenda to carry the milk bottles downstairs. In the hall she paused and ran back upstairs to check the sheets were fairly clean, just in case.

2

Brenda broke into a run as soon as they left the house. A stream of traffic going very fast caused her to halt at the intersection of Park Road and Hope Street.

'Fool,' shouted Freda, walking leisurely behind her.

'We're late,' wailed Brenda. 'We've not been on time yet.'

'Foreigners,' Freda said carefully, 'understand about the artistic temperament.' She walked on in television serials very occasionally, either as a barmaid or a lady agitator.

'I hate being conspicuous. You know how I hate it.'

'You surprise me,' said Freda.

Brenda was so cold she was dressed onion-fashion in layers — pullovers and scarves and a double sheet of newspaper under her vest. She wore no make-up. Sometimes, when she suffered from the toothache, she affected a woollen balaclava that her husband had worn on the farm.

Freda walked towards the sweet-shop to buy her cigarettes. 'Calm yourself,' she called, as the dithering Brenda ran up and down the pavement. 'Nobody will say a word about the time. Not a bloody word.'

Brenda knew it was true. She also knew there was a reason for it, an explanation that Freda refused to credit. Freda hinted Brenda was trying to draw attention to herself.

310

'I ask you,' she had shouted quite loudly, 'is it likely, the way you're got up?' And she had laughed.

Brenda begged her to keep her eyes open so that she would observe the precise moment she was plucked from the bench, but Freda never bothered. She was always turned to Maria, talking about politics or the theatre, and Brenda couldn't very well tug at her arm with Rossi looking on so eagerly from behind the window of his office. Brenda disappeared for what seemed like hours, either down into the cloistered chill of the cellar or upstairs amidst the stored furniture. Freda had never noticed.

Majestically Freda came out of the sweet-shop and strolled up the street. She was like a ballroom dancer moving in time to some slow waltz, pointing her feet delicately as she advanced, swaying from side to side in her purple cloak, one hand raised slightly with wrist arched, as if she dangled a fan. She looked with interest into the basements of the Victorian houses and thought how disordered were the middle classes — the lack of carpeting, the identical shabby rocking-chairs set against the walls, the mania for stripped wood as if under the illusion they lived in log cabins in the outback. She saw herself with Vittorio, sprawled in an embrace upon the bare boards, toes pointing at the ceiling. Brenda was scurrying into the distance: as she ran she brushed the bulky side of a privet hedge with the padded shoulders of her over-large coat — the landlady had discarded it when her grand-dad died, intending it for the bin-men. Freda wouldn't walk with her dressed like that; she made her run on ahead.

The wine factory was on the corner of the street next to the Greek chip-shop. It was three storeys high with its paintwork peeling and the name PAGANOTTI on a brass plate above the door. The lorries parked in the main street and caused traffic jams. There was an alleyway and a

311

fire escape loaded with boxes and plastic containers, and a side door made of iron, outside which Brenda was waiting, shoulders hunched against the wind.

'Please keep your eye on me. It's not much to ask.'

'Shut up,' said Freda, patting her hair into place. No matter how rushed she was for time she managed to paint the lids of her eyes cobalt blue and to coat her lashes with vaseline.

Everyone shook hands with them when they came into work, all the tired bottling men in their green overalls and trilby hats. One by one they took it in turn to step away from the rusted machinery slowly revolving in the centre of the floor. They left the steel rods squirting out wine, pumped up from the cellar beneath into the dark rotating bottles, bashfully to hold the cool outstretched fingers of the English ladies. Freda found the ritual charming. It established contact with the elusive Vittorio, if only fleetingly. '*Bongiorno*', she trilled, over and over.

They worked from eleven in the morning till three in the afternoon. They weren't supposed to have a break for lunch, but most days Freda bullied Brenda into going over the road to the public house to share one hot sausage and one vodka and lime. Maria, who started at eight and left at two, could not bring herself to go with them. She brought sandwiches made of salami, the left-overs from her nephew's restaurant, wrapped up in a headscarf. She wore the black dresses she had carried from Italy twenty years before, and after midday, when the damp got to her bones, she climbed into a mail bag for warmth. All the same she suffered dreadfully from chilblains, and Freda persuaded her to wear mittens. She worshipped Freda, whom she thought bold and dashing and resourceful. What style she had — the large English girl with the milk-white skin and eyelids stained the colour of cornflowers. How easily she had wrought improvements in their daily labour. Refusing to stoop over the wooden labelling bench, she had complained loudly of a pain in her splendid back and found beer crates for them to sit on. She had purchased rubber gloves from the Co-op to protect her mauve and shining nails; she had insisted that the Mrs Brenda do the same. She had contrived an Outing into the landscape, a day under the sky and the trees. Best of all, she had condoned the wearing of mail bags and advised the use of mittens. At the sight of Freda, Maria's large pale face flushed pink with pleasure; she stamped her feet to ease her chilblains and swung her head from side to side. But for the cramp in her knee, she would have risen and genuflected.

'Hey up,' said Freda, when the round of hand-shaking was completed. 'You're wearing your sexy nylons again.' She was looking at the grey football socks on Maria's stumpy legs.

With joy Maria rocked back and forth on her beer crate. 'Aye, aye,' she moaned, rolling her eyes and darting glances at Freda, magnificent in her purple trousers and hand-made Cossack boots. She understood little of the conversation: the English girl gabbled her words so fast.

The ground floor of the factory was open to the street and the loading bay. In summer the stone walls kept the bottling area cool, in winter the temperature dropped below freezing. The men stamped their feet, blew on their fingers and pulled their trilby hats about their ears. On the stone columns that supported the floor above, the men had glued pictures from magazines — a view of Naples, a stout young lady standing in a garden, someone's son who had studied hard at night, bettered himself and passed an examination. Above the cardboard boxes stacked in rows twelve foot high, there was a picture of the Virgin holding her baby and a plaque of the Sacred Heart, sore wounded, nailed like a football rosette to the green painted wall. The work-benches faced a row of windows overlooking the back wall of the chip-shop and an inch of sky.

In vain Freda had tried to tell the men how low their wages were by other standards, how severely they were exploited. They listened politely but without comprehension. To them Mr Paganotti was a wise father, a *padrone* who had plucked them from the arid slopes of their mountain region and set them down in a land of milk and honey. What did she know of their lives before the coming of Mr Paganotti? They were *contadini* who had grown wheat and corn and grapes, but only with tremendous labour, such as made their work in the factory seem like one long afternoon of play. Sometimes they had managed a harvest of plums and apples. They had kept chickens and a cow or two. In every way they were peasants, dulled by poverty. But then there had been a miracle. Mr Paganotti in his infinite wisdom had picked four men from the village of Caprara and brought them to Hope Street, and when they had settled they sent for their wives and their sons and their cousins and they saved their wages and together bought one house, then two, until in time each owned a little brick house in the suburbs with hot water running from a tap and a lavatory that flushed. Gone were the terracotta roofs of the farm-houses they had known, the stone sinks, the primitive wood-burning stoves. Only the religious pictures remained and the statues of Christ on the cross. As the children of the first generation of workers grew up, their parents were diligent in conveying just how munificent was the generosity of Mr Paganotti. They remained a close and isolated community. No one ever left the factory to take other employment; the sons were encouraged to go on to University and become doctors and accountants. Those who did not have the ability joined their fathers on the factory floor. They had changed little in thirty years — even Mr Paganotti could not understand the language they spoke, the *dialetto bolognese* that was older than Italian

314

and closer to French. If there was a confrontation between himself and one of the cellar-men, Rossi the manager, who alone had adapted himself to the English way of life, was called in to act as interpreter. In spite of their good fortune they still stood like beasts of the field, tending Mr Paganotti's machines.

It was Brenda's job to rinse out the sponges in the morning and to tip the glue from the pot into the shallow trays on the benches. She didn't mind fetching the glue pot from beneath old Luigi's place, but she had to go to the Ladies' washroom to wet the sponges. She always ran straight across the factory floor without looking to right or left, in case Rossi caught sight of her, flying through the door of the washroom and out again with her sponges dripping, as if she was the last runner in a relay race. It looked as if she was really zealous and interested in what she was doing.

'You overdo it,' said Freda. She had slapped the little glittering labels into the glue and stacked a dozen bottles of wine in a neat triangle on the bench top. She maintained it was all the same wine — it was just the labels that were different. Today it was Rose Anjou and it was fractionally pinker than the Beaujolais — it could have been the tint of the glass bottles or dilution with water.

Brenda had only used one tray of labels when she was distracted by old Luigi at the far end of the line of benches. He stood with his feet wide apart to balance himself, on lengths of planking laid over the concrete floor to lessen the cold. He was muttering and pulling faces at the women. Freda, as she worked, talked incessantly and dramatically. She twisted and turned on her beer crate, she thumped the bottles down into the cardboard box at her side, she stamped her feet for emphasis. Each time that she got up to reach with her rubber-gloved fingers for another label, and sank backwards on to her upturned

315

crate, the frail old man rose in the air and settled again. As the morning wore on and he trotted more and more frequently to refill his little plastic beaker at the wine barrel reserved for the men, so his muttering became wilder, his glances less discreet. He loathed the English women; he held them in scorn. He would not shake hands with them in the morning; he refused to contribute to the Outing. Alone of all the Italians in the factory, he neither admired nor took pleasure in the appearance of Freda; if he could, he would have burnt her beer crate in the market square.

Freda was saying to Maria: 'You must support the Unions. It's your duty. It's no good burying your head in the sand. Know what I mean?'

'Aye, aye,' intoned Maria, wiping gently the neck of the bottle with her honey-coloured sponge.

'We could do with a bloody Union man here — the cold, the conditions. Talk about A Day in the Life Of — don't you know about the Factories Act?'

Above the hostile shoulder of Luigi, Brenda saw Rossi's face at the window of the office. She tried to avert her eyes, but he was jumping up and down, jerking his curly head in the direction of the door and smiling with all his teeth showing.

'Freda,' she hissed, out of the corner of her mouth.

'We shouldn't be working in a temperature like this,' said Freda. 'It's against the law.'

'Freda — he's at it again.'

'Old Piggynotty could be prosecuted.' Down slammed Freda's boots on the planking. The smell of talcum powder, dry and sweet, rose from the armpits of her grey angora jumper as she jabbed with her sponge at a completed bottle of Rose Anjou. 'Know what I mean?'

As if lassoed by an invisible rope, Brenda was dragged from her place at the bench. Unwillingly she passed the grimacing Luigi and walked between the avenue of

316

shelves filled with brandy bottles, towards the office. Rossi stood in the doorway waiting for her. 'I have something to show you,' he confided in a feverish manner, and was off, trotting towards the pass door, peering over his plump shoulder at her to make certain she was following. She was convinced all the men were looking at her. They tittered and insinuated, anchored to the bottling plant shuddering in the centre of the floor. They knew, she was sure, about Rossi: his childless marriage to an elderly wife called Bruna, his frequent trips into the basement, his sudden disappearances into the groaning lift in the corner behind the boxes, and always, like the smoke from a cigarette, herself trailing in his wake. Looking very serious, as if the matter was both urgent and highly secret, she descended the steps into the cellar.

Rossi was running across the stone floor beneath the white-washed arches hung with cobwebs. He made a small dandified skip into the air as he leapt the rubber hose that lolled like a snake between the barrels of wine. She always felt at a disadvantage in the cellar. Reverently she tip-toed deeper into the shadows cast by the little hanging lights. But for the sour smell of vinegar and the constant hum of machinery as the hose pumped wine to the floor above, she might have been in church. Rossi was bobbing about in the darkness, whispering 'Missy Brenda, come over here. I have a little drink for you.' He had a white overall, to show he was more important than the men, with PAGANOTTI embroidered on the pocket, and he wore suede shoes stained with wine.

'How kind of you,' said Brenda.

He took a medicine bottle from his pocket and poured the contents into two glasses that he kept on a shelf in one of the alcoves, ready for when he lured her down there. She had only been working in the factory for four weeks and it had started on her third day. He'd said then she ought to learn more about the cooling process.

'You like?'

'Yes, thank you very much.'

'You like me?'

'Oh yes, you're very nice.'

He was holding her wrist, tipping the glass backwards, trying to make her drink more rapidly. It was a kind of liqueur brandy, very hot and thick like syrup of figs, and it always made her feel silly. She could feel him trembling.

'What's it called?' she asked him, though she knew.

'Marsalla. You are a nice girl — very nice.'

She couldn't think how to discourage him — she didn't want to lose her job and she hated giving offence. He had a funny way of pinching her all over, as if she was a mattress whose stuffing needed distributing more evenly. She stood there wriggling, saying breathlessly 'Please don't, Rossi,' but he tickled and she gave little smothered laughs and gasps that he took for encouragement.

'You are a nice clean girl.'

'Oh, thank you.'

He was interfering with her clothes, pushing his hands beneath her tweed coat and plucking away at her jumpers and vest, shredding little pieces of newspaper with his nails. She tried to have a chat with him to calm him down.

'I'm so excited about the election, Rossi.'

'So many clothes.'

'Please don't. Are *you*? Oh stop it.'

'Why you have so much clothes?'

'Freda says she's going to vote Communist.'

'You like me?' he pleaded, pinching the skin of her back as much as he was able.

'Don't do that. Consider —'

'Why don't you like me?'

'Your wife. I do like you, I do really. We saw a funeral today. It was a nice funeral.'

He didn't know what she meant. He was trying to kiss her. He had a mouth like a baby's, sulky, with the underlip

318

drooping, set in a round dimpled face. Suck, suck, suck, went his moist little lips at her neck.

'There were lots of flowers. Freda cried when she saw the coffin.'

He paused, startled. In the gloom his eyebrows rose in bewilderment. 'A funeral? Your mammy has died?' Shocked, he left off trying to unravel her defences of wool and tweed and paper. She didn't know what to say. She was very tempted to assent.

'Well, in a manner of speaking — more Freda's than mine.'

'Freda's mammy is dead?'

She hung her head as if overcome, thinking of Al Jolson down on one knee with one hand in its white glove, upraised. Her own hand, unnaturally pink in its rubber covering, hovered above his shoulder. She was still clutching her sponge.

*

In the Ladies' washroom Freda was mystified. She combed her hair at the blotched mirror and asked suspiciously: 'What have we got the day off for? Why have I got to take you home?'

Brenda didn't reply. She was adjusting her clothing, shaking free the fragments of paper that fell from her vest.

'Have you got your toothache again?' Freda was annoyed at having to leave early. It didn't suit her; she hadn't had her talk with Vittorio. 'Look ,at the state of you. You've got cobwebs in your hair.'

'I'm taking you home,' said Brenda. 'On account of your mammy.'

'Me what?'

'I had to say she wasn't well.' She looked at Freda, who for once was speechless. Her mother had died when she was twelve and she had been brought up by an aunt in Newcastle. 'Actually I said we went to her funeral. I couldn't help it, Freda. You never take any notice of me.'

She was whispering in case Rossi was outside the door listening. Freda started to laugh — she never did anything quietly.

'Sssh,' said Brenda desperately, jumping up and down in embarrassment, releasing a fresh fall of newsprint on to the washroom floor.

In the alleyway, Patrick, the Irish van driver, was inhaling a cigarette. Elbow at an angle and shoulders hunched, he stared at them curiously through a cloud of smoke.

'She's hysterical,' explained Brenda, gripping the giggling Freda fiercely by the arm and steering her out into the street.

Later, in the security of the sparsely furnished room, Freda was inclined to get at the truth. 'In the cellar?' she queried. 'But what does he do?'

'Nothing really. He sort of fumbles.'

'Fumbles?' repeated Freda and snorted to suppress laughter. 'Does he feel your chests?'

'All over, really,' admitted Brenda, not liking to go into details — Freda could be very crude in her humour if given the facts. 'Sometimes we go upstairs among all that old furniture.'

'Upstairs? When?'

'Often. I told you, but you wouldn't listen.'

'You must have encouraged him. You must have egged him on.'

'I never. I never did any such thing.'

Freda couldn't get over it. She stared at Brenda lying full length upon the bed like a neglected doll — cobwebs stuck in her hair, her mouth slightly open and two little pegs of teeth protruding.

'I don't understand you at all. You must be mad. You're not telling me he rushes out while we're all bottling away and ties you up with his bootlaces and rushes off into the

320

cellar? You're not telling me I wouldn't have noticed something?'

Brenda had no reply to that.

'You shouldn't have talked to him so much. You're always talking to him, mouthing away at him as if he's stone deaf.'

Brenda gazed up at the ceiling defensively, the padded shoulders of her coat grotesquely lifted about her ears.

'I'm only saying my words clearly. His English is poor.'

'You look like Edward G. Robinson lying there.'

'You talk to Vittorio,' cried Brenda, stung by Freda's unkindness. She wanted sympathy and understanding, not criticism.

'That's different,' Freda said, and was forlornly aware it was the truth. Vittorio wasn't rushing her down into the cellar to fumble at her chests. She knew Brenda wasn't making it up. Though she lacked imagination, Brenda would go to any lengths rather than cause herself embarrassment. It was her upbringing. As a child she had been taught it was rude to say no, unless she didn't mean it. If she was offered another piece of cake and she wanted it she was obliged to refuse out of politeness. And if she didn't want it she had to say yes, even if it choked her. It was involved but understandable. There had been other small incidents that illustrated her extraordinary capacity for remaining passive while put upon. There had been the man on the bus who felt her leg almost to her knickers without her saying anything, until she had to move because it was her stop and then she'd said, 'Excuse me, I'm sorry.' And the woman with the trumpet who had stopped her in the street and asked her if she could borrow a room to practice in. Brenda loathed music. When Freda opened the door to the trumpet player and told her what to do with her instrument, Brenda hid behind the wardrobe.

'Why didn't you tell me sooner?' asked Freda more

321

gently — she looked so dusty and pathetic lying there — 'I would have put him in his place.'

'I did,' protested Brenda, 'Often.'

Freda started to laugh again. 'How on earth did you say my mother had died.'

'I didn't,' said Brenda. 'He did. I was trying to stop him fiddling with me and I mentioned the funeral we saw this morning.'

'You driva me wilda,' mimicked Freda. 'Justa when I thinka I have you in my graspa you talka abouta da funerelo —'

'Stop it,' Brenda said.

'You putta me offa ma spaghetti —' And Freda shook with laughter.

Sulkily Brenda closed her eyes.

After a moment Freda remembered Vittorio and decided she would go downstairs and ring up Maria to ask her to pop in for a cup of tea. If Rossi had told everyone about her loss it was quite possible Vittorio felt sad for her. Perhaps he had said something tender when he heard the news — like 'Poor child — poor grieving child' — maybe he was only waiting for an excuse to come round and offer his condolences. She had to know.

'Does Rossi ever get his thingy out?' she asked, looking in her purse for money.

Brenda pretended to be asleep; she stirred on the bed and sighed as if she were dreaming. It took some time to bring Maria to the telephone. Such a thing had never happened to her before at work and Freda was worried the pips would go before her message was understood. She had to bellow down the phone to explain who she was. Brenda could hear her quite plainly.

'Maria, Maria. It's me, Freda. You know — Freda — Maria —' She sounded as if she was going to burst into the love song from *West Side Story*. 'Maria . . . I want you to come to tea . . . this afternoon . . . after work . . . Can you iear me, Maria? . . . to tea. Here at my house. You come iere. No, today . . . to Freda. No I don't want any tea . . . I want to give you some . . .'

'Is she coming?' asked Brenda.

'God knows,' said Freda, and she went upstairs to the bathroom, taking a pan of water with her to flush down the lavatory. The cistern had been broken for ten days and the landlady said she couldn't find a plumber to mend it. Only Freda was inconvenienced. Brenda, who would have died rather than let the other occupants of the house know she used the toilet, usually went round the corner to the tube station.

Maria came at half-past two carrying a packet of tea and a bag of sugar. She entered the room timidly, her hands in their darned mittens, outstretched.

'*La povera orfanella*,' she murmured with emotion, embracing Freda, burying her head in the girl's ample shoulder. Awkwardly she patted her back and made little mewing sounds, and when she emerged again her face held such an expression of genuine perplexity and pain that it awakened feelings of remorse in Brenda.

Brenda sat Maria in the armchair by the hearth, to warm herself at the gas fire. Freda moved about the room slowly and with dignity, emptying tea-leaves into the china pot, putting the blue cups on the table, ready for the kettle to boil. Now and then she would stare out of the window with a far-away look in her eyes, as if she was remembering lost faces and lost laughter and the joy of a mother's love. After a decent interval, when the tea was poured and the biscuit tin handed round, she asked:

'And what did Vittorio say? Did he say anything?'

'Pah,' exclaimed Maria contemptuously, slapping the air with the flat of her hand. 'What could he say? Nobody work the day of their Mammy's funeral.'

'I mean, was he sorry?'

When she understood, Maria said Vittorio had looked

323

very sad. They were all sad, but not so sad as Mr Rossi: he was the saddest of them all, pale and dejected-looking as if it was a personal loss.

'She's in love with Vittorio,' Brenda said quickly, in case Freda flew into a paddy on the spot and explained the exact reason for Mr Rossi's dejection. Maria, after an initial moment of surprise, her mouth open, her eyes bewildered, stamped her feet approvingly on the thread-bare carpet. Such a match — the tall young landowner and the blonde English girl built like a tree. She recalled she could read the future in the tea-cups; a cook had taught her when she was in service in a house in Holland Park. She sat well forward in the armchair, black-clad knees wide apart, and stared into the depths of Freda's cup.

'There is a tall man,' she began, 'and a journey.'

Brenda withdrew into a corner of the room, seating herself at the table beside the window. Across the road on the balcony of the third floor an elderly woman in a blue dressing-gown and a hat with a rose pinned to the brim waved and gesticulated for help. Brenda knew her gas fire had blown up or she was out of paraffin or the cat had gone missing. It was unfortunate that Freda had rented a room opposite a building devoted to the old and infirm — there was always someone in need of assistance. Once Freda had become involved with a Miss Deansgate on the second floor, who had been a milliner for royalty; and every day for three weeks she took her bowls of soup and cups of tea, feeding her drop by drop from a tin spoon with a long handle that Miss Deansgate claimed had belonged to Queen Victoria's butler. Freda took Brenda to visit her, but she didn't enjoy it — the old woman had no stockings and her ankles were dirty and she sat on the lavatory and had to be helped back to bed. There was a funny smell in the living room. The sheets were yellow and the frill of the pillow-case stained, as if she dribbled as she slept. Miss Deansgate begged Freda not to let the ambulance take her away; but she was dying, and in the end they laid her on the stretcher under a red blanket, looking very cheerful and christmassy, and off she went, sliding a little on her canvas bed, as they bore her at a slant down the flight of stairs. She didn't come back, and Freda used the butler's spoon with the long handle to eat her porridge with in the morning.

Resolutely Brenda turned her eyes away from the woman with the rose in her hat. She looked at Freda and Maria by the fire, crouched over the drained cup as if the future lay there like a photograph. The murmurings of their voices and the hiss of the gas fire merged. A memory came to her. She was walking down a lane between green fields, bending her head to watch her own two feet in shiny shoes pacing the grey road. Behind her someone urged her to hurry; she could feel in the small of her back the round insistent tip of an umbrella propelling her forwards. She stumbled on the rough road, and as she fell she saw out of the corner of her eye a single scarlet poppy blowing in the brown ditch. She opened her eyes quickly, thinking 'Why can't they leave me alone?' and she was still there on the balcony, the woman demanding attention. Brenda wanted to bang on the window and tell her to go away. She hated the implied need, the intrusion on her privacy. Life was absurd, she thought, bouncing her up and down as if she were a rubber ball. She longed to lose height and roll away into a corner and be forgotten. Distress at her own conciliatory nature rose in her throat and lodged there like a stone. She swallowed and pouted her lips.

Freda found the fortune-telling satisfactory, though the reference to men in uniform and horses galloping was difficult to understand. She had a cousin in the navy but she knew nothing about horses. There was a lot of weeping and wailing and people walking in procession — that was the funeral of course. She was going on a long journey by land and sea — it could only refer to the Outing; possibly

325

there would be a lake in the grounds of the Stately Home and she and Vittorio would drift beneath the branches of a weeping willow, alone in a rowing boat. She would trail her hand in the water and tilt her head so that any sunlight available would catch her golden hair and blind him as he rowed. She wasn't sure about the white dress Maria saw, a long flowing dress with flowers at the waist. White was not her colour — she preferred something more definite. Maria visualised problems, seeing Freda wasn't a Catholic, and Freda said actually she was very high-church and often went to mass. She was a little taken aback at what Maria implied — she herself had not been thinking along such ambitious lines.

'I'm not keen on white, am I?' she asked, looking over her shoulder for confirmation, and saw Brenda at the table, her head silhouetted against the panes of glass, the room grown dark and the sky lying yellow above the roof tops, as if snow was on the way. 'It can't snow,' she cried, striding to the window and peering out into the street. 'Not with the Outing next week.'

She shook Brenda by the shoulder as if asking for a denial and saw she had been weeping.

*

In bed that night Freda wanted to know what had been wrong.

'You were crying. Were you upset about Rossi?'

'I wasn't crying. It was your cigarette smoke.'

'Shall I give Rossi a piece of my mind? I could say I was going to inform Mr Paganotti.' She was elated at the prospect. She saw herself confronting the foreign capitalist at his desk. While she was about it she would tell him the conditions in his factory were sub-standard.

'Don't you dare,' said Brenda. 'I don't want any fuss.'

Below in the street she heard the distant tipsy singing of Irishmen leaving the public house on the corner. From the embankment came the low demented wail of the express

326

as it left London for the North.

'Don't you miss the country?' Freda asked. 'The long quiet nights?'

'It wasn't quiet,' said Brenda, thinking of the cries of sheep, the snapping of twigs in the hedge as cattle blundered in the dark field, the tiny scratchings of shrews on the oilcloth of the kitchen shelf. 'Once his mother locked me in the barn with the geese.'

'Whatever for?'

'She just did. She shouted things outside and threw stones at the tin roof. The geese didn't like it.'

'What things?'

'This and that.'

'What did he say when you told him?'

'I didn't. I didn't like.'

'You know,' cried Freda, sitting up in bed and dislodging the faded pink eiderdown, 'you're a born victim, that's what you are. You ask for trouble. One day you'll go too far.' She lay down again and rubbed her toes together to warm them. 'It's probably all that crouching you did under dining-room tables during the war.'

'I never. I was never a war baby.' Brenda wished she would stop getting at her. Freda had a way of talking late at night that unwound her and sent her off into sleep while Brenda was left wide awake and anxious.

'It did make sense,' said Freda. 'The tall man and the journey.'

'That dress —' Brenda said.

'I don't get that. I'm not keen on white.'

'It's a wedding dress,' said Brenda.

All night Freda heaved and flounced beyond the line of books and the bolster encased in red satin. She flung her arm across the pillow and trapped strands of Brenda's hair. From her throat, as she dreamed, came the gurgle of unintelligible words. Brenda huddled on the extreme edge of the bed, holding her share of the blankets in both fists,

327

staring at the cream-painted door shimmering in the light of the street lamp. She remembered her husband coming home from the Legion, dragging her from bed to look at the moon through a telescope. She hated treading through the wet grass with the hem of her nightgown clinging to her ankles and him belching from his intake of Newcastle brown ale. He balanced the telescope on the stone wall and held it steady while she squatted shivering, leap-frog fashion, amidst the nettles, and squinted up at the heavens. The size of the moon, magnified and close, appalled her; she shrank from its size and its stillness, as it hung there like some great golf ball struck into the clouds. She shut her eyes at the memory, and unbidden came a picture of the grey farmhouse she had left, the glimmer of birch trees down by the stream, the vast curve of the worn and ancient moors rolling beyond the yard. It had been spring when she had gone there as a bride: there were lambs lying limp in the field, and he had freshly painted the window-sills for her and the rain barrel and the five-barred gate leading on to the moor. Her wedding dress, chosen and paid for by her mother, had been of cream lace with a little cloth hat to match, sewn with lillies of the valley. She wanted to wear a string of simple daisies about her neck, but Mother said she didn't have to look like a fool even if she was one. At the reception, when she stood with her new husband, Stanley, to greet their guests, his mother had leaned forward to kiss her on the cheek and bitten her ear.

She dozed and woke as Freda turned violently, tumbling books over the curve of the dividing bolster. It happened every night, the pitching of books into Brenda's half of the bed, and she lay with them digging into her shoulder and her hip, making no effort to dislodge them, her hands thrust into the pockets of her overcoat for warmth. At five the bed quivered as the tube train began to rumble beneath the waking street. Across the park the gibbons in the zoo leapt to the top of their wire cages and began to scream.

3

Brenda picked up two bottles of brandy and made small sounds of disapproval. 'Dear me,' she said, 'these are awful mucky.'

Save for old Luigi working away like a conveyor belt, she was alone. Rossi had gone into the city with Mr. Paganotti, the men were herded into the concrete bunker at the rear of the building and Maria was eating her salami sandwiches on a heap of sacks near the loading bay. Tut-tutting as she went, Brenda grasped the bottles in her arms and walked to the wash room. Freda's shopping basket on wheels, loaded with dirty washing, stood against the wall. She put the bottles on the stone floor and began to drag Mr. Paganotti's wardrobe away from the door of the first toilet. Having made a space big enough for her to squeeze through, she snatched one bottle of brandy by the neck, placed her back to the door and shoved. It was jammed. Turning round in the confined space, she leant against the wardrobe and kicked out violently with her shoe. The door sprang open and thudded against the wall; the noise reverberated throughout the wash-room. She put the brandy behind the lavatory bowl, closed the door and dragged the wardrobe back into place. Trembling, she carried the remaining bottle to the sink and dabbed at it with her sponge. 'Never again, God,' she murmured. 'Never again.'

Freda had planned it. She said she'd better stay at home for a few days seeing she was in mourning. They would think it callous otherwise, now that they knew of her loss. She bet anything old Piggynotty wouldn't pay her for time off. It was sensible to take a sample of the firm's products in lieu of wages.

'I can't do it,' Brenda said desperately. 'I'll have a heart attack.'

'You'll have one if you don't,' warned Freda menacingly. What with the cost of living and the oil crisis they deserved something to make life more bearable. 'Look at us,' she said brutally, 'the way we scrape along. Never a penny over at the end of the week. We can't afford to breathe.'

'We never could,' said Brenda. 'It's never been any different.'

She bent down and adjusted a vest that had draped itself over the side of the shopping basket. It was perfectly clean. Freda had just thrown anything in, mainly clothing from Brenda's drawer. The door opened behind her and the bog-roll man entered the washroom, his arms full of newspapers. He wasn't supposed to go near the toilets until after four o'clock, when all the women had gone home. He was short and bulky with a little moustache thin as a pencil line along his lip.

'I have come to place the toilet rolls,' he said, looking at her in a bold way and lingering on the bolstered front of her tweed coat. 'There are no rolls,' he continued. 'I have a shortage.'

'This was awfully dirty,' said Brenda, giving a last wipe with her sponge at the glistening bottle of brandy, and moving to the door. He put both arms out to capture her, hugging her to his green overalls. He smelt of wine and garlic and Jeyes fluid.

'You want to give me a little kiss?'

'No, not really,' she said, smiling politely and shaking her head so that the bristles on his chin scraped her cheek.

Tearing herself free she stumbled from the washroom and ran back to her beer crate and her labels. She supposed it

330

was the fumes from the wine that kept them all in a constant state of lust. It wasn't as if she set out to be desirable.

Maria appeared from the direction of the loading bay, a beaker in her hand, walking very fast and taking tiny steps as if she was still in her mail bag.

'You're early,' said Brenda. 'You've another ten minutes till the hooter goes.'

'I am to look in the box,' Maria told her, waving her arm in the air and spilling Beaujolais on to the floor. 'I am wanting shoes.'

In the corner, beneath the burglar alarm, were two large crates filled with old clothing of all descriptions. Mr Paganotti had a large number of elderly relatives living and dying in England, and hardly a month went by without his becoming the chief beneficiary of yet another will. A few choice articles of furniture he kept for his mansion near Windsor. Some things he sent to the salerooms; others he stored in the washroom, or upstairs on the first floor. The rest, the debris of a lifetime, he placed in boxes on the factory floor for the benefit of his workers. There were numerous pyjamas and nightgowns, golfing shoes in two tones, yellowing stays and white-flannel trousers and striped waistcoats mouldy with damp. There was a notice pinned to the wall, stating in Italian that Mr Paganotti was delighted if his employees found use for the contents — 'Please put 2p in the tea-caddy placed for the purpose.' Rossi emptied the caddy every two days in case Patrick the van driver was tempted to help himself to the proceeds.

Brenda was thirsty. She tried sipping Maria's wine, but it gave her an ache at the back of her jaw.

'Oooh,' she wailed, 'it's horrible.'

Maria, still rummaging for shoes, cackled with laughter and threw ties, and undergarments of incredible dimensions, on to the floor.

The machine Mr Paganotti had provided for hot drinks was out of order. When Brenda inserted her metal token and pressed the button marked 'Cocoa,' a thin stream of soup trickled into her cup. Patrick, come in from the street to be out of the wind, smiled at her sympathetically. He never knew what to do with himself in the lunch hour — the men he worked with couldn't understand a word he uttered, and Rossi treated him with suspicion, seeing he was Irish, following him about the factory in case he slipped a bomb beneath the cardboard boxes and blew them all to pieces.

'Look at that,' said Brenda. 'It's never cocoa.'

'The machine's busted,' he told her, giving it an enormous clout with his fist. He had large hands, discoloured with brown freckles, and badly bitten nails. One ear was slightly swollen where he had banged it falling down the steps of the Princess Beatrice the previous night, and there was a cut on his lip.

'Everything breaks,' said Brenda, 'All sorts of things break down these days. Electric kettles and washing machines and telephones.'

'You're right at that,' he agreed, jingling the coins in the pocket of his overalls and nodding his cropped head. He would have suited long hair, Brenda thought. It would have toned down his ears and covered his neck, which was broad and mottled with old adolescent scars.

'Our toilet's been broken for three weeks,' she told him. 'We can't get a plumber. The landlady's tried.'

'Is that a fact? Broken is it?'

'Plumbers don't live here any more,' explained Brenda, echoing what Freda had told her. 'It's on account of the high rents. Plumbers can't afford to live. It's the same with window cleaners,' she added.

'I'll fix it for you,' he said. And too late she realised what she had done.

'Oh no really, there's no need,' she protested.

But he wouldn't be put off. 'I'll be glad to. I'm good at the plumbing. Will I bring the tools round after work?

332

'It's not my toilet,' said Brenda. 'I'm not sure that the landlady —'

'I'll fetch the wherewithal from me lodgings and be round when I'm finished.'

'You're very kind,' said Brenda feebly, and returned with her beaker of soup to the bench. She stared at a bottle of Chateau Neuf du Pape and dreaded what Freda would say. She could almost hear her — 'You did what? You asked that lout from the bogs of Tipperary to mend our loo?' She wondered if she could sneak him upstairs without Freda knowing, or the landlady for that matter. Perhaps she could persuade him to wrap a duster round the end of his hammer.

*

Freda was not enjoying being off work. She hadn't the money to go down town and enjoy her leisure. She polished the surrounds of the floor and wedged the window open with Brenda's tennis racket. The room lacked character, she thought, looking critically at the yellow utility furniture and the ladies in crinolines walking in pairs across the wallpaper. There was no colour scheme — nothing matched; there was no unity of design. Every time she made some little improvement, like arranging a curtain round the washbasin near the door, it only drew attention to the cracked tiles and the yards of antiquated piping climbing in convoluted loops up the wall. On the shelf she had improvised above the fireplace were some paperbacks, two library books and a bottle of H.P. sauce that Brenda had carelessly placed. Dissatisfied by all she saw, she went discontentedly on to the landing and carried the milk bottles downstairs. Lying on the doormat was an envelope addressed to her. When she opened it she thought she might faint. It was as if life until this moment had been spent underground or beneath the sluggish waters of a river. Now, as she read the words he had written, she shot to the surface, up into the blinding sunlight and the sweet-tasting air:

My dear Freda,

If it is permissible may I call after work to offer my respects.

Your friend,

Vittorio.

She clutched the note to her breast and flew in her fluffy bedroom-slippers up the stairs. Why can't life always be like this, she thought, smiling and smiling at the lovely room with its cheerful wallpaper and the gay curtain that hid the waste-pipe of the washbasin. She revolved slowly in front of the open window, the street turning with her: the shining bonnets of the cars at the kerb, the spearheads of the painted railings, the thin black trees that were bouncing in the wind. Above the gardens devoid of leaf save for laurel bush and privet hedge, the pigeons rose and dipped and rose again, lifting to the rooftops. A woman in a long plaid skirt blew like a paper boat along the pavement.

Freda couldn't stop smiling. She closed the window and boiled a kettle of water, reaching to the shelf above the cooker for her toilet bag with her own special soap and her own clean flannel. She'd had to hide her things from Brenda, who was less than fussy — who could wipe her neck or her shoes on the dishcloth or her underclothes, all with equal impartiality, if nothing else was available. She'd have to tell her to go out for the evening. Anywhere would do: there was a new film on at the Odeon called *Super Dick*. She carried the blue plastic bowl filled with warm water into the living room and knelt in front of the gas fire. Grown solemn now and a little peaked, the tender sensual smile gone from her mouth, she curled her pudgy toes on the worn hearthrug and began to wash herself. It would be nice to buy a piece of steak for Vittorio. She

334

couldn't afford any for herself, but he'd appreciate her appetite was poor the day after her mother's funeral. And she'd provide a salad of lettuce and green peppers and make a real dressing of garlic and lemon juice, such as he was used to. As for Brenda, she could go to the chippie for her supper. She was always saying she didn't care for food, that it was sheer affectation to put herbs in things. People who baked food in the oven, she said, were daft — you could fry everything in a pan twice as quick. Despite her private schooling and her advantages, she'd been brought up on spam and chips and powdered eggs, and it was no wonder her husband Stanley had gone to the Little Legion every night. She couldn't understand why suddenly she felt such resentment towards Brenda — the thought of her was spoiling her anticipation of the night to come. She frowned and slapped the soapy flannel against the soft contours of her arm. It's my room, she told herself. I found it. I have every right to take my chances, to live my life. She felt refined out of existence by the sameness and regularity of each day, the brushing of her clothes in the morning and the cleaning of her teeth at night. 'There is something more,' she murmured, her lips moving, her eyes fixed on the mutilated pattern of the rug. 'I am not Brenda — I do want something.' She had been squeezing the flannel in her hands, and the carpet was quite sodden with water. Shuffling backwards on her knees she dried herself on a towel. It would have been better if Vittorio had given her more time to prepare for his visit: she hated rushing down town and returning home with minutes to spare, her face all red from the hair-dryer. How should she behave when he came? There was no question of outright seduction — not when she was so recently bereaved. Perhaps she could be silent and rather wistful — not exactly droopy, but less aggressive than he had previously known her — so as to arouse his protective feelings. Come the day of the Outing she might then lay her hand on his sleeve and thank him for his understanding. Absently she stroked the edge of the wooden fender, thick with dust, and tilted her head backwards to avoid the heat of the fire which already had begun to mottle the smoothness of her pale cheeks. She stared at the ceiling and her mouth opened to emit a sound half-way between a sigh and a groan — 'Aaah,' she went, kneeling as if in supplication. 'Aaaah, Vittorio!' Was she right about his feelings for her? He must like her. Otherwise why did he spend every afternoon chatting to her? And she'd seen the way his eyes flickered up and down her jumper when he thought she wasn't watching. He did fancy her, but how could she encourage him? God knows what Brenda had said or done to get Rossi into such a state of randy expectancy, but whatever it was it wouldn't work for Vittorio. He was a man of sensibilities and everything was against her — his background, his nationality, the particular regard he had for women or a category of womanhood to which she did not belong. By the strength of her sloping shoulders, the broad curve of her throat, the dimpled vastness of her columnar thighs, she would manoeuvre him into her arms. I will be one of those women, she thought, painted naked on ceilings, lolling amidst rose-coloured clouds. She straightened and stared at a chair. She imagined how she might mesmerise him with her wide blue eyes. Wearing a see-through dressing-gown chosen from a Littlewoods catalogue, she would open the door to him: 'Forgive me, I have been resting — the strain you know. My mother was particularly dear to me —' All Italians, all foreigners were dotty about their mothers; he would expect it of her. She would not actually have to gnash her teeth but imply that she did so — internally. Rumpling her newly washed hair, the black nylon sleeve of her gown sliding back to reveal one elbow, she would press her hand to her brow and tell him the doctor had prescribed sedatives: 'Do sit down, we are quite alone. Brenda has elected to go to the cinema.' Against her will her mind

336

dwelt on an image of Brenda in the cellar, cobwebs lacing her hair, and Rossi, hands trembling, tearing her newspaper to shreds. I will rip you to pieces, she thought; and her hand flew to her mouth as if she had spoken aloud. Beyond the romantic dreams, the little girl waiting to be cuddled, it was power of a kind she was after. It is not so much that I want him, she thought, but that I would like him to want me.

Slumped dripping upon the carpet, she gazed into the glowing mantel of the fire and rehearsed a small wistful smile.

*

Brenda waited a long time on the stairs to see who would arrive first. She had read Freda's note suggesting she go to the pictures — it was not so much a suggestion as a command: there was even 40p left on the mantelpiece. She must have been to the post office to draw out her savings. There was a bowl of salad on the landing and a lump of meat, curiously flattened and spiked with garlic, lying on a plate beneath a clean tea-towel.

At four-thirty the landlady came up from her basement flat on her way to her pottery class at the Arts Centre. She unlocked the back door and turfed the pregnant cat out on to the concrete patio.

'Damn thing,' she said, smiling at Brenda crouched on the stairs.

The cat, with sloping belly, stood on its hind legs and scrambled frantically with outstretched claws at the pane of glass. Freda said the landlady hadn't enough to occupy her time, going off to throw pots like that; but Brenda thought it was an inconsiderate judgment: they had never seen what she did on her clay wheel — she might have been another Henry Moore for all they knew.

'Shut up,' said Brenda when the landlady had gone. She

peered through the bannister rails at the cat running on the spot, irritated by the noise of its paws on the glass panels of the door.

She had come home exhausted from her thieving. Repeating her performance with the wardrobe, she had retrieved the brandy bottle from its place behind the lavatory bowl and buried it beneath the load of washing. When she wheeled the basket down the alleyway, she imagined the bottle breaking and the liquid trickling through the slats of woven straw and Rossi, like a blood-hound scenting the trail of alcohol, running up the street after her, nose quivering, black curls blown backward in the wind. He would call the police and have her arrested. Worse still, he might seize her by the arm and whisper insidiously into her ear his sensual desires, demanding she remain passive while he committed an offence in exchange for his not informing on her.

Outside the back door the agitation of the cat increased. She thought about letting it in, but she didn't dare: it might ravish Freda's steak and piddle on the lino. From behind the basement door came the piteous cries of its last kitten. The landlady had kept it, out of concern for the mother's feelings, but lately the cat had taken to biting it ferociously about the ears. Freda thought the animal ought to be sent to the vet and aborted: it was sheer wantoness to produce more offspring — she pointed out that if human beings had the same fertility rate a woman could have three hundred babies in five years. She said you'd need 2,000 eggs a week to give them all a good breakfast.

'I wonder,' said Brenda aloud, 'what the kitten thinks now its mummy doesn't like it.'

She wished someone would try to savage her every time she made a friendly gesture. She was just working out how happily she could exist, left entirely alone, when there was a knock at the front door. She wanted instantly to hide, but she knew it was no use, so she ran down the stairs with a fixed smile on her face, ready to leave immediately should it be Vittorio with his little silken Zapata moustache flopping above his mouth, or Freda back from her shopping. It was neither. It was Patrick in a shiny black suit and a clean white shirt with a badly frayed collar.

'My word,' she said, letting him into the dark hall, 'you do look smart.'

His appearance alarmed her. He was so evidently out to impress, she would not have been surprised if, like a conjurer, he had whipped a vase of flowers from behind his back and presented them to her.

'Ah well,' he said, holding a canvas bag for her inspection, 'didn't I leave early to get me tools?'

She led him up the stairs, pulling faces as she went to relieve her feelings, sticking her tongue out at the brown-painted walls, telling him silently to drop dead and leave her alone. As they turned to go up the second flight of stairs, passing the cooker and the pungent slice of meat under its tea-towel, she was forced to smile at him and say insincerely: 'It is kind of you, Patrick, to give up your time.'

The bathroom had a geyser riveted to the wall above a large tub stained with rust.

'It's old,' said Patrick, looking at the four curved feet splayed out upon the cracked lino and the dust lying like a carpet beneath the belly of the bath.

Outside the window, open to relieve the odour of stale urine, the yard lay like a jigsaw puzzle, dissected by washing line and paving stone. On the back wall, above the black and barren stem of the rambling rose, stood a row of tin cans and broken bottles placed to repel small boys.

'That's it,' said Brenda pointing at the offending cistern in its bed of cement. Patrick climbed on to the lavatory seat in his sparkling boots and fiddled with the chain. 'It won't flush,' he said. Along the line of his sleeve appeared

339

beads of plaster and a smear of rust.

'Your clothes —' began Brenda.

But already he was removing his jacket and handing it to her for safety. Lifting the heavy lid of the cistern, enough for him to get an arm in up to the elbow, he splashed about in the water, his shoulders raised so that she could see the elasticated top of his underpants holding his shirt in check.

'It's the ballcock,' he volunteered.

'Is that bad?' she asked, praying it was and he would give up and go home quick.

'Don't you fret. I can do it,' he assured her. 'Nothing simpler.'

He jumped to the floor and looked in his tool bag for a spanner and a ball of string. She could see the damp cuff of his shirt clinging to the shape of his wrist.

'Look at that,' she said. 'You're ruining your shirt.'

'I was wondering,' he asked, his brylcreamed head bent low. 'Would you have any objection to me removing me shirt?'

'I don't mind,' she cried, though secretly she did, and her eyes narrowed as she spoke.

Without his shirt, his hands and head looked as if they belonged to someone else, so red and full of blood against the white softness of his trunk. He had a nice chest, not at all pimply, with only a dusting of freckles between his shoulders. When he swung up a sleeve to release his shirt she glimpsed the bright ginger pit of his arm. Back he climbed on to the lavatory seat to probe about among the pipes and the plaster, and she hung his shirt on a nail behind the door and caught a faint smell of mould, as if he never aired his clothes but packed them half-dried into a drawer.

'Jesus, it's cold,' he said, feeling the chill air coming from the window.

'You could borrow my dressing gown,' said Brenda, and he protested there was no need, the small pout of his beer

340

belly overlapping the waistband of his trousers as he twisted to thank her.

'But you must,' she insisted, thinking there was very much a need; she couldn't bear to have him standing there half-naked. She went down the stairs, closing the bathroom door carefully behind her. She stood on the landing for a moment in case Freda had returned, but all was quiet and she crept like a thief into her room and went to the wardrobe, lifting out her dressing-gown, tugging it free from its place between Freda's dresses hung in polythene wrappers. The bottle of brandy, wedged in the folds of a purple cloak, fell on its side and rolled to the edge of the door. Thrusting it further into the recesses of the wardrobe, she ran back upstairs with her dressing-gown still on its hanger.

'That's nice,' he said, as she helped him into it.

Her fingers brushed the top of his arm rough with goose-pimples, and she stepped back not meaning to have touched him. The sleeves only came down to his elbows, and when he climbed back on to the lavatory the pleats of the bright blue dressing-gown swirled out like a skirt above his trousers and the gleaming tops of his cherry-blossom boots.

*

At first Vittorio sat on the chair by the gas fire where Freda had placed him, but she needed a man to open the bottle of wine he had brought and they both stood by the table, she fiddling with two glasses and he with the bottle between his knees to drag out the cork. He wore a black polo-necked jumper and a coat of real leather with two stylish vents at the back.

'It's strange,' she said, sipping her wine. 'I loved her, but we were not close.'

'Yes,' he replied, averting his eyes from her black nylon negligée, looking instead at the cheap utility furniture and

341

the curved railings of the balcony reflecting the light of the street lamp.

'Are you close to your mother?' she asked him, not quite at ease, wishing almost he hadn't come. He said No, she lived in Italy.

'To your heart,' she persisted, touching her breast and looking at him earnestly. She was dreadfully hungry. The hairdresser had made her wait a long time and she hadn't had any lunch.

'Brenda has gone to the pictures to see *Super Dick*, she told him, thinking it was a provocative title. She walked back and forth from the table to the window.

'I would have thought —' he began, but she lowered her head and he fell silent.

'Brenda's different from me,' she murmured. 'When I found her on the Finchley Road I did think —' and she too trailed into silence and left the sentence unfinished.

He had brought her a peach in a skein of tissue paper and she rolled the fruit between her palms.

'How kind of you,' she said, lifting his beautiful coat from the bed and taking it to the wardrobe in case she spilled wine upon it. When she opened the door a bottle of brandy rolled from the hem of her cloak and fell on to the nail of her big bare toe.

'Christ,' she cried, bringing her hand to her mouth and contracting her foot with the pain. 'Brenda,' she told him, voice husky with suppressed violence, 'never puts anything away.'

She stuffed the bottle behind the hanging dresses and prayed he hadn't noticed. She didn't know how to broach the subject of food: if she mentioned the steak it might seem as if she were forcing him to stay — as if it were all planned. She poured herself out another glass of wine and gulped it down. He wasn't very talkative; he was making her do all the work. If he went quite soon she could eat the steak herself and the salad. She hadn't had time to make

342

the garlic dressing, and how could she go out now on to the landing and start messing about with lemons. She was sweating from the pain of her crushed foot and the low rumblings of her empty stomach. Unable to contain herself, she nibbled a chocolate biscuit that Brenda had left on the mantelpiece and listened to the sound of hammering one floor above.

*

'I could do with some tea,' said Patrick, and Brenda had to nod her head as if it was quite all right and tiptoe down the stairs again.

She was always amazed at how seemingly-shy people constantly asked for things without a trace of embarrassment. How could she boil a kettle with Vittorio and Freda only inches away? The gas made a funny whining sound before the water warmed up, and Freda was bound to rush out on to the landing and create a scene. Hardly breathing, she lifted the kettle from the stove and was grateful that it was already half-filled with water. When she struck a match to light the gas, the ignition and flare of the sulphur were like the launching of a rocket. She trembled and dropped the matchstick on to the lino. Suddenly from behind the shut door, Freda began to sing. Under strain as she was, Brenda couldn't help smiling. Freda must have found the brandy bottle. She knew exactly how Freda must look at this moment, having seen her in the same state every Friday night after her visit to the theatrical pub. She would be standing poised like a Greek statue, head bent low so that her hair spilled about her face, one arm raised high in the air, one knee slightly flexed. Clicking her finger and thumb together, she would begin to glide in a small circle, round and round:

MacArthur's Park is lying in the rain...
I don't think that I can take it,
For it took so long to bake it,
And I'll never find the recipe again.

The kettle began its weird sighing

'Oh-o. no. ohohoh,' roared Freda behind the door. 'Ohoho-oh-no-ohoh...'

She's always thinking about food, thought Brenda unfairly. She felt obliged to tell Patrick why the tea was lukewarm.

'You see, Freda's got a friend in and I'm not supposed to be here.'

He looked at her over the rim of his cup and didn't understand.

'A man. She's got a gentleman caller and she told me to go out.'

'It's your room,' he said. 'You've every right to occupy your own room.'

'Well, it's difficult. I quite see I'm in the way.'

She felt a bit foolish. She was conscious she was clipping the ends of her words and mimicking the way he spoke, as if she too came from the bogs of Tipperary.

'She expects you to leave your room if she has a fella in, then?'

'It's reasonable, I'm thinking,' she said, and blushed.

'You know,' said Patrick, 'I think a lot of you. No, honest to God I do. I don't like to think of her making a monkey out of you. Why, if I thought that, I'd throttle her — I would so.'

He had little freckles above the line of his upper lip so that the shape of his mouth was blurred. He put down his cup upon the side of the bath and wound a length of string tightly between his clenched fingers.

*

344

Vittorio had sat on the edge of the bed now, because Freda, undulating her Amazonian hips and pointing one foot at him, was moving more and more wildly about the room. He felt threatened by her size and the volume of her voice, and there was a rim of dried blood along the cuticle of her big toe. He scuffed his suede boots beneath the iron frame of the double bed and kicked a book across the carpet.

'I read a lot,' said Freda, coming to rest beside him, the halo of her washed hair fanning out about her rosy cheeks. 'Poetry, Philosophy, Politics. The three pee's.' And she gave a loud, moist giggle.

'Such a lot of books,' he said, moving his feet about and shuffling more volumes into view, and she found she was telling him about Brenda and the way she couldn't bear they make contact in the night.

'She puts them right down the middle of the bed. It's frightfully inconvenient.'

'The books down the bed — ?'

'Well, you know — she doesn't want to run any risk.'

'Risk?' His eyes were wide with astonishment.

'Oh, come on — you know.' And she dug him quite painfully in the ribs with her elbow. 'It's like this,' she said, speaking very slowly, remembering the way Brenda talked to Rossi. 'She is afraid of life. She does not want to communicate. Know what I mean?'

The way he sat there so obviously not knowing what she meant, his handsome face solemnly gazing at her, filled her with irritation. 'What's the matter with you?' she asked. 'Why don't you relax?'

When he smiled she noticed there was a gap between his front teeth. It gave him the look of an urchin and minimised the sensitive modelling of his face.

'You've got gaps in your teeth,' she cried, and fell heavily against him.

He did kiss her then. He put his arm round her, and

345

they thrashed about on the double bed. She clung to him and fastened her teeth in the woolly shoulder of his polo-necked jumper.

'I have to go to the toilet,' he said, struggling to his feet and striding to the door. She was left with a shred of wool stuck to her lip, alone on the rumpled bed. Another little drinky, she told herself, lurching sideways to the floor and going to the wardrobe to find the bottle of brandy. She didn't want to be drunk. She didn't like the way things were going; but going they were, and she unscrewed the cap of the bottle and took a swig of the alcohol and wiped her mouth with her hand. The peach he had brought lay like a road casualty, squashed into the carpet.

When he returned she was aware that he was uncomfortable. He tried to make love to her but it didn't work.

'What's the matter?' she asked aggressively, pulling his hair quite viciously as he lay stranded upon her.

'The toilet,' he said. 'There are peoples in the toilet. I could not gain entrance.'

He was minus his shoes, but he still wore his trousers and his jumper that was a bit chewed at the collar.

*

Brenda could hear knocking at the front door, growing louder and louder. She watched Patrick screwing a hook into the ceiling above the cistern.

'It's a bit Heath Robinson, isn't it?' she ventured, as he wound a length of string from the ballcock up to the hook in the plaster and down again to the metal eyelet of the lavatory chain.

She unlocked the bathroom door and stood listening. Freda had stopped singing, and the nurses on the ground floor had let someone into the hall. There was a murmur of voices, then silence, until she heard the dialing of the telephone. She couldn't hear the conversation, but quite soon the receiver was replaced and someone began to climb the stairs. Whoever it was halted outside Freda's room and rapped repeatedly on the panel of the door. She won't like that, thought Brenda, and then she heard the voice of her mother-in-law.

'I have come to see Brenda.'

'I'm afraid she is not at home.'

'I'll wait then.'

There was a pause before Freda answered, her voice charged with hostility. 'You can't wait. It's not convenient.'

'I shall wait none the less.'

Turning the curve of the stairs Brenda saw Mrs Haddon on the landing and Freda, hair dishevelled, straddling the threshold of the door.

'It's all right,' called Brenda. 'I'm here.'

'I want my photographs,' said Mrs Haddon, turning to face her.

'I want those pictures of my Stanley as a child.'

Brenda hadn't got them. She knew they were still in the kitchen drawer of the farmhouse, where they had always been, beneath the pre-war knitting patterns, but it was no use telling her so. Mrs Haddon was smiling firmly, nodding her head, the ends of her floral headscarf tied under the determined thrust of her chin.

'Go downstairs,' ordered Brenda. 'I'll get them.'

She frowned meaningfully at Freda who stepped aside, overwhelmed by her air of authority, and allowed her to enter the front room. Vittorio was standing at the foot of the bed, flushed and untidy. He wore a jumper that was unravelling at the neckline and he clutched his shoes to his breast. Brenda ignored him. She stooped to pick a book at random from the floor and went out again on to the landing. Mrs Haddon, a large plastic handbag at her feet, had obediently retreated down the stairs and was grasping the bannister rail for support. Fancy her coming all that way

347

from Ramsbottom, Brenda thought, all on her own on the coach in her nice camel coat.

'Here,' she said, holding out the book. 'They're all inside.'

They looked at each other. For a moment it might have been Stanley pleading to be understood — the same round eyes filled with perplexity behind the rims of the light-brown spectacles, the same wide mouth puckered at the corners. I can't say anything, she thought — nothing that's true.

Mrs Haddon lowered her eyes and bent to pick up her handbag. Freda, looking down, was taken by surprise at her appearance — such a pretty woman, rouge on her cheeks, a little tilted nose. She was taking something out of her bag and showing it to her daughter-in-law with an expression of eager expectancy that was quite touching to watch. From the way Brenda spoke about her in the past Freda had imagined her with cow-dung on her gumboots and straw in her hair.

'Why?' she heard Brenda say in a flat voice, not at all grateful — and then there was a scream. The sound, shivering above the well of the stairs, caused Freda to tremble from head to foot. She saw Brenda strike Mrs Haddon somewhere about the chest. The spectacles balanced on the bridge of the tilted nose jerked forward. A hand holding a gun swung upwards to save them. Brenda shouted: 'Don't —' and 'Why?' This repetition of an earlier question was spoken on a whining note. She cringed in her tweed coat, her red hair hanging limply upon the checked collar.

She's bent on destroying herself, thought Freda, and at that moment there was a small plopping sound as Mrs Haddon squeezed the trigger.

To see Vittorio hurtling down the stairs, his shoes falling to the carpet as if in pursuit, made Freda admire him all over again. A man was needed at this moment and he was

348

here acting on her behalf, and it gave her a feeling of comfort and pride, for she was still trembling. At that moment Patrick the van driver, wearing a short-sleeved garment of powder-blue material, flung himself round the curve of the stairway and in two bounds leapt to join the struggling Vittorio below. How opportune, thought Freda, too shocked to question further. They held Mrs Haddon by the arms; they encircled her waist lovingly. Patrick reached for the gun raised high in the air and entwined his fingers in hers. They swayed, arms dipping up and down, as if energetically dancing. Brenda, standing apart in the recess of the ill-lit landing, put her hand to her mouth and bit the ends of her fingers. She was thin as a stick and behind her closed lids her eyes bulged, round as marbles.

'Pet,' cried Freda, launching herself down the stairs at last. 'My poor pet.'

The men, having manoeuvred Mrs Haddon into the front room, placed her in the best chair by the fire with such force that she lost her balance. As she tipped backwards, her feet in their neat court shoes flew upwards, and she uttered a tiny cry of outrage. Vittorio, refined by his experience, put the gun on top of the wardrobe out of harm's way.

'That's my property,' Mrs Haddon said. 'I should be glad if you would give it to me.'

Vittorio stroked his drooping moustache and looked at Freda for instructions. She was standing at the window with Brenda in her arms, observing the police car in the street below, its blue light flashing as it cruised at the kerb.

'Look at that,' she cried. 'The police have come.'

'I phoned them before I came upstairs,' said Mrs Haddon. 'In case they were needed.' She half-rose to her feet and was thrust downwards again by the two men. They were not taking any chances.

'Answer the door,' commanded Freda, and Patrick did as he was told, running out of the room with the lapels of his dressing-gown falling open to expose his paper-white chest.

'We ought to make a cup of tea,' said Brenda, looking at Stanley's mother. 'She's had a shock.'

Mrs Haddon stared back without pity. 'I was only aiming at your vocal chords. You always talked too much.'

'Murderer,' cried Freda, quivering with indignation as she held Brenda to her breast. 'You should be put away.' All the same, she couldn't help being awed by the smart little woman on her chair, come all the way from the North by rail or coach, her handbag on her knee with her powder puff inside, her purse and her little black gun.

Two plain-clothed men and two in uniform came pounding up the hall. They asked a lot of questions about the old lady's relationship to Brenda and how she had come to be in possession of the pistol. Mrs Haddon said she only wanted to frighten Brenda to punish her for leaving Stanley and that she'd saved up her pension for three weeks to buy the weapon. She'd told the lady in the shop it was for her grandson and the lady had been very helpful. She gave her a card to go with it. She brought out of her handbag a paper target in red and black to show them.

They looked at it in silence.

After a time the uniformed policemen took her outside to the car, and the chief inspector and a sergeant made them all re-enact the drama on the stairs. Brenda felt silly holding out the book to the inspector, who was pretending to be Stanley's mother. She had to hit him quite hard on the chest and bite her lip in case she smiled. They wanted to know how they could contact Stanley and where he would be at this moment.

'At the Little Legion,' she said. 'But you better not ring there. He wouldn't like it.'

Freda shouted interferingly: 'Good God, he ought to be told. It was a gun she carried, you know, not a bunch of flowers.'

350

'It wasn't a gun,' muttered Brenda, 'it was an air pistol,' though she didn't know if it made any difference.

Freda told the sergeant that Brenda was separated from her husband. 'He gave her a very rough time in my opinion.'

'Quite so,' said the sergeant, looking at her and at Patrick still clad in the blue dressing-gown.

There was a knock at the door. The two young nurses from the ground floor, little white caps pinned to the frizzed nests of their hair, wanted to know if they could be of assistance.

'It's quite all right,' Freda told them frostily. 'It's just a small family party.' And down clumped the two girls in their crackling aprons and sensible shoes, desperate at being excluded from the excitement.

The police·inspector asked Brenda finally if she wanted to make a charge.

'Definitely we do,' asserted Freda, and Brenda shook her head and said No, she didn't want to, thank you. Whatever would her mother say if she did and it got into the papers?

Freda didn't even bother to show Vittorio to the front door. She was tired now and grumpy. 'Get to bed,' she ordered Brenda, and she jumped between the sheets still in her negligée.

Brenda lay in the darkness unprotected by the bolster and the row of books. She had tried to re-erect the barrier, but Freda cursed and told her to bloody well stop messing about.

'He didn't make it,' said Freda, mouth crushed against the pillow. 'He couldn't get into the loo.'

'Ah, well —' began Brenda, and thought better of it.

'I wonder if those were Maria's men in uniform?' mused Freda.

'What men?'

'You know — Maria's men — in my cup.'

'They weren't on horseback.'

'No,' said Freda. 'You're right. What the hell was that

Patrick doing running round the house dressed like that?'

'He was just passing and I didn't like to say I was going out.'

'You're barmy. What you see in him I don't know.'

'I don't see anything,' protested Brenda. 'He was just mending the toilet.'

'Half-naked?' said Freda. 'You must be mad.'

When she closed her eyes the bed whirled round and round. She had to force herself to concentrate on the outline of the window pane.

Brenda said: 'I don't think she meant any harm. She was just trying it on.'

'You need help,' murmured Freda. 'You're a victim. I've told you before.' In the light of the street lamp the room was glamorous and bathed in silver. The wooden foot of the bed glowed like genuine mahogany. 'Isn't it nice?' she said.

'Stanley's mother must be furious she missed me. She always hated being thwarted.'

Brenda wore a small gratified smile. She understood perfectly why Mrs Haddon had wanted to do her damage. Inside her own brain she had on numerous occasions perpetrated acts of brutality against friends and enemies alike.

'She needs putting away,' said Freda, beginning to fall into sleep. 'You all need putting away.'

4

For several days Freda was not herself. She suffered outbursts of rage followed by long periods of silence. The rages, which were habitual, did not disturb Brenda as much as the moments of moody reflection; she could not bear to witness her friend slumped on her beer crate or in the armchair by the gas fire, deaf to all overtures. It was unnerving to live with. Freda was so fond of verbalising her emotions. She never brooded. Pain felt, or insults endured, made her the more articulate. In adversity she saw the funny side. She would spit out words describing in precise detail just how badly she was wounded, until her shoulders began to shake with the burble of huge choking laughter that finally burst from her.

She took to lying awake at night, counting the prison bars of the balcony palings reflected on the curve of the ceiling. She watched intently the plummeting bird of the hanging lamp, the bunch of dried leaves in the mantelshelf vase stencilled upon the gleaming paintwork of the door. When she looked out into the street it was bright as day. The lattices of windows, the lids of dustbins, the metal flanks of parked cars flashed in the moonlight and dazzled her. Brenda lay in darkness, the lower half of her face shot away — only the rim of her eyelids touched by light.

'What's wrong, love?' asked Brenda over and over.

But Freda, eyes glittering with fatigue, refused to tell.

She did go to see Rossi. She told him that if there was any more nonsense with Brenda in the cellar she would go to Mr Paganotti and have him dismissed.

'Just because you're the manager,' she told him spitefully, 'it doesn't mean you can wreak your vile will on Brenda.

'I do not understand,' said Rossi, shrinking behind his desk littered with test tubes and sheets of litmus paper. 'What is this wreaking? We only do a little fun.'

'Fun,' she thundered. 'Man, I don't think Mr Paganotti would call it that.'

He hated her. He clenched his chubby fists and scraped his wedding ring across the desk, stuttering his denials. He made the mistake of trying to humour her.

'You are a woman of the world,' he said. But she quelled him with a glance. 'Watch it,' she warned, her arms folded, her nostrils flaring, her silken face poised and tinted like an angel above the powerful wedge of her body.

He lowered his eyes, and back she strode to her bench and the quota of Nuits St. Georges.

Maria was curious to know what was wrong, but Freda shook her head with an air of martyrdom, as if her burdens were beyond comprehension. She had thought Vittorio would never wish to speak to her again after that deplorable evening when she had drunk too much; but surprisingly he asked her several times if she was feeling better, if she was recovering, as if it had been she who had been shot at, for she had forgotten she was in mourning for her mother. He even wanted to take her out to dinner, but she refused. 'Later,' she told him, not caring to shut the door entirely. The thought of a visit to a restaurant, the clatter of knives and forks, the blaze of lights in gilt mirrors as they drank at the bar, filled her with panic. The effort of keeping her elbows off the table, her knees together, her voice down and delicately modulated, was beyond her. The scene on the stairs was imprinted upon her imagination; the inspector's request to know the particular relationship between the old lady and Brenda rang in her ears. Brenda was surrounded by people who claimed her as their own. Her father sent postal orders, her mother wielded power by the headings of her letters — 'Darling' meant Brenda was in favour; 'My Dear Brenda' spelled disapproval, as did the absence of those inked kisses penned at the bottom of the page. Stanley's balaclava hung on a hook behind the door. Under the bed, face down in the dust, lay a wedding photograph of Stanley arm in arm with Brenda, her dress smudged with flowers. His mother had ridden across the country with a gun to prove she was related by marriage. And Freda had no one to call her own except the distant aunt in Newcastle.

'I must be ill,' she thought, 'bothering about such trifles.'

She went to the theatrical pub to be among people who understood, and was unwise enough to tell her version of Mrs Haddon on the stairs. She performed modestly and with seriousness, rolling a cigarette nervously between finger and thumb, and was distressed at the wild hoots of mirth that interrupted her narrative. She joined in the laughter — tears squeezed from the crinkled corners of her eyes — but she was hollow inside.

Brenda tried to expiate the trouble she had caused. She said how well Freda looked, how revolting Patrick appeared in his overalls — that hair, those badly bitten nails . . .

'You're no oil painting yourself,' said Freda, cutting her short. She was grateful to Patrick. After all, the lavatory was mended, even if every time the chain was pulled the hook tore plaster from the ceiling. Brenda carried her coffee to the bench and lifted bottles whenever they were needed.

'Leave off,' cried Freda sharply. 'I'm not an invalid.'

Stanley telephoned later in the week. Rossi called Brenda into the office, Freda marching behind with a slender bottle of Spumanti still in her hand, and he fled from his desk like a rabbit and busied himself at the brandy shelves.

'I can't come down, Brenda,' said Stanley. 'I can't leave the hens.'

'I don't want to see you,' mouthed Freda.

'That's all right,' said Brenda. 'I don't think there's much point.' She was already flattening her vowels to accommodate him.

'What's that you say, Brenda?' he shouted at the end of the wire.

'There's no point you coming down.'

'I can't come down, Brenda — not with mother in hospital. They're sending her home in a day or two, Brenda.' He would keep naming her, as if there was some confusion in his mind as to who she was.

'What's he say?' asked Freda, tweaking her severely on the arm, and she said: 'They've put his mother in hospital.'

'Who's there, Brenda?' he said. 'Who's that with you, Brenda?'

'No one. What's the weather like your end?'

'You what, Brenda?'

'Nothing,' she said. 'I've got to rush now.'

She replaced the receiver quickly and tried not to think about him. She knew he would continue to stand by the windowsill for several seconds, calling her name down the dead wire, scratching his head when he finally realised she was no longer there. He would go out into the yard, the doves with pouting breasts asleep on the guttering of the barn roof, and stand with mackintosh bunched about his waist and relieve himself on the nettles by the ruined pig-sty. At the splattering of water on the leaves, the doves would rise with a flutter of wings and scatter the bantam hens pecking in the dirt.

'You're not firm enough with him,' reprimanded Freda. 'You're too soft with him.'

'I was always waiting for him to come in or waiting for him to go out,' said Brenda, as if to excuse herself. She was curious to know why Freda had defended Patrick earlier in the day. 'You never used to have a good word to say about him,' she reminded.

'I don't see the point,' Freda informed her, 'of denigrating anyone for the way they look. Certainly he's not of your class — that's one thing. But the state of his finger nails has nothing to do with it.'

She looked at Brenda so contemptuously, at the neglected growth of hair and the parched texture of her skin, that Brenda brought her hand to her mouth to cover the front tooth which was chipped since childhood.

Nevertheless Freda sought out Patrick before she left the factory and told him to leave Brenda alone.

'There are things,' she said, finding him in the loading bay, the chill air empurpling his face, 'that you can't know about. Far be it from me to tell anybody how to live their life, but —' and she waggled a rigid finger at him, 'you should look for someone of your own age.'

'I like her,' he said stubbornly, ignoring his fellow workers shifting crates of wine on to a lorry. 'I'd swing for her, that I would.'

'I hope,' said Freda, bewildered by his headstrong declaration, 'it won't come to that.' And she turned on her heel and went to collect Brenda who was in the washroom rinsing out the sponges for the morning.

'I can't understand it,' she said. 'Whatever did you do to that Patrick?'

'I only let him mend the lavatory,' exclaimed Brenda.

She looked so plain and dowdy in her shabby coat and worn shoes that Freda smiled. It was ridiculous to

357

think of her as a *femme fatale*. Neither Rossi nor Patrick would be described as the catch of the year — unlike Vittorio with his noble birth, his beautiful moustaches and his expressive brown eyes. In only two days time, on Sunday — for Mr Paganotti was too stingy to allow them a day off work — they would go on the Outing and picnic together under the trees, discussing where he might take her for dinner. She would tell him how depressed she had been, how lonely. Looking at her reflection in the mirror, her face appeared fragile and tinged with silver. She felt the beginnings of restoration.

*

That night Freda slept more peacefully. At dawn she was awakened by the sound of rain pattering thickly upon the roof. The noise increased in volume and she sat up to look out of the window, the hem of the white sheet sliding to the folds of her belly, and saw a troop of horsemen flowing along the river of the street. Drowsily she admired, as if in a dream, the elegant khaki riders, the swelling calves of their legs bound in puttees, the rows of mustard-coloured hats bobbing up and down as they cantered toward the crossroads. She didn't move, she didn't blink an eyelid — afterwards she thought she might have cried 'Hurrah' or tossed a rose from the balcony — and they were gone, the stylish riders and the taffeta-brown horses beating a tattoo on the crest of the road.

It was all going to come true — she knew that now: the journey by land and sea, the uniformed men, the white dress with flowers at the waist. Perhaps they would live in a flat in Hampstead and have drink on the sideboard, meat in the fridge and Mr Paganotti to dinner once a month. After they were married she and Vittorio would visit the house-proud aunt in Newcastle and litter the hall-way with their pig-skin luggage. She would drop her engagement ring into the glass bowl on the dresser for fear she tore the skin of his back when she held him in her arms. She would smoke in bed and spill talcum powder upon the rug. What disorder she could create with her paper hankies, the cellophane wrappings of her cigarette packets, the pointilistic pieces of confetti still trapped within her garments! Auntie would have to lump it. In the summer, staying at his parents' castle outside Bologna, she would open the shutters in the morning to let in the sun and shield her eyes from the blue surge of the sea sparkling beyond the dusty line of the olive trees that his father owned. Brenda could come too, if his mother had no objection — and why should she, surrounded by her grandchildren, her lovely bouncing bambinos gurgling beneath the lemon trees?

'You do look well,' said Brenda, propped up on the pillows, a plate of porridge balanced on her stomach.

'I am well,' cried Freda, already dressed, sweeping about the room with the transistor radio held to her ear.

*

She couldn't wait to tell Maria about the soldiers on horseback.

'You were right,' she said, clasping Maria's hands in her own and dancing her round the cardboard boxes.

The sky was so overcast it was almost dark. The little naked bulbs hanging from the ceiling glowed like small red stars. Outside the row of windows the rain fell heavily and began to stain the concrete wall of the chip-shop.

Brenda thought Freda must have been dreaming. She hadn't heard anything, and what was a troop of horsemen doing at that hour of the morning in the middle of the city?

'Exercising the animals,' explained Freda jubilantly, 'before the traffic got going.'

'But we've never seen them before.'

'We've never been awake at that time.'

'I have,' said Brenda gloomily, thinking of the times she had watched the first streaks of the dawn appearing above the rooftops of the grey houses.

Now that Sunday was so near, Maria had begun to wonder what she might wear on the Outing. She had found a frock in Mr Paganotti's boxes. She pulled it out from under the bench and draped it across her portly body, waiting for Freda's opinion. It was made of silk, with a pattern of miniature daisies on a band round the hem of the skirt.

'Haven't you got anything of your own?' asked Freda dubiously, looking at the plunging neckline and the absence of sleeves. 'It's winter, you know.'

'Certainly I have nothing,' Maria said, and she whirled about with the hem of daisies flaring above the folds of her grey football socks, whooping with laughter and growing red in the face at her exhibitionism.

'I think it's very nice,' said Brenda.

'By all means wear it,' cried Freda, too happy to bring Maria down. And she looked about for Vittorio, anxious for him to know that her period of mourning was over. After all, she knew now that there was something in store for them both. The premonition of it was becoming stronger by the moment. She felt giddy at the thought of the future, and she longed to experience that shudder of excitement the sight of him might bring. She plunged down the steps into the basement, her large buttocks quivering in the brown trousers she had made herself, searching about among the barrels and the yellow containers, and calling his name for the pleasure it gave her. He wasn't there.

'He's in the office,' said Brenda, when she returned disconcerted to her bench. 'Him and Rossi.'

There were clients tasting the wine when she entered.

360

A middle-aged woman dressed in black and a young girl in a grey coat with a velvet collar.

'Oh,' said Freda, 'I *am* sorry. I thought Vittorio was alone.' She looked at him tenderly, flashing messages with her eyes, and he hung his head as if suddenly shy in her presence. 'I wonder if I might use the telephone — to confirm the van booking for the Outing.'

She was all sweetness and light, her gestures theatrical and charming, her blue eyes wide with candour. The girl in the grey coat bent her head and studied the kid gloves on her lap.

'Later,' said Rossi. 'I am busy just now.'

He spread his fingers expressively and spoke in Italian to the middle-aged woman, who was staring at Freda with polite bleak eyes.

'Of course,' agreed Freda, 'how stupid of me. Do forgive me.'

It was fortunate for Rossi that she was in such a good mood. She seemed not to notice how eager he was to be rid of her. She lingered and postured, leaning against the shelves packed with pretty coloured labels. Finally she asked Vittorio if she might have a word in private. He went unwillingly to stand in the open doorway, and she laid her hand on his sleeve and said she was able to have dinner with him — that very evening if he wished. She smiled at him.

'Ah, no,' he said rapidly, trying to cover the sound of her voice by the breadth of his shoulders. 'I have made other arrangements.' And in spite of himself he gave a brief nervous glance over his shoulder at the group sitting about Rossi's desk sipping their wine in silence.

Freda made a gesture as if to touch his cheek, and he stepped backwards.

'Ah well,' she said, 'till Sunday, then. Tomorrow I will be preparing food for the picnic and washing my hair. I do want to look my best.'

As tall as he, she fanned his face with her breath and ruffled the fine hairs of his drooping moustaches. She fought to keep calm at this unexpected set-back. It hurt that he wasn't in the same frame of mind as herself. She was helped, however, by the sound of her heart palpitating in her breast, for all the world like the beat of horses' hooves.

'It is Madame Rossi,' informed Maria, when told of the women in the office, 'and her niece from Casalecchio di Reno.'

'Is it indeed?' murmured Freda, and she fixed her eyes on the office window and waited for the visitors to depart.

After a time a row of faces appeared at the glass and stared out at the factory floor, watching the workers at their labours. Deliberately Freda touched her lips with the tips of her fingers and blew Vittorio a kiss.

'You are awful,' complained Brenda. 'Rossi must be wetting himself, with his wife watching everything.'

'Rubbish,' said Freda. 'It should be obvious that Vittorio and I are close.'

There was an air of festivity in the factory. The men drank copiously from the barrel of wine and fooled with the women. They had never known Freda so animated.

At two o'clock, Salvatore, splendid in golfing shoes and a muffler of green silk, embraced Maria on her beer crate and received a blow on the cheek.

'Aye, aye,' she wailed, drumming her heels on the planking. 'They are mad for the Outing.'

She scrubbed at her face violently with her fist, to be rid of the moist imprint of his mouth. Salvatore, half-understanding her words, nodded eagerly at Freda and rolled his eyes with mock excitement.

Freda waited in vain for Vittorio to come and speak to her. She clung to the belief that she must not let go of him, that he was destined to be her true love, that he knew it too, only he had not begun to accept it. And yet, remembering the way he had recoiled from her outside the office door, she could not help but wonder. Was it the same for him? She shivered with the cold and drooped at the bench. She was dreaming now, rather than thinking clearly. She wandered among the ginestra bushes and the olive trees, and the cool white rooms of the flat in Hampstead. She rose in a giant jet above the toy blocks of the airport buildings and began her long journey over land and sea. Now and then she was aware of the dismal factory, the hum of machinery in her ears, the tenderly smiling face of the Virgin Mary high on the green-painted wall. Had she been alone she would have swung her head and crooned her love aloud.

Finally she was empty of images: no more pictures left in her head. There remained only an insatiable thirst for all the joy and glory of the good times to come, the life she was soon to know.

5

Mercifully it was not raining. There was even a faint gleam of wintry sunlight. Brenda wore a black woollen dress, black stockings and green court shoes. Freda had hidden the tweed coat the night before; she insisted she borrow her purple cloak. Brenda didn't want to wear the cloak, but neither did she wish to annoy Freda. Protesting that it was too long, she draped it about her shoulders and looked down at the green shoes and an inch of stocking. Freda, in a mauve trouser suit, a sheepskin coat gaily worked in blue thread down the front, and a lilac scarf casually knotted at the throat, wrapped two cooked chickens in silver foil and placed them in the basket. There was a tablecloth embroidered in one corner with pink petals, a lettuce in a polythene bag, some french bread and two pounds of apples. In a small jar, previously containing cocktail onions, she had poured a mixture of oil and lemon and crushed garlic.

Having packed everything, she looked in her handbag and was dismayed to find she only had five cigarettes. She asked Brenda to lend her some money.

'I haven't any,' lied Brenda. 'You made me pay for one chicken and I bought the shampoo.'

It wasn't that she was mean, but she wanted to be prepared for disaster — the 40p in her purse was to get home if she was left stranded at the Stately Home.

Freda was livid. She kicked the basket roughly with her foot and threw herself on to the bed.

'How can I get through a bloody day like this on five ciggies?' she shouted.

'But it was your idea. You got us into it. I'd much rather sleep all day.'

'Shut up,' said Freda.

She looked at her wrist watch and noted the time. She had ordered the van for seven-thirty but had no intention of arriving at the factory before eight o'clock. It restored her good humour, prolonging the agony for Brenda, keeping her in suspense: she was probably dying inside with embarrassment.

'You shouldn't have spent your money on that,' said Brenda desperately, glancing at the table laid for two with the bunch of dried leaves removed from the mantelpiece and set in the middle of the cloth.

There were wine glasses too and a bowl of real butter, and stuffed olives on a saucer. God knows where they had come from, but two napkins, starched and folded, lay beside the blue-rimmed plates. She went to the window and stared out at the flats and the deserted balconies. At the foot of a tree a cat stretched and sharpened its claws on the bark. It shouldn't do that, she thought, and she heard Freda telling her not to hang about. 'We don't want your Patrick dying of a broken heart.'

It was five minutes to eight when they let themselves out into the street. The basket tipped on the steps and a loaf pitched to the ground. As Brenda carefully closed the front door, a huge gust of wind tore at the purple cloak and engulfed her in its folds.

'Christ,' said Freda, reaching for her hair, which was blowing in all directions, and retrieving the long thin bread from beside the dustbins.

At the corner of the empty street Brenda said: 'Honestly, Freda, I don't want to go. It's going to be awful. Couldn't I be ill or something?'

'Be quiet,' snapped Freda, pushing the basket ahead of her, head bent against the gale.

A hundred yards from the factory the wind dropped and the sun came out quite strongly. Maria, a brown paper bag blown by the wind wrapped round her swollen ankles, ran to meet them with outstretched hands.

'There is a delay.. We have no van. Amelio is not come.'

From beneath the hem of her working coat Mr Paganotti's frock, edged with daisies, hung a full two inches.

'My God,' said Freda. 'I might have known.'

She brushed past Maria and looked about for Vittorio. He was nowhere to be seen. The men stood in a row against the wall holding briefcases and carrier bags. They nodded and smiled, raising their wide-brimmed hats in greeting. It looked like a gathering of the Mafia — the street deserted save for the line of men dressed all in black, shoulders hunched, standing in front of the great doors of the factory, and the blonde girl taller than all of them, marching up and down with a face of thunder and a roll of french bread held like a sten gun under her arm.

Brenda tried to pretend she wasn't there, that she was alone at the top of a mountain. Just then Rossi, who had been poised in the middle of the road staring in the direction of the High Street, turned and saw her. Exuberantly he ran to her, his hostility to Freda forgotten in the joy of the occasion. How he had longed for this moment, this day to begin, driving into the countryside unaccompanied by his wife, as if he was an Englishman.

'*Bongiorno*, ladies,' he cried, '*Bongiorno*.' Rubbing his hands together he positively jumped up and down on the pavement.

'What's going on here?' asked Freda officiously, folding her arms and looking at him with deep suspicion. 'I ordered the van for seven-thirty. Amelio should have been here a quarter an hour ago.' She had to bother about the details — the arrival of the van she had organised — even though she was sick to her stomach at the street empty of Vittorio.

Rossi shrugged his shoulders. 'The traffic, maybe. It is only a little waiting.'

'Traffic, you fool? At this hour?' She leant viciously on the wing of his Ford Cortina, and the car lurched slightly. 'I knew it,' she said to Brenda, as if the others didn't exist. 'I knew it would be a shambles.'

'It is only a little hitch,' reasoned Brenda, smiling at the row of workers ashen-faced with the cold.

Round the corner of the street came first Vittorio, then Patrick.

'There's no sign of it at all,' called Patrick, striding ahead in a belted raincoat and a cloth cap over his outstanding ears.

Brenda was surprised how like Stanley he appeared, in his mackintosh and his dark blue tie in a strangle knot at his throat.

Vittorio said something in Italian to Rossi, who shrugged again and consulted his watch. The men murmured and dug their hands deeper into their pockets. At the kerb stood the four small barrels of wine donated by Mr Paganotti. How old and worn, thought Brenda, are the faces of the men in the daylight. Indoors the lighted bulbs, the constant nips of wine, had tinged their cheeks with pink.

'Good morning,' said Vittorio to Freda. 'And how are you this wonderful English morning?'

He was mocking her. He was laying the blame for the weather at her feet. He was telling her how ridiculous she had been to conceive of this Outing.

'We're fine,' said Brenda quickly, smiling so hard that her jaw ached. Much more of this and her toothache would come on with the strain.

Vittorio was so beautiful in her eyes, his immaculate duffel coat fastened with white toggles, his chunky boots threaded with laces of bright red, that Freda was compelled to be off-hand with him.

'Oh hallo,' she said, as if she hardly knew him; and she turned her back. It annoyed her how confident he seemed. She was conscious that for some reason she had lost ground since the visit of Madame Rossi to the office.

'Are you not in a joyful mood?' he asked, and she pretended she hadn't heard.

'You are looking very nice,' Rossi told Brenda, looking at the purple cloak and catching a glimpse of black ankles above the shiny green of her shoes.

'Hmmmph,' cried Freda, and she flounced several yards away.

'Is the great manager getting out of the wrong side of the bed?' asked Rossi unwisely. He was so happy himself he could not believe Freda was angry.

'Please, Freda,' begged Brenda, following her. 'Please behave.'

Brushing her aside, Freda returned to Vittorio. 'Look here,' she shouted. 'I hope you don't think it's my fault that the bloody van hasn't arrived.'

He raised his eyes at her outburst, and the men at the wall shuffled their feet and looked politely at the sky. How vibrant she was, always arguing and gesticulating, waving her loaf of bread like a battle flag in the air.

'She should get herself seen to,' said Patrick, gazing at her in disgust and admiration.

The sound of Freda's voice was suddenly drowned by a great bellow of rage from the street corner, at which appeared the missing Amelio on foot, shaking his fists and in the grip of some huge irritation. The men broke ranks and surged to meet him. A babble of voices rose in enquiry. What was amiss? Where was the van?

Amelio had risen from his warm bed at six to drive from his house in the suburbs to Hope Street. He had parked his small black car outside the factory and gone on foot to the garage off the Edgware Road to collect the van. They had told him that no such vehicle had been promised for today. He had remonstrated. He had pleaded. He had mentioned the name of Mr Paganotti. But there was no van.

'There is no van,' cried Rossi, turning to Freda.

'No van,' she echoed.

'No, no, no,' moaned Amelio, and he broke through the circle of workers and wrenched at the side door of his little black car. Rossi tried to reason with him. He placed an arm about Amelio's shoulders. He clutched him like a brother. He shook him until his own plump cheeks wobbled with passion and entreaty.

'What's going on?' asked Brenda, clinging to Maria, who was scarlet in the face with emotion.

'Amelio have a car. Salvatore and Rossi have a car. Nobody else. He want Amelio to drive us in the car to the picnic.'

'Oh God,' groaned Freda, crumbling the french bread into the gutter.

After a time Amelio freed himself from Rossi and got into the driving seat. He waved his hands at the window in a gesture of dismissal. Rossi stepped back to the kerb, and they all watched the black car slew in a half circle into the middle of the road and move towards the corner. It came to a halt, and then crawled cautiously into the High Street and vanished from sight.

'Poor bugger,' said Patrick.

The men stood for some moments not knowing what to do. A torn poster, advertising some long-finished event, whirled upwards and bowled along the road after the departed Amelio.

369

'Why can't we use one of the firm's vans?' demanded Freda.

'We cannot go in Mr Paganotti's business motors for a picnic,' reproved Rossi.

Freda felt discredited. She stood shaken, her scarf ends and her ash-blonde hair mingling in the wind.

'Give over,' she whispered to Brenda, who, dreadfully perturbed, was already picking her teeth with a matchstick.

After an interval of indecision, Rossi, seeing his excursion in danger, began to issue commands. He ordered Salvatore to the wheel of the red mini. He held up his right hand and indicated with his fingers that there was space for three. The men looked at each other and gripped their briefcases more securely. He propelled Brenda to the front seat of his Ford Cortina. 'In, in, in,' he urged; and she was bundled inside to find Vittorio in the back seat, where he had gone earlier to be out of the cold. They didn't speak. Brenda peered out of the window at Freda holding the mangled loaf to her heart. Rossi, skipping about frenziedly, and acting as if the street was on fire and must be evacuated immediately, motioned Freda towards the car. He held open the rear door, and she bent her head. As she made to enter, Vittorio vacated his seat and leapt out into the road.

'Bloody hell,' said Freda, white-faced and utterly demoralised, endeavouring to accommodate herself and the basket on wheels inside the cramped interior. The car sank on its axle.

'I wish I could die,' thought Brenda; and then again, 'I wish I was dead.'

There was a great deal of shouting going on in the street. A small boy on the far side of the road, intent on his paper round, stopped to stare. A face loomed up at the window of the Ford Cortina. Brenda unwound the glass, and Anselmo, in a slouch hat, brought his sad face on a level with hers and proceeded to kiss her, first on one cheek, then on the other. He went away, and his place was taken by Stefano, who contented himself with shaking her hand.

'You take my place,' urged Brenda, looking down at his hand lying like a little cold piece of cloth in her own. 'Honestly I don't mind in the least.'

'Ah no,' he said, 'you are young.' And he backed away clutching his carrier bag filled with bread and salami, the tears standing in his eyes.

Vittorio was arguing with Rossi and Aldo Gamberini, the overseer of the loading bay. They gripped him by the arm, one on either side, and attempted to drag him from the pavement. He resisted strongly. Rossi winked and grimaced in the direction of the parked car. He patted him playfully on the cheek as if to say 'Don't be a silly boy', and Vittorio, finally submitting and followed by Aldo Gamberini, clambered sullenly inside the Ford Cortina. The vehicle rocked as he and Freda fought for leg space between the wheels of the shopping basket.

Outside there was an orgy of hand-shaking and leave-taking. Around the bonnet of the red mini the men clustered like tired black flies. Brenda could see Maria waddling up the road in retreat, the hem of the silk frock bobbing against her calves. She ground her teeth in misery and stared hard at the picture of the Virgin pasted to the dashboard of the car.

At last Rossi flung himself into the driving seat.

'We are all right,' he assured them over and over, clutching the steering wheel bound in black fur.

As he looked into the mirror to make certain he had clear access to the road, he observed the barrels of wine being trundled towards the red mini. Out he jumped, waving his arms censoriously, and the barrels, all four of them, were transported to the boot of the Ford Cortina.

'Now we go,' he told the silent passengers, and he

371

pressed the starting motor.

The small diminished face of Patrick appeared at the back window. He flattened his pugilistic nose against the glass and made frantic gestures to be admitted. Outside, the farewells of the dispersing workers rose in a continuous murmur like the sea.

'Go away,' bade Freda in a low voice.

He tugged at the handle of the door, the hen-speckled face beneath the peak of his cloth cap distorted with urgency. The door swung open and he tried to squeeze inside. Freda struck him repeatedly in the face with the french loaf and he fell backwards on to the pavement in a sprinkle of breadcrumbs. Brenda slumped as low in her seat as she could. She hadn't the heart to wave. She fixed her eyes on the silver ignition key, dangling from the lock, and the humble smile of the Virgin as she gazed at her bright pink child.

The engine roared into life. The car jumped away from the kerb and gathered speed, passing the homeward-bound men going in twos and threes to the tube station, shoulders bowed in the best black suits worn for a special occasion.

*

Rossi drove as if any moment he was about to be overtaken and sent home. He hunched his shoulders in his casual jumper and pressed his foot down hard upon the accelerator. He drove as if heading toward the Park and suddenly swung left into Monmouth Street, moving at speed past the barred windows of the army barracks and the rows of still-sleeping houses.

'Ah well,' he said, as if speaking to himself, 'it is only a little upset.'

There were few people up at this hour — an old man leaning on a stick, a girl in a caftan, an oriental gentleman wearing silver boots with high heels. Rossi took his attention briefly from the road to watch the girl and was forced to brake hard as the lights changed from green to red. Freda was flung forward in her seat and brought up sharp against the handle of the shopping basket. She said nothing, but her intake of breath was audible.

'Are you all right?' asked Brenda, turning in her seat; but Freda, massive in her sheepskin coat, had closed her eyes.

Beyond the rear window the red mini, bursting with passengers, came into view.

Brenda said: 'They must have been so disappointed — the others — going all the way home again.'

It haunted her: Maria in her silken frock, the prepared food lying unwanted in the black briefcases, the high hopes of the early dawn and the disillusion of the morning.

'They are used to disappointment,' Rossi told her philosophically. 'They have had their lives.'

He looked in the mirror and studied Vittorio and Freda huddled together. He spoke in Italian to Vittorio, but there was no answer. After a pause Aldo Gamberini said something to Rossi, who replied at length with much beating of his hands on the steering wheel. Brenda was glad she was wearing the enveloping cloak: at every gear change he brushed her thigh with his little finger curled like a snail.

She was surprised when she recognised Marble Arch ahead of them. Existing as she did between the bedsitting room on the first floor and the bottle factory down the road, she mostly imagined herself as still living somewhere in the vicinity of Ramsbottom — 'What am I doing,' she thought, 'in a car loaded with foreigners and barrels of wine?' In spite of herself she began to quiver with threatened laughter: sounds escaped from her in small strangulated squeals. Freda stabbed at her neck with her middle finger.

'What's up with you then?'

'I was just thinking about things.'

'It's nothing to laugh about.' But she laughed all the same, a great bellow that engulfed the car and made Rossi feel everything was fine.

'We are having a good time, yes? All is all right now?'

'Oh yes, we're having a good time all right.' And again Freda gave vent to a hoot of mocking laughter that caused Brenda uneasiness.

'I wonder how many fitted into the mini,' she said quickly to distract her, and Freda squirmed in her seat and peered out of the rear window.

'It's not there,' she said.

'Rossi,' cried Brenda, 'the car's not following.'

'It is all right. Just a little delay. They will catch up with us.'

'Those poor buggers,' burst out Freda, 'trotting off home.'

'Every Sunday,' said Vittorio, breaking his silence and lazily contemplating the great white houses of Park Lane and the glass frontage of the Hilton Hotel, 'my family go on an excursion to the sea-side.'

'Oh yes,' sneered Freda, 'we all know about your Outings. I suppose the maids run on ahead carrying the garlic sausages.'

He smiled tolerantly and stretched his arm along the back of the seat to touch a strand of her hair.

'Don't touch me,' she warned, though she was moved, and tossed her head in pretended annoyance. Brushing her coat with her fingers, preening herself, she showered breadcrumbs on to the floor.

'You and Patrick,' said Brenda, 'with that bread —'

'He deserved it. Bloody fool.'

The glittering shops, closed for the day, flashed past the window. The blue dome of a Catholic church, emblazoned with a golden cross, leant against the white

374

cloud-filled sky. A row of well-dressed women, in fur coats and mantillas, linked arms and pranced in a line down the flight of steps.

'Where the hell are we?' demanded Freda, outraged by their red lips and their slim high-kicking legs. 'Where are we going?'

Rossi shrugged. 'It is a little surprise.'

He himself had no idea where he was heading, the original plan to go to the Stately Home had evaporated with the ordered van. He simply drove away from the city and followed his instincts. He only knew that Mr Paganotti lived somewhere near Windsor on the river and it was the countryside.

'I don't want to be surprised,' said Freda. 'I'll kill that Amelio when I see him.'

'Amelio is a good man,' defended Rossi, 'a good worker and a good father —'

'The bloody fool went to the wrong garage. It's obvious —'

Vittorio and Aldo endeavoured to explain.

'It is not Amelio's fault —'

'He tell me he went to the garage you tell him —'

'Maybe you tell him the wrong day,' said Vittorio.

'You have been a little upset lately,' Brenda said, and could have bitten her tongue.

'You make me sick, you do.' Freda hit her repeatedly between the shoulder blades. 'You're always so damn reasonable. A bit upset am I? What about your mother-in-law? Don't you think that's enough to upset anybody?'

'I meant your mother,' whined Brenda, trying to edge forward on her seat to be out of reach. 'The funeral —'

She pushed her hands over her mouth, and laughter spilled from her splayed fingers.

'I don't blame your mother-in-law trying to do you in. Never saying a word out of place.' Her voice rose as she mimicked Brenda: 'She locked me in the barn but I didn't like to say anything. I saw her going to kill the kittens but I didn't like to interfere!'

She thumped Brenda on the head. 'She was doing you a favour if you ask me. You're sick.'

'Now, now,' said Vittorio holding her wrists in an effort to restrain her.

They wrestled together on the back seat, Freda with her lilac scafr crushed under one ear and Vittorio with his duffel coat speckled with crumbs. Brenda felt sorry for Aldo. He was red in the face with distress and bewilderment. She winked at him to show she didn't mind, that it was only a joke.

'Ah well,' said Rossi, 'we will have a little music.'

He turned the knob of the car radio, and instantly Tom Jones was singing about the Civil War. 'I do rememb-bah . . . a litt-al home-stead . . .' She saw the farm again, and all her hysteria left her. She thought of Mrs Haddon dipping behind the hedge outside the kitchen window, a litter of kittens in her apron, going to the stream to drown them. The cat ran from under the rain barrel, its tail arched over its back, hating the wet grass, shaking its paws fastidiously and mewing in despair. When Mrs Haddon ducked under the stile a kitten plopped to the ground, a black rat-like lump, and the cat leapt and caught it in its jaws and streaked off across the field.

'She's so bloody reasonable,' she heard Freda say. 'You can't get the truth out of her.'

'Rossi,' said Brenda, 'how can the mini catch up with us if you don't know where we're going?'

*

At a garage near the approach of the M4 motorway, miraculously the red mini did find them. Salvatore left the driving wheel and accosted Rossi at the petrol pump. He indicated the boot of the Cortina and the road behind them and waved his arms about. Brenda

376

couldn't see who his passengers were. The windows were steamed up. She could only make out a hand, flattened against the glass, and the brim of a hat. She wished Maria could be with them — all those men and just two women making for the wide open spaces. Freda, limp after her outburst, dozed with her head on Vittorio's shoulder. It amazed Brenda. She couldn't think why he hadn't cracked Freda one over the ear and bundled her out of the car. She had called him a bloody Wop; she hinted his mother had never been married. Shaken but civil, he pushed aside the strands of tousled hair clinging to her moist lips and stroked her inflamed cheeks. Perhaps he liked it, thought Brenda. If she had reviled Stanley more, perhaps he would have stayed in to listen.

Rossi was telling Salvatore his destination was Windsor. Fresh air . . . a little jump out . . . a little game of football. He slapped Salvatore on the back and searched his face tenderly for traces of forgiveness. Salvatore hung his head and pointed his toe in the gravel.

Beyond the brown hedge at the side of the road a solitary cow cropped the grass. Salvatore wore a large fedora on his small head. Its brim stuck out above the padded shoulders of his coat and emphasised the elegance of his nipped-in waist. His hand bulged in his pocket.

He's making him an offer he cannot refuse, thought Brenda.

When Rossi came back to the car, he said, 'They are annoyed at having to pay the money for the petrol. They say it is not called for.'

'Well, they did pay 50p each toward the cost of the van,' reasoned Brenda and hoped Freda had not heard. She held her breath as the car nosed out into the thin stream of traffic.

It took some time to find the road to Windsor Park. When they left the M4, they could see the beige-and-grey castle, lapped by a pool of pale green turf, dwarfing the

377

white houses of the town.

'We must be near,' said Brenda helpfully, as they crossed a bridge with a black swan perched on the water. The red mini had once more disappeared from the road. They came to the bowl of a roundabout, heaped with dahlias, and circled it several times trying to decipher which way the sign post pointed.

'There —' said Vittorio.

'No,' contradicted Freda. And they swung yet again around the small island of flowers until Rossi made his own decision and drove straight on. There were no ornamental gates as he had supposed. The pink-washed houses came to an end and the grey road cut through a green landscape spotted with oak trees. He slowed the car almost immediately and swung on to the grass verge. He bounded out into the fresh air leaving the car door swinging on its hinges.

'It's cold,' complained Freda, as Brenda climbed stiffly out to join Rossi on the grass sprigged with dandelions.

'This is the best place for a little jump out,' he cried, pointing eagerly at the woods in the distance, and the flat slanting top of a cut-down oak a few yards from the bonnet of the car.

'Good God,' Freda said. 'You don't believe in moving far from the main road, do you?'

She lumped her basket on to the verge and wrapped her sheepskin arms about herself for warmth, standing disdainfully in the shadow of the car. It wasn't as she had imagined. There were no lush valleys or rising hills saddled with yellow gorse. The land stretched flat and monotonous to the edge of the horizon. To the right was a clump of rhododendron bushes, a blackened oak splattered with the nests of crows, and a timber fence encircling a wood of beech and sycamore. Above her an aeroplane hung low, nose shaped like a bullet. Wings tipped with crimson, it shot in slow motion through an opening in the clouds. On the distant boundary stood the blue haze of a fir plantation, blurred against the white storm-tossed sky. Meanwhile the lorries, the private cars, the containers of petroleum, roared continuously along the road, shaking the parked Cortina on the grass and filling the air with noise.

'Now what?' she demanded. 'Now that you've got us here.'

Aldo Gamberini, his hat hurled from his head by a gust of wind, scampered across the Park in pursuit. His black trilby bowled to the foot of an oak and flattened itself against the trunk.

'Did you tell the others we were going to the Park?' asked Brenda anxiously. 'There must be a lot of entrances.'

'I say here, or maybe I say Windsor,' said Rossi, and he took out of the car a large white ball and bounced it up and down on the damp ground.

Vittorio caught it on the stub of his boot and kicked it high in the air. Hands deep in his pockets, he ran after it as it soared toward the clump of bushes.

'Wait, wait,' called Rossi, mouth trembling petulantly, as he tried to catch the tall young man now dribbling the ball selfishly ahead of him.

Trotting at Vittorio's heels, pestering, he tried in vain to regain possession. The two men ran in a wide circle with the muddy ball bouncing and rolling across the glossy wind-swept grass.

'Look here,' said Freda after ten minutes of this activity. 'I want to see the castle.'

She had been picking at the silver wrapping about the chickens, digging at the carcasses with her nails and licking her fingers. It was a quarter to eleven and there was no point eating yet — she would only be more hungry later on.

'You want to go?' said Rossi. He stopped running and stared at her in surprise, his cheeks rosy from his exercise

379

with the ball, his suede shoes stained with mud. He spread out his hands expressively. 'We have only just come.'

'My dear man,' Freda informed him, 'the castle is redolent with History.' She wanted Vittorio to know how educated she was, to make up for the scene in the car. Also, she felt the need to be near a cigarette shop in case she gained the courage to ask him to lend her some money. 'Besides,' she said, indicating Brenda at the far side of the road, obsessively studying the stream of traffic, 'Madame won't settle until we find the others.'

'There is plenty of time,' protested Rossi. 'If they don't come in a little moment, we go.'

Freda kept her temper with difficulty. She pointed out that she hadn't intended to come here in the first place. She had planned to go to Hertfordshire. However, now they were here she was going to look at the castle.

With some spirit Rossi argued that it wasn't his fault if the plans had gone wrong. 'We take our chances,' he said mysteriously.

Vittorio decided to take Freda's part. He walked to the car and tossed the football at Rossi.

'Let's go,' he said.

How American he is, thought Freda, with his dashing moustaches and his baseball-type boots. The red laces trailed like ribbons in the grass.

She fitted herself into the back seat and allowed Vittorio to manoeuvre the basket through the door.

'We are going?' asked Aldo Gamberini, his hat securely anchored to his head by means of a striped muffler tied under his chin. 'So soon?'

Rossi held the football to his chest. His mouth quivered. 'I want to play the games,' he said sulkily.

'Brenda,' shouted Freda. 'Hurry up.'

They positioned themselves in the car.

'There are little deer,' murmured Rossi forlornly. 'I think you like the little deer?'

380

'I will later,' assured Brenda. 'Honestly, Rossi, I do want to see the little deer.'

They drove out of the Park and back along the road to the flowered roundabout.

Freda thought the castle was wonderful. It towered above the main street, its beige walls curving outwards, the green grass studded with spotlights. She was reminded of a play about a Spanish family of noble birth that she had been in years before. She would have liked to have mentioned it but she had only understudied a rather minor part.

'Isn't it wonderful,' she breathed. 'It's so old.'

She couldn't wait to get out of the car and look at the dungeons. If she couldn't walk through the perfumed gardens with Vittorio, then maybe here where Henry VIII had danced with Anne Boleyn she could find an equally lyrical setting for the beginning of their romance. There were bound to be dark places and iron grills, worn steps leading to cramped stone towers overlooking the country-side. There, above the Thames valley and the blue swell of the Chiltern Hills, he would, looking down at the small fields laid in squares and the ribbon of hedges, see in perspective how puny was the world and how big their love for each other. Accordingly she bustled out of the Cortina and lingered only momentarily outside the tobacco-scented doorway of a sweet-shop. Brenda insisted on writing a note in case the occupants of the mini came upon the deserted car and searched for them.

'After all,' she said, 'we have got the wine. I'll never be able to look them in the face again if they don't find us.'

'You never look anybody in the face as it is,' said Freda; and she drummed her fingers on the bonnet of the car, as Brenda drew an arrow on the back of an envelope, pointing towards the castle, and wrote: 'This way. We have just left.' She signed it 'Mrs Brenda.'

'You're mad,' Freda told her. 'You've got terrible

handwriting.'

All the same, Brenda felt more restful in her mind now that she had left some sign. She stood at various angles from the bumper of the Cortina to make sure her arrow was accurate in its direction.

Freda began to toil up the steep cobbled rise to the main gate, pushed from behind by Aldo and Vittorio.

'We are happy, yes?' said Rossi, and he attempted to put an arm about Brenda's waist. At that moment Aldo chose to turn and see if they were following, and Rossi jumped away, anxious not to seem too intimate.

'He is my cousin.'

'He's a nice man,' said Brenda.

'He is very inquisitive.'

'Does he suffer from ear-ache?' she asked, looking at Aldo with the scarf wrapped about his head.

'It is a pity,' Rossi said, panting from the climb, 'that he fit in my car.' He cheered up and dug her in the ribs. 'Later,' he promised, winking at her encouragingly, and she did her best to look enthusiastic. If his happiness depended on her, who was *she* to offend him? He wanted his Outing, his day of escape. If the missing mini caught up with them, disgorging its quota of fellow-countrymen, then she would not be to blame if he was thwarted. 'It's not my fault,' she thought. 'I can't be expected to take any blame.'

'I've told you about that,' reminded Freda, turning to look at her.

'You shouldn't talk to yourself. It looks daft.'

Above them, carved on the gateway, mingling with the arms of Henry VIII, the Tudor rose blossomed in stone.

'Oh I wish,' cried Freda, 'we had a camera.'

She tripped forward in her purple trousers and gazed entranced at the toy soldier in his red tunic and rippling busby, motionless outside the guardhouse.

*

Salvatore spotted the Cortina with the envelope trapped on its windscreen at mid-day. There was a consultation as to what the arrow meant. Salvatore and his three passengers thought it peculiar that Rossi and the English-women had entered the fortress, but the fifth occupant of the mini, not being Italian, said he understood. He borrowed a pencil from a traffic warden and wrote in English: 'We have gone that way too,' and signed it 'Patrick.'

Murmuring, the four workmen followed him up the hill and stood bewildered on the parade ground. Set at the end of the courtyard was a kiosk, and there was a thin stream of visitors buying tickets. On a pole above the State Apartments, a yellow flag, stretched stiff as a board, pasted itself to the sky. The soberly dressed men, searching for the lost remnants of their party, wandered beneath arches and descended steps. The wind rose in fury and blew them, jackets flapping, along a stone terrace above a garden. Wearily they climbed back to the parade ground and, urged on by Patrick, joined the queue at the kiosk and paid 15p each to the attendant. Entering the doorway of a chapel, they removed their hats and shuffled past the alabaster font. They stared at the carved choir-stalls and the arched roof hung with flags, embroidered with strange beasts and symbols, heavy with tassels of gold. There were no candles burning, no crucifix, no saints bleeding and bedecked with jewels in the shadowy niches of the walls.

Bending their heads, they watched furtively the feet of Patrick as he trod the tiled floor.

*

Freda had enquired and been told that the dungeons had all been sealed off.

'Off?' she repeated, outraged. 'Why?'

Rossi led her away, agreeing with her that it was

383

preposterous.

'These things,' he said, 'how do we know why? What is the purpose?'

And he spread his hands and looked at her with such intensity of feeling that she was quite impressed by him.

He dreaded lest she fight physically with the custodian of the castle and have them ejected. Somewhere, beyond the main portion of the town, stood the family home of Mr Paganotti, set in gardens fragrant with falling leaves and dying roses. From every parapet Rossi leaned and searched the landscape for some sign of Mr Paganotti's existence. Once he had been promised he would be taken to the mansion — he had come to work in his best suit — but something had occurred to postpone his visit. He had waited in the outer office for Mr Paganotti to appear, until the secretary had come out shrugging her arms in her modish coat, and told him that Mr Paganotti had already gone. He did not allow himself to think that Mr Paganotti had forgotten — that was not possible. It was simply that he had so many responsibilities, so many cares — he had been summoned away with no time to explain. He had rehearsed how he would behave the following day when Mr Paganotti sought him out and apologised. He would raise his hand like a drawbridge and tell him no explanation was needed. Between men of business, excuses were unnecessary. He waited a long time at his desk, his hand flat against his breast, but even on the Friday when he went to receive his wages Mr Paganotti said nothing.

Freda was irritated when Vittorio corrected every item of information she gave him about the history of the castle. She understood, but she hated him for it. He was like her in temperament, conscious that he was mortal and determined to have the last word. She fell silent and was genuinely upset that the State Apartments were closed.

'It's obvious,' said Brenda. 'If the flag's flying, she's

here.'

A group of Americans, pork-pie hats jammed securely on their cropped heads, pulled out identical cameras from leather containers, and focussed as one man on the statue of King Charles on his horse.

'She's in London,' said Freda.

'No here,' Vittorio said firmly, striding ahead of her like some monk of ancient times, the hood of his duffel coat about his head.

'If she wasn't here,' said Brenda persistently, 'we could look round her rooms and things. That's why it's closed.'

'Shut up,' Freda said. She didn't see it made any difference whether the Queen was in or out. Nobody actually saw her rooms. It stood to reason that State Apartments were separate. It wasn't as if they were going to catch her doing a bit of dusting.

The Gallery was closed too and the Dolls' House. 'Every bloody thing is closed,' she thought. 'I might as well give up.' The antiquity of her surroundings began to have a depressing effect upon her. What did it matter if Henry VIII had fallen in love all those times and lusted and eaten enormous meals? He was dead now and mouldered. She was further annoyed that she had to let Vittorio pay 15p for her to go into the Chapel. It was degrading, and it made it more difficult to ask him to pay for her ciggies. She stared gloomily at the carved gargoyles above the doorway, the swan and the hart and the dragon, and followed him inside.

The goggling tourists, the orange bars of the electric fires placed in strategic corners, robbed the place of solemnity. Above their heads, circled with motes of dust, stone angels spread their wings and folded pious hands.

'I want to go home,' said Freda, echoing Brenda several hours earlier.

'Isn't it smashing,' Brenda replied, fearful that Rossi had overheard. She sought Freda's hand and held it, trying to

385

comfort her.

'That's Italian, isn't it, Rossi?' asked Freda. She pointed at an inscription on the wall. 'What's it say?'

He studied it carefully. 'Ah well,' he said, 'it is the Latin.'

Ave lumen oculorum
Liberator languidorum
Dentium angustia

'Hail bright eyes,' said Brenda unexpectedly. 'Sleepy liberator . . . bent anguish.'

'What's that mean?' asked Freda.

'It is the sufferers from toothache,' explained Vittorio; and Brenda felt it was an omen. Here, far from the farm and the absent Stanley, someone was caring for her teeth. Is it really, she wondered, trooping round the Chapel, holding Freda's hand in her own? Just thinking about it brought her down a flight of steps with a twinge of pain at the back of her jaw. She winced and stared intently at the warm pink stone ahead of her. They had come to the cloisters, a covered walk of meditation overlooking a patch of grass spread like a tablecloth. They were alone, the five of them, footsteps echoing on the ancient flagstones worn smooth by time.

'That's nice,' said Brenda.

'Let go of me,' hissed Freda. 'For God's sake, get lost.'

Seeing the deserted promenade lined with stone seats, she urgently wanted Rossi and Aldo and Brenda to go away and leave her alone with Vittorio.

Brenda didn't know what to do. She tiptoed self-consciously around the square and trusted that Rossi would follow.

'Lovely,' she murmured in a little more than a whisper. 'How old it all is.'

She went at a slightly increased pace along the southern flank of the cloister, relieved to hear the footsteps behind her. She turned left, fearful of coming back to Freda and found herself in the west wing of the Chapel. High on the wall was the fresco of a king with a white beard and eyes corroded by dampness. She paused and was joined by Rossi, his face pretentiously solemn as he stared upwards at the faded painting.

'Where's Aldo?' she whispered.

'He is somewhere.'

He made as if to retrace his steps, and she seized him by the arm. She had to think of something. Freda would never forgive her if they reappeared. After all she had ruined her assignation with Vittorio the night Mrs Haddon had called with her gun.

'I'm going to be sick, Rossi,' she said. And she pulled him down a dark passage set with little wooden doors and half-ran with him out into the open air and the cobbled forecourt. She headed towards a distant gateway, her arm in his, and found herself on a terrace overlooking a sunken garden.

*

'I'm weary,' announced Freda, and she flopped down on the convenient stone bench. Vittorio stretched his long legs and loosed the hood of his duffel coat. Small flecks of dandruff alighted on his shoulders. Aldo Gamberini, fretting at an archway, stared at the billiard cloth of grass. He cleared his throat. He wished he was working in his garden or helping his eldest son to oil his motorbike. After a moment he walked hesitatingly away in the direction of the Chapel.

'We will all be lost to one another,' said Vittorio.

'Ah no,' she said, 'not you and I.' And she leaned her blonde head on his shoulder.

'You and I,' he said, 'are birds of a tree. You do not let me be the man.'

Now that they were alone he did not mind talking to

387

her freely. His impending engagement to the girl from Casalecchio di Reno was his own concern. At this distance, and with Rossi so obviously in pursuit of Mrs Brenda, he was content to lay his heart bare to the large English girl who treated him with such familiarity.

'I don't what?'

'You are always shouting. Giving orders.'

'I'm not.'

'You are never tranquil.'

'Oh I am,' said Freda. 'Don't you feel like a man?' And unfairly she laid her pale hand on his trouser leg and stroked his thigh. 'You and I,' she warned, 'could be something. I know about you.'

'What do you know of me?'

She brought her face closer to his until the hairs of his moustaches tickled the edges of her mouth.

'You see,' she confided, 'I'm not what I seem. I know I'm aggressive, but I'm not entirely. I'm surrounded perpetually by fools. Given the right opportunity, I could follow. If someone was strong enough to lead.'

She was staring at his mouth, her eyes veiled by the golden sweep of her lashes.

'Ah well —' he said, and his lips quivered.

'I need something serious. Something I can get my teeth into.'

He brought his hand protectively to the collar of his red jumper.

'I'm not fooling. I mean it for real. If I want something I go after it.' She looked at him boldly. He was mesmerised by her blue eyes, the creamy texture of her cheeks, her tinted nails moving softly across his leg. 'I'd do anything for you.'

'I cannot,' he said, 'be less than truthful with you. I have other commitments.'

She had not heard the concluding words of his sentence. She had heard him say he could not be less than true to her, and all else was drowned and deafened in the flood of joy that filled her heart and suffused her face with colour. He did love her. He could only be true to her.

'I will never let you go,' she breathed.

She clung to him and raised her lips to be kissed. An old man came out of a recess in the wall and passed them by. Clad in a long black gown bunched at the waist by a length of rope, he hurried deeper into the interior of the Chapel. Vittorio drew away from Freda and looked curiously at the open door.

'It is his home?' he inquired.

'Never mind,' she said. And she fondled his neck and twined her fingers in the tendrils of his soft brown hair.

It was easy now to be tranquil and happy and kind. She was sickened by her unkindness to Brenda; she wanted everything to be lovely and safe, like the warm clasp of Vittorio's arms. She desired with sudden urgency to show him where she was born, where she had gone to school, a view from the top of a hill, the surface of a lake near her home, clay-brown and pitted under rain. She wanted him to tell her that he too had seen a film years ago that only she remembered, that he too could listen with closed eyes to a certain melody. These few and fragmented reasons for believing love existed and could be unique stayed alive and sweet for perhaps thirty seconds in her mind — and faded as she looked beyond his shoulder, and the pale outline of his ear, and saw a line of black-suited men walking in single file along the opposite side of the cloister. Patrick, his cloth cap and pleasant face glimpsed in profile, strode in their rear. Freda pulled Vittorio's head down to her breast and closed her eyes. At that instant, Patrick, glancing casually across the square of smooth grass, saw them. He ran like a whippet beneath the pink arches and confronted her.

'You,' she said, stealing his thunder. 'How the hell did you get here?'

'Where is she?' demanded Patrick, his cheeks glowing like apples from indignation and the biting wind.

Vittorio bent to tie his shoe lace. He was worried inside; he felt that something had not been clearly understood. He dwelt fleetingly on the curved dark profile of Rossi's niece by marriage and wondered at Freda's formidable instinct. Was it possible she knew him better than he knew himself? Did she think she could take him by force?

'What have you done with her?' Patrick was asking.

Vittorio was not clear what was at issue. The Irish van driver was an unknown quantity. Nobody had explained what he was doing in the bathroom the night he had visited Freda. Maybe she had allowed him too to take liberties with her Rubensesque body. The remembrance of her billowy flesh and her grasping little hands pulling his hair made him giddy. He strolled casually away from the bench and appeared to be studying the grass.

Freda, seeing how he deserted her, was filled with hatred for Patrick. She wished the loaf of bread had been a broken bottle. Spitting, they faced each other, and Patrick held her by the shoulders.

'Help me,' she cried and twisted round to appeal to Vittorio, but he was no longer there.

'Swine,' she shouted, 'beater of women.' And she struggled with the Irishman, pinning him with her knee in his groin against the surface of the wall.

Vittorio in the main chapel, waited for several minutes. He would have liked to have run for it, but Rossi had disappeared and he was next in order of seniority. Mr Paganotti would have expected him to do his duty. After an interval, Freda, quivering with anger, swept round the corner.

'What sort of man are you?' she raged.

'Sssh,' he said, fearful of the reverent tourists and the black-garbed priest climbing to kneel in prayer.

390

'He hit me,' she said. 'Where were you?' Her eyes blazed reproachfully.

'I do not want a scene.'

He turned and made for the exit, conscious he was a coward but terrorised by her loud voice and the strength of her arm.

*

Salvatore and his party were hurrying forlornly down the hill toward the car. But for the wine in the boot of the Cortina, so generously bestowed by Mr Paganotti, and the money they had already contributed to the Outing, they might have headed for home. It was just possible that Mr Paganotti might inquire if they had enjoyed themselves, and how could they disappoint him? They could not imagine what had happened to Patrick. One moment he had been ushering them forward and the next he had vanished into the shadows. He had abandoned them. They called his name softly, but there was no answering voice. Gino, an elderly man who had been once to visit his son in America and never forgotten the experience, said it was a sign of the times. 'Such a hurry they are in.' Speed and violence and a lack of consideration. He shook his grey head and looked up at the North tower, as if Patrick might be seen clambering inconsiderately about the battlements. They trotted down the hill and huddled inside the interior of the mini and watched the women outside in the street.

'Please don't,' Brenda was begging, her teeth chattering, her back against the wall of the parapet.

Beneath her, the sunken garden, heavy with late-flowering shrubs, heaved in a spasm of wind. Rossi, his hands inside her cloak, his black curls blown over his forehead, took no heed.

'I am warming you,' he said, and he nipped her skin

391

between his fingers and gobbled the tip of her reddening nose. She was looking foolishly at him and grinning toothily. He could not understand why she was so friendly to him and so resistant. It was torture to him. He respected his wife. He did not wish to break the sanctity of his marriage vows or lower himself in the estimation of Mr Paganotti, but what was he to think when the English girl allowed him so much freedom? If he took no advantage she would think him a cissy. Perhaps Mrs Freda, with her apparent contempt for men, was indeed the true woman, open to advances.

Beneath them, the massive rhododendrons pitched under the scudding clouds. A ray of cold sunlight, salmon pink, washed over the grey stone. Across the valley, the beech trees with stripped trunks paled to silver.

'Look,' he said, 'how beautiful it is.'

She escaped from him and hugged the stone parapet and leaned as far as she dared, her thin hair hanging about her cheeks, and wished she was down there among the plump yew hedges, walking the paths littered with fallen leaves and the red berries of rowan. She thought of the commercial traveller who had stopped to give her a lift when she was going into Ramsbottom to buy groceries. In vain she said she was married, that her husband was big as an ox. He inveigled her out of his car and bundled her down beneath the bridge, his big feet snapping the stems of foxgloves, and panted above her. She wished Mrs Haddon had done her job properly, had put an end to this aimless business of living through each day. She squeezed her eyelids shut, but no tears would come. Rossi was behind her now, the muzzle of his face worrying her hair.

'Does Mr Paganotti live in a very big house?'

'Ah yes. He is a very big man in business.'

'What sort of a house?'

But he would not be put off. He dug his ferret teeth into

her neck and redoubled his efforts.

Perhasp Freda was right. She was a victim, asking to be destroyed. With any luck Rossi would manoeuvre her to such an extent that she would topple from the wall and be dashed to pieces. If ever I get out of this, she vowed, I will never be friendly again, not to anyone. Please God, send someone.

At that moment she heard a voice torn by the wind and saw Aldo Gamberini propelled along the terrace like a black angel, his arms flapping like wings, the cloth of his trousers whipped into folds about his prancing legs.

Rossi spoke to him heatedly. He clenched his fists and berated the cellar worker. Aldo Gamberini hung his head and seemed near to tears.

'Stop it,' said Brenda. 'The poor man.' And Rossi stalked away as if not trusting himself to say more, and returned abruptly, face sullen and voice harsh.

Severely reprimanded, Aldo followed them through an archway on to the parade ground and slunk down the cobbled hill. At the bottom he made to enter the red mini but Rossi would not allow it. Overcome with emotion, Aldo sank into the back seat of the Cortina and unwound the muffler from his head. His hat, limp over his collar, drooped like the ears of a whipped dog.

There was no contact between the two cars; no horn blowing or festive cries. Salvatore hesitated to remonstrate with Rossi — he looked so thunderous and out of sorts.

At last, through the gate at the top of the hill, came first Freda and then Vittorio. They walked separately, shrouded in emotion, until Freda stopped and asked Vittorio for something. He felt in his pocket and counted coins into her hand. He climbed into the car and it was agony for Brenda, faithful to her vow of half an hour earlier, to keep silent. She watched Freda enter the tobacco shop and reappear snapping the clasp of her handbag shut.

6

Freda laid her embroidered tablecloth on the ground, and it flapped upwards immediately and threatened to fly into the branches of an oak tree. She knelt on her elbows, bottom raised in the air, and told Brenda to help her. Between them they anchored the cloth at its four corners with the basket, the cooked chickens, the bag of apples and a convenient stone. The men were shy of placing their provisions on the cloth. They held tight to their briefcases and carrier bags and sat self-conciously on the grass. Stealthily — for hours of stalking each other about the castle had given them an appetite — they tore pieces of bread and chewed salami.

'For God's sake,' entreated Freda, 'put your food all together.'

She was like a matron, starched and encapsulated in her stiff sheepskin coat, ordering them to take their medicine. They did as they were told, heaping the loaves of bread and the fat lengths of sausage in front of her, and munched in silence.

Some children ran through the grass and stood at a distance looking at the barrels of wine perched on the slaughtered oak.

Freda served Vittorio first. 'Have the best part of the chicken,' she urged. 'Go on, have the breast.'

Brenda looked at the ground. Freda handed her a shrivelled portion of wing and a piece of skin. I want chips, thought Brenda, in this weather.

'Come, come,' called Rossi, smiling at the children and gesturing toward the food.

Freda scowled, and the children scattered and ran to the parked cars.

The morsel of chicken stuck in Brenda's throat. She longed for a mug of hot tea. 'It's nice here,' she said, and scoffed a hunk of bread and looked up at the road for signs of Patrick. Freda had said he had gone home. It didn't seem possible — he hadn't said goodbye.

Freda recollected that there was a safari park nearby. She said it would be nice to go there later in the afternoon. 'You know,' she said impatiently, 'it's a park full of wild animals.'

'Wild animals,' repeated Rossi. 'You are thinking of the little deer?'

'No I'm not. I'm thinking of the little lions and the little tigers — wandering around free, not in cages.'

The workers watched first Rossi then Freda, eyes flickering hopefully back and forth in an effort to understand.

'But it is dangerous,' said Rossi. 'We will all be running.'

'In the car, you fool. We go in the car and they're outside wandering about.'

Rossi liked the idea, once he felt it would be safe. He translated rapidly to the men, who murmured and looked at each other in wonder. They eyed the stretch of grass and the parked mini as if measuring the distance they might have to run.

Gino, whose son had gone to America, refused to eat communally. He had deposited his carrier bag in a pew in the chapel and forgotten to reclaim it.

'For God's sake,' bullied Freda. 'Feed, you fool.' And she thrust into his hand a yellow scrap of meat.

He shook his head politely in denial and turned his face to the wind, the unwanted food lying on his palm.

Vittorio ate heartily. He enjoyed Freda's salad and the dressing in the bottle. He put his bread on a paper plate and saturated it with oil. She watched the juice run down his chin and his fingers slippery with grease. She was repelled by his unabashed vulgarity, the common way he wiped his hands on the grass.

The wind slowly abated, the sky cleared and the sun shone. A dozen cars slowed to a halt and lined up on the grass verge. The men were warmed and revived. They filled their celluloid cups with wine and stretched out on the ground. Too polite to speak in their native language in front of the English girls, they remained monosyllabic.

'Stick this,' said Freda at last, when she had eaten her fill, and she rose to her feet and wandered away in the direction of the beech wood. She hoped Vittorio would follow. She was in a state of suspense as to his intentions. His declaration of true love, his betrayal moments later, had confused her. Still, she was not too distressed. The gradual turning of the October day from storm and cold to balm and mildness filled her with optimism.

Rossi wanted to play games, he tried to explain. He spoke in English to Brenda and in Italian to the respectful men.

'In the woods . . . a little jump out . . . you will count and we will hide.'

They looked at him without enthusiasm. He pointed at the woods and at Freda slowly perambulating round the perimeter of the fencing and covered his eyes coyly with his hands.

'We will hide and you will come to find.'

He jumped to his feet and urged Brenda to stand up.

'No,' she said. 'I want to rest.'

'Ah, never. We are here for a little jump out, yes?' And he pulled her quite roughly to her feet and she cried, 'No, no, later,' and sank down again among the dandelions.

The men averted their faces. They had had enough of

finding and seeking. They knew well who would be found and who would be lost.

Rejected, Rossi went slowly to his car and returned with the stained football. He kicked it high in the air and the men lumbered to their feet and brushed down their clothes and ran about, eyes dilated and legs stiff from lack of exercise. Vittorio did not follow Freda across the park. Instead he discarded his coat and, luminous in a red jumper and trousers of black velvet, joined in the game. In contrast to Rossi, who trundled, garments flapping, in a furious rush along the pitch, he ran elegantly with arms outstretched, placing the heel of one foot precisely against the toe of the other, as if balanced on a tight-rope. After a few moments several players stopped in mid-field and bent over, heads dangling, and fought for breath. If they felt the day lacked real splendour, they were too polite to declare it. It made no difference that the sky now drifted baby-blue above their heads — there were no village girls to dance with, no perspiring members of *la banda* blowing golden trumpets flashing in the sun; the wine balanced on the stump of the tree was contained in barrels of brown plastic. Digging their fists into their stomachs, the men jostled and stumbled together on the turf. They erupted into sly bursts of hysterical laughter as one or other of them, lunging too energetically at the flying ball, lost his balance and slipped on all fours upon the green grass. Patches of damp darkening their knees, and clumps of earth sticking to the soles of their winkle-picker shoes, they dashed back and forth between the oak trees.

*

Freda, lingering at the edge of the timber fence, watched Vittorio in his fiery jumper, flickering beneath the autumn leaves. She went very slowly round the curve of the fence

397

and entered the beech wood. Singing in a slight acrid voice a song her aunt in Newcastle had taught her as a child, she started to march at a rapid pace, with swinging arms, along the path. After one verse, the bracken crackling beneath her boots, she stopped abruptly and listened. Faintly from across the park, now lost to view, she could hear the sporadic cries of the gambolling men, the drone of an aeroplane above her head and somewhere, deeper among the trees, the distinct noise of someone moving. She had the feeling she was being watched. She tried a few experimental paces further along the path and was sure she was being matched, step for step, by something invisible and level with her, screened by the stippled bark and the dying leaves of the beeches. She halted, and all was quiet. It was probably children playing Indians, stalking each other, unaware of her presence. Above her, the vapour trail of the vanished plane rolled wider and mingled with the clouds. Uneasily she continued along the path and tried not to feel afraid. She was nowhere near the safari park: it couldn't be a wolf or a runaway lion. There would be notices all over the place if she had wandered into the lion reserve. She paused and pretended to be examining the curve of a leaf. This time she saw the shape, human in form, of someone gliding behind the trunk of a tree. It's a dirty old man, she thought, relieved, but turned all the same and walked back toward the park. It would be funny if it was Mr Paganotti keeping an eye on them, watching to see if there was any hanky-panky going on in the forest. She wouldn't put it past him. He acted as if he owned his employees body and soul, handing out his cast-off clothing as if he was God Almighty.

A pebble, spinning from the bushes, glanced her cheek. Instantly she was filled with anger.

'Who the bloody hell did that?' she shouted, brave now that she was approaching the fence.

Another pebble, bigger in size, pitched on to the path a few inches from her foot. She went stealthily as a cat through the tangle of bushes, cuckoo spittle on her boots, and stooped to select a large stone from the undergrowth. Peering into the trees she flung it with all her strength into the gloom. There was a pattering of torn leaves, a thud, and an audible intake of breath.

'Serve you right,' she said and half ran, for fear of reprisals, round the curve of the path and into the park.

She trudged thankfully toward the running men and the tilted barrels perched on the oak table. She thought Brenda looked ridiculous, still wrapped in the purple cloak, attempting to kick the ball without exposing her legs. Freda said nothing, but she gave one of her mocking smiles.

'Do join in,' called Brenda. 'It's good fun.'

Her hair was messy and her ankles were braceleted with stalks of grass.

'Don't be absurd,' snapped Freda, and she lowered herself on to the ground and propped her back against the stump of the oak.

She rubbed at her cheek with a piece of twig, trying to scratch it though not wishing to draw blood. Vittorio, peacocking across the pitch, hunched his shoulders like a baseball player and ran to her.

'Where have you been?' he asked.

She held her cheek and shook her head. He squatted on his haunches in front of her. Lip beaded with perspiration, his face bloomed like a rose.

'Ah, you have hurt yourself,' and he touched her soft cheek with one exploring finger. 'What has happened?'

'There was a maniac in the woods,' she said, 'hurling stones at me. I shouldn't be surprised if it was Patrick getting his own back.'

He found it difficult to understand. His eyes widened, and he waited for more words, but she bent her head and kept silent. She hadn't thought of the Irishman until this moment. Surely he wouldn't dare to chuck stones at her? Maybe it had been children. Perhaps some irate parent would come soon over the grass leading a bleeding child by the hand.

'Come,' said Vittorio caressingly. 'Be on my side. You play the ball game with me.'

He was challenging her, she thought, asking her to show her allegiance in front of the workers.

'I'm not keen,' she demurred, and he coaxed her to her feet, holding her hands in his. The men faltered and gave a few encouraging cries as the ball raced across the pitch.

'Why didn't you come for a walk?' she asked.

'But I cannot leave the men,' he said. 'It is not possible.'

Still entwining his fingers in hers, he dragged her some yards across the grass and then loosed her. She floundered as if in deep water among the sea of men, striking out, first in one direction and then another, in a breathless endeavour to intercept the ball kicked from side to side.

'That's it,' encouraged Brenda. 'Get at it, luv.'

She was in her stockinged feet, with one toe protruding from a hole, hopping up and down with excitement. There was no goal mouth to aim at — Freda wasn't even sure whose side she was on. She saw a row of black hats dumped on the ground and kicked out wildly with her boot. She missed and fell heavily on to her bottom. A faint titter began and died away instantly. Vittorio and Brenda, taking no heed, ran together, bumping and shouting after the bouncing ball.

Struggling to her feet, the tide of players rushing away from her, Freda returned, scarlet in the face, to the tree stump and turned the tap of the wine barrel.

Presently Vittorio came to see if she was all right. He looked at her spoilt face and disturbed hair.

'You want a little rest?' he said.

400

'My back,' she said abstractedly, as if it was an old burden she was used to bearing alone. She refused to meet his eye and winced bravely and bit her lip.

'Have you hurt your back again?' asked Brenda, leaving the game and looking at her anxiously. It seemed to Freda that wherever Vittorio went, Brenda followed. She stood very close to him, as if they were both united by their concern for her.

'Play on,' said Freda nobly, waving her hand selflessly at the make-shift football pitch, though she would have liked to catch Brenda a stinging slap across the face. She sank down with extreme caution on to the grass and closed her eyes.

'She's got a bad back,' said Brenda. 'It plays up from time to time. That's why she has to sit on a beer crate to do her labelling.'

'Perhaps a little sleep will do her good,' Vittorio said, as if speaking of his grandmother; and they went away together.

When Freda opened her eyes, her head turned resolutely from the happy team of workmates, she was astonished to see a row of horses at the boundary of the field, flowing along the blue line of the firs. She sat up, shielding her eyes from the sun, absorbed in the sight, touched by some chord of memory, and watched them turn from mauve to chestnut brown as they swerved, two abreast, away from the trees and began to canter across the park. At this distance they resembled an illustration she had seen in a war book, sepia-tinted, of cavalry on the march. They came nearer, the thud of hooves muffled by the grass, and she saw that there were three riders each leading a saddleless horse on a long rein, and they were no longer brown but jet black from head to tail with trappings of dark leather burnished by the sun. Now she knew who they were. She could see quite clearly the peaked caps of the mounted men, the mustard jackets buttoned at the throat. The game of football broke up. The workers flocked to the tree stump to refresh themselves with wine. They gazed in awe and pleasure at the animals and the proud uniformed men sweeping toward them.

'It's them,' cried Freda, getting to her feet and tugging Brenda by the arm. 'The other morning in the street — there were hundreds of them.'

She stared in recognition at the riders, red-cheeked and bright-eyed as if risen from Flanders field, the dead young ones come back to ride again.

'It can't be them,' said Brenda. 'We're miles away.'

Rossi, cherubic face beaming with hospitality, ran to the horses. The men reined in and slowed their mounts to a walk. Circling the oak, Rossi at their rumps, the animals snorted, flared nostrils lined with purple.

The soldiers looked down at the ill-assorted group, at the blonde girl in her sheepskin coat, the dishevelled black-suited workers, the paper cups strewn on the ground. Brenda, with her formidable nose in the air and an utterly misleading expression of haughtiness in her somewhat hooded eyes, spun on the grass like a bird caught in a net. She was terrified of the prancing beasts.

'You will have a little wine?' said Rossi, and he twinkled back to the barrel and turned the tap and rinsed out grass stalks from the cups, pouring the red wine on to the ground and refilling the beakers to the brim. Like a woman holding up refreshments to the liberating troops he smiled coyly and held out his arms. The three young soldiers dismounted. The horses pawed the turf and bent their necks, the clipped manes standing like a pelt of fur along the curve of their necks, the tails, dense as soot, swishing flies from their dark and steaming haunches.

The riders were on a training course from Aldershot. They were exercising the Queen's funeral horses.

'Funeral horses?' said Freda, eying the satiny flanks of the wicked-looking animals.

402

On great occasions, the soldiers explained, the death of military leaders, the laying to rest of Dukes and Princes, the Queen's horses, glossy black, pulled the gun carriage with the coffin on top.

'Of course,' said Brenda, remembering the death of Churchill. She looked discreetly at the rounded bellies, trying to ascertain what sex they were.

'Are they ladies or gentlemen?' she whispered to Freda. 'I can't see.'

'Geldings,' pronounced Freda, though Brenda was no wiser. 'You can't have stallions at a state funeral —'

'Why ever not?' asked Brenda.

'They're too fruity — it stands to reason. They might go wild and stampede down the Mall dragging the coffin at breakneck speed.'

'How awful,' said Brenda.

'They're very carefully trained. In Vienna it was an art in itself.'

Freda spoke as if she knew all about it, though in truth she had only ridden once, and that on a donkey at Whitby Bay when she was six years old.

The soldiers, young boys from country districts with soft burring accents, ate pieces of salami and crusts of bread washed down by the wine. In return, unasked, they offered the two women and one of the men a ride on the horses.

'Oh, no,' said Brenda instantly, 'I couldn't possibly — honestly. Thank you very much all the same.'

She stepped backwards, as if fearing they would fling her into the air by force and strap her in the saddle like some sacrifice to the gods of war. The workers, having been picked once in their lives by Mr Paganotti, hung back, not expecting to be chosen again. Vittorio made a token attempt to stand back for Salvatore, but it was not serious, and he and Rossi mounted. Freda, her delicate back forgotten, flung down her sheepskin coat and was hauled by two soldiers on to the large gelding, the plump curves of her purple calves echoing the rounded swell of the horses. Admiringly the men watched her swaying under the sky, her peach face shimmering amidst the golden strands of her blown hair. Vittorio, the red jumper giving him a military air, rode at her side. The soldiers mounted their own beasts, the long guiding reins streaming out behind them, and began to canter slowly away from the pitch. Last went Rossi, hair clustered in damp ringlets upon his brow, bumping like a schoolboy across the neck of his horse. They rode through the air, level with the distant hills and the black fingers of the thorn trees, and Freda held an imaginary crop in her hand and tilted her chin imperiously at the sun. She was Catherine of Russia at the head of her regiment; she was Lady Barbara riding beside the young squire. Vittorio could not take his eyes from her: she was so majestic, so splendidly rooted to the black horse. She knew he was looking at her. She parted her lips, and a dimple appeared in her left cheek, and she thought, just at this moment we are one, you and I, only a little lower than the angels. They swept in a wide arc around the park, the scent of the firs mingling with the sweat of the horses, and turned at the curve of the timber fence, bending low to avoid the branches dipping in their path.

As they flashed past the beginning of the beech wood, Vittorio thought he saw someone in a peaked cap and a mackintosh running along an avenue of trees. For a second he imagined it was the Irish van-driver, but he remembered that Freda had said he had long since made for home.

'Thank you so much,' said Freda graciously, as the horses stopped once more at the oak tree. 'It was so nice.' And she slid, light as a feather, it seemed, to the green grass and stood patting the nose of her horse.

Her knees began to tremble, her thighs ached; she had

not realised how tightly she had gripped the belly of the saddleless animal. Exhilarated and unsteady on her feet, she smiled with childish satisfaction at Vittorio and said gaily to Brenda: 'Oh, you should have come. It was beautiful. It was so beautiful.'

They sat on the ground and lay in the sunshine. They drank thirstily from the barrels of wine. The soldiers, standing in their stirrups like jockeys, rode in a circle about the tree stump and made for the verge. Stepping delicately on to the gravel, the black horses swayed sedately toward the town, hooves clattering on the surface of the road.

'What did it really feel like?' asked Brenda.

'It was a bit like being on a swing,' Freda told her. 'Something gliding and rushing through the air. It was —'

'It didn't look like gliding. You were all jogging up and down like bags of potatoes.'

'Rubbish. I was —'

'You have ridden before?' asked Rossi.

He made it sound like an accusation. He was aware that he himself had cut a poor figure in front of the cellar workers and was grateful that Mr Paganotti had not been present.

'Several times,' lied Freda, and she lay on top of her sheepskin coat, the wool curling in little fleecy knots about her purple limbs, satisfied, in spite of what Brenda had said, that she had been stunning in her deportment. She no longer needed to talk to Vittorio. For the moment she was sure of his admiration; she could afford to relax. She lay dreaming on her back, still experiencing the motion of the horse, the muscles in her legs trembling with fatigue. Behind her closed lids she indulged in fantasies: brandishing a riding whip, she leapt fences of impossible height and reached Vittorio, motionless in a meadow ringed with poplars.

The men went for little walks into the bushes or sat

in the shade of the several oak trees and dozed. The parked cars had long since departed. The children, whining for sweeties, had gone from the grass. Brenda, not liking to lie down, in case she inflamed Rossi, propped herself on her side with her back to him and, leaning for protection as close to Freda as she dared, dug small holes in the soil with the tips of her grubby fingers.

After a time Rossi rose to his feet and wandered away in the direction of the fence. She watched his low-slung body amble across the park. He turned and waved, and she lowered her eyes and pretended she hadn't seen. Even at such a distance, his very presence in the landscape chafed her sensibilities. He was like some persistently hovering insect buzzing about her ears. She longed to swat him and have done with it. I ought, she told herself severely, to be able to speak my mind: I can't spend the next year or so running away from him. The thought of time lived as it was, spreading ahead of her — a long procession of days in the factory and evenings with Freda — filled her with gloom. She dwelt on the possibility of renting a room of her own: she would sit all day at the window without being disturbed, without having to respond. It occurred to her that she had escaped Stanley only to be dominated by Freda. Why do I do it, she thought, looking up abstractedly? And there was Rossi at the fence, fingers still fluttering in an absurd gesture of beckoning friendliness. Once and for all she would put him in his place. She jumped to her feet and strode purposefully over the grass. If he had been nearer it would have been easier. She had to walk quite a long way, and by the time she reached him she had been forced to smile once or twice and return his hand-waving. She trod on a snail and gathered it up on a leaf and brought it to him, cupped in her hands, to where he stood in tall grass and flowering weeds of red and purple.

'Poor thing,' she said, gazing with horror at the trail of

slime oozing from its shell.

'It is the nature,' he assured her.

Impatiently he took her hand so that the leaf dropped to the undergrowth.

Anger revived, she asked snappily: 'What do you want?'

'We go for a little walk, yes?'

'No we won't.'

'We go now — come.' And he darted away as if he was a dog anticipating a flung stick and returned immediately. 'You come for a little walk?'

'I am not keen on a little walk.'

'A little walk is good. We see the little deer.'

'No.' She began to blush. 'I won't.'

He stared at her as if she was not well, eyes round with concern.

'Freda wouldn't like it.'

'Ah,' he said expressively, relieved that the problem was so simple. 'But she is not looking.'

'She may not seem to be, but she is.'

He looked at the mound of the blonde woman lying like a ripe plum on her coat of wool. 'She is having a little sleep.'

Brenda felt threatened. She had kept her eyes fixed on his in hopes of subduing the wild beast in him. Now, as he still advanced, she wavered. Her glance shifted to the trees beyond. She thought of the shadowy hollow to which he would lead her, the bugs in the grass, the spiders walking across her hair.

'No,' she said. 'You mustn't push me about.' Almost as soon as she had uttered the words she was sorry for them. She wouldn't like anybody to feel she was nasty. 'It's not my fault,' she said. 'I am thinking of you too. You see Freda said she would tell Mr Paganotti if you ever tried to interfere with me again. You wouldn't like that, would you?'

He couldn't deny it. Expressions of misery and doubt

407

wrinkled his flushed face. 'She would tell things to Mr Paganotti?'

'Yes, she would – I mean, if she sees us going off, she would tell.'

'She would not dare –'

'Freda? She'd dare to do anything. She doesn't give a fig for Mr Paganotti.'

She had stabbed him twice, put in the knife and twisted it. The colour drained from his cheeks.

'It is impossible,' he said.

But she did not wait to hear any more. The longer she stayed with him the more likely was it that she would find herself in another awkward situation. She turned her back on him and called over her shoulder: 'We should go back to the others. Freda will think there's something funny going on.'

The men had resumed the game of football under the captainship of Vittorio. His beautiful velvet trousers were crumpled now, his backside grey with dust from the ride on the horse. Brenda weaved her way between the sporting players and flopped down on the grass beside Freda. She was smiling.

'I did it,' she said.

'You what?'

'I told Rossi where to get off.'

Freda's eyes snapped open. 'Good for you. What did you say?'

'I said you were going to tell Mr Paganotti.'

'Whatever did you say that for? Why did you involve me, you fool?'

'But you said you'd tell Mr Paganotti. You said if ever –'

'You didn't have to tell him I would. You should bloody well have said *you* were going to.'

All the joy went out of Brenda's victory. She hugged her knees and despaired of doing the right thing.

'I thought you'd be pleased.'

'Why the hell should I be pleased? It's nothing to do with me what you get up to with Rossi.'

'You never said that before,' protested Brenda. 'If you hadn't been so nasty to Patrick he would have protected me.'

'Me — nasty to Patrick? That lout tried to hit me.' Freda was outraged at the recollection. She sat upright and combed her hair with agitated fingers.

'He never. You hit him with the french loaf.'

'Christ,' bellowed Freda. She jumped to her feet, snatching up her coat and waving it wildly in the air. A shower of grass and the gnawed bone of chicken slid to the ground. 'He attacked me, he did — in the Chapel, he tried to punch me on the jaw.'

'I don't believe it,' whispered Brenda, though she did. She couldn't think what Freda had done to make the Irishman so violent. 'What did he say?'

Freda was staring across the field. Rossi and Vittorio, beyond the surging line of workers, seemed to be having an argument. Like dogs about to leap snarling into combat they padded in a small circle around each other. Vittorio's voice carried, harsh with anger, on the still air.

'What did he say when he tried to hit you?' persisted Brenda.

'Get off,' Freda said. 'What's it about? What are they saying?'

'It's foreign,' said Brenda sulkily.

*

Rossi had boldly asked Vittorio to take Mrs Freda into the woods. Though Vittorio was nephew to his beloved Mr Paganotti he would surely understand. Vittorio was appalled at the suggestion. His impending betrothal to Rossi's niece made such a thing out of the question: he was not a boy burning with lust, he was a man of honour.

409

Rossi said nervously he was in bad trouble with Mrs Freda, and if she too could be disgraced then she would not be able to go to Mr Paganotti and report him for his conduct towards Mrs Brenda. Vittorio retorted that if Rossi had behaved indiscreetly with Mrs Brenda then he must take his punishment. He had dishonoured his family by his demeanour. He could not expect that others should lower themselves in order to protect him. Besides, he pointed out, the English women were different. No matter how many times he took Mrs Freda into the woods she would not feel disgraced, she would be flattered. She would run wantonly from under the trees and tell the whole of Windsor Park how beautifully she had been dishonoured.

Though Vittorio was nephew to Mr Paganotti, Rossi was bold enough to lose his temper and speak his mind. He shouted and shook his fists in the air.

The workers turned their faces to the sky, the ground, the flying ball, and missed nothing. Gino, the brother of old Luigi, smote his forehead and murmured his disapproval.

'Whatever's going on?' fretted Freda. Her plump cheeks, childish with dimples and tendrils of disordered hair, quivered as she tried to understand what the two men shouted.

'Did Patrick do that to you?' asked Brenda, looking at the graze on Freda's face.

But she wouldn't reply. She fidgeted with the sleeves of her coat and longed to join in the battle.

'It's probably something to do with us,' said Brenda unwisely. 'Maybe he's telling Vittorio about you going to Mr Paganotti.'

'You're a bloody menace,' hissed Freda, convinced that Brenda was right. 'Why can't you stand on your own two feet without dragging me into it?'

'But you interfere all the time. You wouldn't let that

lady borrow our room to play her trumpet in . . . You wouldn't let me talk to Stanley on the phone.'

'What lady?' asked Freda, bewildered.

'If you hadn't got rid of Patrick he would have stopped Rossi getting at me, and I wouldn't have had to mention Mr Paganotti.'

'Your teeth,' said Freda, 'are terribly yellow. You should try cleaning them some time.'

The workers, caught between two sets of protagonists, played all the more noisily. They wore themselves out kicking and shouting and running to the limits of the pitch.

Brenda saw Vittorio take hold of Rossi's hand. They're making friends, she thought, and she watched curiously as Rossi clutched his wrist. He seemed to be removing something from his arm.

After a time Vittorio stalked away from Rossi and left him alone at the fence.

'What's going on?' called Freda. 'What was that all about?'

He ignored her completely, running like a bull at the dribbling ball and giving it a tremendous kick in the air. It soared away and hit the branches of an oak tree and fell in a shower of leaves to the grass.

'You'll get nowhere talking to him like that,' said Brenda. 'He can't stand domineering women. You frighten him off.'

'How the hell would you know?' Pink with contempt, Freda put her hands on her hips and erupted into scornful laughter. 'You wouldn't know a real man if you saw one. Rossi and that bloody Irish van-driver —'

'Stanley was a real man. Stanley wasn't —'

'Stanley?' The way Freda pronounced his name conjured up visions of a monster with two heads. 'You're not claiming he was a real man? Dead drunk all the time and —'

411

'Only some of the time,' corrected Brenda, in spite of herself.

'Good God! Any man that lets his mother run amok with a machine gun —'

'Please,' begged Brenda, 'don't shout.'

She didn't want it to go on a moment longer. The hatred she felt frightened her; she tried at all costs to surpress it. As a child her mother had terrified her with moods of violence, had ranted and raved and thrown cups upon the tiled kitchen floor. 'Come to Mummy,' she would say when the pieces of crockery had been swept into the dustbin, holding her arms out to the shrinking Brenda as if nothing had happened. The depths of suffering Brenda experienced and the heights of elation when Mummy returned, with tinted hair combed and nose powdered, had caused her for years to feel confused.

'Don't you like me talking about your Stanley, then?' said Freda. 'Is your Stanley not to be talked about?'

Brenda said: 'If you don't stop shouting at me I'll say something you won't like.'

'What?' Freda was curious. She stared at Brenda and asked almost tenderly. 'What do you want to say? Go on — get it out.'

Brenda had wanted to say that she looked like a long-distance lorry driver in the sheepskin coat, that she was a big fat cow, that she had wobbled like a jelly on the back of the funeral horse. She wanted to hurt her, watch her smooth round face crumple. But when it came to it, all she could murmur was, 'Sometimes you're very difficult to live with.'

'That's rich,' retaliated Freda. 'When I think what I have to put up with from you — you and your bloody bolster.'

'Well, there's things you do at night when you're asleep.'

'What things?' Freda was stunned.

'Well, you roll about and hold yourself —'

'I what?'

'You do. You cup your — your bosoms in your hands and jiggle them about.'

'I don't believe it.'

'You do — you do —'

'Well, what's wrong with that? I'm only dreaming. What's wrong with me holding — me — me —' but Freda couldn't go on. It was too intimate to talk about. Why do I do that she thought. Is it cancer, or lust, or what? Absently she began to walk in the direction of the rhododendron bushes.

'Where are you going?' called Brenda helplessly. It wasn't fair that Freda was walking away. It left her feeling wicked and burdened with remorse.

'As far from you as possible. And don't you dare try to follow.'

Freda's voice was subdued. She lowered her head thoughtfully and trailed her coat in the grass.

'They've been weeing all over those bushes,' warned Brenda.

But Freda never looked back. She pushed her way through the thick stems, fragments of mauve jumper and yellow hair showing between the dusty leaves, and disappeared from sight.

*

Rossi, biting his cherry-coloured lip in agitation, hovered at the fence, hands dug in his pockets, suede shoes scuffing the turf. He ignored Brenda who, curled up in her purple cloak, with cheek laid against the grass, was festooned with ties and waistcoats thrown down by the perspiring workers and touched here and there by points of silver, as cigarette cases and sleeve garters of expanding metal flashed in the sunlight. Though drowsy, she kept

413

her eyes fixed alternatively on the spiralling ball and the dense mass of the rhododendron bushes. Several times the ball thudded against the dark leaves and bounced backwards on to the pitch. Finally, after a spectacular kick by Salvatore, it hurtled over the bushes and dropped from view. Rossi, seizing his chance to re-enter the game, trotted forward and thrust his way into the foliage. There was a beating of undergrowth and snapping of branches. A small bird fluttered upwards. Propelled by invisible hands, the ball was flung back to the waiting players. She won't like that, thought Brenda. In the mood she's in she may very well punch him on the nose. Her eyelids drooped, and she drifted into the beginnings of sleep. Now that Freda was no longer alone she felt she could rest. The cries of the footballers receded. She was having a long serious talk with Freda — it was so real that she felt the drag of the grass as her lips moved — the earth rustled and crawled in the cave of her ear. She half woke. Vittorio was again holding Rossi's hand. He was attaching something to Rossi's wrist . . . The clouds whirled above her head . . .

When she fully woke and became aware of her surroundings, it was to see Rossi stumbling past her toward the car. He looked sick, as if he had a stomach upset from all the wine and scraps of food. She watched him climb into the back seat of the Cortina and close the door. She thought maybe Freda had said dreadful things to him, had told him he was ugly and squat and that his trousers didn't fit. She felt very tender. He was really a very nice little man. He loved Mr Paganotti. He worked from eight till six every day, and he'd never stolen anything.

She got up slowly and went to the car, ready to pretend she didn't know he was there. When she came level with the window she thought for a moment he must have got straight out the other side. He wasn't on the back seat.

Puzzled, she stared over the roof of the car at the deserted field. On the edge of the horizon there was a machine with whirling blades stuttering across the grass. She watched it for several moments until a sound somewhat like the mewing of a cat came from the interior of the Cortina. It was Rossi, crouched on the floor with his knees drawn up to his chin and his arms covering his head, moaning.

'Oh dear,' she said, opening the door. 'What's wrong, love? Whatever's wrong?'

She had to pull his hands away from his face by force and was shocked at his expression of fear.

Scrambling into the car, she wrapped him within her arms, asking: 'What did she say to you? You mustn't take any notice. She never means what she says. She's kind really — you mustn't take it to heart.'

She examined his face anxiously for signs of assault. Though the skin under his watery eyes appeared bruised she couldn't be sure it was inflicted by violence. He spoke in Italian, teeth chattering, pouring out a flood of words, and she laid her finger to his lips and said, 'Don't, little lamb,' as if he were Stanley or someone she knew very well. 'It's no use,' she told him, 'getting yourself into a state. I've been through it myself — I know. Just try to forget what she said, try to block the words out.' And again, but rather more self-consciously, she pressed his head to her purple cloak and rocked him back and forth. Oh God, she thought, whatever did she say?

After a time he became calmer. He leaned his head against the seat and asked her what hour it was.

'I don't know,' she said, and she took his wrist to examine his watch. The glass was shattered and the time stopped at twenty minutes past four.

'Did she do that?' asked Brenda, but he remained silent. Fine rain began to spatter the windows of the car.

'Can't you tell me what happened?' she coaxed. 'Did she mention Mr Paganotti?'

A spasm of distress flittered across his face. He struggled from the floor and half-knelt on the plastic seating, nose pressed to the streaked glass, staring out at the clump of bushes as if expecting to see Mr Paganotti in his camel-hair coat advancing through the rain.

'Now that you're more composed,' said Brenda, 'I'll leave you alone, shall I? I'll go and find Freda.'

'No,' he protested, gripping her by the arms, and she sank against him on the seat thinking he was his old self again and just as randy. She might even have submitted, if only to make him less unhappy, though she did wonder how they could manage in the confined space of the car and what she would say if the men ran in to be out of the wet. I could pretend it was artificial respiration, she thought and looked over his shoulder to see how the game was progressing. Out on the grass, standing beside the wine barrels, was a figure in a peaked cap and mackintosh.

'Patrick,' she cried and she thrust Rossi from her and opened the door and ran over the field.

The workers crowded about Patrick, curious to know where he had been. He was smiling, one eye elongated at the edge by a jagged cut beaded with blood.

'I don't think there's much left to eat,' said Brenda. 'Did you bring your sandwiches?'

She looked inside the shopping basket and disinterred pieces of bread and the cores of apples. She wished Freda would come and help. Even though she might be hostile to Patrick, she was awfully good at looking after people — in a jiffy she would have produced quite a substantial little meal.

'I'm not hungry,' said Patrick, looking toward the road.

Vittorio seemed uncomfortable in his presence. 'You have been in the town?' he asked, holding the ball to his red jumper and rubbing it up and down the flat curve of his stomach.

416

'In a manner of speaking,' Patrick replied, and stared at him without blinking for several seconds.

The men began to dress, knotting their ties at the throat, adjusting suspenders to concertinaed socks, taking out pocket combs and tidying their damp hair.

'Freda's gone to sleep in the bushes,' said Brenda, and looked about for her green shoes.

'I wouldn't disturb her,' advised Patrick.

'But we are all going to the safari park. It was Freda's idea.' She pulled down the foot of her black stocking to cover her naked toe and struggled to keep her balance. 'Rossi's in an awful state,' she whispered, hanging on to Patrick's arm and wriggling into her shoes. 'Freda's had words with him. He's crying.' She looked briefly at the parked car.

'That's bad,' said Patrick. 'That's very bad.'

'I don't know what she said to upset him so much. I know she doesn't mean to be cruel. Honestly, Patrick, she'd give you the coat off her back if you needed it. It's just that she gets carried away.' She felt compelled to defend Freda. She herself had been sufficiently carried away to utter words that she now regretted. She should never have told Freda that she jiggled in her sleep. It was unforgivable. If you hadn't gone on about Stanley, she thought, I would never have mentioned it. She brushed down her cloak and walked towards the rhododendrons. I'm sorry, she said in her head. Don't be cross Freda. It wasn't true.

'I wouldn't wake her just now,' said Patrick. He laid his hand on her arm to detain her.

'Your eye,' she said. 'It's bleeding.'

She sought a way into the bushes, using her shoulder to prise apart the leathery leaves.

'Don't,' said Patrick, more firmly, and she looked back at him and thought he looked quite old, his face shadowy under the peak of his cloth cap.

'Freda,' she called, 'Freda, it's me.'

She struggled through the bushes, hands raised to ward off the bouncing leaves, and entered a clearing floored with tangled grass on which lay Freda, flat on her back with ankles crossed.

'Freda — we're going to the safari park.'

Freda looked disgruntled, her mouth sucked inwards. The blue eyes stared fixedly at the sky. Under the dark leaves her skin assumed a greenish tinge, the cheeks brindled with crimson and spotted with raindrops. For a moment Brenda thought she was weeping. Her painted nails, black in the shaded light, rested on the woollen swell of her stomach.

'Freda,' said Brenda again, and stopped.

Freda's eyes stayed open. A grey insect, sensitively quivering, dawdled on the slope of her thumb. Brenda knelt on the ground and touched the curled edges of hair turning brass-coloured in the rain. She couldn't understand why Freda's face, normally so pale and luminous, now burned with eternal anger, mottled and pitted with irregular patches of brown as if the leaves had stencilled rusty shadows on her cheeks. Only the nose was right, moulded in wax, the nostrils etched with pink. Where are you, she thought, where have you gone? She peered at her, trying to see what was different. It was as if somebody had disconnected the current, switched off the light . . . she'd gone out. Oh, she did feel sad then. Lonely. The terrible pious curve of her hands on the purple jumper — never again to jiggle her bosoms in the dark.

'Please,' she whispered. 'Please.'

She became very thoughtful, as if she had all the time in the world.

'Stanley,' she said out loud and watched a ladybird with speckled back laboriously climb a stalk of grass.

Freda's face, splintered into a thousand smiles and grimaces of rage, leapt at her from every leaf dipping

418

under the onslaught of the rain. She laid her hand fleetingly upon the purple legs crossed on the grass.

'Little one,' she said, and rose to her feet again and left Freda alone.

7

In all the muddle of explanations and beginnings of sentences that were never completed, one thing remained clear. There was some reason, not yet clearly understood, for not fetching either the police or an ambulance.

Patrick had led Brenda to the car and ordered Rossi into the front seat. He called Vittorio, who came slowly over the grass fastening his duffel coat and carelessly holding the embroidered tablecloth.

'There's been an accident,' Patrick told him when the door was closed. 'To Freda.'

Aldo Gamberini, shut outside on the grass, ran to the red mini to be out of the rain.

'But how?' asked Vittorio. 'What has happened?'

'She must have had a fall. When I saw her she was lying on her back. Her heart's stopped beating.'

Vittorio stared at the Irishman and then at the nape of Rossi's neck bordered with damp curls. He waited, but no one spoke.

'She is dead?'

'She is.'

'Her back? She is dead of her back?'

'On her back,' corrected Patrick; and Vittorio shook Brenda by the shoulder, and she said dully: 'No, it wasn't her back. You can't die of a strained back.'

'But we should —'

'Mr Paganotti —' whimpered Rossi. He continually

rubbed the front of his shirt with the palm of his hand, as if fearing that *his* heart too might cease to beat.

'But we must —'

Brenda said: 'We can't be sure that —'

'How does he know?' said Vittorio looking at Patrick. 'He wasn't there. He say he was in the town. How can —'

'Rossi saw her. He went into —'

'I was searching for the ball. I came —'

'You have a bleeding eye,' said Vittorio, as though he had not noticed it before, and he made as if to touch the cut on Patrick's face. He had turned very pale. A tear rolled down his cheek, and he wiped it away with his sleeve. 'Where you get that wound? How you —'

Brenda was folding and refolding the tablecloth, smoothing the petals of the pink flower in the right-hand corner. There was a smear of salad oil and a sweet smell of decaying apples.

'You and Rossi were arguing,' she said, 'up by the fence, and I had words with Freda. She went into the bushes.'

'I see her,' confirmed Vittorio. 'I think she go — you know — she need to —'

'No,' Brenda said. 'She was angry. She said I wasn't to follow.'

I can't, can I, she thought, not now? She hadn't dared to follow either when the soldiers had come to offer them a ride. How brave Freda had been, climbing aboard that monstrous funeral horse with its flaring nostrils and carved head. She hadn't looked like a sack of potatoes or a mound of jelly: she was regal in purple and motionless beneath the sky. She did mean it — it wasn't as if she thought Freda was listening.

'She had a graze on her cheek,' said Vittorio. 'She show me.'

Brenda asked: 'Did you really try to punch her on the jaw, Patrick?'

Vittorio suddenly recalled Freda's return from the

421

beech wood. 'She tell me she saw you in the trees.'

They both looked at the Irishman in the peaked cap that shadowed his battered face.

'I never,' he said, 'and she didn't. It's not me you're wanting.'

Vittorio began to tremble. 'I do not want to think it — you see her first. You came out from behind the bushes in the middle of the football.'

'No,' said Patrick. 'He did —' He tapped Rossi accusingly on the shoulder.

Through the tear-stained glass Brenda could see the red mini sluiced with rain. A faint sound of voices raised in song came from the interior of the car. Freda, she thought, must be getting awfully wet. What would the aunt in Newcastle say? Freda hadn't been home for years. She wouldn't tell her she'd been working in a bottle factory. If she was asked, she'd say she was a secretary, or doing quite well in commercials. Freda would like that. There were the theatrical set at the Friday-night pub in their second-hand clothes, but she didn't think they would hear about it. There wasn't anybody else. There wasn't even a photograph of Freda in the bed-sitting room. She'd never written her a letter or been on holiday with her or shared an adventure — only today and that had gone wrong.

She watched Vittorio and Patrick, heads bent against the rain, walking away toward the rhododendrons. She wondered if the arrangements for the van had been deliberately sabotaged. Perhaps it had been more convenient for Freda's plans that Rossi's car alone had been available for the Outing. It made for a more intimate group. It's a bit too intimate now, she thought, aware of Rossi beside her, still massaging his heart. There stole over her a regrettable feeling of satisfaction. She suspected it was normal in the circumstances. Superstitions were needed at a time like this. The wrong-doers had to be punished

422

in some way. It was not to be wondered at that God had spoken. She remembered that Stanley and her own mother were great believers in the wrath of God. They both in their separate ways called upon him in times of stress and vengeance. 'God blast you,' Stanley had cried often enough when she turned her face to the white-washed wall to avoid his breath heavy with the scent of hops. 'My God,' invoked her mother when hearing of her engagement to the farmer she had met at a Rotary dance.

'What are they doing?' asked Rossi. 'Where have they gone?'

'They've gone to see Freda.' She looked curiously at his white face and his doleful mouth perpetually trembling. 'Tell me what she said to you in the bushes. I won't tell anyone, honestly.'

'Nothing — she said nothing.'

'I don't know what's the matter with me,' she confided. 'I don't feel very upset.'

They stared at each other. The pain in his eyes caused her own to fill with tears, but it had nothing to do with Freda. Every time she tried to concentrate on what had happened she was distracted by something trivial: the particular slant of a raindrop in the window, a piece of grass stuck to the rim of her green court shoe, the spread of veins in Rossi's hand as he gripped the driving wheel.

'*Santa Vergine*,' he murmured.

'Look at my shoe,' she said.

As she spoke, Rossi saw Vittorio and Patrick returning, running past the tree trunk toward the car. Vittorio slumped on the back seat and covered his face with his hands. He spoke in Italian to Rossi, who muttered and shook his head from side to side. Brenda thought she recognised the word 'Paganotti.' How they dote on him, she thought. Whatever will they tell him?

'We can't leave her there,' said Patrick, 'that's for sure. We'll have to bring her to the car.'

'But there's people you have to tell. We —'

'There's more to it,' whispered Patrick. 'You don't just drop dead —'

'Like doctors —'

'Not at her age —'

'She was in an awful state,' said Brenda, 'before she went in to the bushes. Sometimes people have heart attacks when they get angry. I know of —'

'Never,' scoffed Patrick. 'Wasn't she always in a bad temper?'

The implication of his words reached her at last. For the first time since her return to the car she realised that Freda was dead out there in the park, never to live again. She experienced a prolonged bout of shivering followed by noisy intakes of breath and finally began to cry.

*

Twice Salvatore had come to the Cortina and been refused admittance. He made gestures outside the window and was waved away. He told his passengers that Rossi looked as sick as a dog and Vittorio too. They made jokes about it. They said it was the English women that had caused nausea, not the wine. They were in the mood to go to the safari park full of wild lions and tigers: they growled ferociously at one another and clawed the covering of the seats. Salvatore defiantly tooted his horn to remind the occupants of the Cortina that they waited. In the meantime they sang loudly and helped themselves to the remainder of the Beaujolais that they had wedged into the back of the car when no one was looking. They watched the comings and goings of Patrick and Vittorio to the clump of bushes bowed under the rain and speculated as to what was going on. The Mrs Freda had drunk too much and was refusing to come out — they were enjoying her favours, the two of them; she had taken them both in her arms; even the weather could not damp her ardour. They were further amused when they finally saw her being helped out of the bushes — the interior of the mini rang with laughter. They stuffed mufflers into their mouths and watched pop-eyed the sight of Vittorio and Patrick unevenly balancing Mrs Freda under the armpits, the sheepskin coat hanging from her shoulders, her feet scuffing the ground. Aye, aye, they agreed, in smothered admiration; she had drunk enough for them all. Her head hung down limply; the dimmed hair, plastered to her cheeks was like a veil.

'We go now,' called Salvatore sticking his head out of the door as Mrs Freda was bundled into the back seat. Nobody answered. After some time he draped his jacket over his head and ran through the puddles to the Cortina.

'We go now,' he called, 'to safari park, yes?'

Rossi seemed not to hear. He caught a glimpse of Mrs Brenda leaning back exhausted against the front seat, face streaked with rain.

'Do you know the way?' asked Patrick opening the rear window, eyes obscured by the peak of his cap.

'Ah,' said Salvatore, 'we will follow the signposts. You follow me. I lead.'

And he ran enthusiastically back to the car and leapt inside, his coat still over his head, and started the engine. He reversed on to the verge, turned the car and drove deeper into the park.

*

Brenda couldn't turn round. She knew that on the back seat, secured between the bulk of Patrick and Vittorio, Freda sat like a large bedraggled doll, chin sunk on to her chest. They couldn't possibly drive all the way back to London like that, it wasn't right. She ought to be laid

425

down properly and allowed to rest. There was such a thing as *rigor mortis*. She had a dreadful image of Freda, shaped like a sheepskin armchair, impossibly wedged in the doorway of the car. I do wonder where you are, she thought. It was so apparent to her that Freda was anywhere but in the back of the Cortina. Sheep, she knew, just lay and unravelled away, and hens were like burst pillow-cases — but not people, not Freda. She dwelt on the idea of something like an escape hatch under water, through which Freda had slowly shot to the surface, leaving her purple jumper and her hand-made boots behind. Even now she had beached on some pleasant island and was drying in the sun. Smiling, she glanced out of the window and was bewildered to find the car was winding down a slope towards a collection of farm buildings set about with paddocks and gently rising hills. Through the branches of sycamore she saw an ornamental lake ringed with pink flamingos. It had stopped raining. There were people removing raincoats and furling umbrellas and a coach painted like a rainbow outside a cafeteria.

'What the devil is this?' asked Patrick. 'This isn't the way.'

He watched astonished as a mud-caked elephant appeared from beneath the trees and trod ponderously over the grass. The mini halted and Rossi braked; he sat quite still with his hands resting on the column of the steering wheel, unconscious of his surroundings.

Salvatore and his passengers spilled gawping from the car. They ran like children across the gravel and gestured at the dusty elephant beginning to sink to its knees in the paddock.

'Get out,' said Patrick. 'Go and ask what they're up to.' He sounded, but for his accent, remarkably like Freda.

Thoughtfully Brenda joined the workers gazing at the jungle beast settling into the ground.

'But we are out,' cried Salvatore, clutching at her arm.

426

'We are not confined. Where is the tigers? The little children is everywhere.' And she soothed him and said she thought perhaps elephants weren't dangerous, though privately she didn't like the look of the huge animal lying like a heap of ashes on the open field.

They had come to a children's zoo. There were kiosks selling candy floss and a helter-skelter greasily plumeting to a pan of sand. In a compound there were goats with tufted beards nibbling pink-lipped at handfuls of brown hay. 'Poof,' she went, inhaling a whiff of the white-washed stall and observing their stern yellow eyes fixed upon her.

They looked at donkeys and a calf splotched with brown lying woodenly beside a cow, and above them in the grey sky patched with blue an aeroplane swam like a duck towards the city. Aldo bought a postcard of a monkey eating a banana to take home to his children. 'To remind me of this day,' he told Brenda, grinning at her from beneath his wierdly buckled hat; and she ran conspicuous with swollen eyelids out of the gift shop and up a hill to a line of telescopes pointing like guns at the far-off park. She put her eye to the lens and swung the black cylinder in an arc, trying to find the cut-down oak and the piece of grass on which they had laid the tablecloth. It all looked the same. She couldn't tell one piece of ground from another: the trees stood identical, the road ran like a grey ribbon to the castle. She was searching for Freda. As she examined the magnified ground, she caught the Cortina enlarged at the side of the path and the blurred shape of Rossi slumped behind the wheel. Guiltily she ran down the hill to the car and said the men were determined to go to the safari enclosure. As she spoke, she closed her eyes to avoid confrontation with Freda.

'Sweet Jesus,' blasphemed Patrick, 'what are we to do?'

'We cannot tell them,' said Vittorio, 'we should perhaps

427

turn round and go home alone.' He was desperate to be out of the car and away from his silent companion, yet fearful she would slide sideways at his departure.

'Wait,' said Patrick, 'I have to think. I have to decide what's best.' And he frowned and fingered the congealed cut at the corner of his eye.

There was no longer, Brenda thought, any possibility of turning back. It seemed to her that they should have driven hours ago to a hospital or a police station. A faint curiosity rose in her as to the outcome of their actions.

'Why can't we tell them?' she asked, watching Salvatore and his men licking ice creams at the side of the road. It was awful not being able to turn round and look at Patrick. She wanted to ask him things. She would have liked to know what he was afraid of.

He said: 'Be quiet, I'm thinking,' and he drummed his fingers on the back of her seat.

Aldo Gamberini came to the side window. 'We go now.' He pointed to the hill and the row of telescopes. 'The wild ones are that way.' He peered through the glass at the silent Rossi.

'Tell him it's all right,' prompted Patrick. 'Go on.' And he prodded Rossi, who stirred at last, listlessly and with great effort as if emerging from a deep sleep. 'Tell him we'll follow.'

The two cars moved down the road away from the helter-skelter and the dozing elephant. They passed a house behind a wire fence and an open air cafe. Above painted tables the multi-coloured petals of aluminium umbrellas still dripped from the rain. There were public conveniences marked 'Tarzan' and 'Jane', screened by saplings of silver birch and a toll box manned by a ranger in a boy-scout hat.

Vittorio paid the entrance fee — Patrick hadn't got any money and Rossi never moved. Brenda didn't think he was mean. It was just that he was in a state of shock

428

and nothing got through to him. Since her own fit of weeping she was feeling much better, and she couldn't think why he was still so upset; he made her feel she was shallow for recovering so quickly. She wondered if it was safe to let him drive them through a herd of wild animals — they might all end up in a ravine.

The man in the toll box thumped the roof of the Cortina and told them to get out. 'You can't go through in that. Everybody out.'

'We can't get out,' said Patrick. The mini, revving its engine a few yards ahead, tooted an impatient horn.

'Why he tell us to get out?' asked Vittorio, gripping the handle of the door in alarm.

'It's the sliding roof,' explained Brenda. 'It's not safe. The lions might rip it off.'

'Down there,' directed the helpful ranger, pointing further down the path at a rustic shelter thatched with straw. 'Catch your bus from there and park your car under the trees.'

*

They waited some minutes for the bus to arrive. They sat in a row with shoulders pressed together as if they had got into the habit of leaning on each other. Overhead the sky paled in patches leaving dark pockets filled with rain. The red mini waited for them, the men hardly understanding what was happening — they glanced curiously at the Cortina parked under the trees with Mrs Freda alone on the back seat.

The safari bus when it came was painted with black stripes like a zebra. It looked as if a whole pride of lions had hurled themselves at the rusty bonnet and ill-fitting windows and torn the tyres to ribbons. The driver was dressed in a camouflaged jacket of mottled green and a hat to match, one side caught up at the side as if he were

429

a Canadian Mountie. When he opened the double doors at the back of the van, Brenda saw he was wearing plastic sandals, bright orange and practically luminous, and striped socks.

She nudged Patrick, who was edging forward to climb into the bus, and he stopped abruptly and asked 'What's up, what's wrong?' frowning and looking about in an alarmed way. The driver was beckoning her and she couldn't tell Patrick about the socks.

'Nothing,' she said, 'nothing.' And she clambered into the van and sat near the window.

'What's the matter?' asked Patrick sitting heavily beside her and tugging at her cloak.

'His shoes,' she whispered, 'and his socks.'

'His what?'

'Look at his feet.'

'For the love of God — what are you on about?'

She sighed and settled herself more comfortably on the wooden bench. The driver stretched out a speckled hand shaking with palsy and started the engine.

'He's got Parkinson's,' she said. 'He shouldn't be driving a bus.'

Patrick was staring at Rossi's hand, braced against the green slats of the seat in front.

'Will you look at that?' he said, nudging her with his elbow.

'Not Rossi — the driver. Either that or he's over a hundred.'

'Do you see his watch?'

She looked without interest at the damaged time piece. 'He broke it playing football.'

'Is that what he said?'

'He didn't say anything. I don't think he cares about his watch being broken.'

'When we got — her — up from the ground there was bits of glass — there was a piece stuck to her jumper —

430

at the back.'

She listened and watched a dead fly, relic of a previous summer, quivering on the window pane. The bus rattled over ruts in the gravel path and bounced down a lane towards a metal fence covered with wire netting and patrolled by men with rifles.

'Oh God,' she said, 'do you think it's dangerous?'

'Will you listen to what I'm saying. Rossi was in the bushes with her before anybody else. His watch is bust. I told you — I seen the pieces.'

'What pieces?'

'Sweet Jesus,' he murmured. 'Your brain's addled with the shock. I can't make you see how serious it is. I can't get any sense out of that Vittorio and none out of you.' He sounded pained as if she had let him down. He stared gloomily ahead and watched the barricade slowly rising in the air.

'I'm sorry,' she said, 'but I don't seem able to take it in. I don't know why we didn't get a policeman. I don't —'

'For God's sake, will you think about me. I was seen. Wasn't I seen in that Protestant chapel having a barney with her?'

'But you said you didn't hit her,' she said primly.

'I didn't. I didn't lay a finger on her. She thumped me. She pushed me into some hole in the wall and shut me in. I had a devil of a time explaining what I was doing in there.'

'She locked you in a hole?' Her mouth began to turn up at the corners — she couldn't help admiring the spirit of Freda.

'And she hit me in the eye with a bloody big stone.'

'Where?'

Vittorio turned and looked at them. He had dark circles under his eyes and his lashes were stuck together. 'What is wrong?' he hissed. 'Everyone is looking.'

'Sssh,' reproved Brenda. 'People are looking.' After a

431

few moments she whispered: 'Where did she hit you with a stone?'

'In the woods.'

'You said you didn't go into the woods.'

'Well, I did. I was minding me own business, throwing pebbles at birds, and she chucks a bloody big boulder through the trees at me.'

'You shouldn't have thrown pebbles at birds,' Brenda said, shocked at his unkindness.

They drove through a field of ostriches who fled bedraggled at their approach and disappeared into some trees. It didn't look like a park. The grass was patchy and littered with lumps of dung; the leaves hung tattered from the branches.

'Isn't it messy?' she whispered in Rossi's ear, but he didn't reply. He was holding his wrist with one hand and hiding his shattered watch.

Brenda went pale. Beads of perspiration broke out on her temples. She struggled to open a window.

'You can't,' said Patrick. It's not allowed to open the windows. What's the matter with you?' And he stared at her ashen face and her pale lips parting as she fought for breath. 'Get your head down,' he ordered, and thrust her roughly towards the floor littered with cigarette ends. The blood pounded in her ears.

'Siberian camels,' called the driver, 'to our left,' and a murmur of appreciation rustled through the bus.

Brenda didn't faint. She revived in a moment and her sensitive skin became blotchy with colour and she lay back deathly cold and very frightened.

'Bear up,' said Patrick. 'Take hold of yourself.'

She longed for him to take hold of her. She wanted to be protected. She wanted her hand held, but she couldn't be sure that it wasn't he that frightened her.

'What are we doing?' she asked, in much the same way as she had asked the dead Freda where she had gone.

432

'I'm telling you,' he said. 'I'm thinking. I've got to be careful.'

'But if Rossi — hurt Freda —'

'Do you think we'll get that bunch to split on him?' said Patrick scathingly, and he looked through the driving window at the red mini crawling between two ragged llamas. 'That lot will stick together. They'd be out of their minds with fear that Mr Paganotti would give them the sack. It'll be me that'll get it. They'll all swear that I vanished for hours and came out of the bushes with me eye cracked open.'

They had come to a second gate and there was a further delay. At a squalid ditch another batch of flamingos pecked at the bank and teetered on Belsen legs over the mud. They looked obscene, as if they bled all over.

'Was she bleeding?' she cried out loud, and Rossi twitched as if he had been stung.

'Sssh,' Patrick said. 'Her neck was broke.'

It occurred to her that he was cleverer than she had ever imagined. Worn at a jaunty angle over his large ears, the cloth cap she had previously thought common became stylish in her eyes. His face assumed a strength of character she had not noticed before. Vittorio, turning anxiously to look at them, moustaches lank, seemed insipid by comparison. Even the boots with scarlet laces appeared a shade affected.

'Sit up,' said Patrick. 'Pull yourself together.' He was altogether like Freda.

The bus passed under the second gate and traversed an empty field strewn with cabbages and turned sharply left into an arena of sand and dead trees, the whole fenced about with sheets of tin, dark green, dented in places and emitting a weird moaning noise as they vibrated in the wind. On hillocks of baked mud men postured holding whips, rifles slung upon their backs. Clothed in rags, the inmates squatted in the dirt and dipped bald

433

heads and ripped their breasts apart. 'Vultures,' breathed the passengers and shivered in their seats. The men with guns stood motionless posing for photographs. The snout of a baboon was seen at the top of a slope. 'Ooooh' went the occupants of the bus, levelling cameras at the window and craning their necks to see beyond the slopes. 'Wait on,' said the driver, tooting his horn, and the armed guards ran up the hills cracking their whips. Barking like dogs, a hoard of baboons, pink-arsed and hideous, swept over the ridge and bounded across the grey sand. They leapt to the top of a large rock and huddled together holding their young.

'Poor little things,' said Brenda. They were so ugly, so human in their aspect, so vicious in their glances.

'They'd have your guts for garters,' Patrick said. 'They'd tear you limb from limb.'

She thought of Freda sitting in the car under the trees, growing cold — it was a pity they hadn't let the Cortina into the reserve. Nobody would ever have known: a door jerked open, a quick shove — they could say her heart had stopped. She shivered at her own audacity. She tried to remember how Freda had looked when she cantered over the park on the black horse, but she couldn't. It was as if a chasm had opened between them, leaving Freda on one brink and herself on another. The gap was widening hour by hour. She felt like crying and asking someone for forgiveness.

'Listen,' said Patrick. 'You believe I didn't touch her?'

Her eyes were shining, the tears only just held back and she cleared her throat before she replied. 'Yes, I do. Don't be silly.'

'You're sure?'

'I am, I am.'

It was meaningless really, and he knew it. She had the kind of temperament that stopped her from being truthful. All the same, he thought he might persuade her.

434

'What we do,' he said, 'is to get her back to London and put her somewhere while I think how to make Rossi tell us what happened. In your room —'

'No,' she said. 'Don't do that.'

'For me.'

His face loomed over her; he bared his teeth like a baboon. He'd told Vittorio he had never been in the woods. She had heard him. He said he'd been in the town. He was so anxious they shouldn't go to the police... Freda had a graze on her cheek... He was looking at her imploringly. She wondered if he guessed what she was thinking; despite herself she couldn't help recoiling from him and pressing closer to the windows.

As they left the arena a solitary monkey leapt to the top of the slope and stood upright. Dangling a long thin penis like a scarlet lupin, it swung its arms in rage.

The lions and tigers were a disappointment. They lay in lusher pastures under the feathery branches of horse-chestnut trees and slept.

'They are not wild,' cried Rossi, and he unclasped his hands and banged on the window with his fist.

When they returned to the bus shelter, Patrick suggested they should all go for a cup of tea in the cafeteria. Aldo Gamberini tiptoed slyly to the Cortina and rapped with his knuckles on the glass.

'For God's sake,' shouted Patrick, and he leapt across the gravel and knocked Aldo on his back upon the grass. 'Haven't we had enough agitation for one day? Can't you see the woman's sleeping it off?'

The men murmured at Aldo's rough treatment. Patrick put his hand to his forehead and forced himself to smile. He helped Aldo to his feet and brushed him down with his large mauve hand scratched in a score of places. The workers were not rash enough to criticise him; every week he came into work with his face gashed or his mouth bruised from asserting himself outside the public house

435

on a Saturday night. They closed ranks about the demoralised Aldo, and Patrick led the way down the road to the café with Brenda and Vittorio lagging two paces behind.

They had tea paid for by Vittorio, who seemed quite ready to put his hand in his pocket, and packets of dry little biscuits gritty with raisins. The men sprawled across the soiled tables and passed the postcard of the monkey from hand to hand. A waitress with enormous breasts wiped at the plastic cloths with a square of rag and was openly admired. She had yellow hair and a faint ginger down on her narrow lip. Freda, thought Brenda and closed her eyes, but already she could no longer visualise clearly that round face with the painted lids.

After a time Rossi left the café and wandered about outside, hands behind his back and chin sunk on his chest. Patrick nudged Brenda and indicated she should go outside and talk to him.

'No,' she protested, pursing her mouth edged with crumbs, and he pinched her quite hard on her thigh and frowned.

'Talk to him, that's all I ask.'

He wasn't as he had been in the bathroom. He was no longer shy and full of reverence. She bridled and moved her leg away and chipped a raisin from her tooth.

Vittorio was perpetually in the dark — the strange accent of the Irishman and the mumblings of Brenda confused him. He listened politely to the men discussing the placid lions, nodding in all the right places, his eyes continually flickering from Brenda to Patrick and back again. Under his fingers the picture postcard buckled at the corners. Patrick removed his cap and laid it on a ledge. Exposed, his flaring ears burned pinkly beneath his copper-coloured hair. I don't like him without his hat, thought Brenda. Come to think of it, she didn't like him at all. She actually preferred Rossi with his troublesome ways and his black and tangled curls. Excusing herself, she pushed her way from the table and went outside on to the lawn. They paced in silence for a time, up and down the path outside the window. They could hear the clatter of cups and the hiss of the coffee machine. Now and then she sensed Patrick's face at the glass, and when they reached the corner of the café building she took Rossi by the arm and marched him away to a ditch at the side of a fence and leapt clear over it into a field. He dithered on the other side and was reluctant to follow.

'Come on,' she said. 'I want to tell you something,' and he scrambled awkwardly over the cut in the ground, dipping one foot into muddy water and shaking it like a dog, one suede shoe turned black and the turn-up of his trouser soaked.

'Never mind,' she said impatiently, and she ducked down behind a hillock of damp grass and smoothed her purple cloak. 'You must know,' she said, when he had sat down beside her, fussing about his saturated shoe and sulkily wiping at it with a handkerchief, 'that what we've done is very wrong.'

He was like a child being scolded. He tossed his head at the injustice of it and refused to speak.

'Police,' she said, thinking of the night they had taken Mrs Haddon away, 'ask an awful lot of questions — all sorts of things that don't seem to have anything to do with what actually happened. They'll want to know what she said to you when you went into the bushes. Patrick's hinting something funny went on.'

He said: 'It is all happening too quick. I cannot think.' But he was once again the cellar manager whose eye was anxious, almost calculating.

'Well, you'd better. I'm warning you. Patrick thinks you hurt Freda.' She was speaking too quickly for him. 'Don't you see? He's got that cut on the eye and he had a fight with her in the church.'

'He never like Mrs Freda —'

437

'He threw stones at her when she was in the woods —'

'He knock Aldo to the ground. He is a violent man.'

'Yes,' she said. They were piling blame upon the Irishman, brick by brick; they sat there silently remembering.

After a while she said: 'You've got nothing to be worried about. We ought to go to the police now.'

'No.'

'It's your car she's sitting in. You've got the licence.'

'It's not my fault.'

'Well, they'll want to know why you let them put her in your car.'

He did see what she meant but he shook his head. 'No police.'

'Why on earth not?' She was getting quite irritated by him. She wanted it all settled and the landlady told and the aunt in Newcastle informed — she might even ring Stanley. 'Patrick,' she said loudly, speaking very slowly and pronouncing every word clearly, 'is trying to blame you. He says there was glass under her jumper. And I saw you go into the bushes. I'll have to tell the police. If you tell lies they always find out and it looks worse.'

'What glass is this?' he asked. 'What glass under her jumper?'

'Not under it. Stuck in the fluff in the back. And he wanted to know about your watch.'

'My watch,' he repeated in a low voice and stared blankly at the smashed time-piece on his wrist.

A long sigh escaped him. He played idly with his mud-stained handkerchief.

'It's all for the best,' she said.

Haltingly he began to tell her a story.

'When Mrs Freda come into the office and say she tell me to leave you alone, I am very angry. She mention Mr Paganotti...'

438

As he remembered the incident he flushed with renewed rage. She had been so bullying and unladylike, thumping her fist on his desk like a man. He had not known how to deal with her. When his wife had come to the factory with her niece from Casalecchio di Reno he could hardly breathe for fear Freda would march in and denounce him. When she did come, and asked him if she could use the telephone, his heart had nearly stopped beating. How could he let her use the phone with his wife sitting on her chair, listening? Hadn't he told his wife that Mr Paganotti had arranged the Outing long ago and no women were going? Freda had stood there smiling, shuffling his beautifully ordered labels on their shelves. He did not dare tell her to go away. Her pink lips had glistened; she had been so confident. And later Vittorio had seemed upset and anxious. Twice he went to the main door of the factory and looked up and down the road . . .

'But I didn't believe her. I think she just say it to upset me.'

She was always upsetting people, he thought, interfering between him and Mrs Brenda, causing everybody trouble. She had made advances to Vittorio. She had invited him round to her room and given him brandy stolen from Mr Paganotti. She wanted him to take her out to a restaurant. In the office she had whispered into Vittorio's ear as if they were betrothed. . .

'And Vittorio did not want to come on the Outing. In the street I have to persuade him. He want to go home. He say she is always arguing.'

Vittorio had made him ring the coach firm and cancel the van, so that nobody could go into the country. It was not good having to ring the man and tell him he did not want his van. He had felt ashamed doing such a thing. Vittorio had said they must go to the factory on the Sunday as if nothing happen . . . then they would all go home . . . only, when they got to the factory, it seemed a

439

pity to waste the day, he had his sandwiches . . . besides his cousin Aldo Gamberini insist they go, and Salvatore have his car . . .

'When we play the football I think we are all having a good time. The little confusion in the fortress — pah, it is all forgotten. When we go on the horses I think Vittorio too is happy. He look at Freda as if he love her.'

It was true. Vittorio was an educated man: Mr Paganotti, his uncle, had put him through college. He had studied art — poetry. When he had looked at Mrs Freda on her horse it was as if he were reading something in one of his books. He was learning something. It was not just the wine that made him smile at her so. It had seemed a simple thing to suggest that Vittorio take her into the woods. How could he refuse? The sun was shining — the little birds were singing.

'I want us all to be happy, all to go into the woods for a little jump out. I ask Vittorio to take Freda for a walk. The men are happy playing football — the four of us — but he is angry. He say Freda will tell his uncle, Mr Paganotti, that he go to her room and try to get into the bed. I want to help my friend. I wait a little.'

The wine had made him excited. When he had walked over the grass his head was filled with pictures of Freda — alone in her room in a black gown drinking Mr Paganotti's brandy — lying on her back in the sunshine. When she rode the black horse her buttocks were like two round melons.

'I go into the bushes to ask Freda not to go to Mr Paganotti.' Rossi began to tremble. He crumpled his handkerchief into his palm.

'Go on,' said Brenda. 'What did she say?'

'I do not see her. She is talking to Vittorio.'

'She couldn't have been.' Brenda was bursting with resentments. She didn't understand why Vittorio had told lies about Freda; she didn't understand why Rossi pre-

440

tended Vittorio had been in the bushes. She wanted to hit the little Italian sitting there not telling her the truth — she wanted to go home.

'Well,' she said nastily, 'it seems fishy to me. And I don't suppose the police will like it either.'

Suddenly she didn't want to wear the purple cloak any longer; it wasn't her property. She unfastened the collar and shrugged it from her shoulders. She didn't know why she was so bothered about the truth. Who was *she* to sit in judgment? It wasn't going to make any difference to Freda.

More patiently she said: 'But I did see you come out of the bushes. I didn't see Vittorio. And you were crying in the car.'

'I walk around for a few minutes. I look at you and you are like a little girl on the grass. Then I see Vittorio go away and I go into the bushes again. I am thinking she is asleep. And when I realise —'

He stopped and lowered his eyes beginning to fill with tears. She began to cry too, out of sheer tiredness, quietly, with a great deal of sniffing.

It was almost dark now. The cafeteria was closing. There were lights coming on among the trees and the distant sound of metal doors being bolted. A cart with a hose attachment moved slowly along the road toward the lion enclosure. Patrick was disturbed that she had been absent so long. They had gone to the car to look for her. The men had called her name along the hedgerow.

'I didn't hear,' she said.

He took her by the arm and stood murmuring into her ear. The men sat on a low fence and looked in the opposite direction.

'Did he say anything?'

'He said Vittorio was in the bushes before he was.'

Patrick swore.

'Will you give up now?' she said. 'Can't we go to a

441

police station?'

They were cheating Freda out of her death. She knew that if it had been her that had been found dead under the sky, Freda would have beat her breast and shrieked her lamentation. This way, this stuffing into cars and secret consultations, was belittling to her. You'd have thought Patrick would have known how to treat the dead, being Irish — all that weeping and wailing and fluttering of candles through the night. She gave the purple cloak to Vittorio and told him to tuck it about Freda. It wasn't until she was actually sitting in the car that she realised she was dressed all in black; her woollen dress, her dark stockings, even her shoes in shadow beneath the dashboard were entirely suitable for a funeral. She would have liked to tell Rossi but she didn't want to be flippant. He was adjusting the driving mirror, twisting it this way and that — possibly he was trying to avoid the reflection of Freda's head sunk upon her breast. She tried to escape into sleep as the car wound down the path, the red mini in front of them, but she was wide-awake, her brain teeming with images: the edge of the table cloth blowing upwards in the wind, horses racing beside the trees, the white ball leaping toward the sky. The headlamps of the Cortina caught the distempered wall of the open-air café; the metal umbrellas wavered and were gone. She thought as they began to climb the hill that she heard the sound of an elephant trumpeting down in the paddock. Patrick and Vittorio began a desultory conversation interspersed with long silences — something about the climate of Italy. They sounded as if they had just met while waiting for a train.

'In the south it is different.'

'So I've heard. I read a bit once in a paper about Naples.'

'That too is hot,' said Vittorio.

'Dirty place by all accounts,' Patrick said.

'It is a port. You know, the docks — refuse — fruit.'

'Terrible stink in the summer. Like bodies rotting.' He reddened. Even in the dark Patrick blushed like a woman, though no one could see him.

When they entered the north side of the Park, Rossi drove very slowly. The red mini was out of sight. Already it had flashed past the picnic area and was out of the Park approaching the roundabout.

The headlamps of the Cortina pierced the darkness. Brenda saw the dull gleam of the timber fence in the distance. The car crawled along the verge and stopped. Rossi switched off the engine. There was a little silvery noise as the key dangled for one instant in the ignition. They could hear one another breathing. When the wind rustled through the black grass it was like a long-drawn-out sigh.

'Well,' said Patrick, 'we got to get something settled. Between the four of us.'

Five, thought Brenda. As her eyes grew accustomed to the darkness she could make out the shape of the cut-down oak and the grey mass of the bushes beyond. They'd left a barrel of wine on the stump of the tree. If they intended to go on hiding Freda, they ought to get rid of that barrel — it was circumstantial evidence.

'It is best,' said Vittorio, 'if we tell each other the truth.' He sounded a long way off, as if he was outside somewhere, calling to them. 'For myself I have nothing to hide.' He could not however help putting his hands over his face in a gesture of despair.

'Well, I have,' Patrick said. 'I've been in trouble before with the police.'

Brenda stopped herself in the nick of time from turning round. She trembled at the narrow escape and the implications of his words. She'd been alone with him in the bathroom for hours — she'd even locked the door — and she'd have gone a walk with him in the woods if he had asked her, simply to get away from Rossi.

He said: 'Nothing I'd be ashamed to tell me own mother. Fights, I mean — having a drop too much. I don't want to put meself in their hands. Before you know where you are, you've said one thing, and haven't they written it down as something else?'

Brenda wished he wouldn't talk in that ridiculous accent. Everything he said was a question. She knew the sort of trouble he meant. Stanley didn't like the police either, though God knows why: they had often brought him home when he had fallen into a ditch on the way back from the Little Legion. The park at night reminded her of the countryside she had left: the lights of the town twinkling away to the right, the spidery branches of the trees — if she opened the window she might hear the hooting of an owl.

'Isn't it peaceful,' she murmured, though nobody heard.

On the rare occasions when she and Stanley had gone out together, walking the three miles to the village, she had always complained of a stitch in her side. More than once she had sneered at the type of entertainment offered in the Legion — the smart alec in the teddy-boy suit clutching a microphone and singing 'Delilah' at the top of his lungs. They thought her stuck-up in the Legion, even though she broadened her vowels when she spoke to them, even though she tried to play billiards. It wasn't as if she was too different from the others, there were plenty of Polish labourers left over from the war, and Pakistani immigrants who worked in the mills. She was always very polite to everyone. She never made a scene, not even when Stanley fell down the step into the Gents and cut his forehead, but he seemed constantly uneasy in her presence. He struck her repeatedly and painfully on the thigh and told her to sup up. When they were given a lift home in a car the farmhouse sat in the valley like an orange square, tiny — his mother's window was lit by a lamp that was never extinguished, not even in sleep. The white gate at the roadside shone in the head-lamps. The path down to the house was worn with rivulets of rain. Stones littered the way. Sheep floundered to their feet as Stanley ran zig-zag down the slope, urinating as he went. The whole earth swelled upwards like a vast warm bosom.

'It was my fault,' she suddenly said. She was unaware that Rossi had cried out a moment previously the name of Mr Paganotti. 'I shouldn't have been nasty to her. I shouldn't have upset her. Then she wouldn't have gone to the bushes in the first place.'

'For Christ's sake,' shouted Patrick. He leaned forward in his seat and attempted to put an arm about her shoulder in an awkward gesture of sympathy, and Freda slithered slowly downwards along the plastic seating. They got out of the car in a panic, slamming the doors and running to the tree stump as if it was a place of refuge. Rossi was moaning. He ran in a circle round and round the oak and the empty barrel of wine. All at once he darted away into the darkness. They could hear for a moment the rush of his body and the low keening he made; then he had gone. They strained their eyes trying to see into the blackness.

'Where's he gone?' whispered Patrick.

'He will come back,' said Vittorio. 'He is very highly strung. Very sensitive. He will come back.' He had a nice voice, caressing; he sounded full of compassion.

Brenda was shivering without her cloak. The men went back to the car and called her when they had propped Freda upright. She hurled herself into the front seat and curled up with her arms about her knees and pressed her chattering teeth against her wrists.

Patrick was giving up the idea of trying to make the Italians confess. They were too foreign — Vittorio clammed up like a shell and Rossi somewhere out there in the darkness blubbing like a baby. They must get back to London quick and put Freda somewhere for the night. He regretted that he had wasted so much time rushing about the countryside. In the morning he would either have thought of something or would get on the boat home and leave them to sort it out. He had a radio he could pawn, and a fellow he knew at the bar of the Waterford Castle owed him a few quid. Brenda was no use to him. She never said what she meant. She would hide him one moment if she was asked, and betray him the next.

Vittorio had a pain in his chest. His head ached. Had she been alive, Freda would have been stroking his thigh in the dark. Perhaps she was the lucky one, to go quickly and so young. For himself, years hence, there might be disease — pain: like an olive left on the ground he would wither and turn black. Gloomily he shifted his knee and imagined Freda had grown very cold: the chill of her shoulder as it pressed against him, struck him like a blow. The rim of her ear, dimly seen through the fronds of hair, burned like ice.

Now and then a car came swishing up the road; light splashed over the windows like a deluge of water and drained away instantly. After a quarter of an hour had passed Rossi came back to the car and lowered himself into the driving seat. He was breathing heavily as if he had run for miles. Vittorio said something to him and he nodded his head. When he switched on the engine, his fingers in the tiny illumination were soiled, the nails rimmed with dirt.

On the motorway the Cortina kept to the slow lane and was constantly overtaken.

'Faster,' urged Patrick, but Rossi took no heed.

Brenda hated going fast: it was dreadful having to trust her life to someone else. At any moment Rossi could lose control of the wheel and spin them all to pieces. Danger

446

was all around her: the people hurtling along the road, the aeroplanes overhead coming in to land, sailing like railway carriages above the fragile fences — an aircraft, leaving the landing strip of the nearby airport, zoomed upward on a collision course. She kept one hand on the button of the door, ready to jump out should the car swerve or the planes begin to fall.

'Step on it,' said Patrick, like a gangster in a movie. 'We've got to dump her somewhere for the night.' And they rocked together as they drove.

Brenda was searching the outskirts of the town for resting places for Freda. She recoiled from the word 'dump' — surely he couldn't be serious? So many discoveries about him in so short a time made her tremble all over with misgivings. She saw the doorway of a church, a partially demolished house. At Shepherds Bush a black angel flew on a plinth amidst the poplar trees. They passed the green dome of the Music Hall. They spun through the park — a dog stood frozen in the yellow wedge of the headlamps — and into the glare of the High Street. The clock outside the launderette stood at five minutes to nine as they turned the corner and drew up outside the shuttered factory.

*

The mini took a wrong turning just off the M1. The men were philosophical. They had the remains of the wine to sustain them.

'Such a way to behave,' said Salvatore, thinking of the wanton figure in the back of the Cortina.

'But splendid on a horse,' Gino observed grudgingly. He preferred thinner women; he was himself puny in stature, brittle in the leg and cavernous in the cheek.

Aldo seemed disconcerted that once again his cousin had disappeared. He had come to the factory in Rossi's

447

car and dreaded lest he have to return by tube. He was fuddled by the Beaujolais and weary from his game of football. Salvatore was willing to go out of his way and take him to his door, but Aldo wouldn't hear of it.

'I came with him,' he said stubbornly. 'I will return with him.'

It seemed obvious that Rossi would take the English women to their house. Possibly she would have to be lifted in some way up the stairs. They agreed they would have a lot to tell their fellow workers when they met in the morning — the coming and going in the fortress . . . the argument between Vittorio and Rossi . . . the rowing between the two English ladies . . . the return of the Irishman with his face torn . . . the sight of Mrs Freda being supported from the bushes . . . If only Amelio and Stefano had been there to see how it was.

There followed a time of silence while they thought of the less fortunate members of the party who had never journeyed beyond the wall of the factory.

'Surely,' said Aldo, 'they will have their money back.'

*

They almost missed Rossi's car parked at the side of the road. They had not thought it would be there; they expected to find it outside the house of the English girls. They stopped and walked back to the alleyway. The shutter was rolled up. It was unheard of; it was unauthorised. How could Rossi be so bold as to enter Mr Paganotti's business premises after closing time? Never, except at Christmas when Mr Paganotti held a little party in his office and danced stiffly with his secretary, had they known such a thing. They stole up the alleyway and hovered outside the pass door. Gino removed his hat. Pushing the heavy door inwards, they crept down the passageway to the bottling floor. It was dark save for a single yellow bulb burning beneath the roof. The plant stood silent under its ragged cover; a rat rustled beneath the cardboard boxes. Mrs Brenda was slumped on a crate by the wall. Vittorio and Rossi, heaving and straining, were pushing Mrs Freda, stretched out upon a trolley, into the mouth of the lift.

They ran in their best clothes, slapping the concrete floor with their damp shoes. They bent over the sprawled figure, shoulder to shoulder.

'Don't look,' began Vittorio.

'*Madre di Dio*,' cried out Aldo Gamberini, rocking and wailing, already in his black.

*

Brenda had scurried home along the familiar street. The scene in the factory, the weeping of the men, the wild exclamations of Rossi and Vittorio — all restraint gone now they were not alone in their predicament — had embarrassed her. She found it difficult not to smile. She turned her face to the wall and bared her teeth. When Rossi and Vittorio took Freda up to the first floor, the men ceased their lamentations. They turned their faces to the ceiling and listened to the rumble of the trolley across the boards. After an interval the lift descended. The men lined up inside, jostling for space, each with a hat held to his breast — they were like a family posing for a photograph. The dim bulb raked their oiled hair with auburn light. Creaking, the lift ascended — a line of shoes, caked with mud, merged into the darkness.

She waited a few minutes but nobody came down. Freda's sheepskin coat, mingled with the purple cloak, lay abandoned on the dusty floor.

She decided they had forgotten her.

When she entered the bed-sitting room she saw the table set for two, the saucer of olives, the silver slab of the

449

butter. The sight of the folded napkins beneath the blue-rimmed plates affected her far more than the lilac scarf trailing the edge of the funeral trolley. She could not bear to lie down on the bed. She dared not approach the chair at the side of the grate — the worn cushion bore the imprint of Freda's weight. There was nothing of herself in the room: everywhere she saw Freda — the magazine beside the window, the lacy brassiére dangling above the gas-fire, pinned to the marble top of the mantelshelf by the ticking clock. She wilted under the continued presence of Freda. She would rather have stayed in the car, the factory. She had not realised how like a garden of remembrance the room would be. If she listened, all she could hear was the ticking of the clock and the minute crackling of the dried leaves on the dreadful table spread for a romantic supper. After a moment, trapped in the centre of the carpet, she heard a tap on the window. Someone was throwing gravel at the glass. She laid her cheek to the pane and peered down into the street. It was Patrick.

Rigidly he stared up at her, his legs tapering to a point on the paving stones. She ran to the landing wild with relief at not being on her own, and stopped. Freda had called her a victim, had said she was bent on destroying herself — it was possible Patrick had returned because she knew too much. When they had carried Freda into the factory the Irishman had supervised, held open the door, fumbled for the light switch. By the time they had laid her on the trolley he had gone.

She stroked the bannister rail. She remembered Patrick in the bathroom winding the length of string tightly about the hook in the ceiling. She clapped her hands to her cheeks and her mouth flew open. She must at all costs preserve herself. She went back into the room and struggled to lift up the window. Propping the tennis racket into place, she crawled out on to the balcony.

'What do you want?' she called. She saw he was holding a bottle of wine.

'Let me in.'

'I can't.'

'Let me in.'

'The landlady won't let us have people in after midnight.'

'For God's sake, it's only after ten.'

She couldn't believe it. She thought it was the middle of the night — they had got up so early, the day had gone on and on.

'I'm tired.'

He made to climb the steps. He lifted his hand to pound the brass knocker.

'Wait,' she called in desperation, fearful the two nurses would let him in. 'I'll come down.' If he attacked her on the step she would scream or run toward a passing car.

'What did they do with her?' he asked, when she had opened the door.

'They've put her upstairs among the furniture.'

'Let me in. I'm parched for a cup of tea.'

'I can't.' She sat down on the step and shivered.

'I pinched a bottle of wine. Do you not want a drop of wine?'

'I'd be sick,' she said.

He put the bottle on the step beside a withered wallflower. He removed his cap and sat down. He looked like a grocer's boy — he ought to be riding a bicycle, she thought, delivering butter and eggs, and whistling.

'What will they say?' she moaned. 'Whatever will happen?'

He tried to smile at her but his mouth quivered.

'I don't know what to do,' he admitted. 'I'm wore out.'

'It's awful up there,' she told him. 'Her things — her clothes — everywhere.'

'I'm wore out,' he repeated sullenly, as if she had no right to burden him. A door opened in the flats opposite.

451

An old lady leaned over her balcony and called quaveringly: 'Tommy! Tommy! I've got your dinner, Tommy.'

'Upstairs,' said Brenda, 'the table's laid.'

'I'm not hungry.'

'No. I mean for her and Vittorio.'

'Not for you?'

'No,' she said. 'Just for them.'

The leaves of the privet hedge fragmented in the light of the street lamp. Shadows shifted across his face. He drew a handkerchief from the pocket of his mackintosh and laid it between·them on the step. He unfolded it. There were a few pieces of glass.

She said: 'That's Rossi's hankie.'

'I know. The glass is from his broken watch. They were in the bushes.'

'What did you bring them back for?'

'I didn't,' he said. 'Rossi did. When we stopped on the way home didn't he go off into the night? I pinched it from his jacket when we went into the factory.'

'Oh,' she said, 'you *are* clever' — not quite sincerely. She didn't know what to think and was having difficulty in concentrating. Even if she wanted to stay on in the bed-sitting room, could she afford it? Could her father be persuaded to send her a little more money? When people found out about Freda it was bound to get into the papers and her mother would tell her father not to send her any money at all, just to force her to come home.

They'd go out shopping, and her mother would tell her to stay in the car so the neighbours wouldn't see. She'd tell her what clothes to wear, throw out her black stockings and buy her a pink hat from the Bon Marché. They'd put her in a deck chair in the garden and treat her like an invalid, only sternly. She'd never be allowed to stay in bed in the morning, not after the first week. Now that my moment has come, she thought, my chosen solitude, can I stand the expense?

452

'I'm going in,' she said. 'I'm dropping.'

He twisted his cap in his hands round and round between his drawn-up knees.

'Suit yourself.' He plopped the handkerchief with its glass fragments into her unwilling hands. 'I'll leave this with you.'

She held the handkerchief at some distance from her as if it was in danger of exploding. She didn't protest, because she was so glad he didn't insist on following her into the house.

'Good-night,' she murmured.

When he said goodbye she couldn't hear for the slam of the door. She took a pillow and blankets from the bed and went upstairs to the bathroom. If anybody tried to use the toilet in the night it was just too bad. Freda said the man upstairs was a dirty bugger anyway — he probably peed in the sink. The busybodies on the ground floor were hopefully on night duty. Before she bolted the door she remembered the open window.

When she crossed the room she put an olive in her mouth, but it tasted bitter and she laid it down again on the cloth. Freda's brassiere trembled in the draught.

8

Maria was told by her brother-in-law Anselmo. Appalling contortions distorted her face. He clapped his hand over her mouth, for fear she screeched like a railway train, and lowered her into Rossi's chair behind the desk. Though normally she would have leapt upright out of respect for the manager's office, she now remained slumped in her seat, eyes rolling above his bunched fingers. It was a blessing Vittorio had a small glass of brandy ready for when she was more composed — under the circumstances she drained it at one gulp. She flapped her pinny to cool her cheeks and waited while Vittorio fetched Brenda from the washroom, where she had been more or less all morning retching over the basin. The two women embraced and drew apart sniffing.

'It's God's work,' wailed Maria.

'Yes,' said Brenda, although she couldn't be sure. She felt really poorly: her stomach was upset. She was tired out from her night in the bathroom, vivid with dreams.

'We must prepare her. We must see to her.' Maria had laid out an aunt and an infant son of Anselmo's but never in such conditions.

'I can't do anything,' cried Brenda in alarm. 'I'm not going up there.'

Outside the window the men were grouped thinly about the bottling plant. Throughout the morning they had gone in pairs into the ancient lift and visited Freda,

454

returning with calm faces and eyes glittering with excitement. They whispered frantically. The machine rattled and circled. They looked up at the Virgin on the wall and crossed themselves. Rossi had been called into the main office by Mr Paganotti an hour previously and had not returned.

'I have to have water and clean cloths,' said the dedicated Maria, '— clean garments to lie in.' It was inconceivable that they should use the sponges on the bench.

'I could go home and get her flannel,' offered Brenda, 'and her black nightie.'

Maria wouldn't hear of the black nightie — there must be nothing dark — but she accepted the flannel and asked her to bring a bowl and powder and a hairbrush. It seemed silly to Brenda, such a fuss twenty-four hours too late: Freda wasn't going anywhere.

The telephone rang, and Anselmo said Mr Paganotti wanted to speak to Vittorio. They all went very quite, thinking of Rossi and the state he was in. Perhaps he had broken down in the main office and told Mr Paganotti that there was a body upstairs among his relatives' tables and chairs. Vittorio nodded his head several times. He stood very straight, inclining his head deferentially as if Mr Paganotti were actually in the room.

'Go, go,' said Maria, shooing Brenda with her pinny toward the door. 'Fetch the cloth.' To fortify her for the task ahead she allowed herself a little more brandy.

*

As Brenda opened the front door the nurse from the downstairs room came out into the hall in a dressing gown and slippers. 'Oh, it's you,' she said. 'Aren't you working?'

'I've just popped back,' Brenda said.

The nurse let her climb a few stairs before she called: 'Is your friend in?'

Brenda clung to the bannister rail and stopped. 'She's out just now.'

'Well, will you tell her I'd like my serviettes back. I lent them to her yesterday. She said she only wanted them for one evening.'

'Serviettes?' said Brenda, her heart pounding.

'I want to take them in when I go on duty. I can have them laundered for nothing.'

Brenda looked down at her. She had an almost transparent skin and dark eyes that were used to detecting signs of rising temperature and internal disorder.

'Actually,' said Brenda, 'she went away last night — abroad.' Freda had been saving for years to go on the continent. She had never gone because she had never saved, she had a post-office book that she put part of her wages in every month and drew them out the next.

'Lucky her,' said the nurse dangling her hospital towel. 'I expect she could do with a break after her mother dying like that.'

It was simple to explain really, once she got started. There was a bit of money due from Freda's mother's estate, not much but enough for a holiday: and her Uncle Arthur who was in a good way of doing had advanced her funds so that she could get away. She'd always wanted to go to Spain — she was very interested in flamenco dancing — so she just went off all of a sudden. Made up her mind, packed her bag, and went.

'How long for?' asked the nurse, scraping an envious cheek with the handle of her toothbrush. Brenda said it depended on the weather. It was winter after all — it wasn't as if she was going to lie on some beach. She might come back next week or she might never.

'Never?' cried the nurse.

Brenda was laughing. 'You know what I mean. She

456

might, she might not.' She continued up the stairs shaking with laughter. 'Who knows,' she called from the bend of the stairs and she stumbled upwards squealing and gasping for breath.

*

When Brenda returned with the pastel-coloured toilet bag and the washing-up bowl, the workers were crowded into the concrete bunker under the fire escape. She could hear them shouting as she went up the alleyway toward the pass door. The bottling plant stood idle. Alone, old Luigi, undeterred by the drama, was labelling with ferocious speed. Stefano was on guard beside the lift.

'You go,' he said pointing his finger straight up in the air. She said, No, she wouldn't thank you, she'd just brought a few things for Maria.

He told her to fetch Salvatore from the bunker to keep watch while he took the bowl upstairs.

The men, wrapped in pieces of old carpeting, were sitting on upturned boxes, rolling cigarettes and gesticulating.

She felt terribly out of it. The way they carried on, so engrossed, faces drawn with grief, eyes mournfully gazing at their unwrapped luncheons — you'd have thought Freda was a relative. She wondered what Rossi had told them. Surely he hadn't said Patrick had broken her neck — nobody could be certain. Rossi seemed terribly agitated. He was trembling and arguing with Vittorio.

'What's wrong now?' she asked.

Vittorio said: 'Mr Paganotti wants the first floor to be cleared of the furniture. He is going up in the lift this very afternoon to take the look around.'

'Well, she can't stay there anyway,' began Brenda, 'she'll start —' But she couldn't continue. She wasn't

457

sure how quickly bodies began to smell — perhaps here in the factory, with the temperature close to freezing, Freda could be preserved for ever. 'What's he want to shift the furniture for now?' she asked. 'What's the sudden hurry?'

'Mr Paganotti call me in,' cried Rossi. 'His secretary is sitting there, she is smiling and asking me how the Outing go. Did we have the nice time in the country?'

'How awkward,' said Brenda. Mr Paganotti's secretary came from a well-to-do family in Rome. Nobody had liked to ask her on the Outing. She could hardly be classed a worker.

'I look at the floor,' continued Rossi. 'Mr Paganotti ask me if I like the Stately Home. If it had been an interesting Stately Home.'

That was kind of him, thought Brenda. Fancy Mr Paganotti remembering a thing like that.

'Mr Paganotti say he is re-organising his business premises. He is going to get the new machinery, expand — he need more office space. For the ordering, the accountancy. He want the furniture gone from the first floor.'

'I would have died,' breathed Brenda, feeling terribly sorry for Rossi.

Mr Paganotti, it appeared, had noticed how disturbed Rossi had been. He had frowned. He had dug his thumb into the pocket of his beautiful striped waistcoat. He had asked what was wrong.

'I tell him,' said Rossi, 'that the men are very busy at the moment. I say there is the sherry consignment from Santander — the barrels have to be emptied and ready for return shipment tomorrow. I tell him that if the barrels are not ready for return there is a storage charge.' Rossi spread out his hands, palm upwards, to show he had concealed nothing. 'Mr Paganotti understand at once. He say it is a pity but it cannot be helped. He tell me to

458

get on with my work and he himself will go upstairs later in the afternoon and look around.'

'You could tell him the lift was broken,' said Brenda. 'Or not safe.'

'It has never been safe,' Vittorio said. 'But then he go up the stairway.'

'Not if you pile the stairs with furniture, blocking the way.'

'Ah,' cried Rossi. 'That is it.' And the men, when it had been explained to them, thumped the table enthusiastically and scrambled out of the concrete bunker to begin the barricade at once.

'What did you say to the men?' asked Brenda, left alone with Vittorio.

'I say nothing.'

'Did you say Patrick did it?'

'I say nothing. I merely say there has been an accident. I say it will look bad for Rossi and for me. We are not English. The Irishman has a grudge against us. They understand. They do not want our families to be shamed, our children — they do not want to bring shame to the good name of my uncle Mr Paganotti.'

'Didn't they think it was a bit funny?'

'Funny?'

Brenda thought he was incredible; they were all unbelievable. In their loyalty to each other, united in a foreign country, Freda seemed to have been forgotten. She said sharply: 'The girl in my house just asked me for her serviettes back.' He looked at her without understanding. 'For your supper.'

'What supper?'

'Freda was hoping you'd come home with her. She'd bought butter and stuff. And she borrowed things to wipe your mouth on.'

'I do not know about any supper,' he said.

'Well, she thought you might come back. I told the

459

nurse she'd gone abroad.'

'Abroad,' he repeated.

'To Spain. I said she liked dancing.' And again she burst into little trills of laughter, her face quite transformed by smiles.

'You are overwrought,' he said, and he poured her some wine from the jug on the table. While she was still laughing, stuffing her fingers into her cheeks and showing all her teeth, a thought struck him. He began to tremble with excitement. He ran from the bunker and went to find Rossi. Brenda fell asleep with her face on the table amidst a pile of sandwiches.

*

When Brenda woke from a dream, she didn't feel ill any more or cross. She had been in a cinema with Freda: Freda was wearing a trouser suit and one of those floppy hats with some cloth flowers on the brim. She complained bitterly that she couldn't see the bloody screen. The men in the row behind said 'Sssh!' loudly and kicked the back of the seat. Brenda whispered she should take her hat off. 'Why should I?' said Freda; and Brenda remembered a little doggerel her mother had taught her, something about a little woman with a great big hat . . . went to the pictures and there she sat. Freda shrieked and recited rapidly . . . man behind couldn't see a bit . . . finally got tired of it. Somehow it made Brenda very happy that Freda too knew the little rhyme. She beamed in the darkness. She turned and kissed Freda on the cheek and woke instantly.

Gone was the worry and the fear, the underlying resentment. Freda would have been the first to agree, it didn't matter how she had died — it wasn't any use getting all worked up about it now. Life was full of red tape, rules and formalities, papers to be signed. Hadn't Freda always been the first to decry the regimentation of the masses? If Rossi and Vittorio, still alive in a puny world, fought to protect the honour of their families, did it really matter very much? No amount of questions or criminal procedure or punishment would bring her back. Brenda was almost prepared to go up in the lift and see Freda all nice and clean from the ministrations of Maria.

She wandered into the alleyway and through the pass door to the factory. Aldo Gamberini and Stefano, doing the work that eight men had done before, were running giddily after the rotating bottles on the machine. The labelling bench, save for old Luigi, was deserted. She went into the office to find Rossi fiddling about with litmus paper and glass tubes.

'I'm all right now,' she said. 'I don't mind whose fault it was. I'll give you your handkerchief back if you like.'

'My handkerchief —' and he clapped his hand to the pocket of his overall, forgetting that he had worn his best trousers and a jumper on the Outing.

'It doesn't matter,' said Brenda, and was only slightly shocked to see the purple cloak and the sheepskin coat hanging on the back of the door. 'Have you blocked the stairs?' she asked. 'Have you stopped Mr Paganotti?'

'He has gone out,' said Rossi. 'I think he has not remembered.'

'What are you going to do tomorrow, then? He won't be out every day.'

'It was you,' he said, rising from his desk in admiration. 'You have given us the way.'

'Me? What did I do?'

'You tell us about Spain. You give us the idea.' And he paced about the office, face illuminated with appreciation. 'We will put her in a barrel — in a hogshead. It is simple. Gino is even now sawing the lid off for her entrance.'

'You're not going to put Freda in a barrel?'

'Listen,' he said. 'We now bottle the sherry. We take the

461

sherry from the hogshead. When the barrels are empty the man come and we load the empty barrels on to the lorry. They go to the docks, back to Santander.'

'With Freda?'

'Why yes,' he said. 'It is finished.'

She looked at him. Smudges of fatigue showed under her sceptical eyes. 'And what happens when they open the barrels at the other end? Or take out the bung or whatever it's called — at Santander?' It was a lovely name; there were bound to be flamenco dancers.

'We mark the barrel as no good — bad for the wine — tainted — it is leaking. They throw it in the sea.'

'In the sea? Are you sure?'

'But yes. I have seen it when I am training. I know about these things — the unworthy barrels go in the sea.'

She didn't like to mention it, but she felt she must. 'Rossi,' she said, 'what if there's a strike at the docks? There's always some kind of a strike going on somewhere.'

He stared at her. 'What for you worry about a strike?'

'Well, she might begin to — to smell!' His mouth fell open. 'You ought to put something in the barrel with her — like brandy. To preserve her.' She couldn't look at him. She gazed at the floor.

'But we cannot use Mr Paganotti's brandy — it is very expensive — very good.'

Still, he was beginning to see what she meant. Perhaps just a little brandy. The lid would have to be clamped down very securely, so as to avoid leakage. The English girl was right. There was bound to be some kind of a strike.

'We do it,' he said. 'We put a little brandy in the barrel — just a little.'

'Well, that's very satisfactory,' Brenda said and wondered who was going to tell the aunt in Newcastle that Freda had fled to Spain.

*

Maria wanted flowers for Freda; she said it was no good without flowers. She came out of the lift all heated from her work, the sleeves of her frock pushed up to her elbows, her pinny streaked with damp. Vittorio said he would donate money and some should be bought from the shop on the High Street.

'Lots of flowers,' reiterated Maria, and she held her arms out to a certain width and rolled her eyes.

Brenda thought it would cost a fortune.

Rossi said in alarm: 'No, we cannot go to the High Street shop. What for are we buying flowers? Mr Paganotti might see — Mr Cavaloni the accountant — the secretary from Rome.'

Maria drooped in disappointment. Never had she laid out anyone without flowers.

After some moments it occurred to Rossi that when his wife bought washing powder earlier in the week she had returned with a plastic rose. 'A free offer,' he said excitedly.

'The washing powder isn't free,' said Brenda.

He waved his hands impatiently. 'We all buy the powder — we all go one by one and purchase the powder with the little rose.'

Throughout the afternoon the men went to the supermarket and returned with packets of powder and the free offer. Brenda paid for her packet with her own money. She felt it was a gesture. She was scandalised that the little rose turned out to be a sort of tulip on a long yellow stem.

*

The boyfriend of Mr Paganotti's secretary from Rome came at six o'clock in his red sports car and tooted his horn. Mr Paganotti's secretary ran out on the dot in her caramel brown coat of fur and whisked herself into the seat beside him. Five minutes later the accountant, Mr Cavaloni, escorted Mr Paganotti to his grey Bentley and held open the door with respectfully bowed head. They shook hands. A child holding a ball scraped the gleaming paintwork with his nail and was admonished. When the grey Bentley had turned the corner, Mr Cavaloni scrambled into his Ford and drove off down the street.

The workers went to the lift and rode in groups up to the first floor. Brenda had been sent by Vittorio to the Italian confectioners in Lucas Street. She had brought dry little buns seamed with chocolate and a cake, *torta di riso*, that Maria said was a speciality of Bologna. They had cleared a dining-room table, riddled like a collander with woodworm, and laid out the cakes and a row of paper cups. Rossi had sent up five bottles of Spumanti. Before coming to pay their last respects, the men had removed their overalls and washed their hands in the yard. The hogshead of sherry, empty and with its lid neatly sawn off, stood ready by the lift. At the far end of the room, candles burning at her head and her feet, lay Freda on a couch strewn with plastic tulips. Her eyes had been closed. She wore a long white gown reaching to her ankles. Maria had removed the hand-made boots and after some thought encased her feet in a pair of tennis socks somewhat worn at the soles. Her hair, brushed and lightly curled, quivered on the grey upholstery.

'Wherever did you get that?' asked Brenda when she had first clapped eyes on the white dress. It was a nightgown, extremely old in design; fragile lace clung to the collar and cuffs.

'In Mr Paganotti's box,' explained Maria, hastening to add that it was clean and aired. She herself had heated an old steam iron found in the basement and pressed it. Thoughtfully arranged, the brown spots of damp no longer showed.

The men shyly poured out the Spumanti. Glasses had

464

been found in the outer office. 'Careful, careful,' urged Rossi, fearful there might be breakages. They huddled at the mouth of the lift amid a pile of kitchen chairs and bric-a-brac, watching the leaping candles at the far end of the room. Brenda still wore her black dress and her stockings and the old coat that Freda had despised.

The men who had not been on the unforgettable Outing revelled in the unaccustomed festivity of the moment. The rest, worn out from the previous day and hours spent emptying the consignment of sherry at breakneck speed, rubbed their creased foreheads, and stifled yawns. Maria sat in an armchair heavy with dust; her legs did not reach the floor. Grey hair, escaping from the bunch on her neck, spilled down her back, as she rocked back and forth gulping her champagne. She remembered other places, other deaths. Her lips moved.

'Ah well,' sighed Rossi. 'It cannot be helped. It is life.'

'Aye, aye,' agreed the men, though life it was not.

Brenda gazed at the distant sofa. At this angle nothing of Freda was visible save for one big toe warm in its tennis sock and a fringe of golden curls tipping the shadowy upholstery. She remembered that Rossi had brought her here two weeks ago. He had chased her round the tables and the chairs. She had jumped over the back of the sofa and stumbled. He had leapt upon her. Down came his little red mouth in a jangle of springs and a flurry of dust. He had tried to unbutton her coat. Squealing, she rolled to the floor and fluttered her rubber gloves in his face. Freda, when told, had been scornful. 'You must be mad,' she had said. 'You wouldn't catch me lying down on that dirty old couch.' Brenda glanced at Rossi to see if he too remembered, but he was examining the barrel at the lift.

'She looks beautiful, yes?' asked Maria.

'Beautiful,' agreed Brenda. Where were Freda's clothes —

her purple jumper — her knickers? I could never do any-thing like that, she thought, looking at Maria, not even if I was paid.

'On her splendid legs,' whispered Maria, 'there are bruises.'

'Bruises?' said Brenda.

'And on her stomach. There are bruises.'

'Oh,' said Brenda, and wondered if the ride on the horse had caused the bruises on her legs. Freda had said she was aching; she had said her thighs hurt — she hadn't mentioned her stomach.

The men were beginning to drift about the room, relaxed by the Spumanti. They opened drawers and looked inside the suitcases and found sheets of music. Gino, exhausted from his labours with a blunt saw, lay down upon a mildewed mattress and went to sleep. He sprawled with his mouth open and groaned softly.

'He is tired,' said Rossi apologetically, fearing it might seem disrespectful. Under cover of the gloom, he put his hand on Brenda's waist and dug at her with his fingers. He drew her to a bookcase standing against the wall and pointed at the shelves.

'I think it is very good, yes? It is very valuable.' He was licking the tip of her prominent nose.

'No,' she said, 'it's mostly plywood. Look at the cheap varnish on it.'

He was offended. Nothing remotely connected with Mr Paganotti could be cheap or tawdry. Still, he did not let go of her waist.

There was quite a hum of conversation growing. The little buns crumbled to the floor. The bottles of wine emptied. The men filled their cheeks with rice cake and munched and munched. Maria, bolt upright on her chair, fingers closed and pointed at her breast, shut her eyes and prayed. Anselmo found an old gramophone with a handle; a voice reedy with age began to warble a ballad.

'*Santa Vergine*,' cried Maria out loud, and the record was abruptly removed. The turntable continued to spin round and round, slower and slower. From below came the sound of heavy banging. Someone was hitting the shutters of the loading bay with a brick. A voice, dulled at this distance, but dreadfully loud outside in the street, demanded admittance. Vittorio crossed himself. He looked about for Rossi but could not see him. The banging began again, louder this time.

'The Irishman,' whispered Aldo Gamberini, face pressed to the windows above the street.

'Let him in,' cried Vittorio. 'He will wake the town.'

Nobody moved. Like a drowning man, Vittorio ran to the lift and sank below the floor.

When he returned with Patrick they were still in their places: Maria in the chair, the men about the table, Gino asleep on the dusty mattress.

Patrick stared at the remains of the cake, the empty bottles, the flickering candles. 'For the love of God,' he said. 'What are you doing?'

The cut on his eye was already healing; in the dim light it was no longer noticeable. He saw the sofa, the hair tumbled on the padded arm, the white mound strewn with stiff and everlasting flowers.

'Where is she?' he demanded, turning on them grouped together for safety. 'Where's Brenda?'

They too looked about at the shadows, at the dull gleam of the cheap bookcase, the black cave behind a mound of boxes.

He ran to the wall. He clambered over chairs. He kicked the boxes to the ground. Clothing spilled to the floor, old books; there was the smash of disintegrating plates. But he had Rossi by the throat, lifting him bodily from the darkness by the front of his jacket, shaking him like a rattle. It seemed to the men that he would shake the breath out of his body. They hurled themselves upon

467

Patrick. They clawed his hair. They pulled him backwards from the gasping Rossi. Brenda, dishevelled, her coat unbuttoned, treading a carpet of broken crockery, stumbled into the light. She peered short-sightedly at the ring of men. She was dreadfully alarmed and confused.

'You —' she said, 'I thought you'd gone away.'

'At a time like this?' shouted Patrick, outraged. He appeared simpler than before, his cap knocked from his head, a button torn from his mackintosh. Maria gave a small dry titter and clapped a hand over her mouth. The men, shrinking from the heavy blows they had delivered, trembled in the candlelight. Rossi straightened himself, he tugged his shirt into place, he adjusted his ruined tie.

'You have no right,' he said. 'You have not the right to touch me.' And his face crumpled at the unfairness of it.

The workers did not know what to think. If anything, they were inclined to be sympathetic to the Irishman; he was so openly broken-hearted at finding Mrs Brenda in the arms of Rossi. They brushed Patrick's raincoat with tentative hands. They picked his cap from the floor and avoided Rossi's eyes.

'Have you gone mad?' choked Patrick, speaking to Brenda alone.

'I'm sorry,' she said, 'really I'm sorry. It's not what you think.'

She would have comforted him if she had known how. It was embarrassing the way he was looking at her in front of everybody.

Vittorio was shouting at Rossi. Rossi had stepped back a pace and was blinking watery eyes.

'How could you?' said Patrick again, as if she had fallen from a pedestal.

'We were only looking at the bookcase,' she whined. 'You know what Rossi's like, I told you before —' and stopped because she never had — it was Freda she had told.

He sat down on the mattress beside Gino as if he was

tired.

'You're never going to bury her up here,' he said, jerking his head at the funeral couch.

'We've thought of a plan,' she said. 'It's quite a good one.' It didn't seem fair to let him go on suffering, worrying that he was going to be found out — waiting for the knock on the door, the uniformed men on the step. 'Nothing can go wrong. You don't have to be frightened.'

'I didn't do it,' he said. 'For God's sake, I never did it.' He jabbed a finger in the direction of Rossi. 'That bastard did it I tell you. I never touched a hair of her head.'

'Oh well,' she murmured, 'it doesn't matter.' Appalled, she saw that tears were squeezing out of his hurt blue eyes. She sank down on the mattress beside him and would have liked to put an arm about his shoulder.

Vittorio came to her and whispered: 'We are going to put her in the barrel. It's getting late.'

'I'm going,' she said, starting up in horror. 'I can't watch that.'

'Go downstairs to the office,' he said, 'with the Irishman. There is something to tell you.' And he put a hand under Patrick's elbow and helped him to his feet. 'Go and wait,' he said.

Brenda took Patrick to the lift. He shuffled his feet like an old man, all the fight gone out of him. They waited for some time, Patrick slumped behind Rossi's desk, herself standing looking out of the window at the factory floor and the stacked cartons.

'They're very kind really,' she said. 'They're nice men.'

'What are they doing with her now?' he asked.

'Doing things — putting her in a container.'

'A container?'

'In a barrel,' she said, 'with brandy. They're exporting her.'

She thought he might laugh, but he didn't. She herself bit her lip in case.

469

'Is it done?' she asked, when Vittorio and Rossi came into the office. She wondered if they had stuffed the plastic tulips in as well.

'No,' said Vittorio, 'the men are working now.' He looked at Rossi and at the Irishman behind the desk. He said something in Italian.

'I want to tell you what happened,' said Rossi. 'It is I.'

The Irishman did not appear to be listening.

'He is wanting to tell you the truth,' said Vittorio.

'Whose idea was it to put her in a barrel?' asked Patrick.

Rossi threw up his hands in despair. He prowled about the office. Catching sight of his reflection in the mirror beside the door he took a comb from his pocket and attended to his hair.

'Tell him,' urged Vittorio.

'It is I,' cried Rossi, turning from the mirror and steeling himself to go quite near the Irishman. He put his hands on the desk and lowered his head. 'I do it.'

'What happens at the other end when they try to fill the barrels up again? Or this end, if old Paganotti mistakes the barrel and syphons himself a drink? By Jesus, there'd be more body in the brandy than he bargained for.' He giggled nervously.

Vittorio said slowly: 'Rossi is wanting to tell you what happened to Mrs Freda.' In his desperation he hit the blotter with his fist and the glass tubes rolled together and jingled. The Irishman concentrated on Rossi.

'It is very bad,' began Rossi, 'but it is the truth.' He looked briefly at Vittorio who nodded encouragingly. 'I swear it.' He brought his hands passionately to his breast. 'I am at the fence watching everyone play football. I see Mrs Freda go into the bushes. I see Vittorio go into the bushes. When Vittorio go out I go back in again.' He flapped his wrist back and forth indicating the to-and-fro among the bushes. 'She is hot and she is

470

pushing her jumpers from her stomach.'

He was standing now with his feet wide apart, bracing himself for some shock or blow about to be administered. Curiously they watched as he rolled his jersey above the waistband of his trousers. There was a button missing, a glimpse of vest.

'I am a man,' he said. 'I am drinking. I see her skin as she breathe in and out with the hotness, the little bits wobbling. I make to put my arms round her but she is too tall. I only reach her here.' He was miming the incident now. He leaned forward from the waist and circled the air with his arms. His curls bounced upon his brow. 'She say to me — she say —' Evidently it was too painful for him to repeat.

Vittorio frowned and tapped the desk lightly with his finger tips.

Rossi continued: 'She take one little step backwards, like so. She falls away from me. Her neck goes like this —' He was staggering in a ridiculous fashion away from them, jumper ruched about his chest; he was raising an arm in the air. Suddenly he reached up and yanked his head violently backwards by the hair. His mouth fell open; his tongue flickered horribly; he made a small clicking noise. He straightened, and sneaked a glance at his audience, who were sitting bolt upright watching him. Vittorio was white-faced and dismal. His brown eyes seemed to have grown larger as if to be ready for all the things he still had to see, feel. His fingers, playing with the edge of his collar, brushed his throat. Rossi pointed at the dusty floor of the office. 'She fall down. Bang. I am falling on top of her.' He landed absurdly on his knees in front of them, scrambling on all fours before the desk. 'My head bump in her stomach.' And he jerked his chin upward as if heading a ball. His eyes closed as he butted the warm swell of Freda's belly.

There was a long pause. Nobody said anything. After a

471

moment Rossi remarked: 'There is a stone under my wrist. When I get up, my watch is no good. It is done for.'

He fell silent. He got to his feet and, red-faced, brushed the dust from his knees. Again he looked at Vittorio.

'I have forgotten nothing,' he muttered, 'nothing.' He took out the comb and raked his hair once more with a tragic expression.

It sounds reasonable, thought Brenda. She had wanted to know the exact details. It was the sort of thing that could happen to anyone, if they were tall and they were grabbed in the bushes by a small man. It certainly wasn't anything you could hang someone for.

'Well,' said Patrick grudgingly, 'just as long as we know.' He sounded as if he had been cheated out of something.

Outside the office window Brenda saw Salvatore and Aldo Gamberini rolling an enormous barrel out of the lift.

*

Brenda wanted Patrick to come home with her and have a cup of tea: the butter and olives were still on the table. He wouldn't. He wouldn't even walk up the street with her. He strode off without a word and turned the corner. Maria said her sister was waiting. She had cried so much in the washroom when the men were battening down the barrel that her face was lop-sided. She had leant against the wall holding Freda's flannel to her eyes and moaned.

'Stop it,' Brenda had advised. 'You will make yourself ill.'

The men had swept up the crumbs and blown out the candles. Trembling at the waste they had pumped a quantity of brandy up from the basement. They had glued the lid of the barrel into place and driven nails. They had marked it as unworthy.

Vittorio jumped in the Cortina with Rossi and an

unsteady Aldo Gamberini. The green shutter was rolled down in the alleyway. Anselmo adjusted the padlock and went to the car to give Rossi the key. Those who were going in the opposite direction shook hands. 'Ciao,' they murmured, clutching their briefcases and their carrier bags.

Brenda didn't want to seem pathetic, so she gave a little cheery wave and walked off under the street lamps.

She was very lonely, she would have done anything rather than walk up the darkening street alone. She couldn't eat anything, she couldn't settle in the bed-sitting room. The clock had stopped above the hanging brassiere, a mouse had nibbled the corner of the butter. She remembered the rest of the doggerel that Freda had known:

> Turned to woman, sitting there,
> See that mouse beneath that chair,
> Little woman, great big hat,
> Couldn't stand the thought of that.
> Up she got and left the house
> Man made happy, saw no mouse.

'Ah,' she said out loud, 'what a cunning man.' She slid the folded serviettes from beneath the blue plates and went downstairs to knock at the nurse's door. Nobody answered. She shook a finger in the dark and sat down on the stairs. Her neck was terribly stiff. She rubbed at it under her hair and screwed up her eyes — and saw Freda falling backwards. Now then, she told herself, just stop it. There was no one to talk with: even the cat had been let in, safe downstairs on the landlady's hearth rug. She was like one of those old ladies in the flats, roaming the balconies for someone to call to. Resolutely she started up the stairs with the serviettes in her hand to clear the awful table. Things should be put in their place. When she went into the room the lamp-shade with the fringeing spun round: Freda was falling — falling. Oh God, she thought, will I

473

always see her like that? She tried to think of her running after the ball, riding the horse. She saw instead Freda trailing her coat across the grass toward the bushes. She saw Vittorio shouting at Rossi against the timber fence. She saw him take something from Rossi's wrist. He shook it; he held it to his ear. She saw Rossi coming out of the bushes. She felt the grass prickling her cheek. Vittorio was running up to Rossi; he was trying to thrust something into his hand. Rossi was standing like a man in a dream, dazed. Vittorio was buckling a watch about Rossi's wrist. Freda was falling backwards. 'I have forgotten nothing,' muttered Rossi looking at Vittorio, 'nothing.' She shook her head and wished she could stop thinking about it. Rossi was such a loyal little man. He would do anything to protect the name of Paganotti. It doesn't matter, she thought, it is no longer of the slightest importance.

She took money out of her purse and went downstairs to ring Stanley. The code number was very long: the telegraph wires ran right across the country, through Ramsbottom and down the slope to the farm-house.

Mrs Haddon answered the phone. 'Hallo.'

'Hallo,' said Brenda. 'It's me, Brenda. Can I speak to Stanley please?'

'Mr Haddon is out at present. Would you care to leave a message?'

'I want to come home,' said Brenda at last.

'I'm afraid it's not convenient. Mr Haddon has made other arrangements. A woman from the village —'

The receiver was replaced.

*

Brenda went to work at the usual time. She had packed her suitcase in the night. She hadn't known what to do with Freda's things: her theatrical programmes and her jewel

474

case with the plum stones. Her father said he would meet her at the station if she was sure what train she was arriving on.

'Need a spot of home comfort, do you?' he shouted down the phone in a jolly manner.

'Something like that,' Brenda had replied.

'Okey dokey, chickie,' he said. 'Mummy will be waiting.'

*

The lorry stood outside the bottle factory waiting for the loading to be finished. Maria was crying. Some men and a woman in a shabby coat lined the pavement.

'Stop crying,' said Vittorio, 'it is looking strange.'

Four men in green overalls, pushing a hogshead of sherry, appeared at the slant of the loading bay. Below in the street, a row of workers in mufflers and trilby hats stood waiting for the work to be finished.

'It's dreadful,' said Brenda. 'I think I shall faint.'

Mournful at the kerb, she put her hands to her face and watched the wooden barrel begin to roll down the slope. A dozen men with lowered heads lifted the hogshead on to the lorry. A plastic flower was laid on the lid. Papers were signed. Brenda, who was easily embarrassed, didn't want to be seen gawping in the road. She declined to look at the back of the lorry, grey with dust, as the last barrel was shoved into place.

'She's going,' cried Maria, and the engine started and the vehicle slid away from the bay, the plastic tulip lolling in the wind.